ALSO BY JAMES McCOURT

Kaye Wayfaring in "Avenged": Four Stories
Mawrdew Czgowchwz

TIME REMAINING

Time
Remaining

JAMES McCOURT

ALFRED A. KNOPF

New York

1993

THIS IS A BORZOI BOOK
PUBLISHED BY ALFRED A. KNOPF, INC.

The author wishes to thank the Ingram-Merrill Foundation for its generous grant in aid of this book's completion.

Library of Congress Cataloging-in-Publication Data

McCourt, James [date]
Time remaining / James McCourt. — 1st ed.
p.   cm.
ISBN 0-679-41266-2
1. Gay men—New York (N.Y.)—Fiction.   I. Title.
PS3563.C3448T55   1992
813'.54—dc20   92-54798
CIP

Manufactured in the United States of America
First Edition

In memory of dead friends pictured within

I GO BACK TO
THE MAIS OUI

*A few days are all we have. So count
them as they pass.*

—JAMES SCHUYLER,
A Few Days

W hen the Oldsmobile convertible Jackson Pollock was driving hit the tree—
       I call myself Delancey. (And why not?) And "Lazy Afternoon" is my song.

When the 1950 Oldsmobile convertible Jackson Pollock was driving at breakneck speed in East Hampton on the night of August 11, 1956, hit the tree on Fireplace Road and flipped over, Jackson Pollock was sent *planing* into the air, some distance into the woods in Springs. His head hit the trunk of an oak ten feet up from ground level, and that killed him instantly. When, after some time, a policeman and a neighbor from Springs came upon him, he looked *like an old dead tree lying in the brush.*

Whereas what about today?

I call myself Delancey. "Lazy Afternoon" was my theme song then, and here and now it's still just that in East Hampton, some distance from here (Sagaponack) toward Fireplace Road in Springs—from

3

here where I've been sitting reading about that night in 1956, on this day, August 28, 1990. That is, *just that* it's a lazy afternoon, and not *just that*, three dots. . . . Just so you know. So that you'll take *what now*, *what next*, etcetera, more in the nature of a promise. (To answer them the way they used to ask you—in the fifties— when they were being sarcastic: *Is that a promise or a threat?*) Like that.

The fact is, if you want to know the truth, I don't know how to do this; I don't. "And *don't* try telling me," I advised O'Maurigan, "that the subject is so compelling, the need so pressing, the proposition so blah-blah, and the proponent so etcetera, because I know what you said all those years ago—you said it more than once and became a little notorious for saying it—about this or that subject in the mouth of said temperament that was so compelling the book practically wrote itself." Notorious. "You said, *Oh really? Then it should go away and* read *itself, and leave the rest of us in peace!*" You know what he answered? He answered, "It's the truth, I used to be withholding; I'm not withholding any more. And to that end—here."

And to that end—it has a ring to it, doesn't it?—here I sit, at the kitchen table in a house near the beach in Sagaponack, far enough all right from where I started, holding—as if it were a relic of that time before I started on the move—the mouthpiece of a forties Dictaphone.

"Kind of resembles the setup of *Double Indemnity*, doesn't it?" I suggested.

"It's *meant* to. First you're Walter Neff spilling the beans to the absent Barton Keyes—who is desperately in love with you, remember—while your guts pour out on the floor, and then bit by bit we listen to you turning into Phyllis Dietrichson coming down the stairs in pompom mules and ankle bracelet. Your voice will tell what's so—that you're both as handsome as Fred MacMurray was that year *and* as feline as Stanwyck. But you're a good boy in the end—and that's what'll knock 'em all dead; that's what'll plow 'em under."

"What good are they to me dead, I'd like to know."

"Just open your mouth and *talk*—there's a good lad."

(I hadn't been called a *lad* since reform school.)

"Freud says," I reminded him, "that when we talk about the past we lie with every breath we take."

"So what?"

(That did it—absolution before the fact, or did he mean that maybe Freud was wrong? Whatever. As the New York State Department of Motor Vehicles Driver's Manual promises [I learned to drive only fairly recently, at the age of—never mind] concerning parallel parking [me approaching the curbside of the past, get it?], *Practice will make you better at backing up and judging distances. Patience and self-confidence will help you master the task.*)

"Just moving a wire," he continued, "through a magnetic field makes a current try to flow. Remember the Irish proverb: *The most beautiful music is the music of what's going on.*"

Ain't science grand? I, presumably, am the wire, and the starry milieu I've moved in (since I got back down to New York from my sojourn up the Hudson) is, it turns out, the magnetic field. And I liked the music idea—although I couldn't help hearing another Irish proverb, an old County Mayo caution: "If music could boil the pot. . . ." Well, in sum the way he put it, it was a little more flattering than Margo Channing's taunt, *and* you, *presumably, are the Paderewski who plays the concerto on* me, *the piano?* It was more like I'm both the piano and the—not Paderewski, surely, but maybe Teddy Wilson? And it really was, wasn't it, I thought, comparable to jazz, what he proposed I try to do—the way poets do—riff the music of language. (I certainly was in the habit of riffing around in the expression department.) The only thing I didn't care for was making myself the subject—making what had gone on with *me* the music of *what had gone on*. I had been out of it, away from it all, for far too many years. . . .

"Didn't you tell me your friend Yeats told you that to the intelligent mind there are only two subjects of real interest, sex and the dead?"

"If I did, I lied in a blackout. Yeats wasn't my friend; he was mother's."

"But what he said?"

"I don't think I ever cared about anything he said—apart from some of what he wrote for the theater and for posterity—but in any case, I prefer the sex and the resurrected, and that means you, my love."

"Are you proposing," I challenged him, "that I reveal myself at the level of the press, radio, and television?"

"No, I'm proposing you do a vaudeville turn."

He had me there.

"But more or less just about me. What I did before the jewels—how I wanted them: like that?"

"Right—just like that."

"So I don't necessarily talk about the Eleven against Heaven, how Odette and I are the sole survivors, or how Odette buried a token portion of the ashes of eight all mixed together—a teaspoon apiece in a Lucite box—on the night of the dark of the moon in the garden site of the former Women's House of Detention—and took the rest of eight in their urns to Europe to deposit them in various rivers and seas and fjords and canals, has been gone for months and hasn't come back, is holed up in your ancestral stately County Mayo home, and we don't know when she will. Like that?"

"You might mention it—in passing."

"That's how I met you, in passing—do I mention that?"

"You might."

"I might. I might stay long in California."

"Like Odette is staying on at Poulaphouca? I don't think so. You belong right here, with Phil, in Sagaponack. Incidentally, you might try phrasing it all a little better, so it doesn't come out sounding like my stately ancestral pile is now the county home in Mayo."

"Meanwhile, I'm not even going to California, so how can I stay long? Anyway, I'd better not tell Odette's story; I think when she finally does come home, she's going to want to tell it herself, don't you?"

"I do—and I like your story, from the very beginning."

"I could throw in Phil and me going to Europe—not to bury the dead, yet in a way. . . ."

"There you are—start."

"But how—with what?"

"With images. Let's say, for example, with Pollock, dead—he was somewhat rough on you when he was alive; maybe he's good to you dead—and with the *kouros.*"

"With Jackson, and with the *kouros.*"

"That's it. And now I'm off, to meet the Skylark."

So that's how I've started—with sex and the dead after all, tabling for the moment the question of the Resurrection. I used to think of sex—Eros—as that Puck in a top hat who long ago graced the logo of the New York *Journal-American* proclaiming *What fools these mortals be!*, whose ballsass naked stone form can still be viewed on the façade of the Puck Building on West Broadway, not far from where Phil and I live in Little Italy (which we do only officially for a couple of weeks each winter season). But taking Jackson Pollock lying dead at the foot of an oak tree thirty-odd years ago and coupling him with the three-thousand-year-old *kouros* we found lying in a glade at Melanes on Naxos, with his leg broken off at the knee—well, wouldn't you know a poet would come up with that connection. A poet and a kind of wizard, really, who as I speak has just gone off to meet his older mentor-poet wizard, the one he calls his psychopomp, and the Skylark. The Skylark is giving one of his rare readings tonight at Guild Hall in East Hampton, and talking of the starry milieu I fell into when I met O'Maurigan in passing—why be coy: in the long and long-gone halls of the Everard Baths, on Twenty-eighth Street, just west of Broadway, the former center of the New York Tenderloin—this reading has attracted them all. To start sounding like the late, great T. C. Jones, circa 1956, doing his impersonation of Louella Parsons, "Mawrdew Czgowchwz will be there, and Mawrdew Czgowchwz's twin sons, Tristan, married to Kaye Wayfaring—who will be there—and Jacob, the *special friend* of poet Jameson O'Maurigan—who will be there." Well, you had to be there—to hear T. C. that is, at Le Cupidon and the Blue Angel, or at *New Faces of 1956* or at *Mask and Gown.* You won't have had to be at the Skylark's reading to—although if it's anything like the one he gave downtown last winter, which was really beautiful, really of another order from the run of those things; really like—well, like a Mawrdew Czgowchwz recital, people said . . . but I'm off the rails, aren't I? I just don't seem to know how to talk without telling you about all the others, all at once. It's an Irish affliction. Did you ever hear an Irishman start to tell a story? You want to shout, "Get to the *verb!*"

Nevertheless, it's groovy: Mawrdew Czgowchwz coming along just now back onto the South Fork, like a great August whale leading the other big fish in her wake—half the arts colony of the Massachussets island of Manitoy have arrived to stay with Boadicea Tillinghast at Nonsuch Stix—because back then in 1956, when T. C. was imitating Louella (and Bette Davis and Tallulah and Judy Holliday and Thalia Bridgewood), Mawrdew Czgowchwz was present and fabulous at the height of her fame, at another stellar event in the neighborhood: a soireé musicale at the Creeks on Georgica Pond, the showplace home of the Domino sugar heir and assemblagist Alfonso Ossorio and Odette O'Doyle's old colleague the dancer Ted Dragon. She was with her not-then-husband, the father of the twins—who weren't born yet, although they were either conceived or on their way: at any rate, they were what Odette's Aunt May Kelleher used to call *in God's pocket*—and they sang a duet (Mawrdew Czgowchwz and Jacob Beltane, that is, not the twins—but you knew that. I don't remember what it was called— Odette would, although she wasn't there: she has a nearly total recall for everything she's ever seen, heard, or heard told—but I remember it had something to do, as it was explained to me by O'Maurigan, who was there, with tears hanging off flower petals). I mention it because Phil and I were there, too, because Mawrdew Czgowchwz and Jacob Beltane drove everybody crazy by singing in the same register—over, under, around, and through one another's voices—and as Birdie says of the Hollywood star at Margo Channing's welcome home party for Bill Sampson who wore the sable coat that Miss Caswell said a girl could make sacrifices for, they would have left with half the men in the joint, had not the news been brought in on that night—August 11, 1956, a night of shooting stars—that Jackson Pollock had just been killed on Springs Fireplace Road. Tears hanging from flower petals, indeed—sex and the dead—with intimations of resurrection, or what?

Everybody was there—everybody, anyway, but Odette O'Doyle, from whom Phil and I have just received a postcard of an Irish castle—in fact, the castle that is the foundation of the O'Maurigan ancestral pile, Poulaphouca, in County Mayo—with this legend, in her spidery (I sometimes think nunlike) hand:

A lurking pale-grey Irish castle by a pebbly river
Like something torn down at Battery Park

Deign on the passing world to turn thine eyes,
And pause awhile from letters, to be wise.

For yet a little while,
And the coming one shall come and shall not tarry
more.
(Priscilla to the Hebrews 10:37)

Which were in sum: a quote from one of the Skylark's poems, "Voyage autour de mes cartes postales," followed by a couplet from a source I don't recognize, followed by the strange Bible reference, whatever it might mean. But that's Odette: you might get the message of her latest fortune cookie coupled with a fragment of Sappho, in Greek, or something from—*Priscilla* to the Hebrews?

A few days are all we have. So count them as they pass. The opening of the Skylark's last great poem. I start counting backwards from today—isn't that what you do when you're under truth serum? Tell it like it was? (Since O'Maurigan put me in the mood with the *Double Indemnity* Dictaphone, I've remembered a detail from another forties picture. *The File on Thelma Jordon? Possessed?* They inject the wayward heroine, and she starts counting backwards as the days peel off the calendar. In the hospital? On the police station wall? Why do I think police station—because I was a guttersnipe put into a reform school, right?)

When the Oldsmobile convertible Jackson Pollock was driving hit the tree—

I call myself Delancey. (And why not?) "Lazy Afternoon" is my theme song.

When the 1950 Oldsmobile convertible Jackson Pollock was driving at breakneck speed in East Hampton on the night of August 11, 1956, hit the tree on Springs Fireplace Road and flipped over, Jackson was sent *planing* into the air, some distance into the woods. His head hit the trunk of an oak ten feet up from ground level, and that killed him instantly. When, after some time, a policeman and a neighbor from Springs came upon him, he looked *like an old dead tree lying in the brush.*

We went to Greece last summer—Sicily and Greece, Phil and I—for old times' sake. Phil got to cry a lot in Sicily, looking out the windows of trains crawling along slower than the milk train out to Montauk, and standing for intervals of untold length in stations like Caltanissetta and Enna and Castelvetrano and Trápani, looking out over landscapes (to me reminiscent of Arizona, New Mexico, Nevada, and Southern California) he only dimly remembered from childhood, telling me we should have come in spring to see it all green; looking out at families he kept swearing all closely resembled his: whole families that came down to the stations to see one member off—off maybe as far as Palermo, or off to Rome or Florence or Milan. (Phil said most Sicilians had never left their towns, that they were like the Bonackers in East Hampton's Springs, who had never been up island to New York, and never would go. I asked him what was he talking about? What about immigration, the Mafia, *focaccerias*, Bellini in Paris? He said, "Shut up, you know what I mean." So I shut up. I knew what he meant; he was just wrong.)

I was looking at myself in train windows—I admit it uneasily—much of the time Phil was looking out of them, and, if I may get suddenly pluperfect here for a while, one of the things I remember remembering was a night a few winters ago, a night off from going out during one of our Gotham stays. I had the radio on, tuned to the usual respectable call letters—wishing I could listen again to one program of "The Mysterious Traveler" instead of yet another quality evening on "Carnegie Hall Presents," or wishing crazily that Carnegie Hall would present the Judy concert. (We've got the record, of course—I'm *on* it, out of my mind—but we never play it. I'd like to be taken by surprise, but I don't think they'll play it, not in my lifetime.) So anyway, I'm listening, when over the track of a decent enough rendition of the "Appassionata," this voice informs the listener that *this music is not being played by a professional musician.* It is, it turns out, being played by Doctor Somethingorother *Dove* (as in the soap, as in the Holy Ghost). Dr. Dove is a pianist whose work has been recognized, by listeners, *and* the director of Flashbacks, the institute for cosmetic reparation staffed by sensitive artists—dig? I was being invited to ask myself the question: Did I—*do* I—honestly want to keep looking the way I look and *wondering*—

Click. Right?

Such a line of attack was new to me from that station, to which I have for years more or less automatically turned in my moments of repose (few as they are in Gotham). One of the things, though, that the attack made me remember—this looking into the train windows in Sicily—was that travel is wearing and makes you slip up on your sleep, or does me. Because as it happens, I am myself, so far as the upkeep of the face and form is concerned, a devout adherent to the Dolores Del Rio method: long, unhurried excursions into the Land of Nod, *wo die Zitronen blühn* (more reliably, let me tell you, than in Sicily. Dolores, they say, went abroad for up to sixteen hours at a stretch, under a blanket of dried apricots. I can make do with ten or eleven under Scandia duck down, but no matter). I felt myself—listening to the radio at home in New York, that is, well before the scrutiny in the Sicilian train window—well, *assaulted.* Taking a nervous turn for the worse. The gall of such advertising—what would Beethoven have said? Nevertheless, the clock was—well, it wasn't going *tick-tock,* because rather than do what I used to do, put the clocks away in drawers, so as not to hear the tattoo of the march of time, I'd switched to electric clocks: all they do is buzz low—the clocks' hands were still going in one direction only (whatever Beethoven would have said). Like that.

Did Jackson Pollock, a great artist whose work was at last and is for all time recognized, ever think along such cosmetic reparation lines—or did his spouse? Not according to the snapshots of him and her we keep in an honored place in the living room out here. I have—see above—been sitting reading in the new oral biography of the Saint Sebastian of modern art, also the former good friend of the head of this household (who is at his own insistence not represented within, having, as he put it, all he has had to say about the subject to the subject long, long ago), and am amused by one among many odd pronouncements: Willem de Kooning's sputtering indignation in insisting that not for one minute of his life could Jackson Pollock have been considered a faggot. (I like de Kooning. Once I spent an afternoon in his studio blitzed by his stunning palette, and afterwards, in withdrawal, was admiring a collection of pre-Columbian sculpture distributed in the conversation pit of the living room. "D'ya like it? It's my vife's. I dunno vat any of it is, but it's all *autentic.*") Amused, because I think that as specimens, both Pollock and de Kooning were definitely what the Bonackers call *finest kind*—and they knew it. Angels with dirty faces; Satans in stained slacks—in Dorothy Dean's piquant phrase, rough trade *rêve bateaux;* two big bad boys (despite Bill's size). They were *not* nice in the fifties, especially not to faggots. But I don't like thinking about the manifold and multiplex unhappiness of the fifties, great as it was, great as the times were—*and we knew it.* All that sorrow in all that sunlight—express.

How far we've come from the river: Kyle, Mitch, Mary Lee,

Delancey. (*Yes, yes,* the Bonackers say.) Jackson Pollock and Brando, Rock Hudson, and Jimmy Dean. Bent Shoulders cologne. The time goes by, and you say, *Fuck art, let's dance.* That's what we've done: the cha-cha, the way they danced it at the Mais Oui—and always the Madison.

I suppose the image of Jackson and the image of the *kouros* with the broken leg are, as they say, good enough what for, but what I start to think about when I think about sex and the dead is something I've never seen, only heard about: that gay pornography of Tchelitchew's. I want somebody to get it out of the Kinsey archives—they can leave the camera-documented same-sex antics of Glenway Westcott and company right there in the can, thank you—and make a book out of it: a book I can put right next to *L'Amour bleu* and my glorious still-frame enlargements from the great Joe Gage trilogy, *Kansas City Trucking Company, El Paso Wrecking Corporation,* and *L.A. Tool and Die.* How I loved the Joe Gage esthetic, and now it, too, is blasted. As somebody once said to me—or to my shoulder—Sister, I am a child in the world who does still cry for the moon (even having had the stars, or some of them—yes, yes). I was brought up in a sharp school, and it now turns out life isn't *anything* like I thought it would be. *When you wake up in the morning and you don't know what you want, ask an ad.* Remember that? Sufficient unto the day. I wake up pure—but sometimes I do want to be *enveloped* in Je Reviens. . . .

How far from the river—whichever—can you *get* in Manhattan? And let's not forget Marilyn, or Monty, either. (Why did Monty turn down *Sunset Boulevard:* do shadows know?)

It isn't just the Joe Gage esthetic; it's the whole matter of pornography and color film. For years now they've been turning out por-

nography on videotape, and videotape is to film as acrylics are to
oils—like that. Joe Gage was the painterly realist of homosexual
pornographers.

This girl—you heard me, I met her on the Old Met line—she used
to dress all in black: black leotard, brown-and-black tweed skirts,
black sweaters, very existentialist—asked me to take her to her
senior prom. I didn't have to rent anything (and contrary to gorilla-
hash gossip in certain low quarters, she didn't have to rent me; I
was flattered); Phil got me the full-dress regalia. (I remember I
asked him, "Is this *off* anybody—anybody you used to know, up
till last week?") It was beautiful, forties, boxy trousers and wide-
lapelled off-white dinner jacket, much with high two-toned
midnight-blue-and-black cummerbund; I still wear it, to those summer musicales on Long Island's glittering South Fork, at which my
Versace combinations might be considered (just that) too emphatic.
The affair was at the Statler, in the ballroom with the big eagle
over the bandstand. We danced the cha-cha and the Peabody, and
we fox-trotted and waltzed. She was wearing Je Reviens—a lot of
it—and looked like a million dollars in a long-line white satin number with kick pleats. I remember the Peabody especially, because
it was the first time I'd ever had the chance to lead in it. (Not that
I wasn't butch; I was butch, if it matters. Phil always told me I
was a real butch entertainer. Only that he always led in the Peabody.) We went to the Copa after, got our pictures taken and put
on matchbooks, and then to Reuben's, where we ate eggs Benedict
and poured Hennessy from my hip flask into the coffee. (That was
the kind of thing you did in the fifties.) Then over to the Plaza
sidewalk to take a ride in a hansom. She slapped on more Je
Reviens. We didn't do *anything*. (I was not about to have those
beads rattled on the line, is what I told myself, and anyway, she
seemed to like me, as we used to say in those days, for myself.)

When we got back to the Plaza, I asked the driver could he drive us from there to the Met by way of Seventh Avenue and Broadway—the Mawrdew Czgowchwz route. It was very early on a Saturday in June, but we knew that they would all be there: the ballet line for the Bolshoi (the one the fifties goon flagwavers picketed). They were sleeping overnight. "As long as it's down Broadway, right down the middle," the hansom cabbie insisted. "I used to drive a crosstown bus. You wanna know why I stopped? The two rivers." So we got our tickets to Ulanova's last *Giselle*—my prom date arrived dressed back down in black—and we stayed friends. I stayed very cool about the whispered things; I showed I was what Ralph would call *umbothered.* I used to put on Je Reviens from time to time. I'd skid through Macy's on the way up to the line and spritz it on from the samplers. It used to make Phil crazy in the dark standing room—and I knew that; I knew the old wop couldn't wait to get out of there and get me home to our tastefully appointed mirrored boudoir and jump on my bones. Later, when we got rich and joined the Club (Faggot Central) in the Grand Tier—but that's another story.

One strange thing about that hansom cab ride through Central Park. Remember, it was my first actual (heterosexual) date. Well, all I could think of riding along, with the skyline showing here and there through the night trees, highlighted by park lanterns—and particularly as we passed by the terrace of Tavern on the Green—was a crazy chorus of kids back in reform school, tramping along in the woods near the bank of the Hudson, smoking and singing, *Oh how we danced on the night we were pantsed!*

All right, why *did* Monty turn down *Sunset Boulevard?* (The correct answer's *not* "To get to the beach house at Malibu.")

From Sicily to Bríndisi to Athens, to Iráklion to Santoríni to Naxos; back to Athens, through Yugoslavia to Venice. In two weeks. In

Knossos, I found the entrance to the Labyrinth in the queen's toilet, just behind the throne, but we didn't go down. (I *dreamed* I did, but that's another story.) The *it*, the *what happened*, happened on Naxos, birthplace of Dionysus (my patron deity, according to the old publicity), Ariadne's way station.

We'd run into Kiki and Clio Fragousikia (a.k.a.—can we talk?—Fafner and Fasolt) having dinner on Santoríni in a swanky joint called the Kastro, overlooking the harbor formed by the left-over rim of a volcanic crater (left over from the eruption of when-ever forever ago that buried the city of Akrotiri and raised the great wave that destroyed Knossos), and decided to sail with them to Naxos on an ordinary boat, with the people. Attention: the trip was horrifying. Kiki kept saying over and over that something must have happened—*turned* was her word—but Clio, grimly, resolutely candid, kept correcting her. "Bullshit, Ki! You talk as if you didn't know why *we* got out. And why we most certainly will *never* come back. It's *over*—*very* over!" After a seven-hour sail—the watchword was agony—we chugged into Naxos harbor. Leaning overdeck, Kiki went into a kind of forced—nearly faked—orgasmic rapture, re-membering the concert Mawrdew Czgowchwz gave there in an-other lifetime (at which event it was evident she—Kiki, that is, but maybe, come to think of it, Mawrdew Czgowchwz, too—had ex-perienced the real ripple), when she stood in the portal of the Temple of Apollo and sang *Es gibt ein Reich* to a regatta of the advanced elect. "Don't go looking for *her* in Hellas, either," Clio snapped. "After they disposed of what was left of Maria in these troubled waters and the currents carried it back to Colchis, Czgowchwz, too, realized what was over in the way of an era."

(*Es gibt ein Reich, wo alles rein ist: es hat auch einen Namen: Totenreich.* You'll notice, I said to myself, that the one M.C. was not part of that televised tribute to the other M.C.—the one that features about eleven minutes of herself and eleven hours of all the self-promoting foghorns who claim they ever crossed her path, physically, mentally, or spiritually—close as they'd been. And we were *there*. Which reminds me: I was walking past the local Korean grocer the last time I was in town, and you know how they can't spell things—well, advertised on a sign stuck in among the African daisies, birds of paradise, and gladioli, there they were: *Callas* lilies. In New York; I thought it fitting.)

Whatever kept Ariadne on Naxos was not what kept us— unless you believe that all legends (even, for example, the legends of Jackson Pollock and Mawrdew Czgowchwz, which although recent seem nevertheless to be fading in the acid rain of contemporary life) are cover stories for epochal weather reports. Some do. We were anxious to get up to Míkonos and from there over to Delos to spend a day in the last divine place in (as Clio correctly, if acidly, named it) Hellas, but the wind came up—the one they call *Melteme*. (Not the one they call Mar-*eye*-a from *Paint Your Wagon* that John Raitt used to sing on "Your Show of Shows.") It held us there for three days, until a boat big enough—and full of a better class of people, is the truth—to make the voyage docked. On the afternoon before it did, leaving the women behind among the bronzed German nudists in their cunning thatched-hut Tahiti colony along the straits facing Páros, we took a bus ride in search of something I'd seen listed in the guidebook, called the *kouros* of Melanes.

(Who was it—I can't now remember: it wasn't Odette O'Doyle— who, when dressing up to go out on the big town, and applying a little rouge and eye shadow, used to crow *Paint your wagon, Emma—paint your wagon and go out and make a dollar!*)

Kouros means boy—as in the Dioscouri, the two boys, the twins Castor and Pollux, who stand together in the National Museum in Athens ballsass naked in Parian marble, much with the arm of the one thrown over the shoulder of the other (who is holding inverted the ritual torch, which signifies that he will die, abandoning the other), while Demeter—isn't it?—one-third scale and off to the side, looks askance (*"Wouldn't* she!" I can hear Odette say to O'Maurigan, as if they were reading beads on somebody's Irish aunt). The Dioscouri are too painful for me to look at, even in my mind's gay eye. The Faggot's Impossible Dream has always been the same: the Double, the complementary other (who is, in fact, the same, only more so); the one who comes into view getting away—remember the Madison? (No, I have no regrets to speak of—openly—and yes, I love Phil, the insatiable old—after all, *only through the embrace of Pan, whose hairy thighs rub us raw even as they bring us ecstasy, can we learn to be fully alive.* And Pan means Pan, not Peter Pan—*"the* Pan, not P. Pan," as Odette might put it—the man, not the boy—or, completing the metaphor, the goat, not the kid. I said the Dioscouri were the faggot's dream—the faggot's dream before chest hair, before thigh hair: the dream of the smooth, tricky, and elusive Jacob rather than life with the rough-and-ready Esau. Etcetera. Dream lover put your arms around you. Next.)

The *kouros* of Melanes is a giant stone boy, one of those that were attached to Apollonic temple precincts in the archaic period. (I'm remembering what Odette O'Doyle, polymath drag-queen diva, told me, explaining the photographs I took of the statue.) The *kouros* I like best in the National Museum has his pubic hair sculpted into a seven-sided polygon comprising three triangles surmounting a trapezoid—the upper section, in other words, of a five-pointed star, so that it sits like a kind of party hat on top of the things themselves, the things we love, the things of life. Whereas the Melanes *kouros* was abandoned, left unfinished. One day in the middle of whenever—but at least a millennium after the Santorini earthquake–tidal wave—obviously another earth tremor or word of

the landing of hostile forces from the Peloponnese in the harbor—
something, at any rate, of greater moment (as O'Maurigan would
say) than a rustic panic or a long lunch hour—interrupted the work
on this great stone boy, and either then or sometime later he fell
over backward, his right leg snapped off just above the knee, and
there he's lain for twenty-six hundred years. (If you fell over at the
Mais Oui—from too many stingers or too much heart—the patrons
would cha-cha right over your body, but somebody would always
check your breathing at the band break, anyway. You had the
feeling that even if Saint Theresa wasn't so interested, somebody
was. Somebody would pick you up and take you home. Never
your twin, never your opposite number, but somebody with a
story; somebody who'd make you breakfast. Somebody, with any
luck, from the East Side. You remember when *nobody* lived on the
West Side? "Except to do what I did last night," the East Side
breakfast cook would declare emphatically. "I never *go* to the West
Side. All those people pretending to be poor!")

   I lay down with love, and I woke up with lies. . . .

   Phil once told Jackson Pollock that if he would go back to
an earlier style ("Just something *negotiable*, Jack, something
talkative!"), he, Phil, could probably see to it that the resulting
canvases were hung in some of the better Italian restaurants in
Greenwich Village. Instead of which, Jackson continued painting
atomic fission. Phil said, "Okay, I'll shut up and buy some." (My
boon companion, husband, and protector picked up on three right
things in the fifties besides me: Pollock, IBM, and Tiffany glass.
Consequently, we are now what you would call comfortably well
off. Especially me—when you stop to consider everything, that is:
that is, everything I'm off.)

To find the *kouros*, you take the bus to Melanes and walk out of
the town over a kilometer or more of rocky fields, until the path

ends at the base of a high hill, then turn left and start climbing over the stone walls until you find the sacred grove. An old Naxian woman sits at the edge of a rustic hut, selling ice cream. (The easier way is to follow the main traffic road around the town and look for the sign that says "Kouros," but this we found out only on the way back—Cycladic Greeks being profoundly committed to withholding information from visitors, the better, perhaps, either to remind themselves or to assure themselves they are where they are, just. On the way back, having failed to negotiate a return trip on the French-speaking bus tour, we were mercifully picked up and driven to the port by a nice man from Piraeus who was on vacation with his Naxos-born wife, but just then alone in the car—we decided not cruising: just being a nice Greek. His name was Kalegeropoulos. "That was Maria Callas's name!" "Yes, it's the same." "What do you know," said Phil. The conversation went nowhere—perhaps because Mr. Kalegeropoulos hadn't found it necessary to change *his* name to Callas—but he certainly was a nice Greek.)

Phil took my picture sitting on the *kouros*'s chest. Poor gigantic, broken, abandoned boy: features worn smooth by centuries of wind and rain. What significance! What I did last summer in Greece: I had a religious experience on the island of Naxos to beat any Dolores ever could've had in her sleep under that blanket of dried apricots. (Or as has been said better, in a similar connection— even if it was said by one of O'Maurigan's bugbears, a plaster saint—*Du musst dein Leben andern.* Ain't it the truth—day in, day out—but *how*—or maybe that's how *now?*)

I was always particularly interested in Jackson Pollock's stone-dowsing abilities. Apparently, they, the stones, spoke to him from beneath the surface of the earth. He'd hear them, have them dug up, and relate to them regularly thereafter. I think of it nowadays in connection with remembering.

Which reminds me—I'm not sure why, but perhaps thinking

of the concept of relating regularly thereafter—of the time O'Maurigan insisted on dragging me to the MoMA party in honor of Douglas Sirk, and introducing me to the great man—who was, when I offered my hand, deep in conversation with Mawrdew Czgowchwz. I opened my mouth and, distracted as much by her smile as by the Persian-lamb collar on his coat—which he had on indoors—blurted out, "I'm happy to meet you. *Written on the Wind* changed my life." His eyes brightened. "Oh—*how?*" "The same way, I expect," intercut Mawrdew Czgowchwz—right to the rescue—"*Magnificent Obsession* and *All That Heaven Allows* did mine." "Oh, yes, of course," he murmured with, I thought, satisfaction. *Europeans*, I reminded myself: another species of mortal.

I met Phil not at the Mais Oui but at the Cherry Lane. He used to try—sometimes he still tries—to correct me, saying it was the Modern, but I remember that summer almost night by night, and it was the Cherry Lane. Phil gets confused because he remembers Trenchy being the mainstay at the Modern, but Trenchy left the Modern early that summer and went down to the Cherry Lane. We danced, Phil and I, which makes me absolutely certain, because there was no dance floor at the Modern. (Phil says there was no dance floor at the Floradora out in Jackson Heights, either, but they all danced, which is what got all the boys in blue so hot and bothered over at the 110th. But I remember it was the Cherry Lane; trust me.) We danced to the Everly Brothers' "All I Have to Do Is Dream" and "Maybe Tomorrow." Somebody sang "The Man That Got Away" along with Judy on the jukebox. Just another night in fifties gay New York. We did it on the way home—that's something else I remember—in the back of a deserted loading platform on Washington Street. Then we stopped off at Vinnie's Clam Bar—because, then as now, Phil gets voraciously hungry, at any hour whatsoever, after sex. We sat up drinking espresso with Sambuca Romana at Phil's place on Mott Street, watching *June Bride* on "The Late Late Show," and when Robert Montgomery says to Davis, "I'm gay, I'm lovable, and I've got nice teeth. What more do you want?" I turned to Phil, smiled the crazy smile of the clown that used to advertise Tilyou's Playland in Rockaway Park, and asked him, "So?" He answered, "So I'm takin' you away from Rockaway, away from Riis Park, away from Jones Beach, *and* away from Cherry Grove."

Typical Phil, that remark—which certainly clocked my reality. (Reality: everything that is the case, according to O'Maurigan's pet philosopher.) His subtle point about my case (he was on it) was that although I never went near Jones Beach in the way I haunted Rockaway and Riis Park—in the daytime, that is (as none of us did, not even to investigate the notorious *Gay 1*. There was no such thing then as owning a car, and who had that kind of cab fare?)— I *was* seeing a lot of that particular stretch of sand dune off the South Shore in the evenings, and getting there in a Showbiz bus, yet. What had happened was that I'd fallen—fallen hard—for a gypsy in *A Night in Venice*. That was in July. By the Labor Day weekend, many performances of *A Night in Venice* later (which, incredibly, Phil started driving both me and the inamorato out to, night after night), I was spending my last few days in Cherry Grove for twenty-nine years. It was there, away from him—but, I confess, hearing repeatedly in the wind and the waves his lyrical *promessa* to take me the next summer to the real Venice—that I decided on him (Phil). I got the camp name Gay Dawn that weekend. (That was the level of wit at Duffy's in the Grove in the middle fifties— wit, you might say, with fins attached.) It used to make me frantic sometimes to hear about the ascendancy of the Pines—which hardly *existed* then—in the sixties. There I was, by then an idle prisoner of love in uneventful Sagaponack (admittedly, having seen the real Venice, and a lot more); but I know now, absolutely, that I wouldn't have made it, by way of the Grove, to Stonewall.

Stonewall. Let's just say I've always thought it was ironic about Stonewall—and I never have gone in a lot for ironing. I used to say the Mais Oui riots or the Cherry Lane riots or even the Floradora riots would have called out a classier crowd, if you're going to opt for dancing-ground pieties surrounding a Founding-Faggots performance. But I guess I'm prejudiced because I was there *at* the Stonewall—on the first night of the great uprising—and, let's face it, the place was a dump. (So what, you're going to protest, so was the Bastille, right?)

(Is this snobbery? Inverse snobbery? What?)

I don't know why I went there that night, instead of home to our luxurious air-conditioned floor-through on Mott Street. (Phil, turned overnight from lonely child–immigrant bachelor into high-type American husband, had gone to town at Roma Furniture on Grand Street—which suited the wife just fine: I never was and never did become a discerning Bloomingdale's customer.) Except that I was wrecked, I admit it. It certainly was not to look at the go-go dancers. It was hot and I was wrecked. I was also a platinum blond that summer and, frankly, insecure as to my motives; but the big news, of course, and the big *reason* was that Judy was, finally, dead. I'd been up to Frank Campbell's to see the remains of her—one dope-dead doll lying there like the Last Lost Illusion—and was muttering to strangers (and it seemed to me that everybody I saw there was a stranger; where, I kept asking myself, are the familiar faces who were in the audience at Carnegie and the Met—dead, too?). Muttering something a Greek father is supposed to have said once in apology, standing looking down into his little daughter's casket: *Such a big funeral for such a little corpse.* Then, instead of getting on the Montauk train as I'd promised Phil over the phone from the Plaza I would, I swerved out the back door and over to the chic little baths with the embedded-at-all-hours orgy parlor with the jalousies that looked down on West Fifty-eighth Street; left there rather more stained than consoled (we all gave ourselves a *lot* of Attitude in those days), and went down to Kelly's on West Forty-fifth Street to have a few beers. What I must have had in mind was some kind of sentimental tour of my career's doorways, but the next thing I remember is coming to, screwed onto the top of a stool at the Stonewall, looking alternately up into the glassy eyes of a champagne-blond go-go boy and down into the crystal matrix of a stinger.

I saw the amphetamine-crazed drag queen throw the cocktail in the officer's unready face. (He was only there collecting the routine payoff on a Friday night: those boys were carefully picked in those days for such duty—the bars and baths—and simply did *not* incite.) I heard her scream over the blaring strains of The Doors, *That's for Judy!!!* (A fat lot, bitch, I silently declared—sensing more than a decade's demise—you care for Judy. All *you're* wrecked about is Jim Morrison never has and never from this day until the midnight when the horn blows for the General Judgment *will* ask *you* to suck his cock.)

That's for Judy—and, as Bridey says to the judge in the immortal pee-in-the-pot urinalysis story, that's when the fight started. (Or, as Miss Charity would have certified, "That's the *T* on *that*, dihr.") I got out of there in record time—I mean, as you may have gathered, I *like* cops: half the reform-school roster (need I specify, the humpier half) went on the force; maybe that was my chief propeller impetus: maybe I was in no mood, as a platinum blond of uncertain motive, to entertain at an impromptu class reunion at the precinct (say, with another rendition of "America, I Love You" topped off with "The Trolley Song") just so there would be no hard feelings for poor Judy. I got out of there and into a gay cab up the Avenue of the Americas to the heart of the former Tenderloin district. There have always been crises in my life—at least, in my life between leaving that institution upstate (a venue I plan to talk about later) and the padlocking of the parks and stews in these, the plague years—in which the *only* comfort was the comfort of immersion in Everard's glamorous and refreshing bathing pool (No Diving), and there I fled at the hour of decision on that Friday night, until it was time to catch the milk train to Bridgehampton. Poor Judy. You know, at the end they were throwing dinner rolls at her—the Brits—when she sang at Talk of the Town in Leicester Square, and one ambitious (and in his own mind probably compassionate) reviewer had attempted a summation of the situation, saying: *At what must be the end of a long, tumultuous career, it is stunningly apparent that the question* who is this woman that they should pay her cult in blood? *merits this answer. This performer is indeed the very, one and only Judy her shrieking male Bacchantes implore rather than applaud; she is Judy, has played her part—and Show Business has all along and all too well played opposite her the part of Punch.* (It's nice to believe, but hard to be sure, that the Judy-and-Punch-drunk New Yorkers wouldn't have thrown something—like empty amyl nitrite vials—at her had she made it back stateside to sing, say, poolside at the Continental in the Ansonia, then die. I would like to hear the Carnegie recording again because I can pinpoint the *groove* in which the engineers bleeped out Hank's voice as he stampeded down the middle aisle screaming *Juuuudy—sit on my faaace!!!* This is one of the many true-life details you won't be seeing in the proposed—can you believe it—musical of Judy's life. What are they going to call it, *If Love Were All?*)

I remember somebody had sent out for Chinese food and got it delivered to his cubicle—that was the kind of thing you did in the *sixties*—and I got the leftover pork with fried rice and the fortune cookie, along with a little lecture: "I *can't* start mourning Judy yet, baby, I still haven't gotten over Grace Moore" and this caution:

"However, you'd better think twice before you take *my* fortune, cookie. You'd be better off listening to these words of wisdom I was reading before you breezed past my open door. I often read while dining alone. They are the words of wisdom, indirectly quoted, of a Miss Harriet Vane, the *Doppelgänger* creation of the greatest woman Dante scholar of our time, who writes detective fiction on her holidays, upon the occasion of her—Harriet Vane's— having been acquitted of her lover's murder. I think that in spite of the obvious fitness of the act, to read Dante in here would be just a little pretentious—I mean, we're *living* Dante in here, aren't we—so I read this. Listen. *The best remedy for a bruised heart is not, as so many people think, repose upon a manly bosom. Much more efficacious are honest work, physical activity, and the sudden acquisition of wealth.* Now, *tolle, legge,* read it, and if you must weep, weep silently, hmm?" Latin, I said to myself—and German (it so happened, a German word I knew the meaning of: the Double, as in the Faggot's Impossible Dream—see above). Another Jesuit eunuch like the one O'Maurigan used to meet in here all the time; maybe the same one. Latin, and although I didn't right then know, or remember the meaning, I thought I remembered where. . . . "A great thinker, Harriet Vane," the Jesuit continued. "A little later in the same book she remarks, observing a hag jilted by a gigolo, who turns out, of course, to be the murder victim, *Did it come to this then, if one did not marry? Making a public scorn of oneself before the waiters? Are* you going to heed my caution, or are you going to read what Confucius say?" I figured what the hell, things were overdue for a turn; I broke into the cookie and got *You are heading for a land of sunshine and fun.* I've been thinking of that fortune a lot lately—a land of sunshine and fun. It was true that night, although it didn't indicate—or demand—*I* had to have fun there, do or die, but I suddenly decided the Dante girl's girl double was right—actually, both wrong and right. I could have it all—I *already* had it all: the opportunity for honest work through physical activity (I was thinking the landscaping) *and*, at close of day—or at breakfast, lunch, and dinner, so far as he was concerned—a manly breast . . . see above *and* below. There was absolutely no necessity of my making myself or of my being made a scorn of by the waiters—or the bartenders, the go-go boys, and the towel attendants. There was no necessity of committing murder—either quickly by stabbing someone's heart with a stiletto, or slowly by breaking it with cheap and boring infidelities—or of hoping for acquittal. I could just—we could just do what Phil always said we could. Live together. It was all true that night, and it's been true often enough thereafter. A land of sunshine and fun—*wo die Zitronen blühn*, O'Maurigan says (sometimes sings). Where the *kouroi* are all in perfect Joe Gage condition. (And where I'll end up—what? Stationed under the rain tree, signing autographs, prohibiting photographs—unless by then I've given in to Dr. Dove and his ivory-tickling fingers and have had that face-lift—and permitting the curious to fantasize certain delicate liberties with my person, *gratis*, repeating and repeating in all ears, "I go back to the Mais Oui.") And where there's Phil—no *kouros* of Melanes or anywhere else, but clocking *condition*, no Jesuit eunuch. . . .

Penny candy, candy for a penny, I ask for more than a penny now— I've grown very wise, you see. . . . Name the show; name the performer. Next contestant.

Bad art may not drive good out, but it crowds *it*. Who said that? (Name the night; name the—)

After forty hours eating salami and drinking bottled Zeus water (and—after I finally convinced Phil that the train guard who had taken our passports away for the night was, although definitely a Communist, definitely *not* interested in what we were doing be-

hind closed compartment doors—committing sodomy) on the Beo-
grad cannonball, we finally arrived in Venice, then as now—now
as I speak—and for a long, long time before then (in fact, since
that summer after the first: the summer of the promise fulfilled)
my favorite ride in Europe. (After I told O'Maurigan about the
train ride through what was then still Yugoslavia, and about Phil's
attack of paranoia, he agreed with me completely, citing the late
great Zinka Milanov, who, when told most of her most ardent fans
were in the habit of doing just what Phil and I had been doing
when they weren't standing around in her dressing room—and, in
fact, probably as often as not doing it with her records playing in
the background, remarked, *"Zo—vot?* In Zagreb, dey've been doink
dot for *years!"*) After I'd picked up a couple of shirts at Versace,
we went and ate at our little *trattoria* in back of the Teatro della
Fenice. There is a picture on the wall of the rear *salone* there of
us from the fifties, taken at a party we gave for Vana Sprezza—
remember her? She was—still is—the daughter of Phil's mother's
cousin. The party was for the gala world premiere of Trovaso
Corradi's *Livia Serpieri,* written for Vana on commission from some
Pacelli *pastificio* and co-starring the then reigning Adonis of the
Italian lyric stage, Giuseppe di Stefano (*Pippo*), a fellow Sicilian. It
was a smash hit. I still play the Cetra recording—oddly, nothing
of Corradi's and nothing at all with Vana on it has as yet made it
onto CD—and think of Vana, who lives these days—I hope—in
Taormina, up in the back. (We can't be sure; we don't look her up
anymore, there was an altercation.) Both M.C. and M.'C.' (as we
used to write them then) were there—in fact, they came together,
without husbands. (M.C. was almost always traveling without hers
by then, and the spectacular M.'C.' spouse was deep in rehearsals
at the Teatro Nuovo in Milan for the Merovig Creplaczx *Sprech-
stimme* monodrama *Caravaggio.* Creplaczx, of course, had been the
M.'C.' paramour until the year before, when Jacob Beltane, the
husband. . . . It was all very eventful, especially to a dewy-eyed

young New York ex-guttersnipe who'd just been given Venice on a silver tray, as it were.) It was either just before or just after Morgana Neri (yet another Sicilian, but, as Phil says, "We *nevah* bothered with *huh!*") died. I can't remember was she dead yet, only that Pippo told the most hysterically funny Neri stories anybody had ever heard (in the Sicilian dialect). The composer—the oldest living *verista*—conducted. Sets and costumes—never mind.

I recently came across some thrilling words of wisdom—not, need I say, in a cubicle at the Everard. (The Everard, burned out in the late seventies at the cost of perhaps as many as eleven lives. I don't recall the final tally—excuse me—toll; I just remember being there on the morning after—I hadn't been inside; how I got there that time, from East Hampton, in point of fact, is another train-ride story—and looking up at the charred façade, and going back to Twenty-eighth Street sometime afterward to find scrawled in red paint on the boarded-up front doors the proclamation NEVER AGAIN. It had been even then in decline for many years, and never again after Stonewall etcetera could have been called the haunt of the self-styled serious-minded in fugue. It is now a wholesale-merchandise mart.) No, in a book of literary criticism, of which I've been reading a good deal lately at the behest of both O'Maurigan and Odette O'Doyle. (I buy it at the Strand Book Store—where, of course, you encounter, and, if you can think kindly, nod to any number of superannuated ex-Everard patrons; I find it calms my nerves.) *The past's unchallengeable facts account as much as the present's uncontrollable accidents for the tragedies of human fortune. Faith in the fixed idols of anteriority, whether personal or social, serves as well as the ruins of past authority to disorder the conduct of present life.* I ought to pay more attention to directions like these—perhaps have them put on a T-shirt to wear to the gym—like that—and perhaps, when I've come from the showers, don my memories more like a loose (Versace) garment than like a suit of armor. I mean so I go back to the Mais Oui. As Dorothy Dean used to say, to bring me to my senses when I inflated, *big hairy deal!* Phil goes back to Spivvy's Roof and beyond; do you hear him walking around New York talking about it, or singing "Why Don't You . . ." at parties?

(The T-shirt notion reminds me of something else in the Solution to the Problem of Life department—something I read some years ago in *OMNI*, in an article called "Quark City." The scientist author, obviously one of the kind with Plans for the World, had written: *We hope to explain the entire universe in a single simple formula that you can wear on your T-shirt.* I wanted to write to Letters to the Editor, "How about *Love God and Do What You Will?*" but I didn't.)

Nevertheless, I can't stop thinking—here in high summer—about that most recent trip to Venice, or about an eerie attempt—back in the dead of last winter—at re-creating a Venetian experience. Phil and I had to get up practically at dawn one morning during our habitual hibernal stay in New York to go up to the boathouse near the Bethesda Fountain because old (and I mean *old*, like a Currier and Ives winter engraving) Lila Aron, an art patroness and benefactress of note whose childhood companions were J. P. Morgan's daughters, was having the genuine Venetian gondola she'd given to the city launched and floated past the esplanade and past the Ramble promontory—and all this featuring two, both genuine, Venetian *gondolieri* (talk about disordering the conduct of present life and the repose of the citizenry with a piece of private theater). There we stood on a subzero morning, a handful of us, while the *dogaressa* (O'Maurigan's tag) cackled over her *gondolieri* to her gay old heart's content, twigging their dreamy nonchalance. (Each obviously had tucked somewhere into his thermals his open-return ticket, Alitalia first-class, to the Pearl of the Adriatic.) Of course, the eerie little matinee had to remind me of what else but the

Mawrdew Czgowchwz regatta of thirty-odd years before, and of
the radiance of those times—time out of mind—but also, more so,
of the O'Maurigan play *Panache*, in which, if anybody remembers
anything in this age of information exchange, they may care to
recall that I was a bit of a hit in the juvenile lead opposite the
young Kaye Wayfaring. Well, you know how it is with a play: you
never remember a line of your own. But I remember to this day
every syllable of the monologue written for the crazed old fairy
character, Dixwell—the monologue about Venice. It was directed
to me, supposedly as a piece of seduction (my character was spaced-
out on drugs, a kind of sexpot automaton—a lot of people said
typecasting), and it came back to me like a funeral oration for a
funeral—my own—I'd missed that morning, because, well, I suppose the ceremony of the gondola was to me a little, as the French
say, *funeste*, and, as the Irish say, I felt somebody walking over my
grave (or, as if I'd drowned myself—which I would have done, I
know, offshore at Cherry Grove, had things not changed the way
they did—and the *gondolieri* in their long underwear in the gondola
were gliding over same). Anyway, that speech was the hit aria of
the play, and more veterans of that era than can ever have heard
it spoken during the brief run of *Panache* have asked me about it
over the years at parties. For a while it was all you heard talked
about—after the vogue for the anthill-crucifixion passage from *The
Cocktail Party* had passed. I shall speak it now because, although I
hope to God I haven't come to resemble Dixwell, I am now the
age he is in the play—or thereabouts.

> *Situate, uncharted, in the most serene*
> *Republic that was before Napoleon,*
> *(Like so much else upon which more depends. . . .)*
> *In a backwater, a phantom isle, by name*
> Sant'Ariano. *No* vaporetto *stalls*
> *There to discharge* passeggeri. *Never ask*

Of a Venetian where departs. . . . Never tax
A gondolier. . . . For on said isle lie rotting
The bare bones of those miseri *who've not shot*
More or less straight to Heaven by the octaves
Of their viaticumed demises, nor yet
On the anniversaries. . . . 'Til years go by,
And tides erode and leases lapse on their snug
Graves in the boneyard of the Serenissi-
Ma (that was before Napoleon, like so
Much else). We hear The Vatican's most recent
Directive on same indicates though does not
Stipulate, get this: That diocesan pro-
Cedure ought, as in all negotiation
Since So Much Else be flexible, avoiding
The radical boue *of contemporary*
Transalpine thanatology: endorsing
The opinion: only the bones of the souls
In Purgatory may be presumed to have
Lasted in sepulcro. *The bones of the damned*
Rot into the soot that then blackens maggots
Evolving into dungflies. Souls in Paradise—
Ah! leave bones behind that crystallize *o'er night*
Into a kind of marzipan, collected
And stored in the vaults of the Basilica
San Marco. (Marzipan to be dispensed
To those Innocenti *who have taken First*
Communion without incident of gagging.)
Now, about that legendary sacrilege
Committed one night in carnevale *in*
The Serenissima one night long ago
(Before Napoleon) and re-created
At the Venice Biennale in the year—
You remember: the notorious pranzo Dei morti *held on*

  Sant'Ariano:
The supper terminating in a dolce
Of zabaglione, *with slices of that same*
Marzipan. . . . *"Oh, my* God!*" screamed the New*
  York'ress
Overhearing the whole story at Harry's
American Bar. "That's disgusting! *That makes*
The flesh *crawl right off my* bones!*" Like so much else*
In backwaters, uncharted, never ask where. . . .

I sat there at lunch at Cipriani's in the Sherry-Netherland, after the
gondola high mass, eating with O'Maurigan our special-order non-
alcoholic—he calls it *castrato—zabaglione* for dessert, and remembering that monologue again, word for word—and remarking again
to the poet exactly as I had at the time of the premiere, "You may
have spent all those years getting worked over by the Jesuits, and
they may have made you a star turn speaking at communion break-
fasts during the war, where you carried on Sunday mornings working those hotel ballrooms where only the night before maybe
Frances Langford . . . carried on like the adolescent Christ wowing
the priests in the Temple of Jerusalem—all that—but you never did
learn to write like a Catholic—really. No Catholic ever *takes* communion—or, anyway, never did in the fifties. He wouldn't dare—a
Catholic in the fifties *received* communion." (Nowadays, of course,
he might have reminded me, they take it in their fists, but he didn't,
he only nodded slyly, giving me, as they say, my head—a thing
I've always found wildly seductive, especially from a handsome
man so obviously my intellectual superior. It makes me feel like
Mae West.) Then I recited the thing aloud for the company (Lila
Aron cackling away exactly as she had opening night—I remembered the unnerving accompaniment all too well—as if it were still
that year and she'd brought some friends to the first matinee of the
run). Some people can't forget the Gettysburg Address, or the letter
Violetta Valery gets from Giorgio Germont and reads in the last

act of *La Traviata. (Teneste la promessa . . . il barone fu ferito. . . .)*
I can't forget the first night I blasphemed in public and didn't die
in my sleep and go to Hell. (We were all, of course, denounced
from the pulpit at St. Patrick's Cathedral—same as *Baby Doll*—by
no less than the vicious fat faggot then ensconced in his long, long
run as Cardinal Archbishop of New York, and that was the kiss-
off so far as our run went. Religion was in those days more than
the consolation Violetta also speaks of in that same last act; it was
powerful shit.)

(Meanwhile, talking of remarks made in eateries—and what
a category—of Mae West repartee, and of taking [and in the fist]
rather than receiving, let me tell you something that Rhoe, the
great waitress at the Burger Ranch at Fortieth and Seventh, where
all the Met personnel went for coffee, once said to me. I'd come
back from the cash register with change for the tip and noticed she
was clearing the table and had no free hand. "Should I just stick it
in your fist, Rhoe?" I asked, absolutely unthinkingly. "You stick
it in my fist, I'm takin' you *home.*")

You may remember that in *Key Largo,* for which the definitive
Claire Trevor—playing Gay Dawn, a battered alcoholic moll and
(as they used to call them then) thrush—won the Academy Award
as Best Supporting Actress (and let's face this: with very few nods
to the big girls, this has been *the* fabulous gay category over the
years since its inception), Gay Dawn's real name was Maggie Mooney; many people think—or used to think—that I got called Gay
Dawn not just as a joke on Phil and his supposed (or much-
exaggerated) Cosa Nostra connections, but because my real name
was Mooney. My real name, although Irish, wasn't, and isn't, Mooney. (It isn't now the same as Phil's, either—another rumor: that
he adopted me: untrue.) I had known, however, and was beholden
to, a Marge Mooney, and I always think of her in connection with
Venice, because she put me in a motion picture there—the only
one I've made, to date—one summer, and then died there the next.

It all came about in the following way. Years before, I had

been sent from Delancey Street "up the river," as we all used to say, imitating the Dead End Kids. (This was in the era when in the popular imagination children like me either grew up to be manly priests or just got old enough to be put into the electric chair.) Up the river to an archdiocesan correctional facility—a reform school—called Lincoln Hall. The fact is, I got turned around there, through the efforts of a very kind, saintly, and forceful man called Father—later Monsignor—Gregory Mooney, whose sister, Margaret, was this enormous woman with three chins, right out of Dickens, and whose occupation it was to engineer little musical vaudeville shows in grammar schools in the archdiocese. She came up to Lincoln Hall and made me a star at age eleven, singing "America, I Love You." More than eleven years later, sometime after Lincoln Hall (and after the Mais Oui and *Panache*), I was walking across the Piazza San Marco, and there coming out of Florian's, as large as life in the Italian allegorical manner, was Miss Margaret Mooney. "I'm here making a picture," she said, as if that were the most natural thing in the world—as if she'd given up good works and started spending the bulk of her life poolside in Beverly Hills. (Actually, her passion for Italy in summer and her clerical connections had led her right onto the sidelines of the Italian film industry; she'd become as matey with the Cinecittà crowd as she'd ever been with the lace-curtain eunuchs at Villard House.) "I'd heard you'd gone into the profession and from the look of you might be just in time for the regatta scene we're getting ready to shoot. Come with me." That's how I got into—I can't tell you what they finally called it, but Princess Saroya and Richard Harris (remember them?) were the stars. It's never, so far as I know, been released here, but Miss Mooney and I did make the *Sunday News* picture centerfold. M.M. (or should I maybe say M.'M.'?) was playing a sort of Elsa Maxwell American party beast, and she sailed down the Grand Canal in a great draped gondola, and I sailed right down with her, as a Pierrot without whiteface. I got a lot of offers in Europe from that appearance, which I turned down, but everybody who saw it asked me what I was doing, or *thinking about*, in that sequence, because my face read deep mystery. (A similar question, you may recall, was once asked of Miss Garbo.) Well, what I was doing, since I had no character, no script, no direction, was: I was rolling the Sant'Ariano monologue in a slow crawl across my brain pan and *seeing* the island and the supper party on it—although I must tell you, I have never felt the slightest inclination to inquire about the authenticity or whereabouts of that darkly fabled venue, as often as I've been to Venice. (Phil skeeved on it, the whole story.)

Sad to say, Miss Mooney died the very next summer, in Venice, but they shipped the body home, and I went to the funeral. I was by then, and resolutely, no longer in the profession. I remember thinking for a minute while shaking hands with Monsignor Greg that maybe I should go and work with the kids who came from where I'd come from, and maybe find another star, but the Holy Ghost—that dove—sort of let me know in the secret way he has of communicating that that wasn't my line of work, either. I haven't been back to church.

My line of work. For years—decades—nobody's said anything to suggest there *was* such a thing in the world as my line of work—apart from the activities of daily living: the house, the garden, furnishings, and decoration. Odette had begun calling me Harriet Craig—and now, suddenly, this, and Phil going on about the time being right for a book, from me. "Sure," I said—thinking maybe it's Odette who's behind all this: she's sitting on her lard ass over there in County Mayo, probably bored, and has probably decided *I* should get busy—"and you'll get it printed and make sure it gets stocked by all the better Italian restaurants in the *city*, now, right?" He says cut it out with the low self-esteem—he's been looking at daytime television—and that it's time to tell my story; he says he's sure it means something. He says I should put it all down—since

when. I said, "And who's going to look after you after I start
writing books and going back into the profession and going on talk
shows as a faggot grown wise on penny candy?" "I could look
after myself." "You could look after yourself. You could eat *scungils*,
but you don't."

"Well, you ought to think about it, anyway."

(Robber to Jack Benny: "Your money or your life." Long
pause; no response. "I *said* your *money* or your *life!*" Jack Benny:
"I'm thinking—I'm *thinking!*")

"Should I put in what you heard Judy say to Diane DeVors
that time?"

Phil really adored Judy. I guess I did, too; I was always there.
(Does that figure? I ought to try owning up, not merely indicating,
right?) This particular time, just before she went onstage, looking
from the wings over the house filling up, she turned to Diane
DeVors and said, "Why do I get all the cripples?" So, she was in
that kind of mood, poor woman, with God-only-knows what mix
of shit rocketing through her wounded veins. Do I have to repeat
the story? Apparently.

Many years ago now, in the infirmary at Lincoln Hall, I woke
from what was billed as rheumatic fever (really a nervous breakdown—my first and last) hearing children's voices. (The episode
was explained reassuringly years later by Job Gennaio as breaking
the eggshell of latency, and my emergence as an adolescent boychik
diagnosed as, very much against the odds, successful.) Children's
voices alternately crying and calling like newsboys, *Read it and
weep! Read it and weep!* (Gennaio called it my translation of *tolle,
legge.*) The monitors had taken the letter away, and not a word
was ever said about it. (Except by me to me: what was I saying
before about Violetta Valery in the last act of *La Traviata?*) *What
we were doing was wrong, no matter how it felt, no matter what you
told me. Father says it's a question of honor; I should trust him, he
won't tell anyone. But I know if we start again. . . .* You got it?
Good. (I guess it was after I saw Mawrdew Czgowchwz as Violetta

that I started remembering everything—starting with the letter at Lincoln Hall. She had a way of making that happen to me: when she sang Isolde and collapsed at the end, then woke up singing "The Lament of the Hag of Beare," in Irish, I recognized the words—although I didn't know what they meant—and that started off a whole train of associations about Delancey Street and my own . . . another story.) Meanwhile, *my* confessor—grab *this*—had gone on and on about Saint Augustine and God's love and the illusory grandeur of the self. (I'd actually said *I don't know why I'm telling you all this; I don't believe in hell, or in heaven, or in anything.*) The illusory grandeur of the self! You ready? Next. "Fuck *you*, Saint Augustine!" I cried. I had sung "America, I Love You" to over a thousand people and brought down the house. Speculation had run riot that the new Silver Mask Tenor—if not another John McCormack—had been discovered. I had said—almost sung— *I love you* to another human being (*all right*, a guy, a fabulous, spectacular animal male peer). And there's one thing I'm glad of— even Job Gennaio admitted it was paradoxically fortunate—and will be until the day I die, and that's that I had no mother to run to and babble at—no Saint Monica for me, thank you. Phil knows the right thing to do: he pats me on the head; we fuck. That's all I want; that is my absolution. And while you're at it, don't drop me in a sack in either New York river; I'd like to be buried near Jackson Pollock in Springs. In fact, if the world doesn't end first, both Phil and I are, as they say, slated for interment in Green River cemetery. (So you know where to look.) Meanwhile, all that reminds me of something else I've heard of, but never seen, and I sometimes think O'Maurigan made up, but he won't admit he did. In Venice there's supposedly this very ancient Clorox blond who tramps the Lido esplanade in August, wearing *short pants* and a *sailor top*, looking for absolution, in *Polish*, from strangers, for a *sin he cannot reveal.* (O'Maurigan used to say someone should tell him about the pope.) *Catholicism!* (Italics mine.) Love. Lies.

So, should I go on television in the afternoons—give Sally

Jessy and Oprah hot runs for their money (all the while disdaining: we don't need the money—we'll donate it, all of it, to AIDS research—and when we ran into one another that night at the Cherry Lane, it turns out we stopped running, then and there). Should I be the day keeper and diviner invoking the midmost seers of the gay gone life? Should I rattle my beads like corn kernels or coral seeds in lots of four in front of the burnt offerings? (Actually, Odette O'Doyle has planted one portion of all the burnt offerings— the ashes of eight of the Eleven against—in the garden of the former Women's House of Detention and taken the rest away to the rivers, fjords, and seas of Mother Europe. Should I burn some more—the way I still burn my hair bronze?) Then call upon Miss Hildegarde Dorsay, *La Reine Voltige*, upon Miss Charity, upon the ghost of the mother I've just told you I never needed, upon the Good Witch of the North to take me back to—

Naxos and beyond the grove at Melanes. . . . Through the Dardanelles, across the Black Sea to Colchis, where Maria's voice is still growling in the wind as it did on earth over Tito Gobbi's mortal coil, *E avanti a lui tremava tutta Roma!* Or some equivalent. I see her again as I saw her last, at the Metropolitan in January of 1965. She will leave the candles burning now, drop the crucifix on Tito Gobbi's lifeless breast, put the false safe-conduct to Civitavecchia in her beaded bag with her crepe de chine, and leave home—just as I did.

I see four supine figures in a vision (a literary vision, don't lose your whole mind). Jackson Pollock, the *kouros* of Melanes, Judy in her coffin at Campbell's, and Tito Gobbi as Scarpia. I must verify my safe-conduct, sort my memories in lots of four, and—

When they finish reconstructing Central Park, they can seat me in a fanback wicker chair in a pagoda on the promontory of the Ramble. I shall officiate there, singing "Lazy Afternoon" to the Bethesda Fountain crowd, and planning and collecting contributions for the Gay Pride Silver Anniversary Mais Oui Memorial Float. I shall dock my gondola (other people have influential connections at City Hall—and *nobody* is saying the mayor is *gay*, either, or *who with*, okay?), and in the summer evenings, resuming it, I shall circulate among the little rowboats on the lake, garbed in the Venetian peacock-blue ensemble and the carnival mask I brought back last September. (I call the mask Fabrizio: he's painted gold and silver and he's a bit older and a lot smarter than that Pierrot who sailed down the Grand Canal all those years ago.) I shall periodically remove Fabrizio and hold him in one hand while with the other I tell the fortunes of pilgrims who have rowed out to me from Bethesda. And if, before the evening sun's gone down, as it spins red in the sky, the Venetian ensemble proves too hot to wear, I may lay it by and, wearing the T-shirt the scientist whose article I read in *OMNI* will by then have marketed, show off my arms and chest. I may even take up the *Sant'Ariano* monologue again, and inaugurate a new-old craze, or, better still, prerecord it, and counterpoint the playback with a recitation of that single, simple formula of universal life—which I have an idea just might turn out to *be* "Love God etcetera," expressed as an extended equation in calculus. I think I could bring all that off. I'm not so young as I was—as that sixties Pierrot—but I'm still gay, I'm still lovable (I've heard it said), and I've still got the same nice teeth. (They're not, like Peter Pan's, my first teeth, but would you really trust Peter Pan? I never did. He always looked like a woman with an angle, even on the peanut butter jar. Although I have to say Jean Arthur really *was* a boy, even if you knew her angle couldn't possibly be. . . . And for some reason, whereas you can generally believe a boy playing a woman [I mean didn't the same fabulous boy, the Earl of Oxford's protégé, play Juliet and Rosalind, Desdemona and Viola, Ophelia and Lady Macbeth, and, just before retiring, Cleopatra? O'Maurigan says that that's the noise], the *reverse*. . . . Can you *really* believe Sarah Bernhardt was Hamlet? Mae West didn't, even if she allowed, "It wuz a good turn, deah."

They asked her, "Was that before or after she had her leg ampu-
tated, Mae?" "What? Oh *yeah*, lemme see. . . . Musta been *aftuh*,
deah, 'cause she wuz *draggin'* things a bit. Anyway, they're my
big-boy teeth—and I got them the hard way: no nickels under
pillows when the first ones fell out. And I promise I won't drag
things, not a bit. What more could the people want?)

TIME REMAINING
(A CHANCE TO TALK)

One is not free to write this or that.
—GUSTAVE FLAUBERT

Moods change like the landscapes
before a traveler on a train.
—SIGMUND FREUD

THE PROLOGUE

What *more could the people want—in the time remaining.*
That's the part I forgot to write: the last part. (I either
forgot to write it, or somebody told me I must have
forgotten to write it, and what difference, if I write it right, now.
Right? Like that.)

In the time remaining? Was the wanting of the answer as
transparent as all that, or was the truth not that the answer had
been staring me in the shaving-mirror face, mornings, the whole
time? To find out, I started writing again, and the very next thing
I wrote was,

> You want to call in your comments and suggestions?
> The tenth and eleventh callers get two free tickets apiece,
> total of four, all next to one another—so when you get
> there you have an opening gambit.

I swear to you (as in *Howard, I swear to you, I didn't write
that letter!*) that I didn't have in mind what's come about. I swear

45

that when I offered *free tickets so when you get there*, I was talking
figuratively (and, as a matter of fact, using the device of the free
tickets given away to listeners of unsponsored radio programs—
since, as Addison de Witt remarks, they know something of the
world in which they live) to be literary—attempting to produce the
echo of me listening (as reported earlier) and connecting that with
you *listening* now, to me.

Like that. Although to pretend it—what came to pass—was
not right there implicit in what I first wrote, that it was not
already a pretext for Performance Art—but I had always spoken
others' words onstage—as in the O'Maurigan opus, *Panache*—
and, frankly, had been so out of it in Rialto terms that I never
really knew what Performance Art *was*—I mean, how could I
have brought myself to bear the knowledge that it was just you
got up on a bare stage and ranted at people—people who'd bought
tickets—ranted from your own mind? Or as has been said, you
just take what's been bothering you your whole life and, remembering what you love to do more than anything else. . . . Well,
performing is *not* what I love to do more than anything else.
(Neither, really, is sex, much as I. . . .) What I really like to do
best is be alone and think out loud—which some people call
talking to yourself and warn you you could end up in Creedmore
doing. In any case, they got me to do it: it was sort of like
Oedipus, only instead of putting my eyes out and running away
to Colonus—I mean Naxos was enough, know what I mean?—
when the oracle (the Python of Poulaphouca) read me, clocked
me, let me *know* what I wanted the people to want, and challenged me to give it to them—well, I opened on Second Avenue—
cheerily defying Saint Augustine yet again, for it was he who
called the theater *the foul plague spot* and he who denounced *the
voluptuous madness of stage plays*. Well, as the kids say today,
Saint Augustine, *get out of my face!*

There I was—here I still am, on Second Avenue, tonight and every night except Sundays, when I scoot out to the beach, to that little place just two hours from New York that's on Margo Channing's list of. . . . There I stop all day Sunday into Monday, where I officially live, and where of a Sunday afternoon, on my solitary beach walk from Sagaponack to the stone jetty the Army Corps of Engineers built in Wainscott, in my office of Nature Conservancy volunteer, I—get this—*police* the fenced-off nest sites of endangered species like the least tern and the piping plover. (It's on that jetty at Wainscott that I always ask *what for* in earnest. I really can't get into it until I get out into the waves a little, let the ocean breezes clear my head and vividly imagine—what—Atlantis? It was the same at Rockaway when I'd had enough of the rides and the Skee-Ball at Playland, or enough of lying under the boardwalk alone listening to the surrounding heterosexual couples at it. Enough of getting tanked up on the horse-piss beer they poured out in pails at the Leitrim Castle. I'd go and seek solace out at the end of the wooden jetties. The same, too, later at Riis Park, when the gallon thermos of cold sidecars had been emptied, and idle chatter, turning edgy. . . .)

But I'm not now there in any of those other theres. I'm here, onstage (so to speak), feeling sponsored by the ballsass spirit of the woman O'Maurigan refers to as *die ewigweibliches Marlene*. (I see her perched on a Jeep fender parked in a clearing in the rubble in

the Alexanderplatz, Berlin, circa 1945, hoisting her Travis Banton
tailored WAC skirt in a pose duplicating the Scotty Welbourne
publicity still from *Manpower*, 1941, to exhibit those severely perfect Bakelite gams—*Here dey are boys!*) Putting out for the paying
public, singing

> *Want to buy some illusions—slightly used, secondhand?*
> *They were lovely illusions, reaching high, built on sand.*
> *They had a touch of paradise, a spell you can't explain.*
> *For in this crazy paradise you are in love with pain.*

Putting out the way she is said to have put out for this conscripted
Kilroy and that: leading us on—warbling those *R*s to sound like
*W*s—in some version or other of Superman's fight for truth, justice,
and the American Way. (Superman was born the same year I was,
so I get a little sentimental about him, blue hair and all.)

Marlene, the disillusioned girl dressed as the Sick Soul of
Europe, sang

> *Want to buy some illusions, slightly used, just like new?*
> *Such romantic illusions, and they're all about you.*
> *Too bad they fell apart as dreams often do.*
> *They were lovely illusions but they just wouldn't come*
> *true.*

Whereas, as I've already mentioned, I, before I ever learned to
sing *If you hold my hand and sit real still, you can hear the grass
as it grows,* sang "America, I Love You," sang *you're like a sweet-
heart to me.* What if that was a flat-out lie. Was it necessarily
art? Quiz question. Or what if what happened to my feelings
about America were exactly what happened to *Marwene's
iwwusions*—to her *cwazy pawadise* of *dweams* that wouldn't come
twue? As if that were not enough—always leave them wanting you

wanting them more: wanting you to admit to them that once is never enough, they should be angels and buy tickets for another night: you might change a little the performance, O'Maurigan even convinced me to close the show singing the abovementioned— aforementioned, q.v.—"Lazy Afternoon," as if the paradise had never been crazy, or, anyway, as if we'd never found out it was— also commenting by the way that "the Dietrich image is eerily right for you. That picture of her in the ruins of the capital of the Third Reich, decoded, is a sort of apocalyptic, emblematic Goldilocks and the Three Bears, and the story you're telling—strange beds, apocalypse, and all—is a kind of. . . . Well, I won't push it, but it fits.")

Irishmen speak in dark-blue-fire-at-heart-of-emerald riddles. It is O'Maurigan's conceit that the particle *lin* in *Berlin* is the Celtic for *pool*, same as in *Dublin* (Dark Pool). The three bears, apart from being Germanic archetypes and Berlin's very emblem, are, I suppose, Hitler, Himmler, and Goebbels. And who is Marlene, then, Brünnhilde? Well, I said I was going to be a day keeper and diviner, didn't I—in my spare time? Meanwhile, I'm still writing— in my spare time—in the lazy afternoons; backstage making up; on Sundays in Sagaponack—I take pen in hand, so.

Just so you know that *pen in hand* is a metaphor, I haven't taken an actual pen in hand since reform-school days. Having had that go on O'Maurigan's Dictaphone that resulted in the performance piece, I took it up in earnest. It's how we actually open the show, with me sitting talking into it: he convinced me it would create exactly the right nostalgic atmosphere, sort of like opening *La Voix humaine* with a bulbous white telephone—except he insisted *I Go Back to the Mais Oui* was a better show.

It's the story

he wrote in the producer's program intro,

> of a blithe heart-of-gold tough who made good. Who
> never gets bored, because he's a pure-sensation type.
> Whose reminiscences are as bright as paint—or acid—
> and more than an exercise in nostalgia. They are about
> the force of memory, the melodrama of remembering.

(He'd *wanted* to get some compliant journalist to say all that in
print somewhere, the way book reviewers routinely insert publish-
ers' advance copy in their deathless appraisals, so he could then
excerpt it on the poster out front. I said, *"Please,* I have to walk in
and out that *door* every night: don't make me look at such a thing
written on the wall. It was enough what was written on the bathroom wall at Lincoln Hall all those years ago!"*) I mean, that really
is the kind of thing, isn't it, that you put into the past tense and
pin onto the floral arrangements at Campbell's—indoors, where it's
safe. I could well imagine what little additions—in lipstick and
Crayola—would appear on anything left out in front of the theater,
after only a day or two. "And in any case," I added, "my analyst—
who, if you haven't forgotten, is your analyst, too—made hash of
Jung's theory of types in the sixties. The *truth* is I don't get bored
because it is a sin against the Holy Ghost." "Can I put *that* up on
the wall on Second Avenue?" "Well . . . no." "Then trust me—
what they will read is,

He's your type of pure sensation.

It's like subliminal advertising: I've packaged you in blood-red. I
know how you feel: evolved soul that you are, you do not enjoy
fame. The idle dream of fame, yes, but the reality you know is

vexing to the soul, and that makes you wonder why you must put up with it. The more provocative I get on the wall, the better for you—trust me." So I shut up, once again; it felt right.

I almost wrote *here goes nuthin'* up there in the epigraph, instead of that Flaubert and that Freud, but Phil, although he's promised not to butt in, would if he did be sure to slap the back of my hand with a (metaphoric) ruler, declaring, "No low self-esteem!" He'd be thinking in doing so of some of the, shall we say, less appreciative notices *Mais Oui* received here and there on what's left of the Rialto, and their possible effect on its blithe, pure-sensation-type protagonist. He'd also be enacting, as he is some-times wont to do, a parody of the ballsass spirit of the black-bonnet Sisters of Charity of my youth. (Not his: he went to public school, all twelve grades of it, and has never spoken about the Confrater-nity of Christian Doctrine catechism lessons, for which he was released early on Wednesdays. You get the feeling he started drift-ing instead—early—into the *Archestrato* Social Club on Mulberry Street for special instruction in the activities of daily Christian living, *in modo di Palermo*, if you know what I mean—plus bil-liards.)

O'Maurigan said to me something like this. "Although Phil may indeed be wrong about meeting you for the first time at the Modern—I believe you: it was the Cherry Lane—he is absolutely right about everything else that concerns you, and I wouldn't for a minute redirect anything he orders, but I think I may safely augment his argument. With you it is not merely a question of generic low self-esteem; with you it is the slicing of a two-edged sword that cuts up, down, and sideways. For the one, foundlings have a terrible—just ask Erasmus. The second thing is you are an American. What does that mean? Well, it means, for example, in spite of the fact that the greatest American war novel was, like the great Russian one before it, written by a writer who never went to the Civil War, a writer who understood that the battlefield is *the page*—in spite of that, Americans insist on what they take to be eyewitness reporting. Television. What I'm getting at is: Because you had the good sense to decline to visit the theater of the big lost American Southeast Asian war and—call it the good luck or the grace, no matter—to visit the casualty wards merely and not the AIDS battlefield, you somehow languish under the impression that you lack a subject. That you are, God help you, *unworthy* of one. I must advise you in the strongest terms, you are *not.*"

"When you say *foundling,* you really mean *bastard.*"

"*Foundling,*" said he, "was good enough for the Sisters of Charity. Remember?"

Remember? What could I say but, "How could I ever forget?" I had to admit I liked *foundling,* though. It reminded me of something I'd once heard sung—but I couldn't tell you what, when, or by whom.

"Once you start," he advised, "it all comes running."

The black-bonnet Sisters of Charity of St. Patrick's on Mott Street. Of course, they didn't mind low self-esteem; it suited their purposes perfectly, as a matter of fact. They wielded real, not metaphoric, ones: rulers edged with copper strips: really could cut into those little pink boypaws (though that never did stop them— the paws—from growing, did it, into these attractive, manfully hirsute, still-peachy mitts).

"No low self-esteem!" (Phil again, as I return to the moment.) "I read where it lowers the resistance."

"To colds and flu?"

"Just no low self-esteem, okay?"

"Okay." (Okay.)

"And go easy on the modifiers this time, willya, for Chrissakes? Be sparing with the adjectives and the adverbs—and with the goddam parentheses. They're just confusing."

"Confusing? Remember that time I showed you how to diagram a sentence?"

"Just go easy. I read where all that shit is a mark of insecurity—the excess."

"How can I feel insecure with you around? You are all man. Just to hear you say *advoib* gets me excited."

"You know what this is? It's a fist."

"I know, I know—and if I spring it open with one finger, I get the dime that's inside."

"The temperamental ahtist—you're all the same."

"Not really. You wouldn't feature any of the others half as much as you feature me. Anyway, there's an Irish expression: a shut fist never caught a bird. Open your hand and let me kiss it up to God."

Phil's right about the garnish, I know it. Less is—but, you know, I can't help remembering Diane DeVors holding forth on contemporary performing. *Less is* not *more—less is* less! I guess it depends on the temperament, which consists—

I'm going to follow O'Maurigan's orders, and Phil's, and tell this story. I don't want to give you a core dump for your pains and patience, and I don't want to rush, to get all nonlinear and overwrought, but, on the other hand, I haven't got all the time in the world. Let me try, however; let me try to corral, somehow, the time available—in Odette O'Doyle's words, fast approaching the main story line, the true text, the time remaining.

I've just this minute realized, after the second reiteration of them, how ominous those two words sound, especially coming so soon after my little meditation on publicity and the floral arrangements at Campbell's. They definitely would appear to be suing for something more in the strict attention line than you might otherwise be willing to dispense, as if, in spite of what I have

just, as it were, allowed O'Maurigan to say about me, the truth
of it was, *is*—

The truth is I am not ill—not on the face of it, anyway. In spite
of the latest French critical formulation, which dictates that *in
this multidimensional space in which a variety of writings—none
of them original—blend and clash*, necessarily *I am not present*—
dig it—only the writing is. Moreover, *always deferred*: as if it
hadn't had the nerve at the draft board to check the box once
and for all. Writing referring to other writing; signs referring—
I must insist, *your author is not dead—or dying*. What I meant
was the story itself—of Odette, her mission—has a lifeline, a
telling lifetime, after which, perhaps, the life *span* . . . etcetera.
Like that.
    The first terrible thing I realized about this work was that as
soon as I get bored—or is that more properly designated as fearful—it's as if these people I'm writing about—the Eleven against
Heaven—*who are real; they walk this earth, or did, only yesterday*,
are in danger, and if I get bored enough—bored, fearful, what
difference, so far as the effect is concerned—and stay that way long
enough, they're as good as worse-than-dead, as it were, as good as
no-account. I think the most important thing to say about that
conceit is that it represents exactly my original idea of God vis-à-
vis me. I concluded early on that I *had* to keep interesting the
Motherfucker—and if you want to score my language, do so, but
you'll find it hard to dispute my drift: in fact, if you want to get
into theology, I can quote you chapter and verse—through His
agents, in order, literally, to stay alive. Saint Augustine taught me
that—*Confessions* 3:6—his psychological fascination with his own
earlier self, not known to him but known to God, in childhood
and in the womb, and the conclusion from same: that God was
therefore an intermediary, more immediate to him than he is to

himself—*Intimio intimo meo.* Like that. And my substitutions of men for God, or for God-in-men, whatever, had for many years, and still may have, to a degree—I'm writing this, am I not—this bewildering quality of appeasement through agitation and the conviction that it is better to be condemned than to be ignored. *There is no such thing as bad publicity.* Oh? If they say so. Seems to be so. Not even, as it turns out, *There are few torments equal to being locked in a room with a queen on speed.* That's what he wrote—the reviewer in question—purposely vicious, as if he knew (and there's no reason to doubt he'd been advised) about the things I (along with many others having taken certain steps) no longer do, that I am committed to refrain from discussing at the level of the press, radio, and television. I shall therefore take a similar tack in publishing, but put it more delicately. I shall further cite Saint Augustine—on interpreting the text.

> Whoever finds a lesson there useful to the building of Charity, even though he has not read what the author may be shown to have intended in that place, has not been deceived, nor is he lying in any way.

Go figure.

(For example: *He looked like an old dead tree.* Osiris was originally, supposedly, an African tree god. And if you want to think of Jackson's paintings as parts of him—because nobody put himself into his paintings the way he did—then you might say—or I might say—they are a kind of Communion, to be passed around. Or that pieces of the old dead tree Jackson became are like splinters of the new true Cross—you know: Art.)

———

It happened on the Night of the Shooting Stars, August 11, 1991, a year to the night from the Skylark's East Hampton reading, and from the night on which Jimmy Roy—Ethyl—Eichelberger slashed his wrists on Staten Island—laid low, it was widely declared, by the nerve-caustic effects of the drug AZT. Also—I can't help saying significantly, without exactly knowing why—thirty-five years to the night from Jackson Pollock's death in Springs. Moreover, I can't help adding that by then the Skylark was himself among the stellar dead—felled by a stroke in April. Shooting stars—is that significant? When Jackson hit that tree, did he—as represented, for example, in comic strips—see stars, for an instant, before seeing—what? Did the Skylark, who saw more than anybody else, see them, or anything like them, before seeing—what? God—or Nothing? (And could they not be the same, after all? Have you ever seen them together?)

Phil had been on the phone on the Saturday, after the matinee. "Odette's back at last; she's comin' t'th'show tonight, and she'll ride out with you after, so we could finally find out everything that happened."

I was sitting in my dressing room between shows musing not over my beads in lots of four, but (perhaps as a combination emotional recall–sense memory exercise to gear the performance: maybe you'll discern a pattern to the choice) over four of the postcards Odette had sent from Europe. The one of the Irish castle I've already mentioned as preamble to the performance text of *I Go Back to the Mais Oui.* (Just so you know, since this is itself a postmodern document, with the directions on the package, and also suggests to me as I reread it a crossword puzzle that is its own solution, the preamble signifies the remainder of the text from the reprise of *When the 1950 Oldsmobile convertible Jackson Pollock was driving at*

breakneck speed bit etcetera.) The one Phil had talked about most
affectionately ("Some fat old broad backstage in her dressing room;
looks like Odette herself when she comes out to see us and hangs
around the kitchen on Sunday morning in her bathrobe"). Namely,
Toulouse-Lautrec's *La Clownesse Cha-u-Kao*. (I was calling it *Kow-Tow*, and even Odette never got it right—see below—naming and
renaming it in the course of one of her characteristically lepidop-
teran—that's what I said—riffs.) It held the following message.

> Miss Odette O'Doyle, like Miss Banquett, undertook
> this voyage because she was beautiful, not for a holiday.
> In beauty there are no holidays; beauty is a steady oc-
> cupation.
>
> *Should Beauty blunt on fops her fatal dart,*
> *Not claim the triumph of a letter'd heart.* . . .

(First, part of quote from a Laura Riding Jackson story called
Miss Banquett, or The Populating of Cosmania; couplet, source unknown. I mention the Laura Riding Jackson source only to propose
something I'd supposed that, as it turned out in the avalanche of
detail I subsequently was to survive that night, I neglected to verify.
That in Odette's own gay mind Laura Riding Jackson's Cosmania
was equivalent to Very Heaven, to which sphere she had assured
her dearly departed companions' passage by the beauty of her enterprise and the rigor of its execution.)

The one from Venice: a detail of Titian's *Martyrdom of San
Lorenzo*. And one I didn't much care for—I can't even tell you who
did it, but its subject was compelling: of the suicide of the failed
poet Thomas Chatterton. It hangs in the Tate Gallery in London
and was the last card we had before Odette hit Ireland and communication ceased for months. The legend, in couplets—again, from
an unknown source (but I was beginning to infer a pattern)—was,

Should no disease thy torpid veins invade,
Nor Melancholy's phantoms haunt thy shade;
Yet hope not life from grief or danger free,
Nor think the doom of man revers'd for thee. . . .

(The kicker of this last line was that like one of those foreground-background puzzles where you see first one, then the other—and the one you're supposed to see naturally becomes the harder of the two to fix—I kept reading *reserv'd* for *revers'd*. That will tell you something about my habit of mind—the veil it wears, too, like some nun's. Like that.)

"I *told* you why," Phil had reminded me, as the weeks of Odette's absence turned into a season. "When Bush decided last summer to stage the Gulf War, she just decided *fuck it*, and stayed in Europe—and she was serious." Just how serious we knew when she missed both the Night of a Thousand Gowns at the Roosevelt in March and Wigstock in Tompkins Square Park last month. She'd still be over there probably if the war hadn't turned out to be just some flash-forward-then-fizzled American tantrum, and if Schuyler hadn't died. "*A few days are all we have*—but isn't there more days than years?" she'd finally written from County Mayo in June. "Just call me Tarry O'Doyle, and consider, if you will, upon receipt of this, noting the date of dispatch, just what meaning there is in Ireland to the term *haste-post-haste*, reckoning with, as Henry James says, *the Atlantic Ocean, the General Post Office and the extravagant curve of the globe*. And from what I overheard about *Abortion Desert Song*, it was like a rat pack of degenerate hoods from—you will excuse me, dear—south of Delancey, pulling some delivery boy from the local Szechuan takeout off his beat-up bicycle and kicking the shit out of him to prove they can win at something. What a *disgusting* country: where *can* we irenics flee—Cosmania?

I put up all those years with *A Chorus Line,* but this was too much. And now it's over I can't bear to come home to the pathological euphoria rampant there. It's only the death that's made me realize why I have to at all—just to go to his grave, if nothing else. But this, too, dear: just to look at a friend in a *grave* will be something for me after dumping all the girls one after the other into all the rivers of Europe."

"Odette always gets her way—and without destroying anybody, either."

"Well, nobody we know of—nobody we ever cared about, anyway."

"Naw, nobody, I wouda heard. I been around longer than you. Odette's just somethin' unusual, somethin' else. You could say one for the books. A nice girl who didn't finish last. Which is why I'm sure she's done good like she said she was gonna do."

It's true Odette never finished last—or anywhere near it—but for the simple reason that she never competed. At the Night of a Thousand Gowns, for example: she never missed one, but she never entered. "I concluded long ago, dear," she once told me, "that I am essentially *The Whore on the Concourse,* if you take my meaning." So we ended up tear-assing up Second Avenue in a cab to Penn Station to catch the 12:32, me intending to interview my friend on the long ride out. . . . Odette and Delancey: two, how the French ventriloquist would say, *noms de guerre.* The *two sole* survivors of the Eleven against Heaven. Nobody on the Rialto ever called either of us by his rightful name, although you could look either or both of us up in the Hall of Records.

You know about my name; about Odette's I could go on at length. The strapping singing-and-toe-dancing star of the wartime London

and immediate postwar New York revue *Dress Stage.* (As Edwin
Denby put it, "Odette O'Doyle is the woman Toumanova is trying
to be.") Cabareteer at Madame Spivvy's Roof, diagonally across
Fifty-seventh and Lexington from the Menemsha Bar. Diva *diseuse*
at Shirley's Pin-Up Room, lower down on Lexington, and at the
Cherry Lane, way down on Commerce, in old Greenwich Village,
singing *This little frail can do / All that a male can do.* . . . Returned
in glory to England in the self-referential *swinging sixties* to play
the defecting Russian ballerina Stolichnaya in *Carry On, Comrade X*—a very loose cross-remake of *Grand Hotel* and *Ninotchka*—
stealing the picture right out from under the noses of the stock
company that made that series a sort of British farce *Ring of the
Nibelung.* I could go on—how she then got serious for herself and
became O. D. O'Doyle, founding editor of *Terpsichore* (and deviser
of the distinctive logo of same: a silhouette drawn from the negative of Tanaquil Le Clerq in *attitude* balance as that eponymous
muse), and wrote her mouth down on the subject she knew as no
other: what Dorothy Dean called *thub dance.* As O'Maurigan put
it, "She's done dance from A to Z and back again: from Adams
and Alonso to Zorina and Zoritch; from Anna Pavlova to Zizi
Jeanmaire and back to Altynai Asylmuratova." Nobody would say,
least of all Odette, so I won't, either, that she bested Edwin Denby:
even if she could have, she wouldn't have considered it fittin' to do
so—total recall polymath that she was (and is).

　　She did succeed, however, as all must know, in giving him
and all the rest of them a long hard run for their gay money and
keeping them on their eyes' toes, so to speak—and there are those
who would insist that since Denby's sad death (and *that's* some
story, when you're in the mood for it: *You realize, if you don't kill
yourself, you're going to have to keep that appointment with the den-
tist!*) she's been the only *really* authoritative voice of ballet in New
York—that is, whenever she can get it together to publish an
issue. . . .

No, neither of us, castaways both, were ever after called the names on our dogtags. (Odette wore hers entwined together with her pearls in the European theater of the Second World War, and thereafter all the way up till the Vietnam protest days, when she threw them—the tags, not the pearls: she hadn't lost her whole mind—in with the kids' draft cards. I wore mine—my dogtags: I don't wear pearls, although I once did: once only, long ago, at Cherry Grove playing Colette's *Chéri*, opposite Diane DeVors. All wards of the diocese wore dogtags. I gave mine to Phil; he had them bronzed, like baby shoes.)

Odette's pearls: another story. She got them, a rope of them, from an ardent admirer during the run of her first show, *One Touch of Venus*. She was still Danny O'Doyle then, just down from Sedgwick Avenue, and the job, in the chorus—a legendary lineup—was her first. She wore the pearls on her very first drag outing, to, where else, Phil Black's, over a little wartime knockoff-Chanel cap-sleeved black crepe dress.

A legendary lineup, because, of course, it was from it that the aforementioned Roman Catholic Archbishop of New York, a rapacious fellator, plucked the most renowned of his Ganymedes, setting off an intense vogue for such subversive activities as the counterpointing of *Tantum ergo* with "Speak Low When You Speak Love" during Exposition and Solemn Benediction at the cathedral, much to his grace, Bess's, annoyance and chagrin. Then things went further, one Saturday afternoon at the Perpetual Novena, when to the tune of *Immaculate Mary, Our Hearts Are on Fire: Ave! Ave!* the de facto–excommunicated girls' choir broke out into *You tacky old fairy, your purse is on fire: Oi*-ve! *Oi*-ve! and Miss Hope Chest Tone, as they were being expelled, broke into the Judgment Scene at *Sacerdoti*, and carried it all the way through on the cathedral steps to *Impia razza, anatema su voi—la vendetta del ciel* etcetera. Then, stepping into the taxi she'd meanwhile hailed with a whistle between her teeth as loud as her B-flats, and holding the door open as she gave them her last *anatema*, she slunk down in the back seat, lit a Lucky Strike, and ordered "Fortieth Street stage door, Metropolitan Opera," for the *Aida* broadcast, with Mawrdew Czgowchwz as Amneris, was even as she spoke ending up. As Odette says: all this is true.

We kept our civilian names until Fate and Glamour, working as the gay whorish team they are, translated us both into senti-mental favorites on New Nineveh's private performance circuit. (Who was it who said in another context, *To be young was very heaven?* Well, hindsight is what it is, but I might amend the words a little and offer the old showbiz reprise: it was a little bit of heaven being there on those now-legendary occasions, at Leo Lerman's parties, for instance.)

You feature true confessions—you feature the aftermath? Saturday afternoon after confession (which was where I was—am—between the matinee and the evening) had never been given over on the Lower East Side to reflection, especially not to sufficient reflection. After confession and before the fast and Sunday mass and com-munion, all you did was sit around waiting for that first occasion to overtake or not to overtake you: the occasion of sin, mortal sin. Then there was Sunday mass, communion, and more waiting, all through Sunday.

Sunday was a doom-laden day. Sometimes, if the suspense of Sunday was too much, you hurried things along at the movies. An Objectionable-in-Part might do the trick, but sometimes, in the Italian neighborhood in the West Village, there would be a Con-demned—maybe two. That was pay dirt: a mortal-sin double fea-ture. As the girl queried in some voodoo picture of the early forties (not Odette's "the girl," who, as you'll undoubtedly noticed, is a stand-in for any one of "us" queers, but the actual girl in the picture: what they used to call the ingenue, as in Fay Wray in *King Kong*), *"That's a religion?"*

(I'm really no Jacob wrestling with any angel. Not any more, anyway; I gave up wrestling—both actually and metaphorically—a long time ago. In fact, if you want to know, that's exactly how I got into trouble at Lincoln Hall: wrestling. That other human being I said "I love you" to—and who, as I may have pointed out, already was, although human, my very idea of an angel—was on the wrestling team with me. I was the better wrestler, as Jacob was, and while I had my angel pinned to the mat I said the equivalent of *I will not let thee go until* . . . and so forth.)

I had all day Sunday every Sunday—it seemed to me I'd had all the time remaining in the world—for *sufficient reflection*. That was the time needed to make up your mind to commit the mortal sin. There were, as I recall, three things essential. (Just like Merman sang in "The Hostess with the Mostes' on the Ball," remember? *There are just three things essential . . . an ounce of wisdom and a pound of gall and the Hostess*—etcetera.) The three things were: a matter of sufficient gravity, sufficient reflection, and the full consent of the will. It was always the last that could get you off if you dropped dead in midperformance. (Only your guardian angel knew if you had fully consented, and although he was duty bound to report the truth to the Holy Ghost—who was in charge of sending you to heaven or to hell—*nobody alive on earth* could tell what would get put in that report. Consequently, although hell was real—and if you didn't believe in it you would go there on the express—*nobody alive on earth*, not even the pope: who, in any case, was too holy to presume to—could tell you who was suffering for all eternity in it and who not—not even Judas Iscariot. Not even, that Jesuit priest friend of O'Maurigan's, whose name was Strange, once told us both at the Everard, Sigismondo Malatesta: not even after what he did to the Papal Legate, the comely fifteen-year old Bishop of Fano, in the piazza at Rimini. . . . Consequently, we prayed for the repose of Hitler's soul, and later Stalin's.)

Sufficient reflection seemed to vary in extent from seconds to hours—depending technically (and disproportionately, I thought) on the strategy and ugly satisfaction of the sin. For example, if you were going to spoil your confession and communion and the glowing purity of your soul and do the most serious thing in the universe—either with yourself or with others—and make your guardian angel weep out loud in heaven, then usually it took about a minute—sometimes. If you were alone. Otherwise, a minute more to scare up and cajole a partner (maybe even one of the Sigismondo Malatesta cast of mind). If you were, on the other hand, going to do something less weighty, like pick a pocket on the subway, get involved in a heist, or—if you were over twelve—do the preliminary eavesdropping that would in good time lead to somebody's saying goodbye to the world for good and ending up in cement shoes in the East River or under the Pulaski Skyway in Jersey, then more time was needed, and arguments of some subtlety. You were a bit like Jack Benny. "I'm *thinking*, I'm *thinking!*"

(Teaching us all the rules of this, the Sisters of Charity used to rant and rave and thunder, "You'll have all the time in the world—all the time remaining in eternity—to reflect on what you might have done to please Jesus Christ, the Son of God, the Second Person of the Most Holy Trinity, who was crucified for your sins, and like Saint Veronica on the Way of the Cross, wipe away one drop of His precious perspiring blood—or one precious tear His mother Mary shed at the Cross her station keeping on Good Friday— instead of committing that *one* mortal sin—instead of running away naked from Him like the young man in the garden of Gethsemane

in the Holy Gospel According to Saint Mark!" Were they completely *insane*, those women, or what?
They were completely insane.)
Then I remembered that later, much later, and in a rather
more enlightened way, connected to something I do not discuss at
the level of the press, radio, or television (although on interactive
software . . .), I was required to determine and disclose certain
wrongs, and asked to do so in terms of their *exact nature*. I was
stumped. All I could remember was that when I'd been sent away
to Lincoln Hall what I'll call *a voice* said, "I don't know what's to
become of him; he's got brains, all right, and cunning, but there's
no nature in him." To me it was like saying, "He has *no reflection
in the mirror.*"

(When I recounted this to Job Gennaio, in my first analytical
session, he replied, "They were having the correct feeling. You
have the ability to suggest that—that you have no nature, merely
a history—but we'll uncover your nature; that's our existential
task." And, just as I wrote earlier, in another existential connection, *that's when the fight started.* In essence, what Gennaio was
saying was, give me your money, I'll give you your life. Sounded
familiar, but I couldn't decide if Gennaio was a thief or not, and,
more importantly, perhaps, was he the Good Thief or the Bad
Thief?

Judy, if you recall, once asked a similar question of Billie
Burke—and it seems Judy's disciples have been asking similar questions ever since, and in that same strange, querulous voice. And
skipping from the melodrama of the crucified Judy at the Palace,
at Carnegie, at the Palladium, at the Talk of the Town in Leicester
Square, to the melodrama of the crucified Jesus on Calvary, isn't
somebody in the know at least *implying* that the Bad Thief went
to hell? Or is Jesus saying to the Good Thief, "This day shalt thou
be with me in Paradise," and to the Bad Thief, "And you call me
tomorrow, darling." What?)

I remember *everybody* telling the *same* story over and over again. . . .
Could be there's only ever been one story.
(Tick-tock. This-that. Envelope structure and all.)

And will I therefore become, in the words of the narrator of *The
Brothers Karamazov*, concerning Alyosha: *the main*, though future,
hero of my story? Or, rather, is the question like David Copperfield's
*Whether I shall turn out to be the hero of my own life, or whether
that station will be held by anybody else*?
    (You want to hear about Anxiety of Representation? This
is it.)

All that is the residue of the anguish from the reform school.
You've got to keep God interested enough for Him to wake you
up. No alarm bells in the reform school; God woke you up. Then,
when we went one weekend to a monastery on retreat (this happened right after the incident I described earlier, in what they
called Passiontide: that's the two weeks before Easter, when you
were supposed to get all worked up over events leading to the
Crucifixion), He woke us up for matins. Before dawn light we
went—or I did, anyway—still tumescent after micturition into the
chapel, and during Gregorian chant stayed tumescent looking at
the faces and listening to the voices. I never felt so warm and secure,
but I figured they'd never have me: I was such a sex-crazed thing. I
mean, going to *communion* gave me an erection. (Years later, when I
found out—after Vatican II—that they were all doing it in the bushes
at Gethsemane down in Kentucky, and elsewhere . . . Geth-se-
man-e indeed! That was as if the Everard had just gotten itself turned
into The Cloisters—well!)

I remember Phil telling O'Maurigan after the Schuyler reading he's afraid I won't ever write a book—not because I'm lazy, or don't have the self-esteem, but because I skeeve on stealing. (This is true: I've told Phil it makes me think when I tell somebody else's story that I've had no life. Like when I was a kid—around the time of the Oz books—and was taken to see *Portrait of Jennie.* I'd thought *I* must be like Jennie, out of the past, washed up on this shore, let loose in Central Park, but apart from my portrait—on canvas, in a book—nobody, really: not even a has-been, a *never-was.* I still think it when I go out and sit on the jetty and imagine myself being carried away in a hurricane: which worries Phil, so I don't talk about it.) O'Maurigan replied, "Leave him to me, dear; I shall hit him with Deuteronomy 22:3. *And so shall you do with every lost thing of your brother's, which he has lost and you have found.*" One thing I know, and that is that my telling the stories of the dead is in no way bringing order of any kind to a mass of experience the better to preserve it—or anything like that malarkey you still sometimes hear literary theorists peddle. I hold—as Odette would say— with the implications of the painting of Jackson Pollock, and with the ideas of the author of *A Brief History of Time,* the crippled English genius who seems to nearly know the secret of the universe, but who noted,

> Thus the heat expelled by the computer's cooling fan means that when a computer records an item in memory, the total amount of disorder in the universe still goes up.

As it does also, presumably, whenever we make our beds and clean our rooms, and yet we make our beds every morning—as I just had—a habit I got into at Lincoln Hall and never shook off. I make my bed in *hotels;* I used to straighten the sheets at the Everard, no matter how I woke up feeling. (Like that.)

As to who—a genius alone in a room in a wheelchair or a comely dodo alone in front of a dressing-room mirror wondering *what for?*—amuses the Antagonist more—perhaps even *disarms* Him more—I leave to contemporary transalpine radical thanatologists. (For there is no question of life that is not fundamentally a question of death—*that* I know: that goes without saying, in spite of the fact that we can never stop talking about it.)

I'd heard the bell: I had a performance to give.

Whereafter—the performance and backstage rituals—Odette and I were riding up in the cab to Penn Station and I was telling her about that one really stinko review I got—the one I've already mentioned. *There are few torments equal to being locked in a room with a queen on speed.* "Fuck him," she started out, and then the old mouth sailed into "that piss-soaked wedge of Balkan drek. There are only two things to say about *him:* he's never going to know what tie goes with what shirt, and neither the ugly little prick Nature made him, nor the *tiny,* ugly little prick she then stuck on the ugly little prick she'd made, is *ever* going to get any bigger!"

The cab, after crossing west on Thirty-first Street, dropped us not in front of Penn Station but at the entrance between the Madison Square Garden and Felt Forum tower and the Amtrak escalator. (Odette says I may if I choose so designate said portal—her exact words—but that every time *she* goes through it—even when she's on her way, as she usually is, and as we were that night, to the Long Island Rail Road, lower level—it is nothing else but the side entrance to Pennsylvania Station in the majestic shape of the Baths of Caracalla—and, she insists, going into Penn Station by the side door is as *de rigueur* to the truly chic as going into Bonwit's and

Saks the same way—and she is Claudette Colbert running away from Joel McCrea and life in New York, across the splendid esplanade, with the sun streaming through the immense windows, straight into the arms of a gang of protective older men, in *The Palm Beach Story*.) Claudette Colbert running away (silly woman!) from Joel McCrea I wasn't, and I'd been playing truth down on Second Avenue, so for me it was the escalator down to the white neon-at-midnight Amtrak waiting area (no Palm Beach), populated by New York's summer homeless in their droves; they weren't running away from anybody but the constabulary on patrol—none of whom any longer look too much like Joel McCrea (although once in a while a candidate appears, usually an officer going about the business I witnessed—see above—that June night at the Stonewall). And, at that, not running (the homeless), only shuffling, back and forth between the restrooms and the plastic-garbage-bag-lined refuse bins. (I suppose I'm trying to write truth, too, and most probably trying too hard; I'm most probably also—most probably was that night—jealous of what The O calls Odette's bicameral mind—and most certainly of her great overseas adventure. At any rate, one piece of possibly important truth was that—perhaps as a consequence of something so long ago as the letdown and fallout of the variety show at Lincoln Hall, and probably *not* as a consequence of the one or two stinko reviews—which actually made me laugh [a little]—I was beginning all over again to mistrust performing—or Performance Art—beginning all over again to be afraid that in an intrapsychic way, Saint Augustine had been right—ditto Marlene. . . .)

Enter the men: a gang of them, not in the first bloom of carefree youth (it was clear right away as they came barreling in behind us through the revolving door and as, rollicking down the stairs, singing, of all things, and in unison, *Sh-Boom, sha-Boom—ya-dadda, yaddada, yaddada, da* . . . they passed us, stately as we progressed down the escalator). But not the middle-aged members,

either, of the Fun Gun Club (or whatever it was the cardboard
drunks cast by Preston Sturges as the Seven Dwarfs to Claudette's
Snow White called themselves). Possible candidates, rather, all but
one of them, and questions of gender preference and libidinal object
choice to one side, for *Girth and Mirth*, no question. *"They're* not
going to Palm Beach, either," I advised Odette. "No, dear, they're
not." "Where do you think—Jersey?" "Oh, no, dear." (She was
firm, even though if there's one thing about Odette that's exactly
like me—and like Sugarpuss O'Shea in Howard Hawks's *Ball of
Fire*—it's her vague notion of what exactly, apart from Atlantic
City, something called, vaguely, *the Jersey Shore*, and supposedly,
Princeton University, there *is* in the state that borders ours on the
west and south.) "If they were going to Jersey they'd have taken
the Hudson Tube—anyway, just *listen* to them: the accents. Fact
is, they're on the Montauk train, with us—Oh, not all the way, to
be sure. I wouldn't say they were going to be accompanying us as
far as Patchogue, or even Sayville." "Well, how far, then?" She
thought a minute, and as we reached the Amtrak level—and they'd
already gotten as far ahead as the Long Island stairway, and were
singing

> *Life would be a dream,*
> *And you would take me up to Paradise up above,*
> *If you would tell me I'm the only one that you love—*

authoritatively declared "Bay Shore."

"The mascot's called Joey Veneziani." Odette whispered this
to me as we settled into our seats (both of us sporting dark glasses
against the neon light: not trying to look, but perhaps anyway
looking like, two—not women, but, well, ambiguities, of the second type), mischievously pronouncing the mascot's surname the
way she had obviously just heard it: Ven-*eezy*-anni.

"The mascot?"

"The sylph, dear—the one that's unlike the others."

Odette's powers of observation and deduction are, as I may have indicated already, legendary, and the fact that she makes no bones about them, nor has ever been known to boast of them, treating them, rather, matter-of-factly, as if she were merely a good judge of gabardine on Seventh Avenue, or green grocery at Balducci's, merely reinforces the case for trusting her takes absolutely. "Lighter by two stone than the lightest of them, and a few years younger, too—perhaps as many as ten or eleven years younger than the oldest of them—meaning, of course, he's more naturally the heir to "I Can't Get No Satisfaction" than to "Sh-Boom," but obviously head-over-heels in love with them as a team. Probably—almost certainly—the baby in his family—a family, I should think, entirely, apart from him, of girls—probably as many as four or five of them, since the parents wouldn't have stopped until they'd gotten him, a boy— which he most emphatically is. Look at those *bones!*"

I advised myself of the truth: the bone I'd be interested in wasn't in his face, no matter what the face looked like. (I couldn't see the team or its mascot; I was sitting with my back to the partition—why, I don't know: I don't like riding backwards, but the train had been in and the doors open when we'd gotten down to the track, and for some reason I can never remember which way is which at Penn Station.) I then started to berate myself a little for being—but I'm always horny after a performance. The condition would either have long since passed by the time we got out to the South Fork, or I'd get lucky upon retiring at sunrise (an increasingly frequent occurrence). But would I think of it, if offered, as lucky or as . . . and did I ever think about anything else in the end but—as I said, I was berating myself; I stopped.

By the time we'd reached Jamaica, we'd discovered them not as a lot of off-duty security types, but as a group of enthusiasts (and amateur performers) of original rock-'n'-roll who had come from a private-ticket charity function in the Felt Forum, where they had been singing their hearts (but, on evidence, not their lungs or larynxes) out. Odette, although never a rock-'n'-roll girl ("R and R, dear, means to my generation *only* rest and recreation, as in time off from the theater of action"), nevertheless decided then and there that the boys would do nicely as far as they went as an honor guard, as the analogues to Claudette's protectors in *The Palm Beach Story*. ("When they get off, dear—at Bay Shore—we'll just pretend they've gotten *too* raucous and their club car has been detached from the train." Odette identified with many of Claudette's roles— from the De Mille Cleopatra through *It Happened One Night* to *The Best Years Of Our Lives* right to her most recent TV appearance playing Elsie Woodward in the dramatization of the Woodward murder, in that eerie opus that Truman Capote haunts as the model for the narrator, the opus based on the story that shamanistic queens in the sixties used to prophesy would bring no fiction-retailer of it luck. Remember the scene at the Colony lunch? After demolishing Ann-Margret as the girl Truman Capote dubbed Annie-Get-Your-Gun, Claudette calls the waiter over and purrs, "I'll have the seafood salad, Henri, with a little extra vinegar." Odette is so loyal to Claudette, and to her professional severity— the dark side of the moon and all that—that she is one of the few in New York to insist Claudette would have been every bit as good, in a more rarefied way, as Margo Channing—which is one of the great gay questions of moompix metaphysics. And finally, I realized not long ago, Odette loves Claudette merely—and why not— because she is French.) Before very long, we were both dreaming celluloid dreams, because the men were so compelling, with their stories and nostalgia for songs going all the way back to "Sh-Boom," and groups going all the way back to the Modernaires, and moving from there steadily and exhaustively through the fifties, that we *knew*, had we but world enough and time and two Steadycam cameras, we'd wind up each with an Academy of Motion Picture Arts and Sciences award statuette—that's Oscars—no question, hands down, in a walk, out of a paper bag—for documentary.

Whereupon, stopping dreaming of Oscar night, getting down to work, Odette forewent her identification with Claudette (or, rather, with Claudette's fugue. "Well skip to the end, dear: they've gotten back together; you be Joel McCrea. . . . You can handle it, now don't be bashful—or, rather, *do* be bashful, Joel always was—and she's reminiscing. . . ."). She formally presented me with—and I immediately activated—not another forties Dictaphone but the very pocket Sony my subject had herself been using in the work interrupted by the Great European Excursion—her life's work all those years in New York: scouting dance-world dish and in-depth stellar reminiscences for *Terpsichore*. The interview had begun.

THE STORY

"The stories . . . the stories—and the stories, dear, *within* the stories. . . .

"*La nouvelle interpolée*. That's the term for it, dear. I was discussing it with this drop-dead chic girl professor on the train from Amsterdam to Paris. *L'Etoile du Nord* it's called, the train. She'd come into the empty compartment—empty, that is, of all but your mother in man's clothes—and apologized for intruding, but she'd been unable to bear the behaviors, in the compartment she'd been assigned, of a number of Americans on Eurailpasses. Then, of course, she realized, and tried to apologize, but I wouldn't hear of it. I sympathized with her right away and quoted Freud to the effect that such ruthless and overbearing behavior is always that of people traveling either at a reduced rate or, worse, on passes. I felt like Arletty at the Meurice in '44, talking about Schopenhauer over black coffee and *petits fours*. . . ."

Arletty. I breathed a quite audible sigh.

"I know, dear, Arletty—your great role model as a single-name attraction. And you've brought it off—nobody I know is quite as *je suis comme je suis* as you are; nobody knows as well how *tellement simple* is *l'amour*.

"Anyway, there I was, feeling something like—well, it was ever your mother's best and most endearing role, copied from Grady Sutton and honed to fit an earnest deviant from the other side of Tremont Avenue in the Bronx: the flippant, ageless fairy, with deep reserves of dignity. You know, Lynn Fontanne in one of her deeper Valentina moods. She was saying—the professor, dear— that it was exactly like those Russian Matrushka dolls, the-one-set-inside-the-other-inside-the—and I suddenly saw that as a metaphor for the whole saga. It was, it is. The beauty of it also is that like the *film noir* double feature of your youth, or more, really, like a thirties musical, you can come into it at any point so long as you're willing to sit through it again, or sit around *in* it.

"The first thing to say, dear, in talking about the past, is it wasn't the past at the time. . . . I was at that time still carrying the retrieved remains of Miss Faith Healy—with the temperance beverages—in the handled handbag, and I suddenly saw the thing whole, as it were, the metaphor, live, of all the girls, the one invested in the other—the way we all were: the Eleven against Heaven.

"Later—at Poulaphouca—when I thought it over, the only thing about that metaphor I didn't like was the hint of concealment. You know what they used to gargle about Hemingway—that closeted old Dolores—that the apparent text was only the tip of the iceberg? 'The tip of the ice *cube*, you mean,' I'd reply. Well, I

suppose I'm very postmodern, dear—very, as the kids say *po-mo*—
if not, in fact, post-*contemporary*—and *that* is, as they say, as it shall
appear . . . to your midmost seers, for example, as they sort through
the labyrinth of hidden meanings bored by language into the ground
of truth. I don't myself go in for consciously hidden meanings at
all. I like my meanings *manifest*, don't-cha know, the way I like
my men: hung all over the place, and *bulging*, like the plumbing
on the outside of the Beaubourg. All the same, dear, like any
metaphor—like any *man*, too—it works best the first time you get
it up. Later, even an afternoon later, there are bound to be . . .
which doesn't mean you discard it, not necessarily. Only that you
note diligently its deficiencies, and come to terms. Ditto fusion texts
and holograms, cyberspace and autofellatio. . . ."

"People question me. 'You were always smart, but how did you
get to be so *erudite?*' DeVors, for example, who really did expect
to outlive everybody, said to me—not so long before she failed to
do so—'Darling, when you die, *sur n'importe quel prétexte*—it really
will be as if a library has been burned down.' 'Really?' I snapped.
'Well, then, you can go storming onto the Late Night Extra and
do your Elizabeth-Taylor-as-Cleopatra turn: addressing America the
way the Serpent of the Nile addressed Caesar. "You barbarian, you
burned my library!" Gore thinks Americans are the new Romans,
it'll all make divine DeVors sense.'

"Erudite. They want to know—or say they do. Well, first of
all, I tell them, I read books. Throws 'em. I suppose from what
you see around you these days that it might be hard to believe
there was a time in this city when education at the primary level
was not only free, but uniformly excellent—a time when book
banning and book burning were something that was happening
Over There behind the Siegfried Line, and not here in the United
States of America. I read everything. 'Don't *ask* now, where Danny

is,' they'd say. 'He's only off somewhere with his nose in a book.' It was more or less gently said—in spite of the fact that in an Irish family, for every good reason, the primacy of the spoken tale over the written story is an absolute. But I read everything—from Tolstoy right down to the columns, the Prudence Penny recipes and even the pearls of wisdom on the tags of Salada tea bags. To this day I can happily sit down and read through a recipe for *potage parmentier* while heating up a can of Campbell's navy bean soup, and skim Liz Smith. Then, too, there was the discovery in the school library of the Oz books—I never looked back at Dick-and-Jane again, and every time I looked ahead it was through emerald glasses. Now, you know how I adore Judy, and I acknowledge the powerful allure of much of the vision of Metro-Goldwyn-Mayer, but anybody who seriously believes that Metro's *Wizard of Oz* captured Oz—well—

"I do venerate Judy, and I would be honored to ride in a suitable *pose plastique* down any broad boulevard in Manhattan on the float you imagine and propose for the Stonewall twenty-fifth—although the religion that surrounds her sometimes confounds my sense of decorum: those ritual re-enactments that often seem intimations of a strong belief in her second coming in a refreshment of miracles.

"Anyway, I always ever after read—and, if I do say so myself, along the way necessarily developed the skill of differentiating between close reading and wallowing in print shit. I remember that after I finished every Oz book there was, I picked up the *Odyssey*—purely because of the homonym: I figured if it *sounded* like Oz, it might—and, of course, it did. The first time I read *Child of morning, rosy-fingered Dawn*, I knew I was in for a long and delirious trip. It's always been like that. If I feel like killing myself, I read up on suicide—I might even read about Judas Iscariot, in the Gospel According to Saint Matthew. You remember how Paulette—Goddard—always said to her admirers, 'Now don't you bring me flowers, and don't you bring me candy—just bring me jewels, any size.' Well, I said to mine, 'Now don't you bring me flowers, or candy, or jewels, either, just bring me a book you think I'd like.' Well, you can't *imagine* some of the things I got. You know— *Forever Amber.* . . . So then I started saying, 'Now you just bring me *gift certificates* for the Scribner's bookstore on Fifth Avenue.' Bingo. I was building a library. I always had them put on the gift certificates *O.D. O'Doyle*—so that if I felt like going in as Danny, I would, and if I felt like swanning in as Odette—to buy the latest Françoise Sagan, for instance, in French, which they always got in in those days, I could, too. By which time, of course—the time of *Bonjour tristesse* and after—I was a truly educated woman. That was, of course, because of the G.I. Bill. I was a G.I. Billy who speed-read, and the memory of that is *almost* enough to make your mother *patriotic,* if she could only recognize her *country,* the one she—skip it.

"Anyway, in those days, when you worked at night, you had a choice. You could have a stark life, a life of the moment, like the girl who woke up at 4:00 p.m. and ordered *a double Bromo-Seltzer and the evening papers,* or you could do what I did: sleep till noon, get up, take a pill, and go to school in the afternoon.

"You remember *Mother Is a Freshman?* Well, it was a bit like that, only instead of traipsing all over State U. looking irrepressible in saddle shoes, bobby sox, cashmere sweaters, and Veneida hairnets, mother just schlepped it in mufti down to Washington Square. Wasn't gonna study war no more; was gonna—did—study philosophy. And if it was something *pivotal,* in philosophy—or even economics, which, for some reason, I never knew why, was *always* given in the morning—I stayed up rather than got up, and took *two* pills, because don't forget I was at the same time moaning low in cabaret on a fairly regular basis, editing a magazine, *and* carving with my big toe a little niche for myself in the world of *mod*-ren dance—finally ending up doing those seasons with Pierrot Deslieux at the Mawrdew Czgowchwz Theater on Manitoy. The studies helped me—especially in things like *Abraxas* and *Dances of Divided Selves.* The pills, however, turned out to be not such a hot idea—another story for another ride on another train another evening—but I got *A*s, even in economics—which is how I've been able to declare with utmost finality from my own driven-woman experience that the economic policies enacted in this country in the last ten years are the exact equivalent of amphetamine, bound, of course, to have the same horrifying result. Why *won't* people listen to Shakespeare? Put *money* in thy purse—not every piece of plastic issued by every agency of Mammon licensed in the Republic! *Money,* dear, *hard coin*—but why am I telling you all this? You were there on Manitoy, in the hurricane—and you are admirably thrifty. You remember the gutter, as mother does.

"I'd gotten my taste for philosophy in Paris, after the Liberation in the autumn of '44, when the first lectures on existentialism were given at the Sorbonne and spilled out into the cafés. I always hated Sartre—the very *look* of him—but I saw an angelic little man on the Rue Vaneau—he seemed to be walking three feet off the ground with the music of Messiaen in his head—who I was told was Gabriel Marcel, a Catholic existentialist, although he disliked the term—sort of the way I dislike the term *drag queen.* The next thing you know there was somebody trying to explain Gabriel Marcel to me—in English. He, Gabriel Marcel, had said *perhaps something could* be *without* existing, *but the inverse is not possible.* That kind of discussion. I must say it appealed to me, as, well, *Irish.* I thought of it in terms of myself—which in existentialism you were supposed to do. I advised the instructor, as we were sitting in a crowd at Brasserie Lipp. 'Well, it's like *me.*' 'Oh?' he said. 'Yes,' I said, 'perhaps I could always have been a drag queen without ever having put on a dress and performing, but once having put on a dress and performed, I could hardly say I was *not* a drag queen. I think it means exactly that.' He translated; I got a round of applause. Of course, in the Liberation, when the Americans were seen to be—as the girl professor put it to me on the train—in effect *extraterrestrial*, an American soldier drag-queen *existentialist.* . . . Well, I think I was viewed as a performer whose star turn was spinning counterclockwise on the perihelion of the planet Roz. That's really when I fell in love with the French, though, for their infinite tact—that's what I said, bub, *tact.* They treated me exquisitely, especially as I was learning to speak their language—and, yes, you learn it best in bed—*and,* by that time, after Donald and the blitz and all that—we'll get to Donald and the blitz and all that. . . ."

(I'd heard of Donald and the blitz and all that—although not, as yet, from Odette.)

"By that time, I'd become a girl who if treated with kid gloves felt *mauled.* Know what I mean? Achingly sensitive—into Marguerite Yourcenar, who was of course *the* existentialist writer of them all. Not just when she wrote *Hadrian* and *L'Oeuvre au noir,* but earlier, for instance in her translation of Virginia Woolf's *The Waves—Les Vagues:* an absolutely *echt* existentialist text ten years *before* the conflagration. I was a bit in advance myself: I was Audrey Hepburn ten years before *Funny Face.* I was hearing, and believing, things *undreamed* of in America, even in *film noir.* In sum, my case had proved Dorothy Parker wrong: the whore had been led to culture, and had been made to think—or, as I used to say myself, my ignorance—like my vaunted innocence—delicate, exotic, and fruity as it may have been, died, trampled underfoot on Omaha Beach.

   "*Alors,* there I was, back in freewheeling postwar New York, a sensitive existentialist drag queen. Where else was I to go except N.Y.U.? *Perstare et Praestare.* Never did get a degree—your mother

exemplifies performance, dear, over credentialism, and yet, perhaps anomalously, still continues to champion formalism over
advocacy. But I got an apartment in the Village, a more consensual—
existential—grasp of existentialism, the rudiments of Greek
grammar, and lots of information with which to face the postwar
world—ferreting out, as the girl says, entailments and lines of
argument. As the rap ads on the subway say, *They teach you well,
give you a skill, and when it is done you can max and chill.*"

"Whatever those activities are."

"Now, now, Skeezix, don't you start posing as some deadass
decorator's antique maiden auntie. You know perfectly well what
both *max* and *chill* mean—you *know* you do!"

I didn't, but I supposed, as a Second Avenue rapper of sorts myself,
I shouldn't admit it. I knew well enough the meaning of *mix* and
chill, or chill and *mix*, but—and furthermore, I did seriously doubt
that N.Y.U. had anything at all to do with giving Odette the skill
being demonstrated then and there on the train, but I acted as
though I assumed she meant exact philosophical precision, and
asked what max and chill might have to do with *what was the case?*

"Oh, *everything*. For example, whereas Leibniz had postulated that
everything possible demands to be deemed existent, *we* said that
everything existent demands to be deemed possible. Big difference,
of course, between possible and probable. What is it Addison de
Witt says to Eve Harrington? *That I should want you at all suddenly
strikes me as the height of improbability, but that in itself is probably
the reason.* Like that. Also, although never a devout woman, I was
radically opposed to the atheistic brand of existentialism prevalent
then in the Village. I used to insist that the best definition was
that whereas God is masculine, God's mother is feminine: which

means that *authority*, or, if you prefer, *authenticity*, issues from the *matrix*.

"And then years later I went back. I took extension courses—without pills. Do you know what a *charmed hadron* is? I do—and you have to be a little careful how you write it down, or else it turns into a gay name for a boy band. That an imaginary number is also known as an *operator*? Imagine! Then I found the best way of all, and I still by habit follow that path. I stay in nights—most nights—reading things like *The Examined Life* and *A Brief History of Time*, and taking seriously questions like, *Where does this difference between the past and the future come from? Why do we remember the past but not the future?*—you see, some do—and, *Why does disorder increase in the same direction of time as that in which the universe expands?* Which is the same as asking why do I get smarter as my body gets weaker, only to lose all my marbles in the end?

"*Plenty of time to stay in when you're dead*—that's what we used to say. Then I did an about-face and continued my education, becoming, as my mother used to say of layabouts, somebody who was *home through the day*. I also learned about dream work and came to put great faith in its efficacy. Consequently, like you, I sleep a lot. The little segments of this little life are rounded by a lot of little sleeps. I suppose in that respect we're into homeopathy—the pair of us. And who can say that that, too, is not in some measure responsible for our survival—we two of eleven?

"And *now*, in this spare time in which we live, a time in which, as was once said of the Elizabethan age, many choose rather to fiddle at home—and look at 'Dallas' and 'Dynasty' and 'Falcon Crest' and top them off with safe-sex videos—or is that *safer* sex, or is it *save-it* sex? To fiddle at home rather than to go out and be knocked on the head abroad. A time which does seem to fulfill Ezekiel 8, in which it is written that people are *sitting in darkness, each man in his room of pictures*. Yet there is perhaps *too* much staying in. Even I can't *always* be at home reposing with the golden oldies, the educational reruns on P.B.S., and the lesser VCR diversions indicated. After all, didn't we get *you* out of Sagaponack to help invent the nineties—gateway to the millennium? We can hardly expect you to do so alone—brilliant as your turn is, dear—in an old Second Avenue vaudeville house.

"So in these her golden years, your mother, back from harrowing hell, must try to get about a little more—a little lunching in public, a matinee, an early-evening reading: that sort of thing—before coming home, climbing into a lavender bath, then plopping down and spudding out in front of the tube. And as for indulging a little in crap, well, after all, I do go back with Joan to *The Girl in the Red Velvet Swing,* when she attempted to immortalize Evelyn Nesbitt as another Lola Montez. *Tilt,* but gay try. And I do, too, like to take a peek at 'Miami Vice' and 'L.A. Law,' for the clothes and the locations. I mean, if one didn't dip into such little side orders of drek one might turn into a latter-day Dixie Putnam and commence denouncing them as symptoms of social diabetes and late-capitalist decadence—and that *would* be too much for one's staunchest supporters. Although one thing I must say about the video *tournage* that *was* disturbing me last year. I call it the casting of the Saint Sebastians of sex—and I fell into it by accident, when I took out a promising looking Hermosa Beach party–cum–Highway 101 road pic, got ready to take the plunge with the boys, and suddenly, there on the screen—I confess I didn't know what I was looking at until right then and there, bedtime hour that it was, I dashed right back to the emporium and caught the proprietor just as he was locking up the register. 'Ernest,' I demanded, 'what *is* the message? Those Californicators are *pocked,* like fruit bruised in a hailstorm.' He explained. Get this; it's a new development, somewhat analogous to the anorectic girl models one sees here and there in high-fashion print work—you know, the ones with the jeweled dog collars and the artfully faked body bruises—except that the chic is inverted. There they are at it on the screen, and here and there on torsos and limbs is the unmistakable evidence of Kaposi's sarcoma lesions—and on the flaring nostrils, that were wont in an earlier time to put you in mind of wild ponies, the ember glow of popper burns—all veiled in pancake of a shade generally darker than the performer's skin tone, through which the delicate pinks and mauves of the wounds show in that weird color the process features—making the boys seemingly into mauled veterans of more stressful rites than those represented onscreen, but actually into representations either of Christ Himself or of any of the legion of stigmatics swimming heavenward in the blood of His wounds—or, as I've indicated, of living statues of Saint Sebastian, from which the arrows have been removed, the better the gashes may be venerated. You'd need to turn down the sound and play a CD of Lenten Gregorian chants or a Gesualdo motet to get into the right mood—the mood Baudelaire specifies as the proper response to *le dernier éclat d'héroïsme dans les décadences.* 'A revoltin' development, I call it.' 'Yes, and I *am* sorry, Miz O'Doyle,' Ernest replied, most considerately, I thought, considering everything, 'not to have *realized you* are *no* customer for suchlike entertainment. You must take your money *right* back—here—right out of my pocket, with my apologies, and then you must take this home, *avec mes compliments—no* charge—and keep it as *long* as you like. It's four *numi,* absolutely *gleaming* and variously shaded Brazilians—*even-toned* from *brow* to *heel,* each one of them—frolicking in and near Ipanema—more *us,* the Atlantic, isn't it, even if it's in another hemisphere. Guaranteed not a mark on any of them, and the action is as safe as tic-tactoe. *Quadrille frottage*—but never a dull moment. In fact, with the slow beguine music on the track, it's actually, *really* balletic—and I know to whom I am speaking, so *please!'* So I did, and he was right—well, right enough. . . ."

(I have something to report here, and that is that I don't think this story is at all true. Not for a minute because it couldn't be—or that I can't believe that the blasted Joe Gage esthetic could have sunk fathoms to this level—or that Odette was in any sense lying. Odette never lies; she never did; she used to say to me, "I don't *get* lying, or liars." No, it's because since the death of Diane DeVors—who was almost a Community Watch warden when it came to questioning the stories that were passed around town— Odette has, in my opinion, and in O'Maurigan's, too, become oddly credulous. And in this instance I clock the perpetrator— O'Maurigan would say the *allegator*—in the West Village emporium Odette patronizes, whom Odette calls Ernest, as one of a number of characters in contemporary gay life the O and I call the Sons of Trenchy. We call them that in memorial to Big Trenchy, already and again to be referred to in this chronicle, whose inventions and insistences were legend. For instance, in reply to somebody's once saying that Provincetown was so gay that even the mayor was, as Dorothy Dean always put it, A Member of the Committee, "So what? Ever since World War One *all* New York's mayors were gay. That's the secret point," he'd tell his eager customers while slinging Singapores and stingers, "of the most famous Mayor Hylan story—the one about his wife and Queen Marie of Romania at the Saint Patrick's Day parade." More about Mrs. Hylan and Her Majesty later. . . . Trenchy would say things like, "Sure Mayor Hylan was gay. And Jimmy Walker was gay—he was gay with Jack Dempsey. And Fiorello LaGuardia was gay—he was gay with Carmine de Sapio. Bill O'Dwyer was gay: that Sloan Simpson was a beard." "Who was *he* gay with, Trenchy, Toots Shor?" "Very close—matter of fact, with the boxing commissioner." "Oh." And Mayor Impellateri was gay—that was just so silly it was refreshing—but then, when it came to Robert Wagner and—get this—Robert *Moses*—well, the customers weren't buying. . . . And the fact is that Ernest, Son of Trenchy, has the same kind of facility—except that Who's Whorish is categorically passé nowadays, like glimpses of stocking—and so he goes in for alarming observations such as the one I'm convinced he made to rattle Odette, in that same matter-of-fact way, I can tell, that Trenchy used to—with the same kind of aplomb George Sardi had, too, in spades. Like that.

Cultural notes and addenda. All true New Yorkers called their most beloved mayor "Luh *Gardia*"—both during his lifetime and thereafter. And the story of Mrs. Hylan and Marie of Romania goes like this, and is apparently true. They were sitting next to one another at the Saint Patrick's Day parade on the reviewing stand outside St. Patrick's Cathedral, when a regiment of New York's finest marched by. "What a splendid-looking group of men!" the monarch offered enthusiastically. "You said a mouthful *there*, queen!" came the instant reply. And many apparently insist that she was, thereby, talking in transparent code, letting more than a thing or two be known. . . .)

"Nevertheless," Odette continued, "as a rule I stay tuned in to a lot of head shows and to reruns of infotainment ventures like Kenneth Clark's *Civilisation*. I just love the way he gurgles over the Italian Renaissance—it helps me to do my scenes to envision Mantegna's Gonzaga frescoes in Mantua. I have also taken a wild fancy to this latest promoter, Michael Wood. O'Maurigan makes fun of me: he calls him just another Brit boy scout who peddles a markdown Michael York appeal and a potted Anthropology, like it was Sweeney Todd's meat pies—and you *know* that when the O makes a tortured statement like that you're meant to—excuse me—deconstruct and analyze every referential phrase—but I'm enchanted with his vulpine looks and entranced every time he bounds over another rock into the lap of another god, whether in the desert that was Nineveh or in the scrub landscape of Mexico, and looks straight into the camera as if he's going to strip and venerate. . . . And do you know, the odd thing is that he does not look unlike the O himself at that age—but I don't say that, although you may, and may as well do so, and attribute it to me. I can take another lashing of his Irish tongue, and he really doesn't get *so* riled as that—just *don't ever* say *anybody* looks like the young Gabriel Wayfaring. Also, I've continued reading. You know, darling, sometimes I get the feeling that there are only three people in Gotham still actually reading *books:* yours truly, the O'Maurigan, and Donald Lyons. It seems to me that everybody else is merely stacking titles with a view to creating an impression on the morning they're found dead in bed."

The Gonzaga frescoes. Saint Aloysius, I thought to myself, although I don't believe he's featured up on the Duke's wall in Mantua. I do my scenes envisaging—but I've talked about that. Not Saint Aloysius, at any rate. Now, about those aging rock-'n'-rollers on the other side of the partition—what do they envisage? Playboy bunnies—fair enough. Or maybe—just maybe—just one of them envisages Sal Mineo? As Saint Aloysius Gonzaga in the religious picture—one of many—Hollywood never got around to making? What would the statistical probability—how many rock-'n'-rollers were there? I'd forgotten. If, according to the book *The Sixth Man* that came out in the late fifties, one man in six. . . .

"Also, I keep my eyes and ears open on the pavement and on public transportation. One is not forever in taxis speeding to theaters. You yourself have always aptly illustrated the truism that the B.A. and the M.A. are gay, but they'll never replace the I.R.T. and the B.M.T.

"You've got to have a dream, and late last spring mine became an apotheosis: to hold down the Paulette Goddard chair of Existential Philosophy at New York University. And *you* ought to put in for the Paulette Goddard Chair of Memory. If there's any hope, that is, for the future of either Reflection or Philosophy. I have my doubts—aren't *I* original!

"Moreover, your mother hardly knows what's become of the poetry of our time, dear, apart from the bardic loveliness of the O'Maurigan, and what with the quotidian numinosity—what The O calls the *kerygma*—of James Schuyler—"

"The Skylark."

"He was—*part* skylark, dear, and part mourning dove; a great part I think—the latter."

"Shelley wrote *To a Sky-Lark,* didn't he?"

"He did, dear, yes, and I know just what you mean. *I* always thought of Schuyler as our Keats—but also as an older specimen: some troubadour called Jimmy, come to rest in a Templar's château, and some American foundation in the fifties just went and scooped the whole château up—as if it were The Cloisters—and brought it over on the *Ile de France,* and stuck it in the middle of Manhattan—gardens, private chapel, and all—and the troubadour just wanders through it and them—or used to. You used to be able to go over to the Chelsea and see him in it there in room 625—a poet, as O'Maurigan said, made out of a real poet. You could sit there with him at the open window and look at the morning glory sprung up from the potting trough, and all entwined on the vine-pattern wrought-iron balustrade, and at what he called the Bohemian wineglass blossoms hanging out in space over Twenty-third Street. . . .

"And now you can't anymore, and Jimmy's morning-glory vine has been left to . . . they really ought to have kept it up as a memorial to him, not to mention putting a plaque on the wall where you walk in downstairs. And Jimmy's morning-glory spirit, rinsed in the rain and cleared of any trace of—you remember—

madness, fright, is booted up: is doing duty in eternity. Even so, the effect he has on us, left behind in the now-empty room, is much the same—we read *The Crystal Lithium* and *Hymn to Life*, and *The Morning of the Poem* and *A Few Days* and seem to hear him saying in that serene voice: *This day, if you care to notice, you're already here with me in paradise—like it?* I know I do.

"And all along one has tried to keep up with the significant others—with Ashbery's hyperventilated abreactions that seem to extend Lucky's oration from *Waiting for Godot* into infinity, and with Merrill's astral metaphysics. I mean, don't we all wish we knew where and to what end all the ley lines emanating from the Great Pyramid at Giza extend in the world? Never mind, I have reread *Mirabell* many times, and find both the character and his gospel enchanting—or, as I overheard one of those ecstatic matrons exclaim after a reading of same at the Guggenheim, 'Oh, wasn't it just—*celestial?*'

"And I am among the fortunate on John Fandel's mailing list, too—odd about his poems of ecstasy: at one and the same time they are consoling viaticum addressed directly to me, yet might just as well be addressed to *occupant*—but that may be the point of them. However, just lately I must say it's Ashbery who has me by the throat—in fact, I was to pull back, raise a hand to soothe my neck, and say—like Lana did to John Garfield, off the breath—*you're hurting me!* I was terribly shaken in the middle eighties by *A Wave*, and I've just finished *Flow Chart*—and again I say, gay: if I can talk like this, he can write like that. It isn't exactly insane—how he writes. After all, *The Faerie Queene* isn't exactly lifelike. But as it is said of it—*The Faerie Queene*—that the experience of reading it is like the experience of living, so the reading of *Flow Chart* is more than a little like the experience of going insane—and remember, dear, even if you'd rather not dwell on it, your mother is herself no stranger to the flight deck of the Reiss Pavilion. It was the same with *A Wave*; it's like what I think of as Purgatory—not

Hell, mind you, Purgatory. I think of Purgatory as my standing from dawn until sunset in daylight on a day as long as one of the days of creation, at Times Square, forging out my perfectly penitent soul by *reading* the text of a poem such as *A Wave*, such as *Flow Chart*, as it rolls out on the electric Times sign that still coils about the former Times Building. Somebody back in the forties said of the typographically psychotic poetry of Neville Dane that reading it was like looking at mascara running down a face. Well, I see myself standing there, in Purgatory, as all the sinful flesh melts off these bones into a little pool in which the soul's reflection—your mother standing there, *Stabat Mater*—putting up with it for as long as she can—which had better be a good long time, dear, because if she takes the only alternative, and pulls from alongside the crepe de chine in the beaded bag she left home with the little pearl-handled revolver she likes to carry for effect, puts it either into her gay mouth or presses it against what's left of her silvered temple and fires. . . . Well, she gets to go, doesn't she, swirling in the vortex right *out* of the Purgatory her good deeds bumped her up out of Hell into, right back into that same Hell she used to say she was so surely bent on—born to raise. You see, dear, anybody can *talk* like a John Ashbery poem, just as anybody can lisp like Holly Woodlawn, but, after all, just as only Holly Woodlawn is Holly Woodlawn, only a John Ashbery poem is a John Ashbery poem."

"Only Odette O'Doyle is Odette O'Doyle—*Stabat Mater.*"

"Why *thank* you, dear, I hadn't thought of that since going through customs late yesterday afternoon—and do forgive the blasphemy. Mary does: I rang her from the airport the minute I'd cleared the barrier, the minute I'd finished running through *To This We've Come* under my breath. I'll tell you later how you do it— ring Mary, that is; the tessitura of *To This We've Come* is all wrong for you. . . . The other thing I thought, reading *Flow Chart*: the poem has both a progressive and a regressive rhythm, operating something like text and subtext in an actor's performance. Or like two windshield wipers set deliberately out of sync. Now they're going in the same direction, left to right across your rainy mind's glass eye; now they're going haywire; now they're agreeing to disagree entirely and coming at one another from left to right and right to left at once . . . but only once; then they're haywire again—seeming to be what the poet feared: *the incomprehensible messages of tree frogs explicating each other*—until they're both for an instant going right to left. Like that. Now, as to how many readers are going to know automatically what passersby *that look like the Gov and Min in a more strained version* can signify—know even who the Gov and Min are? Well, probably about as many who know who the only Odette O'Doyle is. But I did memorize something one of the windshield wipers said. It said,

> *slippery harmonies abound. In fact, I can't be sure I'm*
> *   not addressing myself*
> *to one or within one right now, but that's no matter.*
> *   I've got to tell this*
> *in whatever time remains to me.*

See what I mean? Of course, Ashbery is, or ought to be, required reading for transvestite narcissists. What are our drag lives, all told, but strenuously painted works in progress all, and all self-portraits in compact mirrors?"

"Wasn't that *convex mirror?*"

"So it was, dear, but you get the point, *n'est-ce pas?*

"I love what O'Maurigan says about why he holds with Ashbery. Not because they go back to the Cambridge Arts Theater the way you and I and the Eleven against Heaven go back to the Mais Oui; because if old Yeats were to be resurrected and come to New York, and attend an Ashbery reading, and read through the publicity handouts—all the awards, all the laurels rained down on the head—he would be absolutely convinced that Aleister Crowley had won the final day, that the Age of Pandemonium had indeed been inaugurated to run its full thousand-year term."

"But back to your mother, and her progress in reading life from Hell through Purgatory into what's advertised as Heaven. Each time I reread *Mirabell*, I wish it, or something like it—something with Mae West in it, actually—were true, and in the offing. . . . And back on dear old earth, O'Maurigan's *Magnetic Resonance Imaging Suite* made me just sit in front of the peat fire in Mayo and sob, but, then, it would, wouldn't it?

"Also, it's been a great treat of late being taken by The O to hear the seminars given at The New School by Professor Harold Bloom of Yale and New York University on contemporary rhapsodics—all those wonderful concepts like *clinamen* and *tessera* and *apophrades* that make it all sound like exotic gardening—even if I find it hard to hold with the contention that American poetry *started* with Whitman and Emily Dickinson. Apart from everything else, as the Brits say, the idea of those two as *parents*, progenitors of a single American sequence, as Professor Bloom would have it, is truly frightening—like the mating, if not of brother and sister, then certainly of two very close first cousins, and that can only mean, dear, that the progeny are *all* going to be shoo-in candidates for the rubber rooms at Creedmore and Camarillo. I mean, whatever happened to James Russell Lowell and James Whitcomb Riley, to mention only the Jameses—and to images such as that lovely frost on the punkins, that first snowfall, and the babes in the wood? It's not as if we've had our last sentimental feeling image, our last regression, even if the word is out that everybody now ought to be consciously *post*-millenarian— which as one girl remarked when told of same, 'Well, honey, they are right *on* about that, whoever said it; hardly anybody you know even *owns* a hat.' But I think the most beautiful thing I heard the

professor say, practically off the cuff, about art and life and nostalgia—
the best thing, really, I'd heard since Paris in the forties—was this:
Paradise is forever there *and our knowing is* here, *but our being is split
off from our knowing, and so it turns out that we still abide in
Eden.* Wouldn't that just take your *breath* away? It did mine—for a
whole day!

"In general, I sense a lack. Nobody *behaves* like a poet any
more, for one thing—in spite of them all running about creation
like traveling salesmen, or evangelists before television, having their
funded experiences all over one another under the rubric of public
address. The Beats used to try to make people believe they were
behaving poetically, but the best thing I've ever heard said about
the Beats was said by Schuyler at the Chelsea only a year or so
before he died. Raymond Foye asked him what he thought of them,
and he said he had never thought of them much. But had he ever
read *Howl?* His answer was, 'I wanted to, but I was having
a nervous breakdown at the time, and Frank wouldn't let me.'
The end.

"And talking of things—splendid things—Greek, it's been a
long time since that truly crazed Ancient-of-Days Laura open-
parenthesis Riding close-parenthesis Jackson paraded around posing
as Finality, being worshiped as the White Goddess, waking up pure
every morning and—talking of millenarian days—wearing her tiara
with 'Laura' spelled out in Greek—a style I wish I'd adopted. It
may indeed have been fashioned of rhinestones, and it may have
long since fallen—like Mélisande's one long irremediable night ago—
into some old cesspool or other, but she wore it once—and more
than once. And shared bananas with this one and that one; they'd
start in eating them at opposite ends. . . ."

This last reminded me of Kaye Wayfaring's necklace: the letters
spelled out "Everything's True" in gold. She wore it at the *Avenged*
premiere. I asked Odette, did she remember?

"Yes, dear, I remember it well—Orphrey Whither had given it to her to wear. O'Maurigan said it was the short form of Blake's *Every thing possible to be believed is an image of truth*. *Not* something a girl could wear comfortably around her neck.

"As for Laura Sibyl Riding Finality Jackson Blake—for she really did consider herself in the same class with the author of *Tyger Tyger, burning bright*—she also, in addition to sporting telling headgear, went tearassing helter-skelter about twenties bohemian London slinging gorilla hash in every direction and, in a gesture I suppose meant to emphasize, if not exactly nail down, Finality, throwing herself out the window. *Bodies have had their day* was what she had proclaimed—along with so much else—and she was evidently giving some sort of demonstration. Then, moving south for a decade-long winter, she got herself into the colorful habit of shrieking her tits off at people and burning bright herself long into the Majorcan *noche*—which I suppose is more like the style that too many of us *did* adopt. Probably, in Tyger Riding's case, the consequence of too many repeated dreams of falling—or, rather, falling again—and of too few clitoral orgasms. And they say that now Mrs. Jackson is waiting on line for death living in a trailer camp in Florida—but, then, isn't everybody these days imprisoned in this society living, spiritually, in a trailer camp in Florida?"

"But back to the poetoids: what *are* they all doing but walking around paradoxically using a combination of the confessional mode and the plea *What's in a name?*—for they are all of them commencing to sound interchangeable. And trying to get people to act as if they believed they were all of them called *Ernest*. Trying to replace dead metaphysical questions which have no relation to the facts of life as we know them with specimens of dead forms which have—metaphysically, *and* theologically—*less* than none. I mean, I suppose Laura Open-Close Finality was a roaring horror—a real Medusa—but at the very least she was a *camp!*

"What she really was, now I come to think of it, was a first-draft version of Jackie Curtis.

"Miss Hildegarde Dorsay really put it to me as well as I've heard it put—perhaps because she rounded it off with a compliment to me that I have never forgotten—and this was some years ago, before she fell mortally ill. She said, 'I have read much of the *material* to which you refer, Miz O'Doyle. Because it is laid out in *labnes*, I suppose we must call it *versa*-tile, but I fail to see why we must regard it as *pob'try*. Such art aspires to—and achieves— the condition of *Muzak*. I greatly perfuh lis'nen to you, deah, waxin' yoah nostalgia to a mirruh gloss—a mirruh gloss I can see mahself in along with all thuh othuhs. . . .'

"I suppose the truth is, poetry is as frightened as everybody else—in the age which, even if we do choose to fiddle at home etcetera, the expression *safe as houses* has nearly lost its meaning. Now when intruders from the savage streets can and do come at you, bursting through the rear windows into the darkened rooms, even as you sit looking for dear life at your cherished moving pictures. That and the fact that anyone who has ever known the muses at all well will tell you that Euterpe is far and away the most highly strung of all the girls—and, incidentally, the only blonde. Which is undoubtedly why, as O'Maurigan has remarked time and again, he takes from Calliope.

"Some wannabe wit said to me just before I left last year on my journey with the girls' remains—at the opening of another can of condensed horror on West Broadway—'Well, this is really an age of satire.' '*Satire?*' I nearly screamed. 'Don't lecture *me* about satire!' Talk about trying to teach grandma how to suck duck eggs. *Satire? Schi'vatz!* You know what satire has become these days, dear? Satire is the girl who's let the ugliness of the world rot her teeth out, and who's decided to stay *irredentist* the better to give

her tired old Johnson better head when he comes to her for consolation in the mezzanine. Or, as DeVors once snapped, '*Satire?*
Wasn't she the Kingfish's wife?'

"I really must stop going on about this. I'm commencing to
sound like a deconstructionist, and you do know, don't you, what
O'Maurigan says about it and about them."

I knew only a little—see above—about what deconstruction is, or
says it is. (What the word suggests to me is the kind of deal
relatives of Phil in demolition who had shit on the former mayor
of New York to reveal made with him and the City Council to
tear down midtown Manhattan and put up what looks like, I
don't know, Omaha? Something, but not the Emerald City. Something I don't like so much that I can't even stop on my way across
Forty-seventh Street from Rockefeller Center to meet somebody
for a Rialto lunch on Restaurant Row to look at the construction
workers down in the holes—and that's bad. I especially skeeve
when I pass the site of the former Lodovico's—but why go on?) I
didn't know exactly what O'Maurigan says about deconstruction,
and, anyway, I wanted to go on hearing (and recording) Odette's
version.

"He says it's nothing more or less than a French reaction formation
to the onslaught of American advertising, marketing, and public
relations. He sees it as a cold war to the death between the Rue
des Ecoles and Madison Avenue—between the Ecole Normale Su-
périeure and the Institut de France on the one side and BBD&O,
Hill & Knowlton, Grey, and N. W. Ayer on the other. And he's
very sure the French will win—they always have, he says, in wars
of the mind—whereupon they will dismantle their arguments and
throw them away on the obsolete-weapons pile, and lie in wait for
the next. . . ."

I avowed I had enough trouble understanding life—what life had become—much less advertising—or what advertising had become since the days of *When you wake up in the morning and you don't know what you want* . . . and *Put your crepe de chine in your beaded bag*. . . . What I wanted—what I was waiting for—was that T-shirt formula the scientist writing in *OMNI* had dared hope he and his colleagues might find. That formula, like those ads, hadn't seemed to me weapons in a life-and-death struggle; they'd seemed like, well, sex. (And with *that* I was trapped. Out of the mouths of babes—right?—and there was the latest buzz rage, the babe within, coming out of my mouth like the voice of Mercedes McCambridge in *The Exorcist*. Sex and the dead.)

"The tragedy of life nowadays, darling, is that not only are death and dying everywhere, but they are preferred. I mean, now that the Sun Belt fascists have finished using Ronald Reagan as the political scumbag he was—using him to fuck the Republic with— and thrown him away, and now that the truly evil George Bush has started slobbering all over television like some compulsive, masturbatory, mentally defective *ghoul*. . . . You know I *always* hated Ronald Reagan, even with Bonita Granville and the Bowery Boys. Of course, I always thought the Bowery Boys were proto-fascists who would have gone to confession to Father Coughlin on a regular basis. You can hear it now. Question: *With yourself, or with others?* Answer: *Wid uderrs, fodda.* And then, of course, they'd start in naming names. . . ."

"Speaking of the New York school, you know I had this *case* on Frank O'Hara—who didn't?—but did *he* ever open up a can of

Franco-American vermicelli! I've always loved O'Maurigan's nickname for him—*Frob*. It tells it all. Well, one night during the last
winter of the girls' demises, I'd just finished watching that darling
Rosa Von Praunheim on 'Closet Case T.V.'—public access—
exhorting committed faggots everywhere to dash over to Shooting
Stars in the meat district for some sanitary, strenuous safe sex—
when on comes this big hulking gladiola reading a *pome* about
Marlon no longer fitting into his Schott black leather *bike* jacket.
Something like

> *You were my hand-job mainstay man, but now what*
>   *are you good for?*
> *Since you climbed down off your Harley, man, and*
>   *went on out the food door. . . .*

I said, out loud, 'Can't fit into his leather jacket? I can't fit into my
stone *martens*, if the truth be told.' The recitation was followed
next by some *theorist*—got-a-minute?—braying some shit like, 'My
ear *automatically demarches* relative measures on the waves and on
the *wavelets—dig?*' As you said about Doctor Dove, face-lifts, and
Beethoven, click. I said, 'Plant you now, dig you later, Manley.'
Click. The mention of Marlon had put in me a chocolate yen for
The Fugitive Kind, for a big slice of him and a hefty portion of
Magnani, too—toot sweet—and DeVors had left me her entire
cinémathèque on videotape. . . ."

"Anyway, Frank sure did know about safe sex, didn't he, even if
everything else he did was so knee-jerk fatal, and even if he never
did succeed—if one may be permitted to say so—in living up to
the epitaph carved on his tombstone in Springs."
    "In Springs, around the block from Jackson Pollock."
    "How you say; where *you're* going—right?—if the world

doesn't end first. Gave me a turn when you said that tonight—I can't think why. After all, *my* world—in case it hasn't already ended and this is a dream train ride into Eternity and you are not you sitting here but really only my memory of you—my world will, in the nature of things, certainly end before yours, if not before.

"Of course, what's the point of measurement—what ever was? Everything's fatal, finally. You can see *why* one is awake so much so late at night. Nearly as much as in '44. . . .

"I was thinking of Frank a lot during your show: thinking how much he would have loved—really—seeing you alive up there, but reminded of him palpably from the moment you brought up the Tchelitchew pornography. It's exactly the same kind of longing he had. He often said, for example, that the world was crying out for a popular edition of the Fuseli drawings, and he and O'Maurigan actually tried to get a serious search going for the Cooper sisters' filthy-picture collection, which *ought* to be up there in the cellar of the Cooper-Hewitt, but isn't. There is something *holy* about the longing for period pornography in this age of California hustlers who will soon outdistance McDonald's in numbers served, and of computer-generated cock-and-balls rockslides. . . .

"Oh, listen to me go on and on and *on! The legs of eternity; the mouth of death.* Remember that? Who said that about me? Which one of you? I can't recall.

> *I can't recall who said it,*
> *I know I never read it*—etcetera—
> *To hold a man in your arms is wonderful, wonderful*
> *In every way—so they say—*

Merman reached her highest peak singing that. *Both* her highest—her *twin* peaks: she was *better* in the revival."

"Listening to you," I said, "retelling the old stories is like that—like Merman in a big Broadway revival. Because of the way you free-associate, it's a new experience—not like listening to a broken record, as is the case with so many of the others."

"Why, what a nice thing to *say* in the middle of the night! I suppose it's true: I don't tend to stick or repeat—but it must be faced nevertheless, Delancey dear, that your mother *was* pressed in the days before Groove Guard, and has been taken out of and put back into her envelope, and played so many times on so many machines of such varied quality, as it were, that there *are* inevitable scratches, of the sort neither Niosôme nor Noctosôme can completely eradicate. However, I do believe I have taken the kids seriously, and to the best of my ability follow their admonition: to walk the talk.

"Which reminds me—does anybody know whatever happened to *Maledicta?* I had a subscription—the O's gift one Christmas—and it lapsed.

"*So many men, so little time!* Remember *that,* speaking of walking the talk by way of walking the streets?"

"So many men," I answered, "and every sixth one is queer."

"That's *right*—I'd forgotten: the *breakthrough* book. Hah, hah, hah, Blanche! Did we *actually believe*—so many men, so little. . . . They put it on T-shirts in the seventies. In the nineties they'll probably be flashing things like *Charmed Hadron. So many men—so little time!* If only we'd known. If only we'd. . . . Would it have made any difference? None—next. If we'd been told in separate private-revelation visions in our efficiency kitchens, like that much-maligned catatonic out in Bayside who has been in recent years advertising on the *subway.* That's how I found out you can call the Mother of God on an 800 line: 1-800-something-something-something-MARY. I've got it written down next to the combination of my safe. Had anybody done so—dialed Mary for a parlez-vous. . . . Listen, if Mary had all those years ago used up all the nickels in all the poor boxes in the dioceses to *call us* and whisper, *A word in your ears, darlings.* . . . Even if she had shown one of us a pageant of the epidemic itself—the way she's said to have shown Francisco and Jacinta and Lucia the pains of hell—we'd never have swung for prophylaxis. Which ought to prove one thing, at least: we're exactly the same sort of creature of Providence as everybody else in America, and, likely, the world. Of course, religion is hardly the answer it once was, when Violetta Valery could get away with expressing the sentiments she expresses on her deathbed, and Minnie could confidently assure us in her Bible lesson of universal salvation through love. Do you realize that *redemption is for everyone*, which even in our youth might have been the spark of a truly stimulating discussion, at least in certain quarters, now can *only* mean that taking your used cans and bottles to the recycling plant will make you a better person? Of course, when the priests started defecting, the gospel was bound to be spread among the people in a dynamic new way—such as to those leisured ladies who *rave* about the work done up on Madison Avenue by that ex-padre from Sunnyside you knew who leaped over the wall right into the arms of Mr. Kenneth, and not so long after took half the joint with him when he went out on his own as a colorist. Talk about *transubstantiation!* Not since Cégeste made Mawrdew Czgowchwz a blonde for a night so she could become Mélisande. . . ."

I had to laugh. The former priest of God, now an eminent beautician, has a weekend house in Amagansett, and only the weekend before, Phil and I had gotten in the mail a flyer from a new recycling plant located there, whose slogan is *We take the pain out of separation.* Phil said, "Remember this, when the time comes to put me six feet under. Maybe there's no such thing as the Resurrection, but this way I could maybe be put to use." I'd laughed then, too—that's what he wanted me to do—but not a lot.

"All the same, dear, I fear a sudden backlash; I do. And then sometimes I remember my mother—a pious Roman Catholic who never missed—never mind mass, but a Miraculous Medal novena, who nevertheless absolutely and resolutely refused to believe in Fatima at all. And do you know why? Because *that the Mother of God would show a child the pains of hell is a thing I can't accept.* . . . God, *listen* to me! And I swear to you I haven't allowed a mood elevator to slip in through these alabaster teeth since I had them riveted in. No, this is *need!* Thanks for understanding that. We all talk too much; that which we must speak of is that which we can *not* hold still in our hearts. Thanks for being here—just here, just now, sitting on this train on the night of the shooting stars. Thanks, Delancey darling, for giving your Odette a chance to talk. I guess the fact is I am as the girl said—have you heard this one? It's the latest, and so, of course, I decided to try it on, and it did fit. *I'm an ambivert. I'm totally exhilarated and exhausted by exposure to company and totally exhilarated and exhausted left to myself.* And if you put it in a book, all the better. I give you permission—unlike poor Miss Garbo and that latest: you *have* heard *it?*"

I had heard it. Whoever it was who went walking with Garbo went walking with a wire in his lapel—like a spy or a Cosa Nostra stool pigeon—and intends publishing the results of his toil in book form. I can't imagine the illustrations; perhaps tasteful representations—*à la* Andy Warhol—of Garbo's old shoes. Who alive in New York, after all (who does not know), does not wonder what she talked about of an afternoon crossing Bow Bridge. Love?

"So I'm not doing the same thing to you now?"

"Absolutely not—I give you permission. Anyway, your

mother does not, apart from the shoulders and the fact that they both created legendary ballerinas on the screen, much resemble Garbo, nor does she hold with her about much—although Stolichnaya sometimes agrees that the pearls are cold."

I leaned over and whispered; I had to know how many. "How many guys are there over there, anyway?"

"Eight, like Brünnhilde's sisters—but prettier."

I was interested only that there were more than five, that there were six, anyway. What I actually *believed*. . . .

"Ja-maica. *All change!* Traina-*Montauk*, track eight!"

"The Eleven against Heaven. The other metaphor I had in mind was the stations—of the cross; but there are too many—like the men. 'I went to him for confession. He told me for my penance, *do the stations*—but I got arrested at Forty-second.' Remember that?"

(It seemed to me that it was Brünnhilde's eight sisters in their unreadable disguises who followed us into the last car of the Montauk train, although it might have seemed to them that it was us—we—who did the—to all, perhaps, but one: number six.)

"Whether or not an unredacted story like this can ever end," Odette continued, settling into a window seat, "we have to pretend, for form's gay sake, that it had at least some semblance of a beginning—*fado, fado,* as the O'Maurigan would say; aboriginally, *in illo tempore,* all the whole long way back in history's mists when. . . . When Thespis first stepped out of the kick line or your mother first stepped into the dressing room with the front-to-back mirrors and the merciless bulbs ablaze in the Mawrdew Czgowchwz manner, and first beheld herself, like the Russian doll, endlessly replicated."

"It was that night on Eighth Street, at the counter of the Riker's. That night that summer, a summer before your time—your time in the Village, at any rate, your time in Carmine de Sapio territory. You were still summering in those days, weren't you, in the same place you were wintering: up in the lovely Hudson Valley. It was that-summer-we-won't-say-which-one, but only that that adorable little- Harry Truman was still walking out every morning along Pennsylvania Avenue, and his cunning little Bess was still dusting doorknobs in the White House. And, of course, closer to home, the Third Avenue El was still up, and that very anything-*but*-adorable, albeit cunning enough, Archbishop Bess was still in her heinous prime—if on the turn—with her teeth soaking in Clorox in a spare silver chalice on the night table next to the canopied bed in which she dreamed her dream of the papacy—its gestatorial chair and its triple crown, and the rest of her going down on the ensuite bathroom doorknob, singing 'Thanks for the Memory' while spending herself into broderie Irish linen hankies. Whereafter the bubble bath, the Listerine mouthwash, and the quick confession required to set her up for the celebration of low mass in the Lady Chapel. That ghoul is the primate that should have died of hiccups—hard to believe there's no hell, whether or not you believe Mary showed it to the children of Fatima.

"Where was I, darling? Oh, yes, the Riker's. Summertime. Suppertime. . . .

"Remember the Riker's hash? There I was, sitting at the counter with a plate of it in front of me—fried egg on top, yolk intact, all crisped around the edges—rye toast, coffee, and a fat wedge of huckleberry pie for dessert. I remember the pie particularly, because I never got to eat it that night.

"They were down around the bend of the counter: Miss Charity Ward and her little protégé. Weeping, weeping—the protégé—what would she *do*, it hurt so *much*. The malignant old nance who'd picked her up in the Fragonard alcove at the Frick, dragged her to some gilt-mirrored fuck hutch near the Queensboro Bridge, and then—because she pleaded an indisposition to continue the shall-we-say *fundamental* deed—had nearly thrown her down the tenement stairs, barking loud after her, 'You want *sympathy*, baby? Look in the *dictionary*, under *symp!*' I naturally assumed she was wailing about being yet a virgin, and about the bruise inflicted upon her still unready heart—until the graphic details erupted, turning the already heavy air a sooty bruise-blue. Willing enough, and, indeed, out already some *weeks*. . . . 'Go *back*,' I muttered— you know how it is: there are always some you want to say that to, right off the bat—nobody in these seats on this train, darling— but you don't, you can't, so you're—well, unless you're a warthog in a gilt-mirrored tenement fuck hutch. . . . Willing enough, she'd been quite unable to accommodate the John—the *secretions*, the *blockage*. . . . I put my fork down, took up the coffee spoon, and beat a rapid tattoo on the countertop. 'Girls, *girls*, my *dinner!*'

"Miss Charity, a woman as yet unknown to me, shot me a look compounded of more or less equal parts of defiance and com-plicity—one that put me right in mind of *Dress Stage* days—then flipped her face back at the suppliant and hit her with, 'Ya knew it was dangerous work when ya took the job!' I loved her from that minute until the minute she breathed her last—and you know how she breathed her last, what her last words were. They were *dangerous work*. It was Miss Charity, by the way, who always said, 'Paint your wagon, Emma, etcetera,' before going out—in case you want to fix it in the show. Although I must say, I do like it the way it is, anonymous."

"Then that's just the way it will stay."

"Thank you, you are—Oh God, what was it that drunken Greek heiress said to you? You know, the one who tried to have the salon and got all those terrible nouveaux riches—O'Maurigan put it into *Panache*. I'm surprised you didn't put it in the show."

"She said, 'You are good, aren't you—but no, you couldn't be . . . *could* you?' "

"Poor woman. Remember what Frank wrote?

I am not interested in good.
It is all like looking in the mirror mornings.
You exclaim good heavens I am handsome! and then,
but not quite as handsome as all the others,
especially the dead.

But where was I, darling?"

"You were in Riker's, being good."

"Yes, to Miss Faith. . . .

"We—already working as a team—sat the patient down in front of the huckleberry pie—and truth to tell, the poor would-be-she looked like something you couldn't give away with a set of dishes. Your mother went over to the wall and dropped a nickel into the phones—God-in-His-gay-heaven, can you *remember* when the telephone was a nickel? So was the rapid transit system. *That and a nickel will get you on the subway.* Dropped a nickel in the phone, got the answering service of the good Dr. Clarence Brown. The doctor would go into the office at ten—and, as I well remember, we even managed between us to cough up the five bucks for the shot. The phone and the subway were a nickel—no, wait a minute, that can't be. O'Dwyer was out of office by . . . Impellateri. . . . It must've been a dime in the phone by then and ditto in the subway. Anyway, I remember for *sure* that a clap shot from Dr. Clarence Brown was five bucks—and listen, stop me before I break out into 'Penny Candy,' will you? We *all* loved the same songs, didn't we. 'Penny Candy,' 'Lazy Afternoon,' 'He Was Too Good to Me,' 'The Man That Got Away.' "

"Not all of us," I replied. (I was thinking just then of the guys across the aisle, and of myself in the period in which, along with the songs Odette mentioned, I shared their taste.) "Some of us also went for 'Walk Like a Man,' 'My Boyfriend's Back,' 'Peggy Sue,' and 'Bye Bye Love.' "

"*Touché*, dear. If you say so; you needn't even insist. . . . In any event, it was some weeks later that Miss Charity Ward's little convalescent bobbed up again on the Boulevard. I remember it was still warm weather—*flawless out*, as Ralph used to say—and we were on the *passeggiata* past the Women's House of Detention. (I went back, dear, on the day before I flew out, to sit with that portion of girls buried there in the garden in the Lucite box, and try to collect myself. Then, flying out, I thought: This *is* the right thing to be doing: my life has become so private, *I* have trouble getting into it.) 'I'm back, and I owe you my life,' the protégé said to us—by then we'd become bosom buddies and I'd introduced Miss Charity to the DeVors, *La Reina*—and sometime in the next few weeks we christened Miss Charity's ward Miss Faith Healy, because her surname *was* that, Healy, and she *swore* she was never going to get that sick again—she was sending through her Aunt May to the Old Country for some holy water out of the saint's well in Ballintubber, County Mayo. The father's family kept a pub there, across the road from the medieval Cistercian abbey, with a separate side door to the priests' snug. And the oddest thing is, you know, she never did, until—I swear, it's as if she only died because Miss Charity and Miss Hope. . . . I can't talk about that now; maybe I'll talk about it later—although it is uncanny. She was *so* fastidious, and had become almost prudish in her voiced cautions. Remember the classic: she said it to everybody, about the evenings at the Saint. 'It's getting so, anymore, you wouldn't kiss your dearest sister, that you don't know whose ass she's just been upstairs eatin' out.' "

I wasn't sure, but I thought I heard the silence from across the aisle in back of me roar.

"And the four of us became the Four in Hand, the core committee of the eventual Eleven against Heaven.

"Sorry to hold up the story, dear, but language is important, how what's said's said. Not nearly enough emphasis is put on the fine points of it any more, on *nuances*, not even in extension courses. It's the *nuances*, dear—as the girl said, make it *nuancical.* Or, better, as the poet I cited earlier wrote: *Je suis un homme qui se noie, montant un cheval à nu et mon ciel est couvert de nuances.* They're part, the nuances, of the glancing narrative—but aren't we all.

"The fine points, understand, are the connections. Make them, attempt them: there's nothing else. It's like I told poor Arthur Bell, God rest her, that time for 'Bell Tells.' It just came back to me when you cited 'Walk Like a Man,' which was, as you undoubtedly remember—in fact, did you not win a *citation* double-thump-stepping to it at the Grove hop?—*the* best uptempo Madison *ever.* 'Let me tell you,' I said to Arthur, 'the kind of girl I am; it'll save you a minute. If you play a game of mental association with me and say *Four Seasons*— well, the first girl wrote down *lunch* and the second girl wrote down *Vivaldi.'* (Actually, sister scribbled *Vivaldo*, but that's her gorgeous hairdresser, so they let it pass.) 'Well, I'd write down "Walk Like a Man"—and then right away think of "Big Girls Don't Cry" as the alternate. Mind you,' I added, 'I don't necessarily hold with either prescription as a way of life—but they are what *Four Seasons* calls to mind.' I wouldn't flash to that overpublicized beanery uptown, nor to either the composer of those fiddle pieces or any of the many terpsichorean seizures taken on them, but I *would*—flash—to those four gorgeous wops from the Platinum Age on 'American Bandstand.' And so would some other men traveling on this train. *Nuances*, dear."

"The years rolled by. You came into the picture one subsequent summer evening, then by and by the others, some singly, some in pairs—well, actually only the one pair, the beauties from Budapest: the first name of the one the last name of the other, and vice versa. Adorable. That was when we first heard that thing about Hungarians, that if you go into a revolving door with a Hungarian behind you, the Hungarian will come out in front of you. So we always used to kid them that whenever we were all out on the town and we came to a revolving door they had to go into it together, that way it wouldn't matter. The Hungarians in later years became symbiotic isolates, the pair of them.

"History—talking about revolving doors—repeating herself like hiccups, went on delivering us all the goods. The Trumans had long since vacated Washington by the time Mercedes Benzedrine breezed in from Havana on a one-way ticket courtesy of that tempestuous Fidel. And speaking of history, darling, weren't we silly and wasn't La Benz all too correct: hasn't that bearded lady turned into a heinous old warthog?

"Will anybody alive or dead ever forget Miss Merced's first excursion to the Statue of Liberty? Disembarked, there the refugee stood, in flowing red, white, and blue—I never saw anything like it again until Big Jessye got herself involved in the *tricolore* on Bastille Day. Even the shades, dear: white rims, red wands, and blue lenses. There she stood wrapped in bliss—murmuring '*Bendiceme*, America!' before the logo of Columbia Pictures in the monumental cast-iron flesh: the logo that had heralded for a decade each and every appearance on the screen of the woman on whom the Cuban boygirl had patterned her very existence, Miss Rita Hayworth—a dedication to that love goddess and to the America that created her which had commenced with the wartime *v.o.* screening in Havana of *Cover Girl*, and the impact of the lyrics— the first English words she learned—*Somehow I think I've found a sure thing in you.* Then she, La Benz, commenced overhearing some earnest schoolmarm from Corona reciting to her assembled fourth grade the famous inscription by Emma Lazarus, the one that opens *Give me your tired, your poor, your huddled masses yearning to breathe free, the wretched refuse of your teeming shore. . . .*

" '*Wretched refuse?!* I came here *first*-class—first-*class!* On Pan American World Airways!' After all, wasn't she the *hija de la hija de la tia del vicepresidente* under Fulgencio Batista, representing the highest-quality people, an ancient Aragonese-Catalan family, on her mother's side? I don't remember what they were called, but Bustamante was the father, so she had a half-dozen elements in her moniker, simplified by the boys in Immigration into Manuel Bustamante y Whatever. 'We were *irresponsible,*' she always used to clamor, 'for any corruptions!' Mercedes was emphatically what they call *alto voltaje,* and determined to be, and be regarded as, a full-fledged woman of the United States of America. So *alto voltaje* that when I attempted to help her do herself over as a Rita Hayworth redhead, spending hours concocting a very subtle preparation to complement her delicate olive skin tone, and counseling her to leave it on for *exactly* forty-seven minutes, she of course went for the burn and ended up looking like Rhonda Fleming—a very seasick Rhonda Fleming. So *alto voltaje* that she finally found herself installed in that archetypal ward eight, the rubber room at Bellevue—consequence, if you recall, of her being found naked and rampant on the public street one January night, stripped of all raiment but a brassiere, and proclaiming herself the diva Mercedes Bustamante of the Havana opera, singing the final scene of Johann Strauss's *Salome.* 'They only put me in there,' she commented later, 'because of that *maricón* cop that told them Johann Strauss didn't write *Salome,* Richard Strauss wrote *Salome.* It was only for that I flunked reality testing.' Anyway, they let her have her straitjacket as a souvenir, which she took home, cut the sleeve-ends, dyed pink, and covered with sequins to wear as a halter to cocktail parties. . . .

"As Old Mother Riley proclaimed, in *Old Mother Riley, M.P.*, when they made her Minister of Strange Affairs, *Time marches on, not sideways. You can't keep a good girl down.* She wouldn't have gotten much out of Relativity; she wouldn't have needed to."

"Reminds me. . . . You know, dear, it was before your time, as was Arthur Lucan in *Old Mother Riley*, but I did use to do the most divine *good girl* Bess Truman imitation at venues up and down both sides of gay Gotham, principally, westerly at the Cork Club on Seventy-second off the Park, and on the East Side of God at Madame Spivvy's, after Johnny Myers's puppet act. I wasn't at all bad as bad Bess Spellman, either. That other Johnny—Donovan—exemplary Catholic boy that *he* was—used to get me to do her—*impersonate* her, that is, at parties, introducing me as Her Grace, Fanny Spellbound—though I shouldn't admit it. What was it the great Countess Madge O'Meagher Gautier once said? 'We don't entertain anybody who entertains the Windsors—unless, of course, they spring for tickets; it's still a free country.' And Johnny did more than merely entertain. . . .

"The Countess—no friend herself of either the archdiocese or the maggoty leftovers of the British royal house—well knew what that gruesome twosome had been up to in Lisbon in 1940—that is, besides him lounging soused in the parlor on his own needlepoint chairs, leafing through his grandfather's collection of the back numbers of *Psst*, perking up his French the better to trade parlayvoos in the Paris of the New World Order: hearing from the likes of Paul Claudel the tidings brought to Mary, his mother, when she was Princess Mae of Teck. And her—Her Grace—barricaded in the bedroom, listening to *fado* on the wireless, and tormenting her vicious dewlaps while practicing her anilinguistic skills on various and sundry of the dreamy, sloe-eyed help. Trying, the pair of them, through channels to get Hitler to agree to nullify the Act of Abdication—that's what—and put them together on the throne of a Nazi-occupied Britain. Somebody had told them about the fascists in Britain, who'd all read up on the situation of World History as revealed to that evil old fairy Alma Toynbee—remember *her* in the late forties on the cover of, what else, *Time?* She was the other half of Ayn Rand, poisoning all those tiny minds on campuses coast to coast.

"Anyway, that was the plan. Poor deluded Wallis would, of course, in such a circumstance have not had what-to-*wear*, since the crown jewels had been stashed *away* with the Elgin marbles and the rest of the nation's valuables and artworks in a slate quarry in north Wales. . . .

"Pity about the war and its aftermath—they cut off the heads of all the lovely cobras in the London Zoo in anticipation of the blitz, whereas those two reptile Windsors went on and on.

"Oh, that Johnny Donovan was a desperate one, though—a queen of the worst Penn Post ilk. He claimed to have been the one who, by screening his home movies for her up there in the Waldorf Towers, taught Wallis Simpson how to rim, which became her, how the Brits say, *fort.* Others sneered at him for his pretensions, saying if anything it was *she* who could teach him the things she learned in a ritzy cathouse in Shanghai, where she went with Ernest Simpson on their tour of China, from some real-life equivalent of Mother Goddam. They insist that the best Johnny could show Wally would be how to dispose of used guests out the rear window. Alas, the provenance of Her Grace's skill may never be known with certitude—anyway, the fact is men are terribly easy to please in that fundamental way, pardon my French. There is an art to it, *toot mem.*

"Whatever's the *T* on Shanghai is, as I say, another pair of tonsils. In my opinion, the Duchess's hold on the Duke was only and entirely that he was a ferocious drunk afflicted with the typical grandiose low self-esteem of the breed manifested in spades—he'd *been* a *king*—in a characteristic penchant for slumming, and that she was able to manipulate that above all else—all else being the fact that he had a thing between his legs approximately the size of Mrs. Tom Thumb's clit. However, Johnny really *did*—and you ought to tell them so—throw that Puerto Rican hustler out the servants' terlet window and down the air shaft as evening shadows fell over sleepy Park Avenue roof-garden walls, and got away with it. There was at least one body that according to Miss Donovan—who perhaps was just then reading a lot of Miss Riding in the bathtub and wearing a tiara with 'Johnny' spelled out in Greek—had had its day. Literally got away with murder—and next day there it was at Chambord taking advice about what a devout woman, a victim of *trop de zèle*, was to wear to an inquest. And rehearsing the story—which, sources said, turned out to be some haughtily sworn rehash of the opening sequence of *Ladies of Leisure:* you remember, where the party girls are tossing the dead soldiers off the penthouse roof onto Fifth Avenue. And to an Irish detective in New York in the 1950s, dear, the fate of an empty liquor bottle would have been, philosophically, morally, and socially, of far greater interest than the corpse of an overexuberant, exhibitionistic Puerto Rican *dancer* lying in the bottom of an air shaft next to his brains—for that was the story told: of a miscalculated *jeté.* You want to talk about barroom, Benzedrine standards: they were his. I wasn't at the party or at Chambord the next day, but more than one witness all but swore the whole thing had come about because of a tantrum Johnny threw over the Ann Woodward publicity. 'You call *that murder?* Why, in a Paris courtroom you wouldn't get two out of seven, much less four to convict; *that* was a *crime passionnel.* I'll give you murder!' Somebody else said they didn't know how he'd gotten into such a mess, hadn't he been reading Sheed lately—you remember, that pious lay theologian who with his wife used to write volumes trying to get good Catholics to embrace the rhythm method? They had a publishing house—in fact, they published *The Confessions of Saint Augustine*, so you would have been affected by them, according to that very moving reminiscence in the show. . . . 'Not *Sheed*, dear,' somebody else kindly replied. '*Gide*.' 'Oh.' The point *being*, you see, that he'd become morbidly obsessed with the *acte gratuite*. Or as somebody put it to me—'He's always hated you, dear, and this is his way of showing you what he thinks it means to be an existentialist.' Like that. All very twisted—like the garbage in the gutters that sometimes gets caught up in the little swirling cyclones engendered by the crosswinds off the rivers when they meet at odd corners. . . . The story then goes on that right there, right then, at Chambord, Lotte Lenya—presumably on her way to the can—stopped in front of his banquette and hissed at him, '*Du hast kein Herz*, Johnny.' Not a story I credit, dear; sounds a little too—much too—well, convenient to me, rather like Barrymore's tag line in *Portrait of Jennie*—similarly delivered on the run, you remember. *How very wise you* are, *my dear!* No, I don't buy that little detail in the portrait of Johnny. Nor people's remembrance of the ensuing brouhaha, which was, to the best of your mother's recollection, and despite the perpetrator's ghoulish hopes, not a *patch* on that surrounding poor Ann Woodward when she blew the face off her Billy. And speaking of bad boys and horsing around, you know, don't you, what his Penn Post pals called him? Well, let's put it dignified: *de mortuis non nisi boner*. . . .

"Johnny Donovan—is there *anything* more revolting than a mick half-breed impersonating a WASP? His was one of those lives, dear, which arrived at the destined pale of its affective worth sometime not long after the subject's first communion, and essentially continued playing fallen-angel reruns ever after. He used to run around telling people he was an existentialist, until I—because I felt it was his due and my place—pointed out to him that living in the afterglow of one's performance is not exactly the same thing as living with the consequences of one's acts. One never did know what the original interest in his performance even *was*, but there was a quality to it that apparently struck a nerve somewhere in the public psyche—probably, come to think of it, the way a nerve in a rotten tooth would. That would explain it in part: you have the tooth out—probably with laughing gas, and in spite of yourself for years after, you find yourself worrying with your tongue the hole it left— recalling dimly, perhaps, what happened under the laughing gas. . . ."

"Well, Wallis Warfield Simpson Windsor never got to woo the inspector in his behalf, like she did on Ann W.'s, nor he to stand at the font at St. Patrick's to witness her baptism by Fulton Sheen. He just died drunk one day—not one day too soon.

"Oh, it's a great mistake, dear, for us sissies, *qua* sissies, to lay any special claim to goodness, just because we are, as Mrs. Behan said of the Irish, very popular among ourselves, and even if, since all the redeemed, according to Revelations 14:4, are male celibates, we have in these latter days become confessional, and now aspire to wake up every morning pure and corrected. Still and all, it is a lovely existential thought: you can't keep a good girl down. If only we knew the exact nature of good. *If only we knew.* The sublime tag line of the greatest play of the twentieth century: *if only we knew.*

"People sometimes tax me, *Why do you go on and on about poor Johnny Donovan after all these years*, and all I can think of is what Miss Davis snapped at the best boy on the set of *The Whales of August. She* was abreacting at some length, as was her wont, about Miss Crawford, and this flippant number said something like what people say to me about Johnny Donovan. She opened up the baby blues full wide, took a long drag on the cigarette, and advised him, 'Just because you're *dead*, doesn't mean you've *changed!*' Did she know *what*, or what?''

''Mercedes, especially after Bellevue, was freaked to her satin-smooth, Mum-scented armpits and gave up wretched excess and reckless chemical experimentation—alas, probably too late—because she feared slipping as-if-back, into a poverty and a squalor she had in fact never known. Consequently she was haunted by the story, noised about in those days as a cautionary tale, of the great Spanish *poule de luxe* Labeja Otero, who once, while dancing naked at Maxim's on New Year's 1900, had flung rubies and un-strung pearls in fistfuls at her aristocratic audience—including, who knows, perhaps the heinous David Windsor's warthog grampa—only to end up in Nice in the years after the Second World War eating out of three-star-restaurant garbage pails. Lick-ing the oyster shells of yesteryear, as if her pearls—no wonder people prefer to forget. What's that great line, 'Here are the stubs; where are the memories?' With me it's the opposite: not a shred of memorabilia. The torn stub has always been to me like the torn stocking—*the laddered hose*, as the girls used to say in *Dress Stage*—out with yesterday's evening papers and that empty box of Bromo-Seltzer. 'Course I know why: though my ducats were almost exclusively comps, *too* too many of them turned out to be extremely ferocious examples of the ticket that exploded: blowing up with terrifying regularity in mother's face. Whereas the mem-ories that linger on—linger on.''

''The gathering and numbering of the ships. Isn't that what they call it in the epic, when at the beginning all the principals are summoned, presented, and accounted for? Let's see, so far we've succeeded in the way of numbering ourselves, you and I, the gay DeVors, Miss Charity, Miss Faith, Miss Mercedes, and the two Magyars: Miss Worthington—commonly known as *Miss Thing*, and later in her career, when she was the co-doorman with Dorothy Dean at Max's Kansas City, and had had her head shaved so as to turn herself into a ringer for Mayakovsky as photographed by Rodchenko, a bizarre and even hilarious turn for a refugee of the 1956 Soviet invasion of Hungary and sometime disciple of Ayn Rand to do, as *Mister Miss Fierce Thing*—and Mrs. Claudia Caswell DeWitt, called *Miss Cass*. That's eight all told, to whom were added, in the Fullness of Time, *Miss Hildegarde Dorsay, Miss Hope Chest Tone—Hojo*—and *Miss Mary Garden Gates—Mae-Mae*. Whereupon, in 1960, we approached the gay talent scout from the William Morris Agency to send us up for that daring print-ad concept 'Eleven on a Ronson.' You were to be the lone wolf, holding the Ronson in one butch fist, ready to service the oral desires of ten receptive women. . . . You were *so* masculine; we were so ahead of our time."

(I myself couldn't help remembering—while wondering were we responsible for the time that caught up with us—the photo session O'Maurigan arranged for the Eleven against Heaven with Avedon, or the comments elicited upon the viewing of the results by the towel boy at the Everard. "Jeez—yiz all soyt'nly come out lookin' like a luscious lotta ta*may*tas. Any-a you goils play some kinda musical instrument?" "Yeah," Miss Charity snapped back. "All of us—the *mouth organ*, why?" "Well, I gotta tell yiz, if yiz cuhd pick up a fiddle ora banjo or sumpin', den look *out*, Phil Spitalne!")

———

"Or were we? I suppose the strict liberationists would. . . . But, then, in my opinion that blowtorch queen you observed on that fatal night at the Stonewall, defacing the officer with a pink lady, has a lot to answer for besides wasting God's own good liquor. She opened up a can of worms, and don't let's mince words—worms that did more than crawl in and out of poor Judy. She opened the way for the tyranny of the liberators—the Body Snatchers. For all those ghastly unkempt mustaches and flannel shirts, for color-coded handkerchiefs and dangling keys, and all the rest of it: the rig, the drill, the deadly perseverance of the captivated. I mean *really*, that practically every fag in Freedomland was forced to go out on the street looking like Zachary Scott at a dude ranch—*that* was supposed to be *masculine?* As the Duchess huffed when the Arabs bought Harrods, *Iniquitous—there ought to've been a plebiscite!*

"You were *terribly masculine*—so demure, so *implicit.* You never would go anywhere in drag, as often as you were sought. The answer was always *next*—until finally, having nothing camp to call you, we called you that, Next. And you know, Next, tonight when you were waxing confessional onstage concerning the gypsy in *One Night in Venice*, I couldn't help wanting to stand up in the audience—such as somebody might have done at one of the divine Edna Everage revues: the *only* authentic evenings-in-the-theater to be had, by the way, in London these days—and ask you to remember and tell a little about the stark revenge you subsequently exacted on showbiz gypsies, when, at Riis Park that first summer of the *West Side Story* run, you succeeded in making the *entire* chorus of Sharks and not a few Jets into the bargain fall head over *fuckman* and *caramba* for you.

"Oh, we were very merry in those days, were we not, and never ever tired. Will you ever forget that time we were all on the Bolshoi line at once—the last Ulanova *Giselle*—Miss Charity picking up that public phone ringing in the shop arcade? 'Yes, I'll marry you—who *is* this?' That was the same night you arrived in the hansom cab on that provocative heterosexual outing you talked about in the show. You had that line *so* worried, despite Miss Hope's calm assurance that in all likelihood the most intimate thing you did with the girl was lend her your comb. Truth to tell, you, Delancey, were either the best bad boy or the baddest best boy there ever—I never have, dear, seen anybody work a line or a room the way you worked them in your salad days: bold as brass, and you already married to Filippo. Guess that's how you could; I never did get marriage. I had all those relationships—or did I? Maybe it was really like the girl said: *Relationships: they never started and they never ended, but I was always there for them.* Well, as to the truth of it all, I never got marriage because I never got married. Next? As Miss Jane Cowl's character in *Payment on Demand* replied to the naive query put by Miss Davis's character, *Because no one ever asked me, dear, and anyone I ever asked said no.* But I wasn't the kind even to ask. I was always Bella Darvi, dear, in *The Egyptian.* I asked for nothing; I never even hinted. Although I'd better watch my own lips on that one—maybe even bite my tongue. Poor Bella ended up much the same way as Labeja Otero—even in the same vicinity."

"Well, that's the lot. Now here we sit, you and I, the ships all in—lined up the way they used to be along the New York waterfront, each in her berth, rumps all rounded at Jersey like a chorus of cancan girls—and what are we about to do but torpedo them, by telling their stories, by dishing them, the way the Nazi saboteurs did the *Normandie,* Diane DeVors's most cherished vessel. Send them each and all to the bottom of the North River the way the Vikings—and that, as they say, will be the price of them.

   "Girl Vikings, or Valkyries. Remember *that* campaign? La DeVors, never one for reticence, simply *assumed* the big Brünnhilde role, and then got very busy and executive assigning the others,

Waltraute to me, because she always said that whatever happened, I'd live to tell about it. Funny, isn't it, how she automatically assumed it'd be herself I'd be telling, at the sanitorium in the Rockies, after one of her legendary marathon sleep cures. Siegmund *and* Siegfried to you, because she said you were to her not only the only boy in the world but the *epitome* of the Eternal Return, and Sieglinde to the baby, Miss Faith. Funny, too, how she didn't like to actually *listen* to Wagner. 'The music is cata-*tonic*, darling, but that story line's got *everything!*' Actually thought it would play better as theater in *modern dress*, spoken to the accompaniment of offstage cocktail piano.

"And like the Valkyries, or like the ships at Pearl Harbor, how quickly they went down when they went down—very much as if together on some other December Sunday morning after some other long, long summer and some other blazing fall. I've got image after image of them, and lately, darling, dream after dream, usually all scrambled. The right girl in the wrong hospital, or vice versa. Vicious parodies of filled-out forms—much with last-name-first and first-name-second, and intimate details catalogued under Sex, Marital Status, Profession, and Religion. Replays of that scene in *42nd Street* of all the girls quick-changing in the bus going from theater to theater, turning back into reality, and it's only your mother, in truth, in the wavering light of a winter afternoon, traveling alone in the bus crosstown-uptown-downtown-crosstown, from St. Vincent's to the heinous St. Clare's—to New York Hospital to the N.Y.U. Medical Center, like an undercover-agent cross between the Spider of the Escorial and the proverbial crab underwater—and, as you well know, that is neither my sign nor my scene. I am, like Marilyn, and Kaye Wayfaring, a Gemini. I am a pair, like tits. Speaking clinically, I suppose a borderline schizophrenic—but although there may be two of me, dear, we are both going, *together*, in *one* direction. *Exalted is the storyteller who can let the wick of his life be consumed completely by the gentle flame of his tale.* With me,

darling, it's more like trying to keep my *hair* from catching fire
from my own flamethrower mouth!

"Then, when I've finished telling the Saga of the Eleven
against Heaven—what? For can I bear to *conceive* of myself not
telling somebody *something?* Sometimes I remember the lines from
This Island Earth, the ones the Metalunan speaks, giving the earth-
lings a tour of his capital city and environs, devastated by inter-
planetary war: *Our educational complexes, blown to rubble. Over
there was a recreation center.* . . . Like that. *If* I survive into another
generation, I see myself giving such a tour of New York to the
new young Japanese landlords, pointing out, for example, N.Y.U.
and the Saint, after not war but neglect and callousness have taken
their final toll, the ozone layer—like Metaluna's ionization layer—
has been destroyed, and the Nips—excuse me. (You can take the
girl out of the war, but taking the war out of the girl. . . .) After
the new landlords have put it all under a glass dome. Or will we,
some of us, as some predict, get off this island earth at the very
last fatal minute and colonize some new green planet in a distant
galaxy. In which case, dear, I don't see your mother on the A list,
so I do *not.*"

"I do so want to tell it like it was, dear, *wie es eigentlich gewesen,*
as *die* DeVors herself would insist in her terminal accesses of Marlene fabulosity and marathon-wild-woman mouth. She used those
very words to me on that last night—*wie es eigentlich gewesen*—just
after they'd shaved her legs in preparation for the last bypass sur-
gery, the one she never made it to the theater for. So I will, starting
with hers, the first ascension into heaven of the eleven against
same, the only one not engineered by that strangely nominated
pestilence, the Acquired Immune Deficiency Syndrome.

"We'd been laughing and laughing, and she'd been doing one
of her sweeping summations—no hint in it of *finale,* just another

one of her famous and oft-recited *précis*. The woman was so per-
suasive, it was as if as long as she was talking she was right, especially about love and duty—*DeVors's devoirs*, as we used to kid.
Somebody once declared Diane was 'fey.' *'Fey!'* Miss Charity
shrieked, and then, calming herself a mite, concluded, 'Yeah, all
right, she's fey—as in Frances Faye.' It was the truth. Remember
Miss Faye's last appearance—in *Pretty Baby?* 'There are only two
things to do on rainy days, and I don't like to play cards.' That
was Miss Diane DeVors to the life. She held with Dostoevsky—in
fact, she more than anyone else I ever knew personified his belief—
that life is full of the comic, and is only majestic in its inner sense.

"I give you the typical DeVors scenario analysis, dear. 'Girl
skips off one night in '62 or '63 to City Center to sit through
Marie Bell and Jacques Charrier in *Phèdre*—he barefoot, she Byz-
antine. Races to the Everard thereafter and translates at breakneck
speed *funeste ardeur* into thanatic sex. Goes to a party on the
weekend and not for the first time suffers the slings and arrows of
outrageous foreplay. The years roll by. Said slings and arrows installed not at the Everard, but at the very modern Club—First and
First. Upshot: sex becomes all foreplay, and more and more outrageous. Nothing but auditions—she might as well have gone into
television. Would footwear on Jacques Charrier have saved sister's
sanity, sister's *life?* Who's to say no?'

"And on politics. 'Forget the revolution, dear. The spectacle
of culture has done away with the idea of revolution.' "

"So there I was, sitting in the coffee shop, spooning up a plain
nonfat Dannon yogurt out of sympathy, and running in my mind
her fabulous self-invented curriculum vitae and filmography—which,
remember, she affixed to the back of all her eight-by-ten glossies,
and which all her admirers were more or less expected to memorize
in order to converse with her—and there she was, upstairs, being

fed a whale's dinner—meat, potatoes, mixed vegetables, bread and
butter, dessert, due to a mixup in the kitchen charts—and as I was
working my way like a mother with a boy gone to war saying the
rosary at an Immaculate Conception novena on a Monday night,
through *Samoan Love Song*, Warners, 1929; *Leftover Ladies*, Warners, 1930; *She Learned to Lie*, Paramount, 1933—off she went, dear,
just like that, in the middle of the stewed kumquats and blanc-
mange—probably at the exact moment when I'd reached her Academy Award performance in *The Most Beautiful Woman in the
World*. I asked myself for *months* ever after, why-did-she-eat-all-
that-food-did-she-not-*understand*? And believe you me, dear, if I
ever do get through to the cow in her ectoplasmic-in-flawless-
eternity self, the very first question I shall put to her is that, and
she'd better answer, too! And then, of course, the touching moment, weeks later at the memorial at Campbell's, when O'Maurigan, by way of eulogy, read the entire filmography out—including
Pert, Boardwalk Melody, Tawdry, The Story of Lorna Lang, before
the tribute closed with the tape of DeVors herself singing 'A Penny
for Your Dreams,' just the way Milanov's service in the same room
had ended with the '54 broadcast *Pace, pace.*"

"With Miss Faith, the last to go—for I really can't bear clicking
them off one by one *ad seriatim* tonight, so this is the synoptic
version of it. You know, generally speaking, I do not approve of
the simile which couples our sufferings in this crisis with those of
the victims of the Holocaust—although very technically, what with
offering the burnt remains of the girls to the great rivers of Europe,
I. . . . However, the one great saying I think we might justly appropriate is *not soevermany taken, but one taken soevermany times*.

"With Miss Faith, it's things like the six pink plastic digital
clocks, set at four-hour intervals for the AZT dosage. So that there
was nothing to do but turn them off one at a time and then reset

them together at midnight. She seldom went out, only to the clinic
at St. Clare's, or occasionally to the Metropolitan Museum of Art,
and never for longer than four hours. And then, the collapse at the
clinic and they put her upstairs—into what she was calling, on
some good evidence, Cardinal O'Connor's death camp, and Dachau. 'It's the original *almshouse*, here, darling: we are the aged,
the infirm, the unruly, and the maniac.' And considering the devastating effects of the toxoplasmosis and the wasting—the ca-
chexia—on her, she tended both to look and intermittently to
correctly voice the part. Whereupon we felt compelled to stage a
rescue. Oh, the doings there were terrible enough: her left crawling
around on the floor, the meningitis tests that went half-done, the
nun who was good, the doctor who seemed unnecessarily cruel:
his sadism—a given, after all, in doctors, and in many ways a
strength—seemingly veering toward the out-of-hand . . . etcetera.
In my anger in the moment, I said out loud to everybody, just
after we got her out, 'If the well, the fit, and the able-bodied
wanted to *picket*, they should go up there and ask for—well, these
people know who they are, as we used to say.' But, no, they prefer
to go over and mess up St. Vincent's, just because some moron
orderly babbled *faggot* and sister fled *fearing for her life*—give your
mother a *coffee* break!

"Anyway, dear, you've heard me on ACT/OUT. Aggrieved
Children Throwing One Uncut Tantrum. After all, some Certified
Horror Show suddenly stands up and screams, *I've lost seven hundred* of my *dearest friends!* And I *swear* to you the only way she
can get away with it is *who's* going to contradict her? Who among the
dead are going to rise from the grave, scream FRIEND?! and thereupon
go into hysterics, laughing themselves to death yet again? The dead,
from all we're told, have more important things to do than to resurrect
just to get a few things clear. I mean *that* was tried exactly once—and
so far as setting things straight, accomplished *what*? These ones are
behaving *exactly* the way the American Publicity Machine—the

strongest machine in operation in the body politic of the Republic—behaves. It is a mistake to say that all Americans want is money; all Americans want is what all rejected children want, recognition and vindication on the primary narcissistic level—always have. I feel strongly that the Sisters of the Perpetual Indulgence, for instance, are more effective all-around than ACT/OUT—just as I *know* that Mae West was and is still more effective against all bigotry than any polemicist.

"I hold with Liz Smith on the ramifications of it all—on outing and all that—as, indeed, on so much else; but then, Liz and I go back together nearly all the way: we're of an age, and behave it, not to mention that, as is universally acknowledged, *there* is one good woman of the fourth estate in a just cause—such as Reconciliation."

·

"We got her—Miss Faith, dear, not Liz—safely installed at N.Y.U. hospital in cooperative care, and the symptoms actually abated—she said it was because of the big stuffed Kermit frog—the *power animal* or confidant that Miss Charity had sent her. So I told her something I'd overheard on the bus that day. 'I signed up for a power hour with this image consultant.' The speaker was one of eight—count 'em, *eight*—little fashionoids going down to Dallas to get some bijou prizeen or other, for which she was going to have to stand up and say *thank you* to three thousand garmentos—*in frenzied anticipation whereof* she was willing to part with a you-can-bet sizeish portion of her hard-earned designing-woman's salary after a *power hour* with an *image consultant.* Try, if you will, to imagine for a spare second Betty Bacall skimping on her coordinated-calorie lunch in order to go to a—Oh, my dear, is your mother ever in the *wrong* business! Anyway, she'd rattle on at it by the hour, Miss Faith, at the frog, and then gradually the symptoms regained their hold, although the Dachau fright had gone forever, until, confusing eras, and returning to what was perhaps the illusory complicities of her childhood-companion fantasies, she would just look at the thing and say, 'Thwack your magic *twanger*, Froggie!'

"Then the meals we took together—until they wouldn't stay on her stomach, and we'd be off down the hall to the toilet. 'God,' she'd say, 'you'd think I was Miss Caswell, auditioning for the sister who burns down the plantation in *Aged in Wood!*' Once, after she'd heaved up her meal, she reminded me about 'Girls, girls, my dinner!' People looked at us funny on the way back to the room, thinking, I suppose, *What do* those *two have to* laugh *about?* Miss Faith with the look of death on her, and this one, looking, at the very least, distracted. . . .

"The week or so before the beginning of the end—one evening after they'd taken down the Yuletide festoons—I remember sitting with her up there in the N.Y.U. hospital roof dining room, trying to get some rice pudding into her, looking out over the East River, watching the very few riverboats and remembering the old waterfront again. I looked down at one point toward the helicopter launching platform and said, 'This isn't really like visiting someone in the hospital at all; it's like sitting in an airport restaurant seeing somebody off whose flight has been delayed—the Lisbon Clipper from the old municipal airport before it was LaGuardia. It, too, took off from the water.' And Miss Faith looked up at me and said, in that strange new voice she'd acquired after the amelioration of the dementia in that environment, 'Darling, I don't think my flight is delayed; they'll be announcing the gate number any time now, and it won't be higher than thirty-one.' Then she went off into a riff on planes and combat, all drawn from her experience of the Second World War and its aftermath—an experience she'd shared with her contemporaries here in New York at the various nabes: R.K.O., Loew's, Skouras, and independent. 'Everybody knew all along,' she said to me, 'that it was kamikaze sex. We knew it was dangerous work when we took the job. That's why we went about it the way we did, in bomber jackets and headsets and stoned to the hair roots; to suggest anything else now in the evening is a lie.' She ended that evening with the Bogart and Lizabeth Scott routine she'd always fastened on from *Dead Reckoning*: where after Dusty, or Rusty, or whatever she's called has been plugged and is dying in the E.R., he leads her along in the final *parachute jump*. I couldn't play it—she didn't much want me to; she did both parts—she was perfect, in both. Then she capped the performance off with a perfect imitation of her girl singing 'Did He Ask about Me?' from the 1958 Vic LP *Lizabeth*. After she was finished, she snapped at me, 'And when you get to Mayo and find May there—she thinks they named it after her, ya know—will you find out what the old whore wants done with her fuckin' bonds and stock certificates?'

"It seems when May went clattering down the stairs that long-ago day—and that was the last he was ever going to see of her or get from her—she'd left her stocks and bonds behind in a Thom McAn shoebox. And she'd never asked after them again."

"Then she started going further off—Miss Faith, that is—going a little closer to gaga again, as she grew more and more tired of the fight and of the expenditure of mouth the fight entailed, and she just held my hand. I thought of the unfinished novel we'd yakked out on the phone over the years—the one about the mannequin in the window at Bergdorf's coming to life with the bolt of lightning, and her progress to the Goddess Lounge high up in the Manhattan sky. . . . Then, for some crazy reason, I thought of the dying words of the Duke of Wellington. He is supposed to have said to the man at his side, *Kismet, Hardy*, but of course what he actually said was *Kiss me, Hardy*. I just leaned over and kissed Miss Faith, and she just smiled—enigmatically, if I may say so, as if the time for language and its employment had just run out—and said, 'You're very kind.' All I could think of was that in both of the two greatest American plays, both of which end with heroines gone gaga, both playwrights have their women say, abstractly, *You're very kind.* And, of course, in both cases they are by then in effect talking to strangers—in fact, the second heroine affirms it—and the fact is, I thought then, that may well be the absolute truth about us throughout our lives, no matter whom we talk to, no matter what we say.

"Although I must say, for what it's worth, that I absolutely do *not* find it true just now, right here on this local train tonight, talking to you, Delancey dear."

I said thank you.

"It was January 25, at 4:00 a.m. I woke from a dream of the two of us on the telephone—of her calling from *'Someplace Else, I don't know where, but I like it; it's like someplace in a Siennese landscape— pink, blue, green, gold.'* When she'd hung up, I went right back to sleep in the dream, thinking of her as Joan of Arc, in the Honegger oratorio, declaring that in the early morning, when her saints appear, it is very pink and blue and green and gold . . . like that. Woke up as usual at eleven, made coffee, called the hospital: she was seven hours dead. I didn't rush right up; I had my coffee, and experienced for the first time in far too long a wild craving for huckleberry pie. I just couldn't get upset. I kept thinking of the pink triangles in the urinals and how we'd giggled about them. That afternoon I went under, didn't I. You said, I realized the dangerous work was done for them, but not for me. Indeed it wasn't, for when I did go up to collect the effects, I found, in the very room where Miss Faith had died that morning, in the same bed, remade, the most beautiful young Italian boy—the face on him almost the exact face of the Saint Sebastian in the Titian *St. Mark Enthroned with Saints*, in the Salute. This beautiful Italian boy, in the bed looking up at the soap opera on the television— and next to him, sitting in the bedside chair I'd sat in feeding and shaving Miss Faith, his grieving grandmother. I stood and gaped, unnoticed, the thought cracking open my mind like forked lightning: *What's wrong with this picture?*

"I know Phil's stipulation—and it never will be revealed where—"

Here's where I clicked off, briefly, the tape recorder. Not to be coy, not really, but to give Odette a chance to slip (metaphorically) into the wings, run around the back wall (the way the kids did at City Center all those years), and re-enter, *apparently* going further along the same route in the same direction, with, can-you-dig-it, me as Prince Siegfried in hot pursuit. . . .

"Next, darling, it was both a great kindness and a stroke of practical genius for you and O'Maurigan to map out mother's itinerary the way you did, in Crayola. It took one right back to *Watch on the Rhine*, reinforcing one's sense of high purpose, of *mission*. Which was why one had ordered, and specifically fitted out with studs and points so that they'd always travel upright, the very same steel-reinforced trunks Dietrich commanded for her progress through perilous war zones and postwar zones as well.

"Dublin, Paris, Milan, Venice, Wien; Budapest, Munich, Köln, Hamburg . . . Stockholm, Oslo, Trondheim, Bergen, Copenhagen, Amsterdam; London, Cork, Ballintubber, Shannon, home.

"Just the names of places is enough to get me going, dear, always has been. *Anaheim . . . Azuza* Cu-*camonga!* Divine. Then, too, the elegance, the thrilling expedition of travel eased by diplomatic and show-business affiliations. You can take the girl out of foreign intrigue, but you can't. . . ."

" 'The last shall be both first and last'—I like that. She *was* the baby, and she did get her way, after a fashion, if only *after* we'd faked our way through the R.C. funeral that the impresario cousin, Jacinta, cooked up to go with the sudden-death-by-stroke story for Faith's true natural mother. How I substituted at the fifty-ninth second of the twelfth hour the ashes of the incinerated diaries, after sitting up all night the way we're doing now, putting them, in a weird neutral voice, on cassette *et*-cetera. . . . I never did blame you for not turning up for those charades, dear, and I have never given you the full *T* on them. I was tempted at the same time to burn up all of old May Healy's bonds and stock certificates, but instead I turned them over to O'Maurigan, and I'm glad I did, because of what happened in Amsterdam. They'd *never* have returned—but I'm getting ahead of myself. The service. 'What's the name of this church?' I asked O'Maurigan. '*Crown of Thorns,*' he hissed back. It took me a second to—and then I nearly—of course, we were in Blessed Sacrament, on West Seventy-first Street. The aftermath: coffee with cousin Jacinta at the Bagel Nosh on Broadway and Seventy-first, then skulking home with the real ashes concealed on my person. More anon.

"Only an Irish girl would have come up with the Healy proposition for the disposition of the only true remains—half of her in the Liffey, on her mother's side of the Old Country, and the other half with her father's people, in the saint's well at Ballintubber. 'I know exactly what you're thinking,' she said to me. 'That he was such a bastard, why would I want—how *could* I even *consider*, in my—Well, I've made my peace with him—dead ahead of me, which is all I had a natural right to ask—and with all the

Healys, and anyway, it was May taught me about Life.' (The father's sister, you remember: she was Thalia Bridgewood's daily-
with-kitchen-privileges for years and years, which was how our Miss
Faith got started, and what saved her when the father threw her
out of the house on Staten Island after Lillian Law entrapped her
in the ferry terminal tea room.) 'It was May taught me about Life.'

"Did you know that Judy at one time wanted her ashes deposited in *three* places: the Palladium, the Palace, and the Olympia?
She meant, of course, *urned, stashed,* in the lobbies, but some
queens, misunderstanding, started shrieking their wussies off.
Scattered! She'll wind up in vacuum *cleaners!"*

"Dublin. O'Connell Bridge—anent the Gentlemen's quayside convenience—to float downstream past the Customs House, past Pool-
beg Light and into Dublin Bay, with the Hill of Howth on one
side and Black Rock on the other. The mother's people were
O'Learys of Black Rock—Jacinta's side. May Healy never had anything to do with them—even had trouble being civil to Jacinta,
whom she'd always refer to in asides as *Gesundheit.* May was a
Tartar, all right, but she certainly rescued Miss Faith—stowed away
in the Bridgewood laundry room and nursed on Dr. Brown's penicillin and streptomycin. Feeding her patient on blood pudding
from the Irish butcher on Third Avenue and the Barry's tea she
kept in the pantry closet in tight tins, she soothed the hellish hurt—
for the clap and the shame had festered—with expressions like, 'Aw,
c'mon, now, Captain Billywinks, there's worse things happen at
sea.' Unhappily, there was the inevitable Irish family falling-out,
when May, years later, after the Bridgewood years and her return
to check the lay of the land in Ballintubber, arrived—Barry's tea
tins, blood puddings, and all—looking to stay *there with the boys*
four floors up on West Seventy-third, between Columbus and Amsterdam, in a household whose stock of comestibles by then in-

cluded much sweeter meats and far stronger potions, pills, and powders. Left, she did, before the week was out, clattering down the four flights, with the one arm as long as the other. Left ten bucks on the table with a note. *It's the last you'll get from me."*

"Well, after I'd measured out the half of Miss Faith into the Liffey as agreed, and had a lovely evening at *School for Scandal* at The Gate, I was anxious to get across the Irish Sea, past Cornwall and the Channel Islands to Cherbourg and Paris on business with Miss Hildegarde Dorsay.

"Paris, the Pont Neuf. Funny, the symmetry of the requests: the specific bridges, the exactitude of the envisioned paths down-river, past this on the left, and that on the right. Quite unlike, for example, *anywhere along the Rhine.* Some of the girls were demanding, others only dispensed on demand. . . .

"Off the Pont Neuf, after a turn around the Place Dauphine and an *accouchement* observing the *bocce* players, the ones Hilda always watched from her balcony at the Hôtel Henri IV. It was past dusk when I re-emerged and walked to the edge of the bridge. The lights of the *bateaux-mouches—Les Vedettes du Pont Neuf—*were on full strength, like blazing foots to feature my performance before an adoring public, when what was wanted was shadow, the shadow of yesteryear, *lorsque descend la nuit,* as Eartha did sing. 'Ah want to float serenely downrivuh, *chérie,'* Hilda had beseeched me, 'unduh thuh Pont des Arts and past thuh Louvre on mah right and thuh old Gare d'Orsay on mah left. It's a museum now, and houses, Ah'm told, thuh most di-vahn Puvis de Cha-vannes. You see, hon, it's like that graffito said—thuh one on thuh station wall at Bastille: *Je suis le seul à comprendre Puvis de Cha-vannes. C'est moi, ça.'* Well, I waited and I waited, and finally a cloud went over the moon, like in the opening sequence of *The Letter,* and there was for a moment not a *bateau-mouche* either coming or going, and I dumped her out, thinking crazily to myself for the first time, it could have been more difficult: suppose she, or any one of them, had said, *I want to float upriver.* And there in the blackness I thought I saw the glint of a gold filling heading for the open sea. . . .

"Hildegarde Dorsay. The Black Pearl of the Chesapeake, Baltimore-born, like Lady Day. How she took to Paris—and it to her! Her impromptus at Bricktop's with the volcanic proprietress became the talk of that town, and I shall never forget her curtain speech that first night of the *Club Ubangi Revue* in '63, or the voice that responded from the back:

Je veux, mesdames et messieurs, vous remercier de tout mon coeur d'avoir fait de moi une vraie femme!

Ça c'est vrai, chérie—tu es divine!

It was truly said of her back then, in her high-shine time, *elle sait son métier de reine.* She did indeed—and she gave it all up to come back and take part in The March and The Movement: a decision that broke her heart, or, at any rate, bruised it very badly—for they turned on her: her very own. . . ."

"They lowered her resistance—Phil says hate can."

"Phil is, as he almost always is, correct—and guess what? That perception keys directly into something I have just decided. I have just decided—wasn't that Rockville Centre we just passed? It was—the hideous illuminated cathedral. More hideous than the basilica at Lisieux—you get a glimpse of that one at almost the same speed when you come down from Cherbourg on the boat train to Paris. I have just decided, definitively, what this is, this what I'm up to this long night. This is the Jackson Pollock abstract expressionist drip method of storytelling—and fuck the begrudgers.

"For, you see, it wasn't just her enemies—or ours—it was the supposed friends. The, pardon my French, *tout comprendre/tout pardonner* crowd—as if anybody ever *asked* their pardon: as if *that's* what we were doing down on our—as if we'd been *born* down on our—born to do floors, so to speak. I shall never forget her calling me up one summer night only a decade or so ago, all in a froth over something she'd read in the *Village Voice*. 'The *Village* Voice!' I abreacted back at her. '*What* do you expect to find out about the world reading *that* wipe?' 'Ah dunno, Miz O'Doyle, but get *this*, from one of yoah precious *lib*'ruls!' It was a piece on Miami, and I remember it tonight because of what it was called—'The Failure of Tantrum Politics'—so you see why. Anyway, it contained the famous hair-raising gaffe, *We took in 79th Street, a strip of which has been taken over by black hustlers and prostitutes, real women and*—and there it came roaring at me over the phone as if *I'd* written it—*those grotesque combinations of fantasy and medical technology that are transvestites.* 'Whut is he *tawkin'* abaht, Miz O'Doyle? *Ah* for wun have got *awl* mah teeth, *includin'* thuh wisdums, an' apaht frum tonsils and appendix, no scalpel has *evuh* touched this beautiful black body! Ah am sick ta *death* uv these ignurrunt, *mean* muthafuckahs castin' they'ah bitter asparagus in mah *face!*' I thought a minute and then I said, 'Not that it matters, really, dear, but I think the fool *meant* to write *transsexuals.*' '*Lib*'ruls' was the single-word comeback—and I had to agree, and to feel a little bit ashamed.

"So fuck the begrudgers—such as that anthropologist I was listening to lecture one night the winter before last—I disremember the venue—who declared *a vital leap in the evolution of intellectual capacity would have been the ability to form concepts, to conceive of individual objects as belonging to distinct classes, and thus to do away with the otherwise almost intolerable burden of relating one experience to another.* What intolerable burden—and what is this *would have been?* Another bubble like *what might have been*—what might have happened in the rose garden. Fuck *would have been;* fuck *might have been;* vot vuz vuz. Relate it; then relate something else—drip, drip, drip, drip. Don't like the sound—can't get to sleep? Put in earplugs. You turn off the faucet, you're dead. No curtain: the end.

"As I've said before, all this is true. Not that I've got anything against fiction—which is easily said, because nobody is writing it any more anyway. Nobody—they're simply writing nonfiction that never happened. Everything I tell you happened, happened—to people. Furthermore, as has been said by somebody cleverer by far than your mother, *the knob is not the door.*

"I took a stroll the next afternoon, across the Pont des Arts to the Musée d'Orsay. Went straight upstairs into the darkened rooms where they exhibit the pastels to stand in front of Toulouse-Lautrec's *La Clownesse Coco* or *Kow-Tow* or *Chow-Chow,* or whatever she's called—I sent you the card. Something like *Cocteau,* but not Cocteau. Stood there thinking of two art-babble expressions, in respect of narration: *distressed out* and *heavily molded.* Nothing of Toulouse's is either, technically, but truly, we can't all get to be immortal in the same heaven worrying whole-cloth *matériel* in the same vocabulary with the same techniques. I think what *Chow-Chow* is saying in that pose is *This girdle is killing me!*—with everything that implies. Have you kept the card? We'll discuss it in the morning.

"Coco. Can't help being reminded of her, every time I splash on the Egoïste. I met her in '45. *Aucune mouche* on that girl, although she was no stainless Thérèse of Lisieux, either, Mademoiselle Gabrielle, what with her legs wrapped around assorted Krauts' ears—and *danke schön pour ton assurance et expérience à l'art de plaire*—unless, of course, as was somewhat overstrenuously rumored later, at the time of the Arletty–Blanche DuBois fracas, there had been all the while a tiny radio receiver nestled like a stray pearl in among the scented brambles, relaying hot intelligence to the *copains* down in the sewers, and that her code name in the Maquis was *Gobelins.* I'd like to believe it's true. Anyway, she was absolutely right about Cocteau—he *was* an insect, he *was* vile, he *did happen* to be a pederast (although I must declare, the mind shrivels like one's dick in the Everard's cold plunge to contemplate the doings), and all he ever *did* do his whole life long was steal things from people. God, remember how O'Maurigan used to *shiver* when it was pointed out that he and Cocteau had the same birthday—July 4, no less. It's indelibly true—*all* Cocteau did was steal things from people."

"Stood there looking at *Kow-Tow* strapping on her hooters, or is she about to heave them off? Either way, she is, in a way, distressed out. Then drifted over to *The Woman in the Black Boa*—more my kind of apparition, really, and, in a way, heavily molded. Spiritually. More Hildegarde's kind of apparition, too—in fact, as I stood there I saw in those wild eyes the same violet gaga stare of Hilda's we all remember. (All of us left, that is, a clutch numerable on the fingers of one hand.) Whereupon did she—Hilda—commence again in memory to bray, and I was back with her at Riker's—all night—listening to her sad tale of Epiphany and the night after—Thirteenth Night, unlucky Thirteenth Night.

"She'd picked up this Southeast Asian boy, at Dick's Hat Band, and, having satisfied herself that he was neither a Communist nor a woman, taken him home for the night to look at her tree, which, if you remember, she used to keep up till Groundhog Day, trying everybody's patience. She kept calling the boy *Cambodge*, and he taught her everything she hadn't so far learned—basically a compendium of love lore from that corner of the earth, the mere recitation of which to me took two full hours. 'Ah never really *liked* slowpokes,' she admitted; 'always felt they were *malingerers*—but this one was nahce—*ve'y* nahce.'

"The trouble came later, when the next night at Dick's she picked up the married towhead ad executive from Bronxville who'd *missed his train*—a type she always fell for. 'Ah always tell them, darlin', that it's a far far better thing they do missin' they'ah train than that they miss the boat—and, you know, they *aw'*ways see

mah point.' She came at him in sections, then got him poached
on those stingers Trenchy made out of Hennessy V.S.O.P. and
Cointreau—the ones you used to pour in both ears, pet, in your
cocktail years, when you followed Trenchy from job to job because
he was, you said, your confessor. She took him shitfaced back to
her place, drenched herself in Jungle Gardenia, and gave him the
fresh-paint gamboge works. She ministered with warm caring hands
to the *chakras,* as per instruction, and played for him as she worked
away the recording of the only white woman whose singing she
really respected, Miss Lee Wiley. I was reminded hearing the story
from *La Reina* how I used to remonstrate with her from time to
time that Lady Day was at least one-half Irish. 'Ah have *heh'yd* of
such a thing as black Irish, Miz O'Doyle,' she'd say back every
time, 'but Ah cannot say Ahm cuhn'vinced.' In any event, Bronxville Blondie came, then fell directly asleep. Demented, Diva Dorsay tore into him—threw him right out into Morton Street, with
the chill wind *howling* off the river. . . .

"Miss DeVors was *very* put out with her. '*Imbecile!* They're
supposed to fall asleep! Who *taught* you to do all that—a Sister of
Mercy? A *whore!* It's not a whore's *business* to come. You can turn
three or four tricks a *night* to try your wares if you get an answering service and schedule it right. In fact, once you get into
accomplished form, you could probably knock them out in forty-
five minutes apiece. You don't take *them* home, dear, you don't
any longer get them to follow you and climb your stairs; you go
to *their* place, and tiptoe *out,* down to the nearest pay phone and
dial *Susanswerphone.* You *do* remember *Bells Are Ringing?* Well,
nowadays Sue and Ella are up all night every night, making a
dollar, same as you!' 'Ah *couldn't* go to his place—he lived in
Bronxville, with a wife and kids!' 'They'd have *loved* you,' replied
the divine Diane. 'They'd have called you *Beaulah* and you could
have taught them how to masturbate, just like Dorothy Parker used
to do.' '*That* is a racist rem'ahk!' 'I know it is—and I'm *terribly*

ashamed.' She wasn't. We were laughing about it only a few weeks before she died, *La Reina* saying, 'Well, of course the poor dear never *did* cotton to Oriental habits of mind, even if she did toward the end evince a hurried and rather fevered interest in the Pacific Rim. . . . She thought of *chakras* as those pretty little things you picked up here and there in your vagrant life and decorated your various temporary dwellings with.' And wondering, the two of us, if answering-machine technology had so effectively replaced the answering services that had once employed true women that a revival of *Bells Are Ringing* might prove incomprehensible to to-day's theatergoing public—'whoever they *are*, anyway.'

"Then I drifted down—like a piece of flotsam on High Art's current—to the Monet alcove, and there was snagged in front of Westminster Bridge for, as it turned out, another long elegy. If a picture is worth a thousand words—and those merely of introduc-tion—then even a casual little squinny can set you off on the replay of an epoch in your life. Can you imagine what it'd be like if Monet had ever come over and painted the Queensboro Bridge? It would hang in MoMA, *tormenting* us. Well, looking at the Houses of Parliament Monet saw I came face-to-face with the pity of it—England—and the terror of it, too."

"*Bab*'a'l'n!"

"*Alors*, there I sat me, in the Musée d'Orsay, gazing into that fabulously contrived mist, and remembered 1944. That's when your mother really was *in* the war, dear, with all the other stout-hearted men fighting for the right to adore one another—at least, that was my interpretation of that piece of theater. Whereas now, in this one—metaphoric war or no—all I'm up to is something like a conscientious objector on mop-up detail—an ironic turn for a girl who has always considered it her appointed task to distract people by inducing delirious amazement, rather than to alleviate their pain.

"I was chiding the ACT/OUT children about using the term *blitz*—same as I did about using the term *Holocaust*—trying, as O'Maurigan suggested later, like Ovid's muse, to encourage them to rehearse love, not war, and suggesting things like instead of dumping wheelbarrows full of horseshit on the steps of the local precinct to protest the mounted police's handling of crowds at a gay protest, what about calling up the evening news with an exclusive: you are going to see how many gay boys wearing only Levi 501's you can squeeze into a telephone booth on Greenwich and Sixth, opposite the old site of the Women's House of Detention. Boost their ratings—and it might start that sexy college-boy trend up again with a telling difference: you know, *out of the closet and into the telephone booth.* Anyway, they rounded on me. 'Were *you* ever in a blitz?' 'Yes, dears, I *was,* and I wouldn't've missed it.' I thought that'd shut 'em up, but no dice. *'Lately?'* Sometimes I want to say to them, *May you never see the sights mother has seen.* Yet I saw the point; change is so fast now—so fast, so relentless, and so craved. As one of the last of the poets who behaved like a poet wrote,

> *In yester times it*
> *was different: the old could still be helpful*
> *when they could nicely envisage the future*
> *as a named and settled landscape their children*
> *would make the same sense of as they did*
> *laughing and weeping at the same stories*

No more."

"That's true," I agreed, "unless you're Kaye Wayfaring's children and have Mawrdew Czgowchwz for a grandmother. I bet she's teaching them to laugh and weep at the old stories."

"A strong point, dear—but can we put them in the ark along with two of everything else to start the world and its weary and worrying melodrama all over again from scratch? Not only are they brother and sister, they're *twins*. Mind *you*, there are cosmological creation myths that specify that very—but is the same old story worth telling yet one more time?

"Mind you, too, moving down a sphere from myth into history, and continuing your mother's melodrama—art thou weary? Worried? Not too, I hope; the day will dawn—I *wasn't* in *the* blitz—the Battle of Britain one. I was in the *doodlebug* one, in February of '44, and in the next one, too, in June, just before we got shipped over to France. People were incredibly brave in England—somehow managing to convey the impression to one another that what was happening across the Channel was some kind of degrading street riot in which they had accidentally become embroiled, and from which they would shortly succeed in extricating themselves. Of course, they were *deluded*, too—but terribly brave. Irish of me, ain't it, talking out of both sides of my mouth like that, but as Mr. O'Hara said to Scarlett, there's no getting away from it. There's no getting away from it, Britannia is like the blind whore: you gotta hand it to her. And to the women of the upper classes running all over London in old furs just in case somebody needed to get warm in a shelter. And people *prayed* then, dear—especially those women, and especially, for some reason, the Cardinal Newman prayer: *O Lord support us all the day long of this troublous life* etcetera . . . *and the busy world is hushed and the fever of life is over and our work is done* etcetera. I suppose, when I think of it now, it was the idea of *hushed* they found most appealing just then. Of course, as DeVors has often justly remarked, true women—either of the one sex or the other—have always known the value of prayer; have always been adept at it. There are no atheists, darling, in fox stoles.

"No, I repeated to myself, sitting there resting my bones, I wouldn't've missed it. There was, first of all, the show, *Dress Stage—*

an enormous success; they *all* came to it. *A lotta soup and fish out there tonight!* the kids would yell back and forth to one another, peeking out through the curtain peephole. *Fancy-pants husband material! Dream on, Snow White!* someone would howl, and sister would snap back something like, *A dream is a wish your hard-on makes, when it's fast asleep. Mine hasn't had a* nap *since Fort* Dix, *if ya take my meanin'!* Now, there were no flies on those Piccadilly boys, but not even they were ready for the unleashed likes of us. We were *mustard*—free for the first and only time in our lives to be both he and she, able to assume on command the curves of a Phyllis Dixey, and as good at it all as any to be found in that man's army or among the Wacs, the Waves, and the Wrens. We knew how many beans made five—and the exchange rate. When we were being women, we were being *strong* women, and no clause elevens, either, singing

> *Roll me* o-ver
> In the clo-*ver*—
> *Roll me over,*
> *Lay me down and do it again!*

"It really was, dear, as *my* auntie, May Kelleher, used to say, a funny old world. Those were the days when an admiral in the U.S. Navy could and did have the nickname *Betty,* and when F.D.R. could say to him, when queried on his and the nation's preparedness for war with Japan, '*Betty,* please don't ask me that.' The days when the King's Dragoon Guards—what was left of them after Benghazi and Tobruk—were called *the King's Dancing Girls.* The days when Mama-cita Hemingway, guzzling Cuba libres and boosting the morale of the nation by issuing frontline communiqués from the vantage of her buzzard's nest down there at *Finca Vigía,* in Mercedes's old country, could *drool* in public over Gary Cooper's manliness and not get clocked. In that period *everybody's* performance seemed to be modeled on Phyllis Brooks as Dixey Pomeroy in *The Shanghai Gesture*—and everybody seemed to be *dreaming* of giving it on that *set*. . . . Oh, your mother was a *name* in *those* days!"

"You're still a name," I offered.

"Yes, dear, I know. I'm still a name—just not a brand name anymore."

"There was the show, and then there was the aftermath. The Boeuf sur le Toit in Soho—where your mother routinely encored the number of the same name made on the Milhaud score that was such a *succès fou* in the show. None of our country boys could say *Boeuf sur le Toit;* they called it *Biff Le Sueur's twat.* And there were the drag pubs off the Mile End Road in the East End—all the sex you could handle, dear, until the dawn—or until one of Jerry's little V-2 valentines happened to have your dogtag number on it and reach you, and you went west in a hot flash. You know the sort of collision—the sex, I mean: vague monosyllables easing into an interlude; long silences, no names—and in those days the address was the stage door, as yours is now, not that you now. . . .

"You might, in the aftermath, be fondling a dogtag and just then memorize the number—sentimental you—but you wouldn't hold on to the information. Maybe the thought would strike you that it might keep him alive if you did—but even a quick study could only keep so many . . . and it didn't seem right to impersonate God. It wasn't, if you will, playing the game. And everything reinforced with Benzedrine, which was the newest thing: Benzedrine came just before penicillin into our mod-ren lives. And for when the V-2's started whizzing, there were the special little rubber *bones* you were given to *chew* on, when your gay nerves were ready to *snap*.

"Your mother got her bone rather imprudently, which is what

I began seriously remembering in front of the Monet, easing the old dogs out of those Tootsie Plohound brogues that looked so—don't they *always* look so chic in the window. On a Sunday, after a quarter-act bit in a benefit matinee at the Chelsea Palace, when I took up for the evening, and for a few evenings after, with a hank of straight Scotch hair and a lanky thing or two more assembled under the name Donald MacLean. A famous name now in the annals of the postwar world—far more so than your mother's—but at that precise moment he was nobody at all, outside the circle of Cambridge fairies he'd learned to fascinate—like a cobra does mongooses—and your mother was, as somebody had already noted, the fourth-most-discussed American in the London *beau monde*—after Wallis Warfield Simpson Windsor, Chips Channon, and Donald Duck.

"Well, Donald—MacLean, not Duck—and his pals followed me from Chelsea into the West End that Sunday night to see the whole of *Dress Stage*, and to celebrate what it subsequently turned out was *our* joint birthday, May 25. I remember four of them in particular, besides Donald: it seemed they were never separated, and went by the names *Solitary, Nasty, Brutish,* and *Short*. I once asked *Solitary* how he could be called that and never be out of the others' company. 'Not British, *are* you,' was his succinct reply. The story—of course, there was a story—was one of those that both is and isn't funny. *Solitary* just didn't care to be, well, *exposed*, as Guy, who was the one who put things, put it: 'One's seen bigger bits of meat than his hanging off the tines of a dirty fork.'

"Donald was exactly ten years my senior. Then, after lowering innumerable gin-and-Frenches and gin-and-Its at Biff Le Sueur's, we drifted back to an entirely—but *entirely*, including the lined curtains and the pelmets—red, white, and blue basement dwelling in Bentinck Street, the habitation of a sadistic Barbie doll-cum–speed freak and drunk name of Guy Burgess, one or two of whose swains called him *Prinny*—a basement dwelling that later, lined curtains, pelmets, and all. . . . As you may have discerned by now, I didn't care very much for Mr. Guy Burgess—although I can still see the mother-of-pearl along the mantelshelf. *Loose lips sink ships*, we used to say, and *he*—well, the truth is, I suppose, we were all a little careless and freewheeling in those days, even if we'd never sit down on a bench marked *wet paint*—us with our Polari slang. As they would say in the west of Ireland, ferocious women we *were* for *trolling*—bold as brass in the Long Bar of the Trocadero on Shaftesbury Avenue, much with the *vardas*, the *eeks*, and the *zshooshed-up riah*, flappin' about like bleedin' Bristol City *polones*, goin' all damp in a girly place over the *omi bonas*, hoping wildly to wind up the night in Mayfair, and ending up as often as not in the Bermondsey Baths. No, I wouldn't've missed it—even though it was all told a happy time, and happiness is an awful thing to remember.

"No, pet, I didn't like Guy Burgess, but as I was thinking back, sitting there in the Musée d'Orsay—and especially having just been looking at the Lautrecs—he—Guy—could draw like the Masters; he was that talented. He did a sketch that festive May night of your mother and her new blitz beau *consorting* in a compromising if inventive position that was, for instance, so much finer than the louche doodles of the aforementioned invertebrate Cocteau, just then working, as it were, the other side of the Long Bar—across the Channel, in occupied Paris, where soon enough we lot were headed—snoods and all—and where, of course, the heinous article was soon enough again sucking up to *us*—the Pernod or the Chanel he gargled with barely masking the reek of sauerkraut. 'Kiss *that*? Kiss *this!*' As one nautical girl put it so memorably, of another, *That one may have come out like a full-rigged schooner, but the last they saw of her she was floundering all over The Solent with her self-steering shot and her tiller arm jury-rigged to the rudder head!*

"The sketch of Donald and me turned up years later in the

Burgess dossiers. Although the ecstatic-looking MacLean was rec-
ognizable, his partner wasn't.

"Donald was seldom ecstatic—although once, in a blitz, he
said to me, 'You know, *Donny*, I feel a terrible, wild joy and
exaltation at the sound and taste and *smell* of all this destruction—
at the lurid sky, the pall of smoke, the faces of bystanders lit in the
flames. It is as if Revelation had come to pass at last.' Whereupon
he broke out into an excruciatingly off-key rendition of Sir Arthur
Sullivan's 'O Gladsome Light.' When he went to Washington—
married—he became wildly depressed and anti-American—he'd
been far from that that night under the pelmets with me, especially
when I'd taught him what Wallis Simpson taught David Windsor.
Talk about learning how to burst joy's grape with strenuous
tongue. . . . In fact, in the words of Miss Davis as Charlotte Vale
in *Now Voyager*, addressed to Miss Cooper as her mother and
divulging the gift of a foulard dress to a retainer, *He was most
grateful.* Unhappily, though, it did no good one's being good to
him; he was basically a voyeuristic, self-loathing Scotch Presbyte-
rian tit-torture slave, and, of course, all along a traitor. Or is that
little detail the least bit important any more?

"As for Guy—whom Donald used to refer to, witheringly, as
Acrasia—his story was more a Three Stooges two-reeler than the
Marx Brothers extravaganza he liked to think it. For me he had all
the allure of a limp windsock. I mean, really, darling, sadism is *so*
tedious, rough stuff *so* unimaginative: all a body wants, really, is a
little *emphasis* now and again. You know what he had hung up in
the swanky toilet—itself quite a modern convenience in bohemian
Chelsea in 1944? Two needlepoint samplers, framed in cherry wood:
God Is Not Mocked and *Jesus Wept*, and a framed copy of Holman
Hunt's *Light of the World* with the inscription '*To Guy—what a
guy, what a weekend! Love, J.C.*' 'How else,' he used to cry aloud,
'in these low times, can anyone behave except badly!' I once had
the temerity to ask him if he and Donald had ever made the beast.

'*What?* God! With *him?* I wouldn't touch him with an *eel spear!*
The *idea* of—it would be like going to bed with a great white
woman!' Well, he was wrong. 'What did you do in the war,
Mommy?' 'Wore army boots, darling, just like your little friends
told you—and fell absolutely head over the heels off them, for a
spy.' "

"I never saw Donald stateside—he was married, and as Miss Davis
as Kit Marlowe says to John Loder as Preston Drake in wartime
New York in *Old Acquaintance, There are things you just don't do
if you want to live decently with yourself afterwards.* You see, he'd
broken down weeping, drunk, and *told* me he—but, you know, we
were allies with Russia then—like we are now—and. . . . Well, the
fact is, darling, all those spies were hopeless roaring drunks—which
is what endeared them to the Russians; the Russians—Stalin, Mo-
lotov, Mikoyan, etcetera—were all hopeless roaring drunks. There's
a line in a bad thirties play—utter drivel, but I've never forgotten
it: 'He taught me that a man can get drunk and not be no different.' Hah! Those Apostles from Cambridge: hard to say what
they'd ever been to start with, but they got nothing but different,
and different again—even as we spoke in the night. *Plus ça change*
is in only one way *la même chose,* dear, and that's in the same hell
the roads go to—the high, the low, and the median. Now, I realize
liberated people will disagree with me and call me Sally Army, and
maybe in the long end-run they're right. I mean, for example, *was*
Miss Jackie Curtis getting only *more so* when she embedded the
ground glass in the instep of Holly Woodlawn's open-toed fuck-
me's, just before Miss Lawn went on at Reno Sweeney's to sing
'I'm Cooking Breakfast for the Man I Love' in one of her very
finest hours? Were we saps to infer a chemical *merely?* We were
correct, of course, factually—there was a chemical *factory:* there
was nearly all of Hoffmann–La Roche, and a smart quart of Gav-

ilan tequila guzzled into the bargain. But would she have—but, then, would there have *been* a Jackie Curtis, boy, man, or wicked woman, but for alcohol and drugs? Would there have been a Guy Burgess and a Donald MacLean? Was Jackie Curtis *born*, or was she poured out of a bottle of Rock 'n Rye over cracked ice at Slugger Ann's? Was Donald—well, I'll never forget Guy hissing at him, *You know, Donald, the best part of you ran down your mother's leg!*

"Of course, there was more to Jackie than evil—much more. The entirely conceived Curtis extravaganza *Nola Noonan: Glamor, Glory and Gold*, starring Candy, Holly, Bobby De Niro, and her own Second Avenue Methedrine self was one for which all true believers in outrage pray and wait."

"The Cambridge sissies ('The Apostles all called *Judas*,' as *Short* had put it) absolutely *hated* women—which was funny, as O'Maurigan used to quip, because what were they at bottom but only silly dames subject to hard mischance. Absolutely—and erroneously supposed I did, too, because I was a female impersonator: they considered the art *not* the sincerest form of flattery, but the most cunning form of contempt. *The whoredom of a woman*, Donald used to quip, *may be known in the pride of her eyes and eyelids.* I would counter with sage words taken from Lady Diana Manners—Mrs. Duff Cooper—and her sister Marjorie, Lady Angelsey, whom I met through David Herbert, the second son of the fifteenth Earl of Pembroke, on the advisability—necessity, really—of learning to keep the eyebrows arched and of avoiding frowns. *Nothing*, darling, is so aging as a frown—*never* be beetle-browed. The corrugations, by their contraction, lower the eyebrows and bring them together, producing vertical furrows on the forehead—that is, a frown. Disemploy the corrugations, Dolores—a girl can get perfectly serious without *ever* knitting her plucky brows. Miss Dietrich had the same advice, pointing out as she did that it is the smile that uses the face muscles in the most efficient and proper way—and Marlene has been nothing all these decades if not both efficient and liberal with glamour tips. Who else, for instance, could have let fall into the public domain the info that a man's linen handkerchief stuffed into the crotch of a true woman's silk underpants makes her bias-cut silk chiffon skirts swirl just so?

"No, I never saw Donald again, but I did see Guy. I was at a pre-sailing bash somebody gave for him the last time he left America. Rotten Rodney Bergamot was there, and Johnny Donovan, both of them howling over somebody in the CIA called John Jesus Anglophile or something like that. Guy did his imitation of Clementine Churchill, and I mine of Bess Truman. I came formal—not in *ladies' long*, dear, but in *le smoking*, and wearing the Eton bow tie Donald had given me, and a matching cummerbund that a Sixth Avenue wardrobe woman of my acquaintance ran up. Guy sketched me—and Donald—from memory, in black Crayola on the linen tablecloth. . . .

"Ah, well, dear, as they say, *Boy's dreams are mothers' night-mares.*"

"Guy sailed with his American boy toy—the saga of who that was, and wherefore, is another mother's nightmare; I'm not at liberty to say, and anyway, I don't remember—but they never did get to honeymoon in Paris. Guy crossed the Channel at midnight with the only available part of Donald—leaving the American at the Savoy, or wherever—and the story goes they left all their men's tweeds behind them in the cabin. God alone knows what they entered France wearing—probably, Rotten Rodney used to quip thereafter, nun drag, but, then, that was his particular fondness. We figured some kind of *matelot* mufti. Anyway, they got to Zurich, then to Prague, and, well, everybody knows the rest—and nobody gives a shit, even after that movie with Coral Browne and Alan Bates. Nobody cares about Guy, except to know maybe— and here's a better movie: let's call it *Troika to the Terlet*—that he ended up nightly cruising the world's most immense tea room, right there in the middle of Red Square in Moscow, under the frozen cobblestones, not far from Lenin's tomb. *Sic transit* Gloria Swanson.

"No, people don't care about dead spies—and anyway, what are they doing in a story about AIDS? Unless you believe conspiracy theories. I mean, it makes as much sense that they . . . as much sense as that the army. . . . People don't care about spies, unless, like Emmy Destinn, they were also divine in some walk of life you could look at under lights. People care about Judy, and Maria, and the Kennedys—and, speaking of the summation of the qualities inherent in these, and of stunning spying, and of serious and effective nun drag, the living Mawrdew Czgowchwz.

"Britannia herself, flat on her back, asphyxiating, with that hideous harridan in Ten Downing Street squat on her gray face, straining for the orgasm she's plainly never had—like those birching masters' assistants at Eton I was told of during the buzz-bombing by the quivering pale boys I held in my long strong arms: public-school head boys who'd sit on fags' heads while masters whacked away at the victims' gardenia-petal bottoms. How I thanked God none of the girls had requested the Thames, in spite of the fact that I did stop off in London, to go on the Terry Wogan Show with Barbara Windsor, helping her plug her bio, and reminiscing delightfully about the *Carry On* days—about that time, for instance, at the height of the Stolichnaya publicity, that I went on 'Desert Island Discs' and when they asked me, after listing the records, what books apart from the Bible and Shakespeare I'd want to take along with me, I answered that as an Irish-Catholic American turned existentialist I was afraid I didn't care to spend the rest of my life reading *either* the Bible *or* Shakespeare, but I'd like to

take along if I might *Moby-Dick*—I assured them on good authority
that it was at least terribly *influenced* by Shakespeare—and the whole
of *A la recherche du temps perdu.* Threw 'em. I dropped in on
Dame Edna Everage, too.

"London in the sixties was *free—young*: it *was.* Do you know
what my image of sixties London is?"

I suddenly saw Odette choke up—and I must say I was entirely unprepared for what came out next.

"Dear, do you remember Jacqueline Du Pré?"

"Of course I do."

"Of course you do. Well, dear, I sat to the side of her once
at the Albert Hall when she played the Haydn and the Elgar con-
certos, and, oh, my dear, I've never seen or heard in my born days
a more beautiful creature anywhere on earth."

As Odette's shaded eyes, filled to the brim with tears, overflowed,
and she turned to her reflection in the window, I heard the conductor call *"Bay* Shore!" and watched, as sure enough, all eight
rock-'n'-rollers marched past us toward the door—and, as they
were swinging off onto the platform, Joey Veneziani, the last out,
looked back, nodded, and smiled. I thought to myself: that's benediction. . . . I nudged Odette, to indicate I wished to recognize her
powers of prescience, and she smiled a little wearily back at me—
I think feeling I was merely trying to console . . . at which task I
have been told I have some skill.

"But back to the spies, *n'est-ce pas*, and to my meditations on them,
enjoyed not a stone's throw from the Quai d'Orsay, font, if you
like, of all espionage since—well, dear, as The O'Maurigan wrote
it and as you recited it, again so brilliantly tonight, since Napoleon.
I thought to myself about the Cambridge sissies, as I got up and

went out down the escalator and out the door of the old Gare
d'Orsay to grab a cab to the new Gare Montparnasse: that was the
price of them, them and their deep game. Espionage—altogether
one prefers the legitimate stage. I was on my way down to Chartres
cathedral, to pay Miss Dorsay's last respects and light a candle in
her name to the Black Madonna there—the first of two trips to
black madonnas. The second came the very next day, when from
Barcelona I motored in a tourer up to Montserrat to pay
Mercedes's—who, you know, also used to call herself *Mercedes del
Talgo*—to the Maria there, before dropping her—Mercedes—into
the Mediterranean at Sitges on the night of the dark of the moon.

"What a relief—her original plan had been for me to sail out
to Majorca, to the Cuevas del Drach, go all the way to the deep
underground lake where for the benefit of tourists assembled in a
troglodyte amphitheater hewn out of the rock, they row a small
orchestra across in a boat, playing things like *Barcarole, you thrill
my poor soul* from *The Tales of Hoffmann* and the music of the
shades from Gluck's *Orpheus and Eurydice*, bribe the boatman to
let me sit at the stern, and dump her—but she decided the whole
thing was too melodramatic. 'Just take me to Sitges, honey, where
the *chicas* go nude, and pour me in the shallows. It's more *me* that
way, isn't it? I was never a girl for the deep water, not at Riis Park
in the old days, not out on the Island—you'd always find me in
the shallows. But didn't I sport the *ultimate* sun wear, always? And
headgear and beach props. *Hermana, si*—drop me off at Sitges at
sunset on the day of the dark of the moon on your way back from
Montserrat.'

"Well, it wasn't at sunset, because at sunset I was to be on
the *Talgo* for Lausanne; it was at four o'clock in the afternoon—
tea-dance time on the Island, which would have *slain* her, were she
not slain, because if there was one ritual Mercedes considered more
ridiculous than any other in the Lavender Book of Hours it was
tea dance on the Island—that suffering and dancing country of the

vague, regardless eyes. She was a true *chica*, dear, never up before noon, and enamored of sitting up plying her fan in conversation, enjoying the cool beauty of the Hispanic night in her heart. God, she was elegant—elegant and dedicated. Even at the very end: hopping out of her sickbed, spending hours getting into slap and drag—including that sequined souvenir straitjacket—and proceeding by private car on the arm of her care partner up to Spanish Harlem, to La Escuelita, to do her turn—redirecting the experience of four decades' walking the ball and throwing shade on three continents in two hemispheres, her art refined—distilled, really—to its rare essence: mixing safe-sex information and referrals for help with her own inimitable exercises in vogueing and provocative read-out. 'I have finally done my political duty,' she said proudly, 'and joined the *Contras: las estrellas contra el SIDA.*' But as I stood there, decorously draped on the nude beach at Sitges, ankle-deep in the shallows myself—my Tootsie Plohounds deposited for safety on a rock formation, in the care of a humpy naked Jose who lay provocatively atop his castoff terrycloth robe absently fingering the shoe straps—I thought to myself, well, he has almost certainly never read, no more than Mercedes ever did, Havelock Ellis's *Psychology of Sex*, with its suggestion of man's saltwater origins. Or had he? Suppose, in the event, he was a Humanities student from the University of Barcelona, just down for the day. . . .

"As I stood there speculating, calming myself and peppering the wavelets with the earthly remains of the Marquesa del Talgo-Benz, I couldn't help remembering her great ambition to play Peter Pan—Pedro Pan—one day. She'd fallen in love with, of all interpretations, Thalia Bridgewood's—in stock, in Provincetown—and particularly with the line that closes Act Three, as Peter Pan is stranded on the island and the water is rising: *To die will be an awfully big adventure.* Then I realized, of course, it wasn't tea time Eastern Standard at all; it was more like 10:00 a.m. And Mercedes at 10:00 a.m. would not have been, for instance, sitting up in bed reading Havelock Ellis; she would have been asleep behind the lace-embroidered sleep mask, with the tasseled earplugs in, dreaming her dream of a reconstituted prewar, pre-Castro Havana, where, at Reyes—Epiphany to us, dear—at the end of her spectacular annual run of *Pedro Pan* at the opera house, she and her minions, on parade along the beach—much like the Sharks at Riis Park on a fifties summer Sunday—would have vogued their spangled wussies off, before vogueing was ever *conceived* up here—perhaps in their own way paying tribute to mankind's marine origins. . . . God, wasn't everything so long ago—*que leya esta todo*. Everything seems so far away from here, from now. *Seems? Is*. It was long ago and in another country, nearly *all* the wenches, all the great adventuresses, are dead.

"*Toot-mem*, sweetcheeks, the three kings had their mission, and this solitary *reina* had hers—in the report on which it appears I've gotten rather far ahead of myself. So, back to Chartres and what transpired there of an afternoon—a lazy afternoon in God's own eternity."

"What is there to say about Chartres? I'd been reading Kenneth Clark—he was a mainstay of my education, dear, up to the point where he got all demented about modern art—and decided to throw him into my luggage with the girls in their urns. I was glad I did, because at several points along the way, when I was feeling all-in, I consulted it—sort of like you might a favorite murder mystery: you know how it's going to end, but—well, dear, what *is* Civilization anyway, by and large, but murder and mystery—which may or may not ever end.

"I can never ride down to Chartres without remembering the wisecracking American dame we met in the sixties on the boat train from London to Paris. She was reading *Is Paris Burning?* and we asked her was it any good. 'It's *dyna*-mite,' she replied. 'I'm going to have to sit up all night on the boat to find out if I should continue on from Calais.' Which got me telling her and everybody in the compartment the true story of Chartres being saved from the Americans—you remember: it was in the path of the *pincer* advance toward Paris—the advance your mother was in, dear, as it happened. There were nests of Germans armed with machine guns in the towers—and, of course, the thing is up on the hill. The American commandant said *blow it to hell.* Can you believe it? Believe it—they didn't; not on the train; thought I was making it up as a sixties antiwar story. Fortunately, the mayor of Chartres had—believed it—and, waving a white tablecloth from La Vieille Maison or another one of those lovely restaurants in the close, had gone up to the German commandant, who said *Mein Gott im Himmel!* and cleared the place out. Oh, there were unsung heroes on both sides, dear. Not evened-up *ranks* of them, but nevertheless. . . .

"So, your mother lets herself out of La Vieille Maison, after one of those sybaritic lunches that constitute the most appropriate prelude to a French religious experience, and across the square into church, and the first thing she notices is how *full* the square is of parked cars—and this a weekday—and no tour buses, either, which anyway always come down in the morning and then turn back to lunch the ladies in the pants suits at Versailles—after which they like to go and have a look at the hall of mirrors and at Barbara Hutton's chairs. Hildegarde could never bear Versailles. 'It is a *royne!* Why, do you know how thuh arts *flourished* there? Racine and Molière wrote plays, the royal Gobelin manufacture produced exquisite tapestries for thuh walls, and *Watteau* painted *numi* pictures of gay picnics in magic parks, wheuh it never rains, to act as a background to festivities and pageantries of court society. What happens theuh *now?* No—go *straight* to Chartres, wheuh what's happened foah centuries is *still happening.*' So I had done, I told her ghost, and for good measure corrected her: *millennia* rather than centuries.

"I entered the south door, as we always did, the better to

come right upon the north window, sat down and looked up at same, and kept looking, as always, for ages, thinking: stained-glass windows in Gothic cathedrals were the first motion pictures: you only have to keep looking at one long enough before its energy and the light of day make it into a dramatic feature of whatever length you can sustain. Similarly, the saints and their lives were the first motion-picture stars and scenarios. I then rose from the contemplation of the mystic rose—remember Jimmy Schuyler's divine line,

Here just for you is a rose made out of a real rose.

Rose and went over to the right of the transept, where the Black Madonna receives her petitioners. Now, I may have told you this, or I may not, but the one place in all the world I can pray to God with the absolute conviction that I'm getting through is in a French Gothic cathedral—and of the French Gothic cathedrals, the uttermost is Chartres. I don't go as far as Péguy, who said that after Chartres everything else was crap—you know these converts, dear, they go overboard—but it *is* definitely supreme—and the fact that it wears two hats is double divine. Two hats in the architectural sense, with the vying splendors of its two spires, but also, of course, two ceremonial hats—the one, as it were, on top of the other—because it was the principal site of druidism in northwestern France. Norma's altar. Yes, the Beauce was, they reckon, on a par with Angelsey and County Mayo for the frequency and intensity of the Old Religion's high mass.

"Which turned out to be the very reason there were so many parked cars. I had come down, coincidentally, on the *solstice*—to mark which, a sampling of the vigorous hordes of God's holy on the earth had zoned in, to step into the famous Chartres maze— *le labyrinthe*—and creep in tiny, tiny steps in a kind of wiccan conga line around the circle. I declare, syncretic Christianity in Europe is—I was *terribly* moved.

"I got caught up in the contrast, which turned out, as always, to be the two sides of the one coin—sort of like ACT/OUT and me: them all ostentatious headgear and me all ruffled tail feathers— in the psychedelic contrast between the expanding rose window and the contracting maze. In both cases, as we've heard before concerning deliberate dilemmas, the way out is the way in. It's hard to talk about these things in New York and its environs. Gotham does not conduce—the wretched refuse do not, it would seem, tend to cart here in *their* bags of needments long memories of rose windows and labyrinthine designs. In Europe you feel everywhere—despite the devastating wars—some sense of permanence. Here—well, darling, nothing is forever, but there must be *something* that lasts longer than Drella's parsimonious allotment of all future tenure in the limelight. Or else."

"*Eye*-slip!"

"A diamond is forever," I offered weakly.

"Is it?" she replied—and, looking out the window, asked, "Isn't the loony bin somewhere around here?"

"Nobody ever had much success interrupting Odette," Phil remarked somewhat later.

"*Great* River next!"

———

"Diamonds," she continued, "always make me think of the cold—of ice, really, as in 'get that ice or else no dice,' and ice is anything but forever. Of course, Miss Charity held that diamonds were forever—they were her birthstone, and I think she'd gotten the strong idea somewhere that *she* was forever. As a matter of fact, she thought the four most beautiful words in the English language were those you just spoke: *a diamond is forever.* She used to say she was like the woman in the Bible—and being Protestant, unlike us, she had Bible reference—she whose price was above rubies: it was diamonds. I'm more of a pearl girl, as you well know, which certain people—with a penchant for reading certain passages in the aforementioned Gospel of Saint Matthew—have tried to suggest suggests I have really all the while been hankering after the Kingdom of Heaven. Could be—although sometimes I do find myself agreeing with Miss Garbo as Grusinskaya in *Grand Hotel* that *the pearls are cold,* and whatever else the Kingdom of Heaven might be, dear, we've never heard it called cold. Another thing about diamonds, dear. One night DeVors was watching the boob tube with me—an unusual concession for Diane, but I'd pressed it on her as educational. It was a documentary about the Hope Diamond—which as everybody knows had a rajah's curse put on it and brought ruin to each and every single one of its owners after it left India. The show ended with some glib comment like, 'Well, now the Hope Diamond reposes in the Smithsonian Institution, and so far as we know. . . .' All the DeVors needed. 'Well, there it *is,* dear—so far as anybody needs to know who wants to know *what* has happened to this country!' Provocative, no? I've thought of it often since.

"Be that as it may—I was looking up at the rose window in Chartres and thinking of that idiotic dictum of George Orwell's about good prose writing being like a windowpane you can see through. See through to *what*—a brick wall? It was *that* kind of thinking, you realize, that led to the destruction of all the stained-glass windows in the cathedrals of Britain. And to the suppression of the Irish language. That enterprise, of course, backfired—which good fortune the English scarcely deserved, but, then, language has no politics, merely a divinely ordained dynamic.

"Give me, I thought, the expanding, unfolding kaleidoscope of the rose window—mimicking as the sun enlivens it the very effect of the same hot sun on the rose itself, as she erupts in the rose garden, her voids accommodating—let me feel the centrifugal force: leading, if you like, to the moment in the rose window. . . .

"And as I came out of the moment, the first thing that way-laid me again was the contrast between that centrifugal force and the centripetal, snaking movement of the devout into the center of the maze. . . . And as I rose from the involved meditation of the one to witness the chaste ostentation of the other, I suddenly thought of something *you* might've thought of in my place, dear, and might install in your mind—perhaps insert in the show some-where, because it is in its way a return-to-the-Mais Oui or *funeste*-Venetian conceit. I thought, what if the long, winding line of these peregrines suddenly commenced getting shorter and shorter—as if, unremarked, each one who reached the center, instead of turning on the still point and finding the way out, stuck for an instant *on* that same point, then *disappeared!* Scapegoated, as the girl said, out of the narrative world. Nobody behind would notice until—and what if I'd begun to be so fascinated by them that I'd joined them, walking around in the circle and praying something like, *Lead me, guides, where my sisters wait.* . . . But not yet! What if after the last of them *had* disappeared, with me the next in line to go, I'd snapped out of it as I'd stepped on a crooked stone, and as a result I alone had escaped to tell you—stalking out in a cold fright into the evening square to find no parked cars there and a squadron of raven gargoyles wheeling between the spires overhead!

"Make a good story—or would it be better if the parked cars were *still* there, like in this *rapture* scenario that's been making the rounds in recent years. You're driving along, saved in the blood of the Lamb of God, and suddenly *shazaam*, you're in heaven—but I believe your old De Soto is left behind.''

"Or your Oldsmobile convertible," I countered, thinking of Jackson Pollock being intercepted in midarc: seized in a rapture maneuver and transported . . . but, then, they'd found his body in the brush—like an old dead tree, etcetera—and the rapturists insist you rocket bodily to heaven, right?

"Whatever. Make a good story, but in order for it to be an *honest* story, I'd have had to stay the afternoon, and suffer, along with them—standing there and clocking them at their snail's pace and observing the play of emotion on each, and, as I said, perhaps nearly succumbing—otherwise it would have been like one of these poems you hear read on late-night television: one hot spasm followed by twenty minutes of diarrhea. But I had the *Talgo* to Barcelona to catch, and anyway, what with the metaphor of the conga line, I had already flashed to the *and then there were none* finale as a parallel to the girls' situation. The situation of all the boys and girls and men and women dead of AIDS—and, why the hell not, of everything else as well: all the old things as well as all the new things killing people in damned new ways, or as was once said in Ireland many years ago of a certain new strain of influenza that was decimating the rural population: *There's people dyin' now that never died* before! You could call the story that—with the metaphor of the slow dance and all: call it *That Never Died Before.*

"Next I was barreling back to the capital on the express— *provenance* Le Mans—with only enough time remaining to scoot up from the Gare Montparnasse to the Crillon, check out, and scoot across to the Gare d'Austerlitz. No time at all, and just as well, to scoot over to the Bois de Boulougne for a chat with the Algerian transvestite hookers I'd been reading about in the waiting room in *Le Figaro*. The most *branché* things in Paris vice, dear, and, it seems, *divided*, if you don't mind, on the question of *les capotes*. That's condoms to you. I had a mind to go and find out from them, specifically, if they had learned any of the local wisdom of Paris from the true women of their trade, such as the wisdom of the whores' devotion to Saint Thérèse of Lisieux—which they insist accounted for the lifting of the plague of consumption from Pigalle in the early years of the century.

"*Divided!* Imagine! Of course, I said to myself—exactly at the moment when we sped through Versailles—'Girl-*friend, mind* your *own business:* God knows it is serious enough business—and leave them to heaven.' This was *not* the moment to go impersonating the late Hildegarde Dorsay by dusking up, slathering on the Jungle Gardenia, and going off to the Bois to lecture *pieds-noirs* in plastic fuck-me's *either* on the virtue and wisdom of the cult of Thérèse of Lisieux or on up-to-the-minute prophylactic techniques of *allure modérée*—which the Belle Epoque signposts still advise in the gardens of the Eiffel Tower. And I do think *capotes* is a scream, don't you? Did Truman ever hear—probably not: he wasn't very conversant in French, was he, apart from '*mille tendresses*' and '*quel* beast.' "

"Great River!"

"Funny, one never thinks of there being any rivers on Long Island. I mean, can you name them? No."

"Oakdale next!"

"No, I didn't read on the *Talgo* to Barcelona; I talked to the people instead—the porter, the waiter, the bartender, Fulgencio. *En Espan-*yol—*diga-me.* . . .

"Ditto setting out the next night on the *Talgo* to Lausanne, chatting up a storm with the help. Well, I was always kitchen Irish, if the truth be known—much with the *digas* and the *no-mi-digas*, the *ombres*, and the *claros*. Which is what Merced used to tax and even taunt me with whenever she got to remembering the fact that I greatly preferred Puerto Ricans to Cubans. Sometimes it would make her almost demented, as when I was instrumental in getting *Broken Goddess* written for Holly Woodlawn. La Benz *hated* the picture—always said Miss Lawn was only and exactly and forever what Paul Morrissey had filmed her as: *Trash*. She had one small point in that Holly could never have reached the heights of tragic pathos she herself, Mercedes, did, in art and life, but then I used to try to placate her by explaining that the greater part of the Woodlawn art was, in fact, the legacy of Yiddish theater and cabaret—Fanny Brice etcetera—and that the rest of it owed more to Mae West than to any of the West Indies—but she was for a time deeply angry with me. She would have said, for instance, were she listening now, that of course I sat up on the Catalan *Talgo* talking to the *help*. The help all talk Spanish; it's the passengers in the club car who speak Catalan. And she'd be right, on the face of it, at least; I don't speak or understand a word of Catalan, but as Lady Bracknell said of German, it sounds a thoroughly respectable language, and, indeed, I believe is so. Mercedes, of course, was taught it at home, in Havana; it had deep cachet in her parental circles there—they were *the highest-quality people*, remember—sort of the way Gaelic does in certain households in New York. And she got to give a television interview in it once, too—in Barcelona, after she'd done a special cameo turn as *Mercedes del Talgo* in Sarita Monteil's big variety show at the Victoria. Very serious interview, all about her childhood veneration of the Copper Virgin, the patroness of Cuba, her adult veneration of the Black Virgin of Montserrat, and about her coming to Barcelona to do penance for the sins committed in the Spanish Civil War—for the corpses of the nuns and priests and mummified saints that were disinterred and exhibited there before jeering crowds. She also said she believed she was meant to do so—penance, that is—because were she and her like not to take the precaution of being cremated, a like fate might very well befall their remains in the coming fascist United States. She certainly had drifted. Then about her New York career as a travesti artiste, about her nunlike life, and about her beloved Shih-Tzu, Pelléas—the great companion and solace of same—whose ears were so refined he could only bear to listen to Victoria de los Angeles, Maria Callas, and Mawrdew Czgowchwz recordings; if you put on Montserrat Caballé, he would jump up and run howling out of the room."

"I was regaling the steward with that very story when, at Gerona, suddenly *another man* entered to share my compartment. The *Talgo*'s compartments for one can be made up into one for two, but your mother had made quite specific arrangements, given the size of the luggage load—in fact, checking onto the train at Sants station in Barcelona, hadn't I been teased by one porter, asking was I perhaps the wardrobe manager of a zarzuela company? Now here was this poor creature—an American academic traveling on a Eurailpass. Seems the computers were down all over Spain, and he couldn't get a reservation. *Had* to be in Geneva to catch the whatever to wherever—I didn't listen at first. Of course, I relented. He wasn't bad looking, of a type, but *that* phase of my life—hot gay sex fun with strangers on trains—is a thing of my long-gone past: a thing out of *Kake* comics and the novels of Frances Parkinson Keyes. Will you ever forget Miss Charity's remark? *The first time I went to Europe, I saw everything they had; the second time, I had everything I saw.*

"My sudden companion looked just about old enough to have had some experience of the Second World War himself, but

I said to myself in the windowpane, 'So *what? You don't: remember* that.' So when he brought it up—in passing—and I only blinked, as if he were talking about Napoleon's campaigns, he dropped it. Anyway, his abiding passion was not, strictly speaking, geopolitical; it was for the *names* of the trans-European express trains. 'I think of them,' he confessed rather shyly, 'as modern mythological deities.'

"I began thinking of them, as he ticked off their names, as his version of the numbering of the ships, and I asked myself, am I going to have to listen to the recitation of *his* personal epic—the way you're doing now to mine—on the night's journey through eastern France to the Swiss border? I mean, at least I gave you fair warning—and anyway, you know me of old—and this recitation *is*, into the bargain, in the nature of an oral examination: my report to the committee of two. O'Maurigan always said I could have been a crack reporter—like Claudette Colbert in *Arise My Love*; said he's never met anybody with a greater retentive grasp of exacting detail. I told him that was no more than a consequence of being a quick study in the theater, coupled with the lifelong necessary faggot-survival technique: knowing as much as ever you could about what *everybody* was up to—in the house, on the block, later in the columns, and, of course, during the war. . . . 'Well,' he said, 'you should definitely have been in military intelligence,' and I replied, 'Darling, only a boy bred in a neutral country like Ireland could say a thing like that, because the rest of us know that *military intelligence* is the ultimate in oxy-*moron.*' Which, of course, is why I'd sooner have posed as a catatonic than get into a discussion with my compartment mate that night on the *Talgo* to Lausanne— he was almost certainly a veteran of army intelligence, a conclusion I came to as soon as Felipe came by at the French border and collected our passports for the night, took our breakfast orders, and tucked us in.

"I thought to myself: if you're being a woman, be an *authen-*

tic woman; *pray.* And I did. 'Please, dear Midnight Mary, Mother
of God,' I prayed, 'from Chartres, from Montserrat, from the
Carmelite Church on Whitefriars Street in Dublin, in your manifestation as Our Lady of the Frontier-between-That-Which-We-
Call-Yesterday-and-That-Which-We-Call-Tomorrow, put him to
sleep after his enumeration of the names of the trains. Let them
be for him like counting sheep'—and do you know, that is *exactly*
how it fell out, or came down, or however it is you care to say it.
It was as if somebody had given him knockout drops and told him
to count backwards from one hundred. No sooner were the *Talgo*
wheels contracted from the wide Spanish gauge to standard European, and we were clickety-clacking through Cerbère, than he was
mumbling like the stooge hypnotized by Carmen Miranda in *That
Night in Rio:* 'The *Pablo Casals:* Barcelona to Bern . . . the *Gottfried
Keller:* Bern to Munich . . . the *Leonardo da Vinci:* Munich to
Milan . . . the *Carlo Magno:* Milan to Dortmund . . . the *Franz
Liszt:* Dortmund to Budapest . . . the *Lehár:* Budapest to Vienna
. . . the *Chopin:* Vienna to Moscow. . . .'

"He drifted off to the Land of Nod, the darling, on the
journey to Moscow, and I wondered, briefly, would he—if, indeed,
he was *international*—wind up in dreamland's biggest tea room,
not far from Lenin's tomb, where Guy—then, prayers answered, I
fell asleep myself, and didn't open an eye or an ear until Geneva,
where I woke to a brilliant morning on the lake out the window,
and a nice cup of coffee with a swizzle stick of Swiss chocolate
stuck in, and the professor already shaved and dressed appropri-
ately—for the *Gottfried Keller* and writing down his impressions in
a little travel diary. He asked me if, on the basis of our conversation, I didn't think a story about traveling all over Europe by
train—as if on a mission—might not be interesting. 'Each time I
get on a train,' he said, 'I think of Teddy Roosevelt and his sailing
down what he called the River of Doubt: "I have to go; it may be
my last chance to be a boy." ' I was *so* touched. I encouraged him

enthusiastically. I even suggested a title—*I Took the Train.* Remember that? I encourage everybody, darling; I always have. Fuck 'em if they can't take a joke. Anyway, train melodramas *are* compelling; remember *The Little Engine That Could?* He'll probably go home to Council Bluffs, knock off what the French call *un sottisier,* make a million, and forget to thank the stranger on the train.

"My train to Milan had no name, but what a lovely ride through the Alps. Then a quick jump-off to check the girls into Left Luggage and dash off in a cab to the Piazza del Duomo, to rub Remo's nose on the cathedral door—the first thing a girl with a past must *always* do in Milan, even before checking the risotto at Biffi Scala. Then up to the roof to gaze at all the saints on their individual stalactite spires—O'Maurigan calls it the standing-room line for heaven—and on the winding stairs down saw an adorable graffito: *Il futuro e nelle caramelle.* Wasn't it Pascal who said, *Moi je dis que les bonbons, ils vont mieux que la raison?* Or was it Wallis Simpson, at the end?

"I then took a turn around Rinascente, walked up the one side and down the other of the Montenape, salaamed to Scala, and dashed back to Centrale to collect the girls and proceed—on the lunch train—to Venice, city of your eternal dream.

"Now, pet, you know me and Venice—it's almost like *you* and Venice. I've always remembered what Kenneth Clark said on television. He said, *The dazzling summit of human achievement represented by Michelangelo, Raphael, and Leonardo da Vinci lasted for less than twenty years. It was followed*—except in Venice—*by a time of uneasiness often ending in disaster.*

"And remember, too, I was—God help me—working that Jones Beach *Night in Venice* you were talking about earlier this evening, and I *remember* your besotted longing for—another story. Only thank God and Mary the Mother of God, in her manifestation as Our Lady Protectress of Vagabond Stars, for Filippo: the story with the happy ending, the ending we all dreamed of—all still dream of. . . . But when I stepped out onto the corner balcony of the Leo Lerman suite at the Gritti and looked around at the surface of the Pearl of the Adriatic—and at that hour and in the heat the watchword was *opalescent*—I said to the girl—Venezia—in those immortal words of Miss Charity to Miss Hope, 'You're not serene, you're *depressed!*' So I decided what I'd do, I'd go over to the *campiello* near Santa Maria del Giglio to the Piazzesi *carteria*, and see if the agendas for 1991—because I'd decided I was going to *adore* 1991: can't tell you why; hoped to same time next year. Also, to have a chat with the truly serene and smart old woman who'd been there since forever ago—one of the most elegant women in Europe, and a bit of a wisenheimer, too, when you got her going; my idea, I suppose, really, of the Sibyl.

" '*E come la vecchia signora?*' I inquired directly to the nice but slightly acerbic fiftyish Venetian woman in charge—after discovering the agendas weren't, in fact, ready yet, and assuming my old acquaintance was at her siesta. '*E morta in gennaio, signore—da l'influenza. Era stancata.*' 'O,' I mumbled, terribly shaken, '*mi dispiace molto—sono desolato. La signora era molta gentile.*' '*Era molta gentile,*' was the somewhat detached and even almost defiant response. '*Ma era molta stancata.*' It made me think, as I stumbled into the *piazzale*, of old Kate Heartburn, interviewed on television, shaking her head faster than the rest of her shook by itself, and declaring, 'You'd better be prepared to stay *interesting*, and *produce* something—otherwise, when you're old, they just *throw* you *away!* ' "

"*Oak*dale—*Say*'v'l next!"

"Do you remember the DeVors's projected sequel to *Summertime*—called *Wintertime?*"

I did. Diane used to love to regale all comers with it—and I can still hear the cackle of her voice as she detailed it: characters, casting, plot, direction.

"Aldrich—or maybe Curtis Harrington. It's the one to put Davis and Hepburn together in—if only to shut Davis *up*, already, on that subject." And Diane used to insist that the *only* reason Davis wanted to do a picture with Hepburn was to see would she be willing to compare notes and dish Howard Hughes. "Maybe Huston, actually; he's worked with both of them. I see it as a little bit of an *in* industry joke. Hepburn returns to Venice in her golden years and finds Brazzi in the same antiques shop, but—now *get* this, it's what they used to call the *crux—married*, for the *second* time, to an *American*—Davis—with the *same name* as the Hepburn character. Quiz question: the name. Ain't that a tease for the French-ventriloquist cinéastes? Seems he always hoped she'd return, and when—in the early seventies—the woman with the identical moniker walked into the shop on her way to cruise the Adriatic, bought some old piece of shit, and signed her American Express gold card with—well, turns out it was her late husband's name, but the *effect!* Etcetera. She never sailed away, and after a night of *Modern Maturity* sex and a whirlwind courtship, they married. Cackle, cackle. Ten years later the *signora americana* is a crazed invalid, looked after by a nurse—we'll get Divine. What *happens* is, Hepburn walks into the shop—where was it? I don't recall the *sestiere*, but let's make it that dingy one near the Fenice that has the sign in the window—NO TOURIST DIRECTIONS—and never seems to sell a thing."

I don't remember the twists and turns, but it all takes place in January—during a spell of high water—which is what reminded Odette of it, when the woman in the printing shop told her the old woman had died in January. I do remember that somehow Davis and Divine get Hepburn to give all her money to Brazzi—I think by letting the affair reach fever pitch (*cackle, cackle*)—then drug her and tie her into Davis's wheelchair. Davis rides on Divine's back—really, Diane DeVors had a truly baroque mind—with the body in the wheelchair in the back of the house gondola. They dump Hepburn in the lagoon, near Sant'Ariano—Remember that? as Odette would ask. Anyway, it ends with Davis and Divine going off together on the train—with Brazzi waving to them from a motorboat, as the water continues to rise. On a train together—like Odette and me. Is the water rising, in the world?

(Incidentally, in the unlikely event that you can't stand it, the answer to the quiz question is: Jane Hudson.)

"*Say'v'l!*"

"*Sayville,*" Odette sighed. "What seraphic joy not to have to get off—although there *is* a lovely little church in the town: St. Lawrence's, as a matter of fact—a propos this night and morning. Some of the truly sentimental girls used to like to go over from the Grove of a Sunday morning, if they'd been up all night—as when had they not? There was a genuinely lovely priest—another story . . . except I may tell you, as the Brits say, he wound up in East Hampton. I was looking at the *Star* one summer afternoon just a few years ago, and there he was, at a church picnic. I remember remarking about it to O'Maurigan, and saying something like, 'Most Holy Trinity used to be St. Philomena's—what did Crown of Thorns use to be?' 'St. Bridey Murphy—and before that, St. Deirdre of the Sorrows; it's had a checkered career, which is why we like to go there.' But it's way too early for church—Crown of Thorns, Bridey Murphy's, St. Lawrence's, or—*Good* Holy *God* in the Dark Dead of *Night,* what is *that*—look at that!"

"What?"

"*That*—that *sign* . . . *hovering* out there—a *nightmare!*"

I looked out—or rather, it seemed, into the depths of the dark window, and saw floating there, in black letters on a white neon field, a sign, "Flatbush Pub," fixed atop a wood-framed house that had become in the days of rum runners in Suffolk County a railway tavern. "Flatbush Pub" gleaming over a fake-brick front. (I thought suddenly of the brick paper you used to be able to buy in rolls, and that they stuck on the common-room wall at Lincoln Hall, cut in the shape of a chimney: a chimney, so Santa could reach us castaways.)

"Imagine that."

"I am doing just that, darling, and have begun to enter into a state of morbid dread. I am imagining them all in there, at this hour of the morning, shitfaced and malcontent, imagining they are back in Flatbush, and planning the next day's raid on Riis Park. I am imagining them in there now, planning a retro predawn raid on the Grove."

I assured Odette that to the best of my knowledge, gleaned from investigation of reliable up-island grapevines, predawn raids on the Grove were a thing of the long-gone past. There were simply too many crew-cut combat-veteran muscle queens out there to mess with these days, and the long-haired, mustached, soiled-shirt boys in the station bars had come to know that fact all too well and were inclined, if only for the sake of losing no more front teeth, and albeit begrudgingly, to behave in accordance with the dictates of (similarly begrudging, but consensual) community feeling—and would most likely continue to do so, so long as gun control held in New York State. Calmed, my companion relaxed her gaze, and I, as they say in novels, for my part, could but urge her to return in spirit and in tongue to Venice, our common favorite—which she was only too willing to do, especially as the train had lurched forward and "Flatbush Pub" was, even as we spoke, falling back out of the frame of the window into the dark and unknown, shapeless Sayville night. . . .

"Patch' ogue, next!"

"I found myself in St. Mark's—the orchestra was playing 'Fascination.' Banners everywhere heralded the Titian show at the Doge's palace, and I didn't need much prodding—so, ten minutes later, I was in, and you'll never guess with *whom* enmeshed in conversation."

"Vana Sprezza—you go back to the Mais Oui too, right?"

"But, my God, are you becoming clairvoyant?"

"We had a note," I assured her, as we pulled into Sayville station, "on stationery from the Grand Hotel *et de Milan*—our first communication in twenty-something years. Phil keeps wondering whether we should've written back. She's sure to have checked out by now." (I was going to remind her of the time Diane DeVors snapped at her for getting on her high horse. "How could *I* know what you felt; I'm not *clairvoyant!*" "No, you're Claire Trevor." I didn't.)

"You could write to the *de Milan*—they'd forward it. You could probably just do what people used to do when writing love notes to Verdi—address it *Vana Sprezza, Italy*. She's still pretty famous there, although nowadays famous mainly as a loose drifter. It's like in the Antonioni pictures: she just gets up, puts on an outfit, and gets on a train—no ticket. She apparently thinks she's being *misteriosa;* Italians think she's merely being *paurosa*. Said remark, by the way, and others to come concerning the former *doppiagista*, diva, and right rip of the fifties lyric-theater scene, courtesy of the bell captain of the Gritti in *conversazione* over a game of *scoppone* with his opposite number at your hangout, the Fenice degli Artiste—a *conversazione* at which your mother was graciously permitted to eavesdrop. She wanders up and down the Italian pen-

insula checking in and out of the grand hotels—but never again
will she cross the Strait of Messina: there was, as you so well put
it, dear, in your case, an altercation. She told me so."

"I saw her before she saw me—in fact, I trailed her for some
minutes and clocked her moves, before I made myself known. She
was standing—in a divine Ungaro: white lace bolero jacket swung
out over a little black silk dress—in front of the *Danae,* and I
followed her over to the *Venere allo Specchio,* then back to Danaë,
then back to Venus . . . like that, until I intervened. She looks, in
the face-and-format department, almost the same now across a
room as she did back when—with all that strawberry-blond hair—
uncannily like Eve on the ceiling of the Capella Sistina, and, as has
been wisely said of that girl, already—a potential source of big
earth trouble. And like that Eve she is, of course, in spite of her
wanderings, completely wrapped up in an old man's cloak.

"There was a joke going around, she told me later, about him
and her—the pharmaceuticals husband, dear, not God. Seems he's
made yet another fortune, this time in double-bag condoms—
striped, if you please, in the Italian tricolor, and marketed under
the name *Calcio.* The joke is that Vana's travels are sales trips, and
speaking of old jokes, all I could think of—and I told her so later
that evening, and she guffawed—was the old joke, 'Mix 'em up;
I'm goin' on a *picnic!*'

" '*Adesso, caro,*' she said, without preliminary, as if we'd seen
one another for lunch and were continuing a discussion. 'I *adore*
Tiziano, but I get fed up, you know, with all these madonnas on
the one wall and all these scheming Italian women on the other,
and all this carnage up on the ceiling.' I said I knew how she felt—
although I was transfixed, absolutely, by the *Martyrdom of San
Lorenzo.*

"For me it was greater than a Caravaggio. And I could have

stood there all afternoon looking at San Sebastian in the right-hand corner of the *Saint Mark Enthroned with Saints* from the Salute: a breathtaking beauty pierced with the single arrow—with his starched white loincloth twisted into an erect codpiece. Of course, that's Titian for you, no matter whether he clothes them or strips them—you even want to rip the clothes right off the *gentiluomo* from the Uffizi, not to mention the *bravo* from Vienna: so splendid, so cocksure, and like so many, then as now, just about to be cut down in his prime. . . . Real one-hander stroke material, darling, and I *don't* mean of the cerebral hemorrhage variety. Even the paint itself—if you're into paint itself, as, for example, you are with Pollock. Which reminds me, dear, I don't agree with you that Jackson was painting atomic fission; I believe he was painting the labyrinthine circuitry of the human mind. And, of course, Jackson *was* Sebastian, wasn't he? He was not only the great martyr of modern art; he was *that* martyr. Sebastian! To give the martyr who was, it has been said, before his conversion the beloved of the Emperor Heliogabalus, a hard-on in Paradise! Profoundly gay. Meanwhile, *is* there any such thing as a form of sexual activity that doesn't either lead to death directly, or lead to contemplation of it in some way? It's as if they were right after all, that playing with yourself *will* drive you crazy. And another thing hit me with stunning force that afternoon about Sebastian and faggots. Do you know why Saint Sebastian was so popular in the late Middle Ages and the Renaissance? He was the protector against the bubonic plague—the Black Death! Does that not add a new and utterly eerie dimension to the configuration? Anyway, I got the poster of him and brought it home. I think it belongs in the Gay Pride Parade on a banner next to Judy. In the Salute, Sebastian stands next to Saint Rocco; I think he makes more sense standing next to Judy, replacing Punch. You carry Judy and I'll carry Sebastian. You sing 'The Man That Got Away' and I'll sing 'Full Moon and Empty Arms.'

"Sex and death, dear, sex and death—you can't get away from their conjunction. As somebody said, *Age comes, the body withers: mere anarchy is loosed upon the tits and ass*—and *that* always reminds me somehow of the single flower growing out of the girl's asshole in *The Garden of Earthly Delights* in the Prado.

" 'But imagine running into you here today,' Vana continued. 'Funny, isn't it,' I said to her, 'and only this afternoon I was in Milan, rubbing Remo's nose at the Duomo, just like you taught me to do all those years ago, after your triumph here at the Fenice, in *Livia Serpieri.*'

"Suddenly she stopped, and stood looking for a long while at the penitent Magdalene from the Hermitage in Leningrad. *'Senti, caro*, what are you doing tonight? Nothing, eh? Come with me to the Fenice. Some children from Trieste are singing in the *salone*, and I gave my word I'd go hear them.' 'Actually, Vana,' I replied, 'I do have something to do tonight. I have to go and throw a dear friend's ashes off the Ponte Malavisa Vechia.' 'Oh,' she countered, in that partly blasé, partly *engagé* social-calendar manner Europeans affect. 'But that's right *behind* the Fenice! We'll take your friend to the children, then drop him off. Anyway, you shouldn't do that kind of thing alone—I'll be the altar boy.'

"The aptness of going to hear a bunch of kids sing before Miss Hope's funeral rites struck me—Miss Hope, you remember, was a schoolteacher—and I was thinking about the Fenice on a couple of counts as you rattled on up there earlier this evening. In fact, I had thought about you while there, in the Apollo Salon of that opera house—for it was there, under the crystal chandeliers, that we heard Le Voci Bianche della Città di Trieste, and not in the main auditorium, where *La Traviata* had its world premiere, where Maria sang Isolde—or *Isotta*—where Visconti filmed the opening of *Senso*, and where Vana triumphed as Livia Serpieri. I thought of you as I was hearing them, and again tonight as you recalled yourself as a child singing in the reformatory. Your Miss

Mooney and the directrice of the Voci Bianche undoubtedly shared a point of view or two—and so far as looking after children, the ministrations of a goodly woman were sorely needed, because on one of the hottest nights of summer, the administration had neglected to provide adequate ventilation—there seemed to be no air conditioning—and there we were, sweltering, and soon enough— as a matter of fact, right into the second number, a charming Viozzi thing—presented with the unhappy spectacle of child after child fainting from the closeness—passing out, dear, one after the other, like little skylarks winged in midflight—until somebody had the sense to call an interval, and epauletted flunkies went about the place throwing open the long windows and admitting the dank vapors off the *canaletti*. Whereupon backstage Vana was to be seen in all her silken splendor—for she had come out for evening wrapped in a purple-and-black Versace number that swirled on her body like a wreath of smoke—attentive as a school nurse all in white with white rubber-soled shoes to the plight of the stricken tots—and most especially, I could not help notice, to that of the sixteen-year-old soprano. I thought to myself, A-*ha!*

"Whereupon to the obsequies themselves. The sixteen-year-old had been presented, as had all the others, with a little white plastic rosary, which I couldn't help noticing Vana, while comforting the child, had pocketed. A-ha-*ha*, was my first reaction—and from it a whole chain of suspicions about Vana on trains, going through luggage, etcetera: the whole Margaret Elliot melodrama of the faded star turned klepto. But then, on the Ponte Malavisa Vechia, when Vana took the beads from her purse and threw them into the *canaletto* on top of the ashes, I got the point, and as if reading my mind, my altar boy explained, 'They are of no use to the little soprano, *caro;* she would only at best have made fun of them, and at worst—well, they have all seen too many sacrilegious northern European films, these young ones, and, well, this is the proper use for them.' I saw the white plastic rosary ring the ashes

I had just tossed over the bridge into the *canaletto*, and observed it gleaming in the lamplight—but *exactly* as Hildegarde Dorsay's gold filling had done on the Seine—and, exactly simultaneously, heard Vana break out, in truly glorious voice, into,

A te questo rosario
Che le preghiere aduna,
Io te lo porgo accetelo
Ti portera fortuna. . . .

"Now, if you remember, the other thing besides intensity that made both critics and public compare Vana to the Meneghini in the late fifties was that already at her age, the younger woman had a wobble you could walk through. Well, it's *gone*—or it was that night. I tell you, dear, I was both shocked and uplifted—talk of the power of *religion*. For a crazy moment, I thought, she is going to rise up whole—Miss Faith—out of the canal, the way Laura did from her bier, and join the Italian boy whose grandmother was watching the television in the hospital—and I cast *her* immediately as the *vecchia signora* from the print shop in the *campiello* near Santa Maria del Giglio—and together they are going to live the life of man and wife here in Venice, in the millennium. Vana, meanwhile, had reached her great moment, far surpassing the old days: the *legato*, the *portamenti*—just as, amid echoes of *gondolieri* and of the Venetian cats, two American boys walked across the bridge twirling electric-light yo-yos from San Marco.

Sulla tua testa vigili
La mia benedizion. . . .

"I was so overwhelmed, I couldn't stop gushing, thanking her over and over, and saying I truly wished she would accompany me on my travels to assist at all the rest of the rites I'd signed on to perform. She was gracious, otherworldly, demure—never more so than when I then asked should we go to Harry's for old times' sake? 'I always *hated* Harry's—and Harry, too,' she responded, making it sound not like a malediction, but like Garbo as Camille, in the country, recalling how she always hated the parties *chez* Prudence. We went instead to Florian, and Vana drank Bellinis—spiking them with her purse full of, well, Stolichnaya, in point of fact, while I sipped my espresso and forked into some heavenly cheesecake. 'You know, *caro,* I was thinking before that my life has been so like the mezzo's career. She starts out singing *A te questo rosario . . . la mia benedizion,* and she ends up singing, badly always, *A te la mala Pasqua!* and *Anatema su voi!* and *Ti maledico, o mia beltà!* What a life, eh?' We then got up and danced a tango in the piazza, before retiring to my corner suite at the Gritti to watch the World Cup. Vana, dancing, observed by many who knew her, had known her, said, 'Noël Coward was right about an awful lot of things, wasn't he—about television, for instance, and *absolutely* about the *potenza* of cheap music. Think of Wagner, for example: everything except *Tristan* really is shit, and he only got *Tristan* right because he wrote it here. Vortice was right in the fifties: it should all be staged on *barche* and *gondole* and in a walled garden right off the Canale Grande, and it should end on the deserted beach at Mestre.' Watching the World Cup, I mentioned the rumor that the referees are owned by the Mafia—and dared broach the subject then of the scandal of Masonic Lodge P-2, said to have ordered the Bologna railway station bombing in 1980, in which eighty-five people were killed. I was trying, of course, to get her to open up. . . ."

"*Patch*'ogue—*Bellport* next."

" 'Yes, it's true,' she said, 'my husband is a member of P-2, and they *do* assassinate people, just as Italians have always done. I'm sure they assassinated the Swedish prime minister. Did the CIA and the Vatican of the Polish pope care who did their dirty work? It's what the Italians have always done: although they did *not* kill the first Papa Giovanni Paulo. He just dropped dead: God was good and took him—fast. Everybody imagines conspiracies in Italy—you know, in 1980 I had already begun wandering on trains, and *my* first thought after Bologna was: Ruggiero is trying to kill me! I thought, he's trying to *kill* me, and I'm not even *forty!* ' "

"What?" I shot out.

"I said *Bellport,* next," the conductor shouted, closing the car door.

"What?" I whispered to the grinning Venetian carnival face reflected in the window, as we groaned out of Patchogue.
     "Exactly—we can both count. '*That* young, Vana?' I said. 'In 1980?' 'Well, yes. I'm not now yet fifty, so—' 'You're not now—' 'No—*cara.* Look, why do you think in 1957, Callas pointed across from table eleven at Biffi's, where she was sitting eating a steak with Mawrdew Czgowchwz, and said, *I'm twice her age.*' I thought to myself, *Vana, you old wild card.* It was Czgowchwz, of course, who'd said that to Callas—in response to the question, '*Be, Mawrdew, chi e quella bionda là su?*' Blonde was all Maria could have seen at ten paces. She wouldn't have known if Vana was sixteen or sixty-one—she could have been asking Mawrdew Czgowchwz about Hope Hampton. Anyway, it certainly wasn't the Magdalene Maria was indicating—penitent or otherwise. Never mind, twenty-one, which is what Vana was that year, was still terribly young to be

edging toward the big time, and to be taking some of the attention
away from the Meneghini at Biffi's—which was, of course, a situation La Divina could feel blindfolded, as if by the shifting of the
ion flow in the room.

" 'Yes, my husband had all my male lovers murdered—and
all the horses they owned as well, which was vile, and insulting to
me—so I'm a lesbian now. Much better for everybody. I will admit
I do *feel* fifty—sometimes. Only last week in Milan, after lunch
casa Gianni—I had to listen to all *his* troubles: you can't *imagine*
what—I went into a little shop on the Via Gesù and said to the
venditrice, the *commessa*, "I want a hat for a woman whose husband
hates her." "But," she objected with downcast eyes, standing there
behind the counter in the attitude of *La Pudicizia Velata*, "the
signora is too *young* for a hat!" You see what I see in girls? I wanted
to take her out from behind that counter *pronto*, and throw her
on the floor, and say to her, "No, once I was as young as you
are—young and proud; now I am only vain, and middle-aged."
Then loose my hair and fall on her. Instead, I'm taking her to the
Ticino tomorrow—to Bellinzona; the day after tomorrow is her
day off.'

"I may as well warn you, dear, that Vana may soon be showing up in New York. I'm afraid I got matey enough to tell her
about the Clit Club on Fourteenth Street. She pretended to be
shocked, saying no self-respecting lesbian would go into a place
called that—the Clit Club. I challenged her: the world had long
since grown tired of club names like Bilitis and Penthesilea, Gan-
ymede and Corydon. She relented. I then let her know that Italian-
American lesbians were, along with Jewish lesbians, in the
vanguard of Sapphic politics in the U.S.A. She replied coolly that
although many of her best friends were Jews, she could *not* cotton
to Italian-American women of any persuasion—especially those who
come to Italy from places like Philadelphia and pretend to be divas.
I chided her for prejudice and prudery—remarking that the rich

wife of a scumbag manufacturer shouldn't make such fancy distinctions as a matter of course, even if the product that kept her in Missoni knits and Ungaro silks was striped like American toothpaste in patriotic Italian colors. To my surprise, she agreed, sadly, remarking, *'Ah, serva Italia—di dolore ostello!'* She then went into a riff about Italy, during the reign of Papa Giovanni Ventitrezza. What a saint, etcetera—Sant'Angelo Roncalli—walking around the dark streets of Rome blessing people, etcetera. You felt safe, you felt loved by the *Buon Pastore* himself; you felt—get this—it was *unnecessary* to sin. Nothing bad could happen: there were no murders, no kidnappings in Italy in those years; there was *La Dolce Vita* and *L'Avventura*, and *Livia Serpieri*, and Mawrdew Czgowchwz's husband in *Caravaggio* at Scala. We laughed remembering *Caravaggio*'s reviews, especially the one that demanded an investigation be held: that somewhere in the world a murder had been committed. Not an allegorical homicide against Music—a murder. The anonymous reviewer of the *Corriere della Sera* had insisted that such music could never have been written down; its only possible provenance was a pistol stuck into an ear and fired, and brains blown out on a sheet of music copy paper; *and* since the composer was still walking about the streets of Milan and eating at table eleven with Mawrdew Czgowchwz and Maria Meneghini Callas, among others, suicide must in all probability be ruled out—unless Czech vampires, etcetera. . . . And therefore somewhere in Bohemia, or in America or in Italy itself . . . like that. And Papa Giovanni understood all and pardoned all—this is Vana again, now, not the critic of the *Corriere della Sera*. He had the hideous metal loincloth on Michelangelo's Risen Christ in Santa Maria Sopra Minerva removed so the people could see and admire, knowing there was no sin in beholding—*venerating*—a glorified male's whereabouts. Paolo Sesto left it that way—wouldn't he—but now this fascist Pole has had the loincloth screwed back on. She connected him—Papa Giovanni, not this cretin who stole his predecessor's names—with Venice, where he'd been the patriarch. Etcetera. Anyway, fair warning: La Vana might be on the next plane, the way Mishima was from Tokyo ringing up Tennessee Williams to take him to Kelly's and getting knocked around as a result. . . .

"Poor Yuriko Mishegas—that's what we called her then. Not for her the superconsiderate rice queens of the East Side, who would have had themselves crucified on Mount Fuji for one evening with her talking about *onegata*s and peonies. . . . Which rhapsodies, you realize, produced some rather grim cultural fallout. It wasn't until Yuriko started babbling about all those Noh plays that feature the head-box mixup scenes that give the *onegata*s their supreme tragic moments—like when the vengeful warlord's lady recognizes her own son's noggin where she expects to see the young lord's with whom she has been carrying on a clandestine, etcetera— it wasn't until he started hanging off barstools at Kelly's and in certain Tenth Avenue haunts of the Westies retailing the heinous, gory details of these exotic Shogun practices and their refinement into the high exquisite by transvestites on the Kyoto Rialto that the vogue for presenting the rival wise guy's *head*—in a Stetson hatbox—ceremonially at the social club to the local *capo* got started. And—fatal rebound—poor Yuriko, hoisted on her own petard, quite lost her head over promoting the chic."

"Meanwhile, Vana very well might, dear, on Alitalia and on wings of song descend among us again—the very way she did early in the seventies when, before the current husband and while still thinking of a Met debut, she shattered the mirror at the Duchess, clearing the place in two gay minutes. *She* claimed it was with her B-flat in *O don fatale*, but any dyke still alive who was there will give you the *T*: it was with a heavy glass ashtray. Sort of like your true story of the Stonewall riots, isn't it? You'd better watch your step, dear, if she gets wind of what you're up to. I can see it now: *I Go*

Back to the Duchess—what would that be in Italian? *Ritorno alla Duchesa?* She'd open in Milan, of course—give Valeria Moriconi a run for her money on the Rialto there, and then, with the scumbag millions behind her, probably open at the Palace—if not inaugurate a new theater *à la* Maxine Elliot. In fact, that's *exactly* what she'd do, if I know Vana. Somebody would tell her how Maxine opened her own place right up the block from the Old Met, and before you could say *Gianni Versace*—or *La sorella di Gianni Versace*—there it would be—right where the Harkness was: Il Teatro Vana Sprezza. Of course, speaking of Versace—of your shared passion—perhaps the two of you could do a *duo* number— you know, sort of *We Go Back to Harry's American Bar?* High cabaret."

"And would you guest from time to time?"

"I might—I very well might, my dear, do that. . . . Whereupon she asked me—speaking of the danger of Italy now—if I was traveling with my pearls. I revealed them underneath my shirt. She declared pearls are really the ultimate: they absorb the *sudore*, and thereby the personality, of the wearer—which brought her in her wanderings back to the Pearl of the Adriatic.

" 'Yet all the same, *caro*, Venice is not really a pearl. Venice is a sapphire. The fact that it is covered every summer with shit and maggots makes no difference whatever—shit and maggots make no impression on a star sapphire. When the rains come, and they're washed off, there is the jewel—*sempre la stessa.* '

"I chose not to take offense at her remarks about summer people, any more than those about Italian-American lesbians—I had heard it all before—and made no protest when she called down for a motorboat to take her to the station for the night train to Milan. It was obviously the next day that she wrote you from the *de Milan*—before picking up her little *commessa* and turning her into a *camerista* for a day. The *Ticino?* I said to myself. Well, there's horses for courses, and, of course, if she took the kid to

Bellagio and flaunted her there, there might well be delivered to the *de Milan* one day not too long thereafter something in a hatbox. . . .

" 'On the train,' she announced, very grandly—she was by then shitfaced drunk—'I shall talk to Americans. Some remember me and play my records—and *some* even take the liberty of wondering, since I am married to a rich man, why my art has not been made available to a new public on CD. Such forwardness amuses me. *E strano.* . . . '

" 'Vana,' I replied, somewhat sharply, 'frankly, I'm shocked!' '*Are* you?' she said, rising to go. 'Well, *cara*, do forgive me if I suggest that perhaps a *travesti* does not really, finally comprehend the pathos of an aging woman with no voice left—*perchè d'amaro sente 'l sapor della pietade acerba.' An aging woman,* I thought, *whose husband hates her, with no voice left, who rides on trains.* Because although I believe, dear, in the action of grace, I think I can recognize in the moment the difference between actual grace and sanctifying grace. Merely because she had sounded so miraculously restored singing *a te questo rosario* on the Ponte Malavisa Vechia was no reason to imagine that were she to open her throat, poor blasted rose that it was, then and there—or dare to do so on any evening in any music on any stage in the world—Vana Sprezza would come off sounding any better than the very late Zarah Leander. And at that there was truth in what she said. A *travesti* has his limitations; he is unlikely to be able to trill in rapid-fire Rossini and Donizetti arias and ensembles, and so far as we know, none of us has ever achieved that other, archetypal trill, the multiple orgasm. Whether Vana herself ever had or not—and I rather think she had. . . . After all, what is it they say about Italian princesses—and she was the very type of one—the jewels may be fake, but the orgasms never. But at any rate, I was quite sure the trills were gone forever, and as for the orgasms, I had the impression, from the skin tone under the artful makeup, that they were at least in abeyance—

and wished her from the bottom of my silent heart then and there the best of luck on her holiday in Bellinzona.

"Then she sat down again and, taking my hand, looked imploringly into my eyes. *'Senti, caro*—listen to me, and answer me in truth. *Ti ricordi*—you remember, don't you—*qual'estate*—that summer, thirty-three years ago—*qui, in Venezia*—*quando, avanti la prima di* Livia Serpieri, *io porteva dal Lido quella roba da spiaggia*— I wore that garment to the beach at the Lido to sit in front of that whole American crowd—*giallo e azzuro col immagine di* Minnie Mouse *ch'io ho comprata in Padova, e* Truman Capote *me diceva*— he said to me *che nessun' portava quagli abbigliamenti sulla spiaggia*—nobody wears that kind of cheap drag on the *Lido da Venezia?* I was all right, then, wasn't I: I was even a nice girl. *Ero una brava ragazza. T'imploro, cara, non è vero?'*

"I answered as best I could. *'Ma, cara, sei sempre brava.' 'Sono brava, ma—stancata!'* she said, rising again, with effort. I thought to myself, *And will you die in January—of influenza?* But said no more. It hit me suddenly that Vana's anxiety—her terror, really—about the days of her extreme celebrity was emblematic of that suicide-inducing saying about all myth: that myth is that which was never true and which always will be. Then, suddenly, she laughed that laugh of hers—the one Vortice taught her for the finale of *Livia Serpieri*, remember, where the libretto parodies the last act of *Tosca*, and the betrayer is shot as the demented *contessa* carries on chortling downstage right. Like that. And then she walked out the door, declaring, *'Sono vecchia, sono bruta, sono sola—ma sono sempre Vana Sprezza!'* "

"She was right about Italy then, though, and about Papa Giovanni. You know, people might take us for anti-Catholic, you and I. We're not; we saw the fat pope together—with Phil, remember? And *there* was a saint of God on this earth, and plain to see.

"I thought of Vana with the Americans, and then I thought if only, before she left like that, I'd thought of our old joke—hers and mine—the castrato aria *E pericoloso sporgersi*, expurgated from Rossini's *Viaggio a Ragusa*. We made it up together in Milan in '57, at the time of the raging controversy over the completeness of the maleness of Mawrdew Czgowchwz's yet-to-be husband, for whom Merovig Creplaczx had just composed his *Caravaggio*. You remember the story—he'd finally had enough of all the *melocheccha crocchio ristretto*, and took himself off to the public baths, causing a sensation, but certainly scotching the speculation. Somebody said at the time he could have done it less sensationally in a private interview with the archbishop, Montini—one day to be pope himself. Those were gorilla-hash days, dear.

"The train from Venice to Vienna was called the *Gondoliere*, and I saw myself in the window, crossing the lagoon to Mestre—and thinking, as always on that crossing, of coming back across Broad Channel from Rockaway to Howard Beach—saw myself again in performance-art terms, in a motion picture: as Divine, cast by DeVors, but alone, without Davis. Only for a moment—coming to myself, I realized just how much, how truly and how terribly Venice is the City of Death, and nearly resolved—again as before and before and before—never to come to it again."

"What a magnificent hotel the Bristol is. Louis Quatorze is supposed to have said—at Versailles—that the mark of a man of quality is his indifference to cold, heat, hunger, and thirst—and, if that weren't enough to make any man decide to be a woman, one night—with or without love—in the Bristol in Vienna would. And *I* spent *two* nights there. Of course, reflecting, there has never been anyone on *earth* as *far out* as Louis Quatorze, except Mae West, and just as surely as *she* was never a *man*, he, somehow, *irregardless*, as the girl said, was *always* a woman.

"Vienna's a little sad, though, I find. . . . So saying, the diva plunged to her death. I mean, it does remind you a little bit of Jo Van Fleet in *East of Eden: I* was *very beautiful once.* I spent the first night in—in a long hot tub, and then in front of the television looking at something called *Mascara.* Murder and mayhem in a drag-queen cabaret—including lip-syncing to the final scene of *Salome,* etcetera; the murderer, of course, a bent sister. Business as usual—let's face it, I said to myself, who's going to make a movie about, well, me, for instance, on this mission? Bresson? Then I thought to myself, well, maybe he would, if I were doing it on foot—barefoot—stopping at Carmelite hostels along the old Irish missionary route from County Mayo to Bohemia, and sleeping on hard boards."

"Next morning I went out walking, in search of the old Vienna that was very beautiful once, and, of course, I found it all around the place—up and down the Kärntnerstrasse. If they make the picture, the lead-in music for this segment is the Beethoven Fourth. I was that morning that exuberant, holding with Lotte Lehmann, *Ach dass ich wieder von dir traumte, du schöne Stadt im Frulingsblühn, mein Wien!* Right around the corner from the Bristol, for example, in the record store across from the Staatsoper, there was a window devoted to Hermann Leopoldi and Helly Moslein—the postwar toasts of New York. Helly was, as much as Beethoven, Vienna itself.

"Further afield—on the Favoritenstrasse, just off the Sudtirolerplatz—I found Dora Krebs, went in, and picked out a few frocks—waltzed right in, dear, tried them on right off the rack, plunked down the gold card, and breezed out, and if any of Dora's *Verkäuferin* thought it strange, in Catholic Vienna, for a man to be . . . they didn't say so. Ah, American Express, I thought: when you put your crepe de chine in your beaded bag and leave home, don't leave home without it. I'll tell the world—even if I can't tell it how I got mine.

"Do you know what that warthog Henry Ford said about women shopping for outfits, dear? He said, *To say it plainly, the great majority of women who work do so in order to buy fancy clothes.* Now, albeit Henry Ford was clearly incapable of saying anything more complicated than that, he *was*, if unwittingly, engaging in allegory—since if allegory isn't fancy clothes bought with one's hard-earned metaphoric coin, what is it? I walked *very* emblematically up the Favoritenstrasse, chin to the wind, to the museum. I made my way through the Italian Renaissance rooms—nodding at the *Bravo*'s empty niche—and sat down for two spells in front of two great allegories: the Arcimboldo *Seasons* and Vermeer's *Fame*.

"There is, to be sure, allegory *everywhere* in Central Europe. Do you know why, when Mawrdew Czgowchwz fled Prague in the single-engine plane, she didn't fly to nearby Vienna instead of all the way to Paris? The Senate committee asked her that, in '49, in the closed hearing that resulted in her being awarded citizenship by the Congress. *Why go east to get west?* is the rhetorical question she put to them in reply. Allegory.

"In Vienna there is allegory even in public transport. Yes, there is something in the *tone* of the recorded voice on the Ringstrasse trolley car, and, of course, there is *no* end of the line. I can't tell you how often I went around in the circle. I'd go into the Rotisserie Sirk, have a coffee, and get on at Opernring, and just ride around again. I did all the things you're supposed to do in Vienna. Nineteen Berggasse—I sent a card to Mawrdew Czgowchwz. Up and down the Mariahilfestrasse on foot—trying to picture Hitler's entry: it wasn't hard. The Belvedere, the Rathaus. Had a pee or two in *the* most outrageous tea rooms, *bar none*, in this plague-age world. And everything so spotlessly *clean*, you'd swear you were in a Sirk movie. I mean, do you want to talk *open house*—and speaking of Sirk—with all those gleaming *vespasiennes* and spotless mirrors, strategically placed over the wash-basins, at a gay tilt. And written—practically *engraved*—in *script*—on the white tile walls, ***Wenn du hast deine Fleischbank offen***—I mean, darling, in Vienna, men *dress up* to go to the terlet. Including *headgear* and *footwear*—that is, Tyrolean feathers in hats, and cunning little buskins, and, yes, dear, *Lederhosen.* Stop me. It was safer above ground, so I rode around, and I *always* remounted, not to ride to the next stop, but once again all the way around and *then* to the next stop."

"*Bell*-port!—Mastic-*Shirley* next!"

"It was the voice—the opposite of Hitler's, and Zarah Leander's, not to mention the dulcet thing we've been hearing on this choo-choo for the past hour and a half—as hypnotic in its way as Judy's in 'The Trolley Song.' Actually, it couldn't have been the opposite of *both* Hitler *and* Zarah Leander, could it? That was badly put—actually, it was about *midway between* Hitler and Zarah Leander, in timbre, but of course it was *warbling* in the Viennese drawl. It was a Helly Moslein voice—even a Richard Tauber voice, since it *was* the voice of a man. Remember *I'm in love/With a man/Plaza O double four double three?* Well, *I* fell in love with the man who announces the stops and changes on the Viennese trolley cars. I couldn't help wondering—and later, alone at the Bristol, dreaming about—*What* did he look like? I wished I knew. What did he look like—was he *six foot seven or three foot two/Eyes of brown, or baby blue?/ . . . pompadour, or not a hair?* I did not care—just rode around. Never went out to the Prater—what for? I've seen *Letter from an Unknown Woman* often enough. From what they told me at the desk at the Bristol, I concluded that the *Lusthaus* had become a kind of Schrafft's, and, well—

"I did dine out—and not on the trolley, but up in the Kärnt-nerstrasse, at the Olympia, upstairs in the back, much with the leather banquettes and the dusty crystal chandeliers and the ersatz gypsy fiddler. I asked him did he know the main theme of the Berg violin concerto. Instead, he played Marietta's *lied* from *Die tote Stadt*, and *Im chambre séparée—Suddenly*, to us. All I could think of was Mawrdew Czgowchwz in that room—on the night she first sang the Rosenkavalier to Leda Freitag's Marschallin— eating a whole goose, with red cabbage, proving the old adage, *Every true Viennese is a Bohemian.* Whether or not the converse is true—in the extended sense of *Bohemian*, that is—I'm not so sure. I'd have to get out my existentialism notes and examine them.

"Then, as if in response to the riddle of the ages, rather than the riddle of an aphorism, as I was paying my check, I heard one of the waiters say to another, *'Denkst-du das er kennt die turkische Prinzessen?'* It was *too* gay to ignore. I just looked back over my shoulder straight into his overstressed eyes and cooed *Ja, ja.* Allegory. Like talent, it can go pretty far. Remember orgone boxes? I swept out of the place, thinking strangely of the head of Mustapha Whatsisface. Somebody cut it off at the time of the last siege of Europe by the Turks—what, four hundred years ago? Nearly. It sits there in the Historical Museum—on my list, too, of things I'll never understand. You know, that ghastly looking Noriega collected severed heads. I wonder if *he* knows the Turkish princess? Mustapha did—he knew a lot of 'em. Ah, dear, it's when you travel that history grabs you by the throat—as if it wants to screw off your head. And if you want to ignore history—and, speaking of the converse, screw your head off—then you go along to the Turkish princess's.

"Good thing I was in the mood for rumination, because the cable television that night featured satellite news of the AIDS conference in San Francisco, followed by a showing of Joan Crawford and Mercedes McCambridge—she who for one simple but no sin-

gle reason was Mercedes del Talgo-Benzedrine's very favorite character actress—in *Johnny Guitar*. Need I say more? Is the pope heterosexual—or is he not at the very least the very last and most
offensive Polish joke?

"I saw two cute San Francisco boys marching with the *From
the Raw Bar* and *Toilets Customer Use Only* T-shirts. *They're still
at it,* I thought, like Carolina snake-handling Baptists, besotted in
their religion exactly like believers in the thoroughly discredited
appendix to the Gospel of Mark: believing they can beguile the
cobra and drink any deadly thing and it shall not harm them, all
because they are wearing the talisman: not ankh, and not the cross,
but the pink triangle.

"The holy pink triangle. You remember, in the hospital with
Miss Faith I went into the men's room—because, when all is said
and done, dear, your mother is a man and pees standing up—to
find that the urinal deodorant blocks were of pink triangular shape.
Such a thing would have been enough in the acting-out days of the
Eleven against Heaven to . . . but what, if anything, did it mean
to me that afternoon?

"Meanwhile, I said to myself, the drag queen's revenge m.o.
is *not* to shriek her tits off, it is to *plot*, and to pronounce, when
through, in the grand manner of the Cobra Woman: *Young men,
young women, children—all must go!* But no, that wouldn't do,
either. What about this, then? What if I agreed not to put down
ACT/OUT if they would agree to stop calling me and my kind
retro masochistic self-loathing detritus of the bad old days? History
is written by the winners, dear, and in this case by the survivors—
a history that contains all the abreactions, all the compensations
for disallowing the complicated feelings of the actual losers, the
dead. But I question my reactions, and wonder, am I not myself
an unwell woman, in some sense? We must make a decision. We
subscribe to the Greek ideal—or pay lip service to some form of
it—and in the Greek ideal it is Eros that binds society together—

all society, dear, not merely the Gay Community, *soi-disant.* Aristotle says the mark of the citizen is that he can be governed as well as govern. Are we to be citizens of the world, or merely denizens of a sideshow, of whom it may be said that it is time we checked in our lips and went home?

"I sat there looking at San Francisco, and remembering us emblazoning *Better Living through Chemistry* on *our* T-shirts, and wearing them to the cathedral to disrupt the benediction. And then, inevitably, sitting in bed in Vienna, with clocks and mirrors everywhere, to musing on the no-win situation of the older entertainer. If you carry on like the Certified Horror Show I mentioned earlier—a crazy, old, basically reactionary and unrepentantly self-loathing thing trying to recapture the irretrievable liberating opportunities—the *dangerous work*—available to youth by leading marches on barricades, you make yourself ridiculous. And if you turn from what the Eleven against Heaven were, into even a mild conservative, you're all too predictable. To quote Frank yet again,

> The song of an old cow is not more full of judgment
> than the vapors which escape one's soul when one is
> sick.

And I *was* getting sick, and remembering all too well my rage at the yuppie faggots who went for Reagan—and not just yuppies, either. We were not among those fairies in the fairy caravan who in 1980 took that sharp right on Flamingo Road directly into the Reagan camp, and stayed on there to vote for George Bush, but an awful lot of our contemporaries—some of the SAGE crowd, for example—were. *Then* they got pissed off when the hets got rich in supply sidings and all they got was PCP. Did they think they were going to get preferential treatment—these same fairies who had drooled over the Kennedy brothers in the sixties—merely because one of them had taught Nancy Reagan flower arranging or because another of them had introduced her to Bill Blass? Of course, these same girls who were such *open* liberals in the sixties were so *only* because they imagined that because both Jack and Bobby Kennedy were fucking Marilyn, that meant *somehow* they were being incestuous with one another. *Sowie es.* . . .

"I felt like Thomas Jefferson, who lamented, late in life, *All, all dead, and ourselves left alone amidst a new generation whom we know not, and who knows us not.* . . . Whereupon onscreen trooped my darling Sisters of Perpetual Indulgence, lightening the mood, redirecting my heart to religion."

"Actually, in '80, Misses Worthington and Caswell DeWitt—those refugees from the Nathaniel Branden Institute—nearly *did* join the caravan, but Miss Charity and La DeVors threatened to beat them to death outside the polling place and *then* tell Bette Davis on them. And another reason the San Francisco shirts upset me was that the Magyars, when they were terminal, went to a shirt party in matched slogans: *Going Out of Business* and *Last Days.* But with the dying, darling, you do *not* quibble taste—nor, perhaps, finally, politics. . . .

"I'd like to believe that when it comes, ours will not be a revolution that marches in the streets or blows up public buildings—or uses AIDS as a cover for the expression of our thwarted narcissistic faggot rage, a rage more about such circumstances as the conventual closure of the baroque fuckpits than about anybody's personal mortality. And in the last analysis, as Margo said to Karen, no revolution can be permitted to succeed. Do you know why? I just read why last year: because then we would be compelled to renounce the liberty of our longing. Grab that, philosopher.

"I gave up finally on the Movement, it and all its talking

hydra heads, black, feminist, faggot, dyke. After the country fell apart, they just appropriated the rhetoric of the oppressor. *Ask not what the Movement can do for you; ask what you can do for the Movement.* I said to myself, *I've heard that one before.* I remembered my response, too. I'd said, *Get her!*—and they did just that, didn't they? Ought to have taught somebody a lesson.

"Of course, as I've said, I do fear that the crackdown on behavior—on *mores*—is in the offing, on the heels of the Depression, as before. Only before, of course—after the twenties and the low, libidinous, and violent thirties—that dark decade whose literature turned into forties *film noir*—instead of a purge they just sent everybody off to war to get the country morally regenerated into a generation of wholesome, God-fearing, and dictatorial conquerors. Now, with nothing left to conquer but the moon and Mars, which may take longer than they supposed . . . well, it's harder to envision than to fear, but already there are strange new *rules.* Only the other day I saw a notice in the subway—next to Mary's phone number. If you deliberately litter, get caught, and don't pay the fine—becoming a litter scofflaw—if you defy them, they will fix you. They will fix it so that you can't—there was a list: get credit, get a student loan, work for the city, or join the armed forces. And don't even *think* of calling Mary to fix the ticket: *she's on their side!*

"Whereupon I chastise myself, saying, *If you want it all blue and gold, woman, just trot off to Miss Faith's heaven. Here in the Vale of Tears there are pink triangles.* And I remind myself that I took the pink triangle and *Don't Tread on Me* out of the ACT/ OUT solicitation and stuck it up in the kitchen. Your mother's not much of a gay politico, dear, all told—dithering in the divide would seem to be her besetting tendency. Don't tell on her."

"I won't," I said. "Father Ritter was conflicted—why not you?"

"*Jeee*-sus, *Mary—that* one! If there is one thing that *will* drive a fundamentally irenic woman like your mother *straight* to the barricades in a taxi, it's these fuckin' hypocrite Helens and male Mother Teresas galloping loose in the world: sitting on federal pornography commissions in the daytime and indulging in a little light cocksucking on the pullout Castro after the network sports final and the weather report. Of course, now that it's getting really *interestingly* evil, with *Contra* aid, gunrunning, and boy prostitution coming into it, and with Covenant House exposed as a front. . . . Next they'll be reissuing Rose Ritter's book on boy salvation. Ever read it? I have; it's a stitch. Confusing times we live in. I mean, I don't really even get Mother Teresa, if you want to know; to me she's just some overpublicized undertaker—is that too awful? Confusing times. No wonder Miss Mercedes, for instance, was getting *her* mind all tangled and confused in her cabaret instruction between against aid for the *Contras* and for condoms against AIDS. She feared she was *not of this world.* God love her, she was far above it.

"However, the truth is—and this will become *the* apparent plague in the nineties, as AIDS was the apparent plague of the eighties—or, rather, the apparent version of the Plague, the perennial scourge, heretofore attributed, like sin and death itself, to infernal forces, and who shall say that metaphor and its long, sad *nouvelle interpolée* has gone passé? The truth is, the whole argument organized around AIDS politics *is* passé. AIDS itself is not the Great Plague. The Great Plague of the age is Addiction—and probably has been, if you count back to the nineteenth century, when the whole country was said to be hooked on pickles, liquor, laudanum, and heroin cough syrup, but certainly since the war, since Benzedrine and Dexamyl made their debuts. I mean *definitely* since the psychedelics, since the new cocaine, since Ecstasy and MDA—*Mary Don't Ask*—which obviously render, along with visions of eternity, immortal longings, and unquestionably imprint ineradicable thanatic codes on the brain. Your mother, on her Carrie Nation rampage, would also proscribe not only Tuinal, Seconal, Thorazine, and Stelazine—the twins—but also Valium, Librium, Quaalude, Ativan, megatonic antibiotics, and Prozac. All must go.

"Mind *you*, the redress of addictions can itself go too far. Why, just before I left New York, at the Gay Pride rally in Union Square, did I not with my own ears hear an earnest, if fraught, young lesbian inveighing against everything that, by trying to cheer one up, gives one a temporary buzz, or titillates one's sense of adventure, leads to the kicker of the moment, low self-esteem. She cited especially four things: exercise, gambling, shopping, and relationships. I felt a strong civic urge to grab the bullhorn and let that young gay girl person in on a few home truths—such as what would Paulette—Miss Goddard—for example, have come to without exercise, gambling, shopping, and relationships—and as a consequence, would not New York University, and the humanities themselves, be today the poorer by those several chairs? Why, even religionists take exercise, go shopping, and certainly gamble for souls by way of human relationships. The Dalai Lama, for the love of God, enjoys the odd caprice! But back to art—a gamble if ever there was one—and its relationship to life and calisthenics. . . ."

"*Johnny Guitar* is called in German *Wenn Frauen hassen*—and did they *not*, Mercedes and Joan, as we know, two of fifties Hollywood's Olympic juicers. Joan's voice was dubbed by a somebody sounding like Zarah Leander in her late days, and Mercedes's by someone sounding like Peter Lorre in *M*. You know, sitting there in the white dress, at the piano, in her saloon—Vienna's, if you remember; her name in the picture—Joan does for a spell become the iconographic epitome of cinematic Temperance. Ironic. Even later, with the noose around her neck and the saloon in flames lighting up the night sky—it really *is* a masterpiece, you know; they're right who list it—when with that noose around her neck she says—I missed it in the German, but remembered the original:

'You'll have to do it yourself, Emma.' Well, *you believe—right then, right there—in the power of the Celebrity Prayer*: 'God grant me the celebrity to accept the things I cannot change. . . .' I was *uplifted—* I *was!*

"Joan in *Johnny Guitar*, sedated and sibylline at the piano, reminds your mother, of course, about herself in that very year, the year it came out. I was just that, doing my motorific late-night turns at Shirley's Pin-Up Room—242 Lexington Avenue, in Murray Hill—and still, I'm afraid, *relaxing* my nervous stomach with paregoric and stingers, which seemed to work. The divine Mabel would drop in, sing Alec Wilder songs, and Mawrdew Czgowchwz—she was still a contralto then, singing Amneris, *Figlia di Faraone!*—would arrive from the Metropolitan with Halcyon Paranoy, the Countess Madge O'Meagher Gautier, Carl Van Vechten, Thalia Bridgewood, Dame Sybil Farewell-Tarnysh, Bea Lillie, and Leo Lerman. Do you know who lived upstairs? Andy Warhol, and his mother. And Ayn Rand lived around the corner, on Thirty-fourth. Sounds like I'm listing the ships again, doesn't it—Mawrdew Czgowchwz, Bea Lillie, Julia Warhola, Ayn Rand: that crowd. All I'm saying, I suppose, really, is that—well, New York was more *interesting* then. I mean, does anybody care who collides with whom, where, nowadays? Does anybody care who anybody specifically *is*—as opposed to, say, what they look like they're coming as, to the Halloween parade?

"Andy was fascinated by Mawrdew Czgowchwz. He was just starting to go to the opera, with Charles Lisanly, and, of course, Mawrdew Czgowchwz was *the* thing—her Amneris, in particular: wiping every Aida except Milanov right off the stage—but it really was the fact that she was Czech. A lot of people have called Andy Czech; wrong—he was Slovak; they were from way down east, nowhere near Bohemia. Calling a Slovak a Czech is like calling the Welsh Irish—which, of course, happened in reverse in *How Green Was My Valley*. . . . Anyway, he used to sit there—at Shirley's—

saying nothing, but we all knew he drew beautifully. I was at the dinner where he drew Dick Banks's cock—you know, dear, *that's* what you ought to be on the trail of, along with Tchelitchew's pornography: Andy's cock drawings. Exquisite things.

"I suppose I identify with Vienna—Joan in *Johnny Guitar*, dear, not the city. There are two words I don't ever want to hear said in succession about me, and they are *was* and *beautiful*—so I cast myself as Vienna, and *them*—the ACT/OUT children—as Emma, wearing a bomber jacket and triangular pink plastic earrings and packin' her pistol, mama—because they would, I feel strongly, burn my place down if it suited them. My place, which stands for me and for the best of Gay Life as I knew it, from *Dress Stage* through the Cherry Lane, the Mais Oui, and the Cherry Grove *little shows—Odds and Ends* and *Heat Wave* and *From Drags to Riches* and *Once Upon a Boardwalk*—right down to Charles Ludlam at the Ridiculous—gone now to God—and Charles Pierce at the Ballroom, and Charles Busch—to name only the Charleses. And Everett Quinton and wacky old Ethyl Eichelberger—gone to meet Charles—and darling Vera Galupe-Borszkh and company. Too many of the young are what Dorothy Dean used to call the Internal Revenue Service: the I-R-*A*."

"*Mastic*-Shirley—*Centah* Moriches next!"

"The *Lehár* to Budapest, and your mother on it, humming all the way—a little obsessively—the melody to 'Oh, What I'll Do to That Young Hungarian'—Betty Grable, *That Lady in Ermine*, Lubitsch-Preminger, 1948, Technicolor. The Danube, beautiful, beige, wide—on the other side, Czechoslovakia, beckoning, perhaps at the very point where Mawrdew Czgowchwz, in the dead of night, had crossed into Hungary in her flight east in the war. A situation pregnant with possibilities for remembering, but everybody aboard seemed to be going to Budapest on business."

"You were going to Budapest on business."

"Exactly—and exactly what I said to myself. *'You're* going to Budapest on business, *Detta;* and no lady—except a cardinal in the Roman Catholic Church—wears ermine in the morning. Plus you're overindicating. Quit trying to figure it; let it unroll, as the kids say.' When you do, y'know, it is awesome—really.

"The old songs, and the old lines, if not the best, are usually the most effective comforts in time of trial. Not so, however, the old gags—they seem worse than they ever were to begin with. So O'Maurigan said to me, 'You'll stay in neither Buda nor Pest, but on Margareten Island, in the middle of the Danube—in the old hotel connected to the spa. It's a Ramada, but don't worry; it's gorgeous—and it's not air-conditioned, which means if some international bozo descends upon the second city of the old empire, the way Millard Bush did last summer, the entourage won't throw you out on your ass the way his did from all the deluxe dumps.' Staying on the island was also the only way to solve the tricky timing issue in the dispatch of the Magyars, who—having made up from one of the many spats that characterized their long, strange marriage and decided to be sent home to God together after all—had requested it as their launch venue, to fulfill the old Hungarian proverb which says that love begins and ends there. Mrs. Caswell DeWitt had requested her Post Toasties be cast upon the waters from the more folkloric Buda side, whereas the more cosmopolitan Miss Worthington had chosen the Pest side. They were to then *meet,* on the current, in death, as they had met on it—swimming off Margareten Island and *kissing shamelessly, one soul embracing itself in two bodies*—in life.

"It helps to know rich and efficient men, doesn't it. O'Maurigan's connections arranged everything. There *I* was, in the sulfur pool, and there they were—the two darling wide-eyed Hungarian-

boy bellhops—one on either side of the island, synchronzied—at
the hour of the angelus—dispatching both girls at once. It was,
when I came to think of it, something like the gag about the
revolving doors. *Something* like.

"I never enjoyed a more relaxed dinner—on the terrace, with
the *real* gypsy orchestra—from that city called Debrecen, actually,
where Mawrdew Czgowchwz hid out before she disappeared into
the Ukraine—playing first a tune called 'The Skylark'—really—and
then what sounded almost like evening ragas. That evening *I* ate
the whole goose, or very nearly. Ah, food! Let us learn to become
what we—as the gay girl who wrote *Zen Flesh, Zen Bones* pro-
claims: *Suck something and become the suckling.* Now *that's* a message, never mind this injunction against shopping! The Russians
seem to have the same idea, in that the infinitive forms of *to eat*
and *to be* are the same word—it's very existentialist, really. *Suck
something and become the*—I thought it was *suckling,* but maybe it
was *sucking,* as in the *act.* That would be existentialist, too, in
another direction. *Suck something* . . . Such as that lovely goose,
for instance: turn into a—but what if you're a gay goose already?
Then maybe you're ahead of the game? What was it Miss Worthington and Miss Caswell always said—check your premises?"

"Yes," I replied, adding unnecessarily, "if you remember, they
were both Objectivists." Unnecessarily, because there was no such
thing as an occurrence anywhere *near* Odette, or near any one of
her *myriad correspondents* (her phrase), that she didn't, it seemed
that night, remember, and rehash (that night).

"Who could *forget!*" she remonstrated—whereupon, fooling
me, she fell silent.

What had happened was this. At one of Ayn Rand's lunatic
seminars at the Statler, or the Roosevelt, or the Waldorf . . . wherever (and at which, as O'Maurigan has graciously reminded me,
the present Director of the Federal Reserve, then one of the Domi-
natrix's many hangdog acolytes, was undoubtedly present) Miss

Caswell, speaking up, addressed a question to Herself, beginning
with the words, "In his speech Galt contends that—" That was all
the speed freak who'd named herself after her typewriter had to
hear. (And was *ever* Truman's *mot* about typing not writing truer
of any published author?) "Galt does not *contend*. If you have read
Atlas Shrugged, if you profess to be an admirer of mine, then you
should know that Galt does not *strive, debate, argue, or contend.*"

Miss Caswell: "But Miss Rand, all I meant was—"

A.R.: "*If* you wish to speak to me, first remember to whom
and about what you are speaking!"

Later, at the Cherry Lane, Miss Caswell, gasping still and
resuming after a few cocktails her smoky Ilona Massey accent,
exclaimed, "I vassn't tryink to make trubble, dollink, I vas only
tryink to *think!*"

Then, in her clairvoyance, she (Odette) picked up my train
of thought—as if she were jumping back on the *Lehár*. "Miss Rand
may have thought Miss Caswell was thinking *pink*. She was a sick
bitch, really she was, that Alice Rosenbloom, and that ridiculous
book—we called it *Alice Drugged*—had a terrible influence on the
abused young, and in particular children of alcoholics. Poor Miss
Hope, for example, actually went around for a while calling herself
'Dagney Taggart' and asking people what were their premises, and
wondering who John Galt *was*, and where was the happy valley in
the Rockies, until we read her beads for her on the subject. Turned
out she was only desperately in love with *both* the boys from Budapest, and was having *horrifying* incest dreams—which was a much
easier hank of knotted gay hair to comb and iron out than Objec-
tivism. Whenever she'd start up we'd say, *Alice is drugged again—
her John called. He's gonna give her such a* beating!"

"Miss Worthington was Budapest born and bred, but Debrecen,
on the Hortobagy plain, thirty-five miles from the Ukraine, was

where Claudia Caswell DeWitt hailed from, and her idea had been to be scattered on the town's outskirts, across the plain, the way Gene Tierney scattered her father's ashes across New Mexico or Arizona or wherever it was in *Leave Her to Heaven*. Then, at the end, she changed her lap-dissolving mind—no longer able to identify even with Gene Tierney—and asked a little weakly—remembering to add her tag line, *I don't want to make trouble*—that a gypsy band from Debrecen play something at her funeral. As O'Maurigan said to me of all the girls' requests, 'Promise them anything, but remember to pick yourself up some Arpège at Shannon. And don't forget what DeVors told you about the Magyars in '88.' There sure ain't no fleas on *that* lamb of God, let me tell you—and it was largely at his prompting that they decided to go into the Danube together. I almost said it was at his instigation that they died at St. Vincent's on the same afternoon in adjoining beds, but. . . . I sent him a card from Budapest saying, *Guess what? The gypsies from Debrecen showed up!*"

With what had DeVors taxed her in '88? "They had just started to show symptoms, both of them in the same week, but had decided to keep up their spirits by keeping up their engagements, and *La Reina* gave me the following blast: 'It's not their *T* cells, dear, I'm worried about.' That *letter* again! If only we'd never even known what it *meant!* 'It's their *B—for brain* cells: alarming diminution of same. It's true we always said they were on all the world's concerns and fashions as of one mind, but did we realize they were actually *sharing* the one meager collection of marbles? I fear they are losing same at an alarming rate. *What* year in this, dear? *Eighty-eight?* And *where*—get this—where were they both last week, dressed to the nines? *Régine's!* I *nearly* asked Miss Thing were they decked out in flared pants and block *heels!*' "

———

"That night in Budapest was a hot night—it had gone up to nearly a hundred Fahrenheit that afternoon—and I left the windows open to catch the breeze off the river. I dreamed I was a boy again and that I was going down with my grandfather—God help me, I nearly said going *down on* my grandfather—going down with my grandfather on the elevator from the Queensboro Bridge to Welfare Island. We had come halfway across the bridge on the trolley from Fifty-ninth Street and Second Avenue—from where you get that cable car now out to Welfare Island, only now it's called Roosevelt Island. We were going to visit my grandfather's first cousin, Charley Farley, in the drug addicts' hospital—where he lived, full-time, as a ward of the state. 'They've put my release on the long finger, Dan,' he said to the old man, who had the same name I had, took a shine to me for that, and called me Danny Boy. 'It's just as well—where would I go? What would I do? At least here I can stand up in the ward room and say, "Do you want to end up like me?" The thing is, did *I* want to end up like me?' I heard all that in the dream just as it happened—or so it seemed. Might be a secondary revision, right?"

"*Cen*-tah Moriches—Speonk next!"

"*On the long finger.* . . . Been haunted by that expression ever since.

"We went into the bathroom. There were row upon row of enormous white bathtubs—which is probably why I had that dream that night, in pure 'Naked City' black-and-white—after sitting in the great sulfur baths in the spa on Margareten Island, between Buda and Pest. Margareten Island . . . feeling of well-being . . . Welfare Island . . . like that. Funny that Welfare Island is now renamed after our most parental president—a middle-class housing mecca of the new Gotham: an environment—like Battery Park

City—I've never set foot in. Actually, to date the dream correctly, it was in pure *Dead End* or pure *Winterset* black-and-white. Anyway, the next thing Charley Farley said to my grandfather—in life, that is: I can't tell you if I dreamed it or not; probably not, since you seldom bother to dream words that have been engraved in your memory as if on your tombstone. He said, 'Sometimes, Dan, when I'm comin' home from a day out of the place—maybe I've been down on the Third Aven-ya El to get some cigars at the Flatiron Building or stopped off at Grand Central for a shine—when I'm comin' home, and I get off the trolley, before I get on the elevator I look up at the bridge that you and I both worked on, and then down at the river, and I remember the story of the fairy who saved the guy's life that was gonna go off the Brooklyn Bridge—remember?—sayin', "I wuz gonna do that once, but I wuz afraid of gettin' the water dirty." ' The thing I remember is that nobody laughed—not my grandfather, not Charley Farley. I laughed about it years later, often, but the next day, in Köln, when I was tossing Miss Mae-Mae into the Rhine, the words came back to me again—and I couldn't laugh, either. And do you know why? Because before I set out in June, somebody actually said to me, *Do you think what you've agreed to do is* safe? And *meant* it—in the public-health sense. Did you *ever?* The poor old thing who asked me that was, of course, a very good argument for ACT/OUT—except that, once again, when you know there's no point in hearing your own voice telling itself how it feels. . . . Another instance of the when-to-hold-it-in-and-when-to-let-them-have-it, I suppose. Sort of like the Taoist doctrine of lying back and massaging your balls in the sunlight, while letting the energy warm your perineum and soak in through your asshole, as a prelude to—guess what—*the conservation of energy.* I don't guess you cotton any more to *that* Oriental habit of mind than does your mother. . . .

"The row of enormous white tubs, in the white-tiled room, in the sunshine, the three of us—then a voice offstage.

Rub-a-dub-dub
Three men in a tub—
Queer!

Sudden quick cut to the bright white light of the *Klo* in Vienna—the white urinals, and the voice-over *Berggasse . . . Mariahilfestrasse . . . Sudtirolerplatz . . . Opernring . . .*
"*Is* life a dream?

"Next morning, scented, serene, Detta boarded the *Franz Liszt* to Köln, to dump Miss Mary Garden Gates into the Rhine, sleep in the station hotel, and—morning after yet again—catch the *Merkur* to Copenhagen, gateway to the North. Is life a *scream?* And so-the-fuck *what* the Magyars went out like a couple from Kansas City that night in '88 to Régine's, or if they went in the fucking New Look—'My *right?*' as the cabbie implored, rhetorically, when, in the course of a long peroration on the text *live and let live*, he declined to infer the Fall of the Republic from the sale of Rockefeller Center to the Japanese. Sometimes DeVors, justly proud, I suppose, of her Bourbon royal blood—although O'Maurigan used to remark there was more bourbon than blood to the attitude— could be a little too Spanish Inquisition on occasion in her *obiter dicta.*"

" 'If those two are going down the Danube together,' Mae-Mae had said, dying, 'I'll go down the mighty Rhine. Actually, darling, since I think I woke up this morning in the acceptance stage, I'd just as soon go down the mighty Hudson from *Rhinecliff*—but, on the other hand, since you'll be going to Europe anyway, it would probably be *withholding* of me to be the one and only one you don't get to do one of your scenes with over there.'
" 'I will do whatever it is you tell me to do, Miss Mae,' I assured her. 'If you like, I'll put you in right under the Lorelei's

rock.' Call me old-fashioned, as Dame Edna would say. I love the moonlight—especially on a river. I love the old-fashioned ways. The sound of rain upon the windowpane—which, of course, it was doing just then as Mae-Mae lay there dying.

" 'Gosh,' she replied, 'that'll be something different, anyway—just making a *suggestion*, never *mind* giving anybody any such thing as a detailed order. I have been on the receiving end of so much *instruction* these days!' And she had been, too, from the diagnosis through the push-pull pharmacology and the blind testing. 'If they'd taken a tenth part of the trouble showing us how to live as they take showing us how to—of course, we *wouldn't* pay them any mind, would we? Drugs, dick, disco, and dish—remember? If anybody—*anybody* on *our side*—had tried to tell us they would turn into dysentery, dementia, despair, and death, we'd have told *them* to go fuck themselves in church and gargle with holy water. And were we *wrong*? Of course, I was very poorly educated—and it went downhill from there. They always said I had a good mind, but—I'll tell you, dear, and this is a bulletin you can give whoever's left out there from me. Of all the things I've lost on my way up this hill, the thing I miss *least* is my mind. I mean, I tell myself, "Mae, imagine *getting* it?" I mean, can you imagine my having to put up with *understanding* what's happening to me? I haven't the. . . . Well, Miss Davis said it best in *Watch on the Rhine*: "I am not brave—I'm not brave at all; but when the time comes, I shall do my best." And she did, too. And maybe *that's* why I chose the Rhine—so that not the Lorelei but Miss Davis will keep watch over me. . . .'

"Then, towards the very end, on an afternoon when the rain had turned to freezing sleet, after listening through the headphones to the 1956 Met broadcast tape of Mawrdew Czgowchwz's Mélisande again and again and again, she decided where she *really* wanted to go: into the *fontaine des aveugles*, in the park of Arkel's castle in Allemonde. Miss Charity got wind of that development as *she* lay dying *her* way, at home. She was at that point talking to *her* power animal, a stuffed bear, and said to it, in characteristic fashion, 'Did'ya hear, Teddy? Miss Mary got born again—musta happened yesterday.' You see, all the while Miss Mary was talking to Miss Piggy, while dreaming of becoming Mélisande, and Miss Faith and Kermit were dreaming of Cimabue and company, Miss Charity was seeing visions of herself and Teddy in her very own heaven: the set of the Joe Gage *Paradiso Garage*, on which she was the executive fluffer—and who shall cast the first rhinestone?''

"Power animals. You know, at the end of that ride across town—I was thinking of that ex–bus driver hansom cabbie you recalled in your show tonight, and *Mona, was he right, and way back when.* I kept overhearing that voice. *I signed up for a power hour with this image consultant.* I often heard the same voice—the same desperate, seeking tone—from Americans on the trains at night in Europe. God knows, maybe the girl ended up on one of them herself—telling Vana Sprezza, for instance, that a power hour with an image consultant is what *she* ought to do. And would she be wrong? I mean, if Madame Marchesi is no longer of any use to Vana, then. . . . I tell you again what I told myself—this old fool sitting opposite you, your mother, is in the *wrong line of work!*

"There being in the world no reliable map of Allemonde, I put Miss Mary into the Rhine, under Miss Davis's protection. Another reason for the Rhine had been, in Mae-Mae's words, 'That way I'll get back to Amsterdam. I always liked Amsterdam.' I didn't like to tell her the Rhine goes into the North Sea at Rotterdam. Amsterdam, Rotterdam, Potsdam, Boulder Dam—what the hell, I decided, and meanwhile decided, too, that since I hadn't been to Amsterdam in a while myself, I'd stop off there on my way back from Scandinavia. Big mistake—or maybe not, after all.

It turned out to be, one way or another, the most memorable part of the journey. But at Köln, I couldn't think of anything to say except *schlaf in himmliche Ruhe*. It wasn't the season, but I kept remembering Miss Mae-Mae's conceit as we watched them singing 'Silent Night' last Christmas that the Vienna Choir Boys never got any older, and still wore the same little sailor suits. I got a little sentimental about my childhood, too, in Köln, because it's where Saint Ursula, her eleven thousand virgins, and their attendant clerical sissies were hacked to bits by the Huns. I was taught by the Ursulines, dear, and that story made some kind of deep impression on all us sensitive children in the class—or should I say both of us.

"Vienna, Köln, the Danube, the Rhine. . . . All cities, dear, are the one city—the capital of Allemonde—and all rivers the one river, whose wellspring is the fountain of the three blind mice."

"I won't say I was near breaking point on the *Merkur*, but—it was like something I read about, a far more stringent circumstance: that of a German Jew aboard a prison train on its way to a Soviet labor camp, listening to the rhythm of the wheels and seeming to hear them repeat '*Warum-wohin? Warum-wohin?* Why-where? Why-where?' And the names of the cities—they're with me still, as if to repeat them were some kind of answer. Budapest, Hegyeshalom, Wien, Linz, Wels, Passau, Regensburg, Nürnberg, Würzburg, Frankfurt, Mainz, Koblenz, Bonn, Köln, Düsseldorf, Duisburg, Hamburg, Lübeck, Puttgarden, Rødby—"

"Speonk!"
    "Speonk," she repeated. *"Exactly!"*
    "But you remember *everything*," I said, unnecessarily.
    "*Everything*, darling, from the foundation of the world—it's a crucifixion."

"*Wes*-hamp'n, next!"

"Anyway, a crucifixion—and especially since total recall is of no help in resolving the very conflict the clacking of the wheels put in train in my mind—that famous one of holding two opposing ideas in conceptual captivity in the same interval. For some reason, all the length of the journey from Budapest, until I rinsed my brain pan clean in the Tivoli Gardens, the two propositions I held— or that held me—were *nothing ever happens twice* and *whatever happens, happens twice—simultaneously: in oneself and in the universe.*"

"You mean," I offered, I thought a little lamely, "like the Crucifixion?"

"Exactly, darling—but let's not, shall we? *Especially* since it's Sunday morning, before mass. Where was I—what town along the way?"

"Lübeck?"

"*Lübeck?* Never. Lübeck is the Speonk of—of course, Thomas Mann was born in Lübeck, wasn't he, talking of travel, free-associating, the Crucifixion, and putting people to sleep. *I* used to put 'em to sleep, you know, at the Everard—exactly like Miss Dorsay did unwittingly. It was usually Sunday morning when I did. On other mornings they were so jittery about getting to work, but if it was Sunday morning they'd sleep on—right through the bells of the Little Church Around the Corner. *That* used to slay me. Nobody ever seemed to know what the Little Church Around the Corner was around the corner *from*—but your mother did. It was around the corner, more or less, from the Everard. Yes, they'd sleep on and I'd talk on—narrating like Thomas Mann.

"Well, like they say, it's only God who's ever *really* listened. Seems to be what God gets off on—listening, watching, waiting. . . ."

"Lübeck, Puttgarden, Rødby—that's the ferry: you go up on deck for an hour and cross from Jutland to Zeeland. Denmark is beautiful, and we truly love the Danes for their heroism in the war— whether or not King Christian did ride out on a white horse wearing the yellow Star of David, or the pink triangle of the fairies, or *nothing at all*—just to torment that awful little boy whose awful habit it was to tell nothing but the awful truth, and give him an erection. . . .

"Then, finally, Copenhagen, which is only and forever about the Tivoli Gardens.

"The Tivoli Gardens are so divine, darling, that to walk out of them is to do so in a dream. The pirate-ship ride is the most beautiful amusement-park ride in the world—not excluding our own carousel in Central Park. I put all the girls in one boat in my mind—just like the old Valkyrie-carousel fantasy—bought all eight seats and rode around and around, imagining Miss Faith, the baby, sitting in my lap. One doesn't know what is going on in the real world, or in one grand hotel or another, or on television, and, wearied, after what often had seemed a long-term sentence of travel, one was catapulted directly from the springboard of the ambience of Tivoli into one's own dream life. In my case that I was Mrs. Brigid O'Shaughnessy and that the Maltese Falcon—well, that's only how it started out. I became many, many other women as I rode around. The pirate queen Grace O'Malley—replacing Miss Wayfaring up there on the screen in her latest, and in some ways most absorbing, triumph. Catherine of Russia, replacing Miss Dietrich, Miss Bankhead, *and* Miss West. Elizabeth of England, replacing Miss Davis. Margaret Thatcher, suddenly transformed into a human being. The ballerina Stolichnaya—my own singular screen role. Diane DeVors, fabulist and *mythomane* in her fantasy Oscar-winning role, *The Most Beautiful Woman in the World.* Audrey Hepburn, my exact contemporary, in her greatest performance, as

Miss Holiday Golightly in *Breakfast at Tiffany's*, in two outtakes
from that film: lunching with Sally Tomato's lawyer at Hamburger
Heaven and transmitting the coded information to his client at
Sing Sing. And all the while I was still in the Tivoli Gardens: even
when I thought I was in Luna Park or on the Hudson River Day
Line. I revived that idea of the ride of the Valkyries on a carousel,
and then transferred it to the vision of the girls coming across Great
South Bay from Sayville to Cherry Grove on great seahorses, to
anchor at Belvedere. I thought of the party there as I walked around
Tivoli—Miss Sally Katt plugged into the wall and walking around
with her extension cord, looking like a summer Christmas tree and
terrifying everybody that she would fall into the pool and electro-
cute them all. I remembered the host, the *pope*, calling himself
Silvestro and appearing at midnight to the prerecorded sound of
the bells of St. Peter's, and blessing the huddled, fornicating masses,
yearning to breathe free in purgation through excess. Tell me, dear,
you who have looked long and hard into these matters, how *did*
the idea of yearning to breathe free translate so quickly into the
compulsion to freebase?"

"Better new friends than old foes, dear, and most especially
that oldest of old foes, Loneliness. By the time I got up to Stockholm on the *Alfred Nobel*, I hadn't had any real company but
Vana's, and hilarious as that had been, it was, basically, Chinese food—know what I mean? I was just *that* fed up with
screwing on and surveying the room with that bold, indifferent
glance of those who dine alone. Your mother was getting to feel,
dear, as she journeyed from metropolis to metropolis, like King
Ahasuerus in the Bible. Remember? Fleeing from himself and
other men."

"How could I possibly remember that?" I countered. "Catholics don't read the Bible. How do you?"

"Remind me to tell you," she cooed, "some snowy night in

front of the fire, how I took the Good Book up. Meanwhile, I wonder—do we get *tsouris* from Ahasuerus?"

"Better ask Professor Bloom."

"I'll do that, darling, the very next time I'm crossing Washington Square on the way to Tower Records—or when I next run up to New Haven to pick the ivy off the walls of Yale, and see him schlepping it to the lecture hall. 'Yoo-*hoo*, Professor Bloom!' I shall call out, and then, having attracted his attention, say to him, 'By the *way*, now that I *have* you, I have a little *bone* to pick with you. I must tell you that in my candid opinion, no woman wrote Genesis. Women are simply not possessed of the specific irony you attribute to J. It is a clear-cut case of right church, wrong pew. After innumerable close readings of the material at hand, I twig the author as one of the innumerable illegitimate sons of Solomon, whose *truc* it was to operate in drag as the nurse-confidante of the Queen of Sheba. It is my belief that he called himself "Vashti." Oh, and of course, he's black.'

"Dining alone had really only worked in Paris, at the Crillon, and only then because I'd remembered what La Dorsay used to say about it, after she came back to the States and started in going into the frog ponds uptown at six o'clock, where she'd sit down—very obviously a black man in a dress—shackled in the *rivière* she'd acquired from gentlemen of consequence in Paris, ordering in her perfect French, and remembering and repeating to herself what I'd told her about the great wartime Tiffany ad *Be Valiant in Diamonds.* Order her dinner like the Duchesse de Praslin, consume it ditto, and pay for it always with a crisp Ben Franklin ('becawse the French a-*doah* him, chile, to this day'). She would say to me, *Il y a dans ce geste tout ce que j'aime dans mes plaisirs solitaires—a la fois de la violence, de la douleur, et un curieux bien-être: une sensation de brulure.* That was Hilda in a phrase: hot stuff on ice.

"She kept the diamonds always, through all the dark and terrible months, wearing them to the Welfare office on Fourteenth Street, where she convinced the kindly social worker they were but rhinestones to keep her ailing regal spirits up. She wore them to GMHC meetings, and in the hospital. Having succeeded in wringing every gay penny she could out of Social Security, only then, dying, she sold them—through a friend who'd risen from towel boy at the Mt. Morris Baths to purveyor of that-which-is-forever on Forty-seventh Street—and gave the cash to the Lambda Legal Defense Fund. Then, as she lay dying, with those of us left to her gathered around her, she turned to the nurse and declared, 'These, Cornelia, are my jewels.' No matter the nurse's name was *Corazon:* Hilda had her final say. *There* was a girl—a *diva*—worthy of the title *Travesti*.

"Also, there is that about Stockholm, of all European cities, where—*pace* Miss Garbo—being left alone is almost life threatening, even in high summer. Perhaps paradoxically because it is *so* safe—that is, when Vana Sprezza's husband and his Masonic co-horts are not collaborating with the CIA in the assassination of the Swedish prime minister. You feel utterly unmolested there, but all the same, you might see your reflection in one too many window-panes in that curious northern light, break it, and slit your throat right there on the sidewalk. . . .

"Anyway, new friends. I liked Barb Vesteralen right away, for her laugh—a laugh, in the words of my aunt May Kelleher, *like a slow drain*. It took me a bit longer to warm to Doug—although he did say very smart things right off the bat, as you might expect from a full professor of Cognitive Science with a passion for base-ball, opera, and *film noir*. Unnerving. He remarked, for instance, that tourism had replaced war as civilization's scourge, adding that the only way to combat it was to follow the instructions of the Maquis during the occupation of France: *Make the* boche *fall off trains; make him fall off buses; make him late; don't deliver his letters. If you are taking care of his car, ruin it.* 'They've done all that to *us*, honey,' Barb drawled back, 'and *we* keep coming back for more. Why's that?' 'Well,' I said, 'they haven't done any of that to *me.*' I should have said *yet*—or touched wood: There was plenty of it there, backstage at the Royal Theater at Drottningholm—but I didn't, so they got me, in Amsterdam. A nightmare. . . .

"You really ought to think about playing Drottningholm—if only in memory of Gustav III. Remember, he was the fairy king murdered at the masked ball—Scribe wrote the play and Verdi the opera, and they both used the girl as the beard for the real story, although Verdi got close casting the page as a soprano. People sometimes say they can't figure out what Oscar is doing in *Ballo*. I can.

"Anyway, we were touring the place, and it's always in an empty theater that somebody says something and I know somebody's just walked over my grave—located right underneath the up-center trapdoor. What happens is I awake in the grave, and they're all supposed to be up there onstage, but they're *not*. Consequently, there's no cue, and consequently, *no resurrection*. I'm dead and buried and that's it—I get to stay in a lot. What the somebody—who was the guide—said was that Gustav was known to be *temperamental*. Something called a temperament. All I can ever hear when I hear that word is *Danny is—well—*tempera-*mental*. The way they always accented the last part—*mental*. As Margo rejoins, when *she's* behaving temperamentally, *cut—print it! What happens now—do I get carried off screaming to the snake pit?* See what I mean? I bet you do."

"Doug Vesteralen is one of those American specimens you hardly even consider here—they've become so numerous—but that in Europe—particularly sitting in a compartment on a slow train through Norway—can make you remember for your scarlet sins *exactly* what *varsity* meant. You know, the shining knight in the Chevrolet: perfection of hair, teeth, bones; line, proportion, coloring, expression. A type which, like the Scandinavian red barns, has become an archetype, a *sine qua non* in the checklist of the American idea of goodness—and need we stress that goodness, of course, has *nu-thin'* t'do with it? Neither, of course, does wickedness—not neces-sarily, anyway; merely only too often. You mentioned Glinda Westcott in the show—she had a good description of one, a soldier she cruised on a bus once—or maybe she watched the soldier cruis-ing somebody else. Anyway, she said the soldier was *exactly like certain portraits of those Nordics, Lombards, or Ostrogoths*—she couldn't, as usual, poor dear, make up her overstimulated mind—*who invaded and ruined Italy in the Dark Ages.* By which she probably meant 1944. . . . The type has always made your mother nervous, maybe because—well, it's a morbid assertion, but to me an awful lot of them, the Doug Vesteralens, look an awful lot like their exact opposite numbers on what was once the other side. Also, because I think that either a disproportionate number of them—on both sides—got blown to ragged body parts in Nor-mandy in '44, or your mother was wearing toe shoes at Omaha, instead of, and not under, her army boots. In fact, they *were* the ones in Doug Vesteralen's life: his uncles and father—dead in France and in the Norwegian campaign—and that's how the war-tourism comparison came up so readily. Consequently, Doug was raised in Minnesota by women, and I'd have to say well, because he was so unfussed by having an old drag queen—but that's jumping ahead. He was initially so *interested* in *everything* that, after dinner in Stockholm, over the cloudberry liqueur, after they told me about this masquerade party they'd gone to the year before, he as a Swiss mountain climber and she as the Matterhorn, I told them both what I was up to: at that point, rehearsing Miss Charity's funeral rites.

"Now, you want to talk about a specific and demanding drill? Cast upon still waters in the fjord at Ålesund, in the twilight at one in the morning. *How* she *knew* the waters would be *that* still, one must ask her in heaven. Anyway, the details of the Norwegian expedition were spooky—Norway itself gave your mother ripples:

just enough like *Song of Norway* to be enticing, before turning—in Oslo—and, my dear, if you've never been there, *scratch* it *right* off your list—turning into something quite determinedly grim.

"We had a good laugh about Norway on the boat—after the obsequies at Ålesund, when Doug found a flyer at the purser's desk and handed it to me, saying, 'Since you haven't done this, maybe we should. You're into the epic quest, and, as I remember from Classical Lit, in every example of the epic quest, the hero goes to hell and back; it's part of the proposition.' I didn't bother to remind him I'd already done that—that there was even a movie title indicating a lot of us had—I suppose because the men in his life all had been issued one-way tickets, and I was also thinking of the kid who's asked me, *lately?* Oh, but here—I saved the flyer; thought you'd get a kick out of it. If you and Phil ever do go to Norway, you can do it for me, and tell me. The train leaves from Trondheim—the old capital—which *is* a town worthy of inclusion on your itinerary."

"*Wes*-hamp'n—*Quogue* next!"

Odette produced the flyer from her capacious handbag. Printed in black and white, it featured a picture in vanishing-point perspective of a long black train, headed with one of those very anthropomorphic-looking square-windowed diesel engines—very like the Long Island Rail Road, but more *Euro* and sinister-looking—and contained the following information.

> SPECIAL OFFER 4 - YOU ! Would you like to take a day trip
> to Hell-station and a safe return—by train of course.
> HELL-station can issue the famous HELL CERTIFICATE.
> The station office is open from 7:15 a.m. to 14:45 p.m.

From Trondheim 9:25 a.m.   Platform no. 1
From Hell   11:32 a.m.   Platform no. 3*
                              Arrives Trondheim 12:00 p.m.
Price Trondheim - Hell - Trondheim NKr. 25.-
Information 52 64 69   * (Platform no. 1 Saturdays)
Go by train and save the environment

"I think the part I like best is the telephone number," Odette remarked, as I pored over the text. "Sort of represents my idea of your mother's measurements, when she finally decides to let go and let God fatten her up for the worms."

Once again, I couldn't think of a single thing to say. All I could remember was everybody at Lincoln Hall giggling crazily in Church history class about the Diet of Worms.

"But I'm ahead of myself again. It was still back in Stockholm, drinking all that cloudberry liqueur, that we concocted the scheme that got your mother *through* the Norwegian fjord experience. Or you might argue that the scheme was itself that same experience, so *signal* was—I don't know—but to use one of Doug Vesteralen's pet words, it was the m.o. that *obtained*.

"It came about when, in an effort to be sociable—and I suppose, well, you know, more *normal* or something, after scattering all the info about the *pompes funèbres*—I asked Doug if he was carrying any pictures of his kids in his wallet, which of course he was. Four pictures, two kids, one of each, two informal, two formal: high school graduation mug shots—lovely. Then he asked me did I have any of the girls, which of course I did: the one of all of us together, with you, at the Palm Gardens, that DeVors posed and took with the delayed trigger—in the pose for 'Eleven on a Ronson.' Do you know what? Well, two things, actually. You have another admirer in Barb Vesteralen—don't be surprised if a note appears soon one night backstage and a smiling couple arrives after curtain call. And secondly, there was an actual resemblance between Miss Charity—rawboned Scandinavian knockout that she was—and the Vesteralen daughter, a very intelligent-looking, perhaps rather precocious, and obviously alluring girl, bearing a striking resemblance—more striking, really, than that to Miss C.—to the young Dorothy Malone, as she appears in the book shop in *The Big Sleep.* I suppose I thought that especially since—slanting back in the other direction once more—I recalled that *La Carità* had patterned her entire life performance—successfully, against the odds, if you come to think about it—on the Dorothy Malone of a decade later, in *Written on the Wind.* Oh God, dear, will you *ever* forget her just zooming in every chance she got with *You mean* usually; *You've* had *it; I'm filthy,* period; and *She saw the end of a marriage, and the beginning of a love affair!*

"Anyway, we got on the subject of offbeat resemblances, and Doug actually said I reminded *him* of his *mother*—at which Barb's slow-drain laugh suddenly went manic, and turned into a case of hiccups. Now, as I indicated earlier, I remember from one dead pope just how serious hiccups can get—although it *was* rumored that Pia Pacelli got hers because she opened the Letter from Fatima before it was supposed to be opened in 1960. So I said so. 'Huh?' Doug wondered; they're not Catholic. 'I *mean,* Our *Lady* of Fatima,' I corrected myself, 'Mary the Mother of God, *not* King Hussein of Jordan's great-great-great-etcetera-grandmother, Mohammed's *daughter* Fatima.' 'There was a cigarette called "Fatima," ' said Doug. 'Remember?' But Barb went on hiccuping away. People have funny reactions to their in-laws. Actually, I'd already decided that Doug was that very type of man—the median—they say always marries his mother—so that when he said *that* about *me.* . . . Well, the upshot of the whole thing was that finally Barb— whose train of thought to hell and back was obviously the same as mine—held her breath for about two minutes and just *guffawed* for about another two minutes—I mean, my dear, the pipes underneath the drain had *burst*—and then suddenly turned very casually to me, as though for the past ten minutes she'd been concentrating at bridge rather than having an episode, and said 'Dagmar.' *'Dagmar,'* said Doug, 'who's *Dagmar?'* 'Dagmar Vesteralen—*Mrs.* Dagmar Vesteralen!' Barb replied, and of course I twigged the scenario like *that*, then and there, and in about ten seconds I had the voice, and said in it, 'So, what's the setup? Show me to my cabin.'

" 'My mother's name is Mary Jane,' Professor Vesteralen announced at this point, somewhat unnecessarily perhaps, but very much in character. 'So was Mae West's,' Barb replied. 'Yes,' Doug continued, 'well, mother's always been called "M.J.," except by some old friends, who called her "Stretch"—I've never known why.' 'Well,' said Barb, with the authority of an experienced Blanche Bickerson, 'drawing a veil over that subject, if we may, your mother is now called "Dagmar." But what will she *wear?* Do we outfit her in Oslo?' 'That,' I replied, 'will not be necessary,' and, turning to Doug, advised him, in the manner of those mothers who like their daughters-in-law well enough but prefer to let them overhear remarks rather than addressing them directly, 'Your mother keeps a selection of suitably stylish frocks stashed away under the corduroys for just such madcap occasions.' I was thinking of all my pretty Dora Krebs originals and already seeing myself resplendent in them while trying to work out an outfit that would read Woman of Consequence on deck aboard the MS *Elfhaven*, sailing from Trondheim to Bergen two days thence, at six o'clock in the morning. You will appreciate the problem if you give it only a little of the compassionate thought you're famous for—*also* famous for. *Any* woman can walk out on deck looking endowed after lunch, but to walk up the gangplank of what is essentially a gussied-up mail boat at—well, I can't say dawn, because there almost *is* no dawn on the coast of Norway in July—at 6:00 a.m., looking, in the words of Henry James, *possessed of a perfect plain propriety, an expensive, subdued suitability.* And they didn't even ring the angelus.' "

"We ended the night pretty drunk. Doug got rather carried away by the fact that Stockholm had just refused to name a street after Garbo, and started singing, very loudly,

Wenn die Königin von Schweden
Bei geschlossen Fensterladen
Mit Apollokerzen onaniert. . . .

'If you're going to be his mother,' Barb asked me, 'could you practice by getting him to pipe down? It can't be any fun to be taken for disruptive Krauts and flung in the Stockholm hoosegow, whatever you've got on.'

"So, we booked in together in Oslo and gave Dagmar a trial run—up to the palace and back—and I must say the rigout did turn more than just a few heads in the Christiania that was. Oslo was totally unprepared for your mother as the older Glenda Farrell, even dressed down in Dora Krebs. *What*, I said to myself, would have been the upshot had I waltzed out in a Norma Kamali, or even a Jhane Barnes ensemble. And darling, the heads we turned in the Norwegian capital were strictly cabbage—*no* candidates!

"We sailed from Trondheim, the day after the next, at 6:00 a.m.—as an American family."

"It was such a bright hazy day out on the water—and remember, we're talking about an endless daylight day. For an inveterate night-owl it was tantamount to a low-yield mescaline trip. Thanks be to God there was no neon anywhere, or *I'd* have gone into the drink like Ida Lupino as Helen Chernin in *The Hard Way*. Such a haze held that the whole of the legendary Norwegian coast, so veiled, so silhouetted and chalky—the most vivid color being the lacquered walnut of the taffrail underscoring the view—that I felt like I was living through a bleached-out pastel print of *Imitation of Life*, or one of those very long mid-August excursions on the Hudson River Day Line to Poughkeepsie. At least until we passed the land formation they call the Seven Sisters and entered the harbor at Kristiansund—which sort of looked like Sheepshead Bay, if you've even been out in a boat from Canarsie after lunch at McGuinness's. By that time Barb and I had hunkered down in deck chairs and were *being girls together*, like Bette Davis as Charlotte Vale and Who-Was-That-Anyway? Deb Whatsis in *Now Voyager*—and there was a time, dear, when your mother could have gone on 'The $64,000 Dollar Question' and won a lot of money with the correct answers to Who That Was and Deb Whatsis. No more: don't put her on 'Jeopardy' tomorrow—the whole while Doug and some Brit were sitting inside doing a jigsaw puzzle of Trollfjord and trying to figure out when the sun was going to cross the yardarm. 'Odd sort of bird,' Doug remarked later. 'Never asked me question one about myself—or about either of you. I don't get Brits.' 'What *is* a yardarm, exactly?' Barb asked me. I felt so *rounded* being able to tell her, like an accomplished, matey, can-do woman—you know, sort of middle-period Stanwyck—who knew about such things as secants and celestial navigation as a matter of course.

"After Canarsie—Kristiansund—and dinner, suddenly dramatic sheer palisades and ski slopes in the middle distance, and at one point a massive configuration resembling the head and torso of a woman lying facedown. At the fjord at Molde a whole string of snow-capped Alps—and everywhere tiny toy villages with gaily painted homes perched on outcropped clusters at the shoreline, smaller than Breezy Point and Cherry Grove—some nearly only the size of those stone groins or jetties or whatever they're called that Juan Trippe had the Army Corps of Engineers construct—that dart out like skeleton fingers into the Atlantic, supposedly to protect the shoreline of the fabulous, dazzling resort we're barreling out to, even as I speak, only, as it turns out, they, like so much else, do the opposite, and the moral of the story is. . . . Lots of little patio parties—like at the Grove: one imagined little floor shows on the leeward porches, perhaps as exuberant—if not as detailed—as those at Roseland and Belle Rive.

"Southward in still waters, in a timeless interval; the Germans fell silent: there *were* spirits hovering. . . .

"Ålesund is very like Santoríni—the harbor is surrounded by mountains. We walked around the town while the Brits and the Germans went separately into the hotel to get more to drink, and then, when at 1:00 a.m. the boat started up again, we tossed Miss Charity into its wake—in the bottle-green, silver, and indigo twilight. Barb hummed a bit of what she remembered of Åse's Lament from Grieg's *Peer Gynt* Suite, and off we went to bed.

"On the late morning of the next day, en route to Bergen, the boat, slowing to dead-slow, passed through the narrow fjord channels cut by the Ice Age glaciers into a geological area resembling Monument Valley. I was reminded of the fact that for decades I've fantasized flooding that set. Some have said it's because I want to be a kind of Moses in John Ford westerns, others that I'm forecasting the tidal wave and aftermath of the earthquake that will destroy the Los Angeles we know.

"Then, just before Bergen, the landscape resumed the look of Dutchess County as viewed from the decks of the old Hudson River Day Line, and it was as if we were coming down to New York from Nyack. There was a bit of an incident. Doug overheard the Brit he'd been jigsaw puzzling with say, 'Oh, we know a couple of terrible old fairies back home. It's the mothers are the cause of it—terrible old dragons, both of 'em, and when they get *together*—' 'That's funny,' Doug suddenly shot across the salon—loud—'*my* mother here is an absolute *prince*, and I'm queer as a three-dollar bill. So's my sister here—aren't ya, Biff! Anyway, if it takes a dragon lady to make a fairy out of a son, then what made *you* the straightforward mess *you* are, I wonder?' I *did* admire him so, at that moment. As the aforementioned Glinda the Good Witch of the Northeast so wisely counseled, 'It's best not to fight back, but if you feel you must, if you can't help it, then for pity's sake fight *dirty!*' It's the *for pity's sake* I find so adorable, and right to the point—and Doug Vesteralen was at that moment an *absolutely* adorable, right-to-the-point heterosexual male. And you *know* I don't find too many of *them that.*

"Nevertheless, I felt the situation needed a little hosing down—a thing I've always been good at in the heat of the moment. *'Douglas!'* I cut in with strong-backbone matronly severity. 'You were brought up to express yourself like a gentleman, and a gentleman is *never* cruel to a *moron!* If you are at all planning to continue carrying on in this fashion, your mother is going to have to restrict—perhaps even withhold altogether—the poppers and the wheeze!' 'Sorry, mother,' he replied, and then, 'Holy *shit!* Now they know we've all been traveling under false pretenses! Is incest illegal in Norway? Are *drugs?'* 'Never mind,' I huffed, 'they can hardly make us walk the plank—they can only throw us off at Bergen, and we are disembarking at Bergen anyway. In the meantime, may I remind you that we are hardly commercial travelers; we are the Vesteralens of Laguna Niguel. It is unpleasant enough having to be on board this ship of fools—you must learn how *not* to leave yourself and us susceptible to the untoward advances of common tourists!' I was particularly proud of that *untoward.* You never hear an American use the word, and I didn't Brit it up, either. I said it the way Hayes would have—in fact, if I may correct myself, the whole delivery was rather more on the Hayes than on the Glenda Farrell level: rather like Helen's performances in *The Show-Off*, if you remember. People have said a lot of dreadful things about that girl over the years, but there are two virtues that, as they obtain in her case, we ought particularly to consider and prize: she's Irish, and she's still here, the way we are.

"We caught the express from Bergen to Copenhagen, where, in the Tivoli Gardens, we dined at Pepe's Pizzeria. Then the Vesteralens went off to the airport, and your mother, a man again, hopped onto the *Alfred Nobel* to Hamburg, and there—ignoring the blandishments of the Rieperbahn—climbed into her berth on the overnight to Amsterdam."

"The Amsterdam we loved—or thought we loved—the Amsterdam of prostitutes in picture windows and vaudeville at the Tuchinski, is, I'm sorry to have to tell you, finished. *Did* we love it, or were we just being sentimental because of the canals, the art deco at the American, the foreign-intrigue ambience of the Krasnapolsky, and the heartbreaking pictures on the bedroom wall at the Anne Frank house of Ginger Rogers and Garbo cut out from *Photoplay?* Or for the fact that old New York was once New Amsterdam? Whatever—it's disappeared, dear, vaudeville, hurdy-gurdies, foreign intrigue, and all. The American still features the art deco, but even that. . . . What's left—that is to say, always apart from one's old, dear friends—is canals and prostitutes in picture windows, the diamond market, of course, and drugs and dealing and stoned punk children along the banks of the Prinsengracht making ugly remarks at tourists coming out of the Anne Frank house, and a contemptible new breed of predator dispatched in swarms by some malevolent submarine agency to the Central Station, there to fan out over the unprotected platforms and with uncanny instinct mop the most valued pieces of your luggage the minute you descend and turn your back to seek porter assistance.

"It happened—right in front of the station police office—faster than the magician's sleight of hand in the Tuchinski vaudeville, and what they got—in the studded trunk, of course—was the diary, all the Dora Krebs originals, several pairs of comfy shoes, lots of mother's bijoux and all the little *ricordi* of the trip, *and* the rest of the remains—the remains of the remains of Captain Billywinks—slated for deposit in the holy well at Ballintubber. And, of course, you can be sure without my telling you—because I'm telling you I didn't see it happen, they were that good—they hauled the thing off sideways, so that undoubtedly the shoes fell out of their pockets, the dresses fell off their hangers, the diary probably fell out of its case, and Captain Billywinks—Miss Faith—there in the urn. . . . Not that that matters—in fact, it sort of reminded me when I thought about it in the station restaurant of what happens when, as I have heard, surviving spouses arrange to have their incinerated deceased encased in functional hourglass egg timers. But all the same, the ugliness—and that first sickening feeling, when I turned and realized—and the scene with the police shortly afterwards. The meaningless forms, the listing of the contents—costumes, private papers, and, since something deep and Continental told me *not* to say the remains of the dead, a box of very expensive Scandinavian *talcum powder!* Of course, the minute I'd said all that and watched the secretary write it all down, I thought, God forgive me, I'll never dust with Ashes of Roses again!

"But, then, as always, friends—theatrical friends—proved the surest balm, and, as always, a bath—well, dear, of all there is about your mother that says Blanche DuBois the most telltale is her deep love of the solitary soak. There she was, so, on the Rosmarijnsteeg, deep in a lovely rosemary-oil bath, while Jenn and Robbie put their heads together in the kitchen as to the best way to get Miss Faith Healy's remains returned—providing that they weren't already sunk in their urn rightside-up, upside-down, or sideways deep in the Amstel. As it turned out, they weren't; the thieves seemed to have had gypsy wisdom in them, or available to them, and so had kept safe what they knew was someone else's more-than-sentimental property."

———

" 'The play's the thing,' said Robbie, as I emerged, feeling refreshed and restored, in self if not in raiment. 'The thing to catch the conscience, isn't that the idea?'

"The conscience of the king, I thought, not of common thieves—but then I thought again: but conscience doth make cowards of us all, no? Or words to that effect. Quoting Miss Channing, *How does it go, groom? I played it once in stock in Wilkes-Barre.* And, musing expansively: what a nice thing to be able to say across a table, *groom*—and marking what a lovely groom Robbie makes, how courtly, how attentive, after so many years. . . . Your mother can get *very* sentimental over heterosexual marriage, dear—consequence, I rather imagine, of having had a mother and a father.

" 'What sort of play did you have in mind?' I asked. *'Antigone? Mother Courage?* Something by Beaumont and Fletcher?'

" 'Not a play, exactly,' the groom responded, meditatively. 'More of a *skit.*' "

"Well, I hadn't done anything you could call a skit since the early eighties, when Diane DeVors, Hildegarde Dorsay, Mercedes Benzedrine, and I teamed up with the Downtown Sissies in Revolt and that all-girl band at Danceteria in Haoui Montaug's No Entiendies cabaret to raise money for what was then called GRID. And that had been really a reprise of sixties Cherry Grove Playhouse routines like *Open Arms* and *Toots Sweet* and *Star Quality* and *All Woman.* What was the name of that all-girl band?"

"Pulsallama," I reminded her, remembering the evening perfectly, "and perhaps you remember a rather frantic girl on the same bill who made a nuisance of herself and called herself Madonna?"

"You know, I don't—what with so many people loitering about. . . . Of course, Pulsallama—what fun they were. I felt so revived by the kids in the early eighties—by their defiance in the face of Reagan. It was as if, in New York, at any rate, the Reagan eighties were not going to happen after all. You can almost, can't you, hear the thugs in Washington laughing, 'Hah, hah, *hah*, Blanche' at us all. And Haoui was adorable—like a kindlier Oscar Levant; now he's dead, too.

" 'More of a *skit.*' With his lovely South African accent, Robbie always hits his *T*s. Like in his first response to Jenn's idea of making a public appeal to the thieves, to be left on a placard leaning against the statue known as *Het Lieverdje—The Little Rascal*—that stands in front of the Athenaeum bookstore. 'Fat chance!' he said—but it came out sounding like *fett chahnce. Fett* as in *fetlock* and *chahnce* as in Chance Wayne, the way Miss Page said it in *Sweet Bird of Youth.* Anyway, the skit was Robbie's idea, and so I was put back in the way of thinking skit, and further away, as my hair dried, from the bathtub fantasy of actually going on some fine day in a charity benefit as Blanche DuBois or Alexandra del Lago.

"We three sat up all night that night, devising the skit for the Mickery, which turned out to be—but you know."

I knew. Odette had sent O'Maurigan the videotape made at the Mickery in Amsterdam (a theater now itself sadly defunct) of *Cave of Seraphic Acrobats*, which, after a tantalizing delay—the tape required conversion to the American VCR system—we programmed as a Halloween entertainment out in Sagaponack, inviting a select crowd of companionable (surviving) crazies. (What Odette declared on the train that night about Helen Hayes was something we'd decided was true of just about anybody, Irish or otherwise, about whom over the years we might have felt and said sharp things: just the fact that they were still *around.* . . .)

Made the summer before Martha Graham's death, *Cave of Seraphic Acrobats* opens onstage at the Mickery with a videotaped "interview" between the pythoness Ancient of Dancing Days (Jenn Ben-Yakov, in a plaster-of-Paris mask onto which the Graham head, shot circa 1980, had been phototransferred) and Stolichnaya, the most illustrious of all the terpsichorean defectors from all the Russias, joining the Graham company for one last gala before her scheduled return-in-triumph to the Motherland. ("I throw myself on President Mikhail Sergeyevich Gorbachev's *perestroika*, also on sovereign Soviet people's great understanding of artist soul-agony.") Graham, nodding, issues a statement from the echo chamber of the mask: *All artists bleed to death today. They will resurrect tomorrow to atone for yesterday's political and bureaucratic crimes against humanity.* Blackout and Fate theme from *Swan Lake*.

The Fate theme from *Swan Lake* segues into the serene opening of the second act of *Giselle*. Stolichnaya, as Myrtle, Queen of the Seraphic Acrobats, enters grandly *en bourrée* from upstage left, and after a few crosses disappears into the stage-right wings, to emerge moments later in backless carpet slippers, and trailing a long white scarf, in imitation of Nikya in the Kingdom of the Shades scene of *La Bayadère*. Schlepping it to center stage, where are grouped *en attitude* the corps de ballet—beefy boys in spandex gym tights and double sets of shoulder pads with wings affixed, led by a big blond Dutchman called Willy—she does a number with them in which all get hopelessly entangled in the white silk scarf. Willy, extricating himself, presents Myrtle with the gamekeeper Hilarious—Robbie Hahn, dressed like the statue *Het Lieverdje*, in short pants, wearing horn-rimmed glasses and carrying a butterfly net—apprehended by the acrobats while attempting to trap a black swan. Reprise *Swan Lake* theme.

Myrtle, in mime, tells Hilarious he is way out of his class, yet she feels for him—and starts first feeling him up, then wrapping him up in the white scarf, from which the corps has meanwhile disentangled itself. Enter Black Swan, a young, strong, slightly sickle-footed Surinamese classical ballerina. She and Willy immediately launch into the Black Swan pas de deux. Hilarious breaks free of Myrtle's embrace and attempts to cut in, offering the white silk scarf. The Black Swan fingers it like a customer, then she and Hilarious begin a parody of the *Bayadère* Act Two pas de deux. Myrtle, furious, turns on Hilarious, seizing the white silk scarf. The acrobats seize Hilarious, and the black ballerina goes into her thirty-two fouettés routine—but to the tune of the French cancan from the Offenbach *Orpheus in the Underworld* ("Orpheus in His Underpants" we used to call it when Ballet Theatre did it in the old days)—kicking the victim in the face with each one. Hilarious falls down dead on the floor. The acrobats cover him with the white silk scarf. Myrtle, distraught at the lengths to which jealousy has driven her, pulls the white silk scarf off Hilarious and, rolling all over the floor, entangling herself in it (yet again), goes yet again mad. The acrobats are bereft.

Act Two. Mad Myrtle descends into the Underworld in search of Hilarious. Voice of Jacob Beltane on the soundtrack from one of his fifties LPs: Orpheus singing *L'espoir renaît dans mon âme.* A great oven is roaring upstage center, processing the dead, who arrive as corpses on a conveyor belt from stage right and go out as little urns stage left. Jenn as Martha Graham appears as Dementia, Queen of Hell. She is impressed with Myrtle's dancing (a wild Graham parody of contractions and leaps), and when Myrtle pulls out from her mouth—in the gesture meant to be symbolic of her helpless longing— the white silk scarf, the two begin to haggle over a trade. Dementia snaps her fingers, and from the corps of red devils the hunk who had played Willy in Act One arrives with the urn containing the Hilarious ashes. This is Dementia's final offer: the scarf for the urn. Ecstatic, and cured of her madness, Myrtle straps her toe shoes back on and *bourrées* offstage with the urn, accompanied by Gluck's Dance of the Blessed Spirits, leaving Dementia to wrap herself up in the white silk scarf. . . .

On the way back up to the entrance to the Cave of Seraphic Acrobats, Myrtle is tempted out of her *bourrée* by the big blond devil who was Willy, and, giving in, unlacing her toe shoes once more, goes into a parody of Graham's Medea-Jason pas de deux. At its climax, devil Willy throws Myrtle to the floor, and the corps makes off with the urn containing Hilarious's ashes, tossing it back and forth across the stage like a volleyball. Utterly defeated, barefoot, and distraught, Stolichnaya comes downstage, and, after a weak attempt to mime it, gives up and, as Odette O'Doyle, addresses the audience. As she tells the story of Miss Faith Healy in English, Jenn translates it into Dutch. . . .

It was really something, even on the videotape, watching Odette work that room. It used to be said of her turns that she left not a dry leg in the house; of this one it could truly be said that hardly a dry eye remained. She told it as the great New York story it is—the exile from Staten Island, the Bagel Nosh funeral, and all—but invoking everything she knew about the Amsterdamers' sense of justice and fair play and praising, without fawning over them, their energy and ingenuity, and reminding them more than once that old New York had been New Amsterdam. She declared that although she didn't absolutely hold with all the lengthy extensions of the metaphor of AIDS as a new Holocaust, she would trust them, as a people who had lived under siege and tried to do what they could for human dignity. . . . She concluded in Dutch, turned, and walked upstage into the dark. Phil and I sat there crying like teenagers.

"We played *Cave* for three nights at the Mickery, and in the afternoons we went and checked the flea market to see if any of the Dora Krebses had surfaced. Nothing—and then, on the third night, a note in Dutch, concluding *man en paard noemen*, was delivered to the stage door directing us to the statue *Het Lieverdje*. There, around the statue's neck, was a key on a string—a key to a locker at the Central Station, number 666. The Black Swan girl with the slightly sickled foot didn't like that at all, and warned us that the locker would probably blow up in our face when we opened it. I said the only terrorists

who'd ever come after me had been Roman Catholic priests and the
I.R.S., and that so far as the number 666 was concerned, what it
meant to me was a tall building on Fifth Avenue at Fifty-third Street
with its address lit up at night in red just like the RCA Building a few
blocks to the south and west and the Pepsi-Cola sign a mile or so east
across the river in Long Island City. So off we went at midnight, just
as the time was up and they were coming around, with determined
Dutch precision, to empty out the lockers, and there it was—they
were: the urn and my diaries, but, of course, not a thread of the drag,
nor so much as a buckle of a shoe. Fair enough. We went out to
celebrate at a gorgeous Indonesian place in Nova Zembla and brought
Miss Faith along, exactly as we'd done when we carted her from
Crown of Thorns into the Bagel Nosh—only this time she got to be
guest of honor at a divine *rijstafel* meal, and instead of the Muzak,
which had treated the mourners at the Bagel Nosh to homogenized
versions of 'I'm a Native New Yorker' and 'I Will Survive,' there was
a lovely tape of Javanese gamelan music to lull her shade, or that half
of it, anyway, destined for the holy well at Ballintubber."

"Happy ending," I proposed.

"It's getting near that time, isn't it," she said. "Well, happy end
of curve of loop, anyway—and you see now what I meant when I
said I was glad about leaving old May Healy's bonds and stock certificates with O'Maurigan. I knew I'd catch up with her—I felt I would—
and while I was willing to tell her about the Bagel Nosh funeral, I
was somehow unwilling to tell her about Amsterdam—or, for that
matter, about anything to do with the trip except that I'd dumped
Captain Billywinks in the holy well at Ballintubber and decided to
drop in on her while I was in the neighborhood.

"But meanwhile, the neighborhood *that* puts your mother back
into is back on the Continent, on the train with the girl professor and
the *nouvelle interpolée*, bound for—where are we, by the way, anywhere near *our* destination?"

"Quogue," I replied. "But first tell me one thing." I'd either forgotten or had never known, and confessed it. "Did Stolichnaya have a Christian name?"

"Oh, very definitely—Agrafena."

"Thanks."

"And a patronymic, too—although seldom used—Alexandrovna. Quogue? Not bad. . . . Back on the *Etoile du Nord*—Paris bound."

"Hamp'n Bays will be the *next stop!"*

"On the *Etoile du Nord,"* she repeated, "talking about American literature."

"You said you'd been rereading *Moby-Dick,"* I suggested. "It's about this whale."

"She wouldn't've gotten it—too serious. No, like every other ostentatiously educated American on a train in Europe, I was actually reading—rereading—Henry James. *The Ambassadors*—I'd grabbed it off the rack at the bookstall in Central Station. I hadn't looked at it since N.Y.U., when and where—need I tell you—you weren't allowed to *open your mouth and say 'boo'* if you hadn't read it. It and at least a half dozen others, and unless you'd also taken—or, at any rate, audited—Leon Edel's course. And had formed—or let's say *forged*—as a *direct consequence* of your reading and explication of the texts a *point of view on adult life.* That was just the way it was. At Columbia you couldn't get laid by *anybody* unless you had taken Lionel Trilling and Jacques Barzun, read the metaphysical poets, and gotten into the habit of staying in on Saturday night to listen to De Koven so you could rave on all week long about Locatelli—the composer, not the cheese. And at N.Y.U. you couldn't get anybody to even show you his snapshots of the Amalfi coast or play you his Piaf records until you said something about poor old Hattie Jaques. The undergraduates who

used to go to see the *Carry On* films on Forty-second Street after the
Met and before the Everard had started calling the Master that, and
I took it up as part of my nostalgia for London—never *imagining* I'd
wind up on the screen opposite the girl herself."

"And that," I remarked, "was how you fell into discussion with
the professor."

"Exactly how. As I said, do you know any American who has
not, at one time or another riding on a train in Europe, had a conversation about a Hattie Jaques novel?"

"Yes—me."

"*That's* because *you* are more interesting than anything Hattie
Jaques *ever* observed or thought up.

"Anyway, there I was, with *The Ambassadors* in my lap, staring
out the window at Brabant and remembering the summer I took the
Edel course: one novel per lecture for a month—hilarious. I wanted
to do my paper on the so-called *little thing* that makes the fortune
the sexpot we used to call Chapstick Nuisance lives on in sin on the
Rive Gauche—the commodity he's supposed to go back to Asshole,
Mass., to oversee the manufacture of, the better that his offspring and
theirs and theirs might live lives of leisure on blind trusts. I decided it
was toilet paper. Edel was not amused, so I did one on 'The Polish
Joke as Paradigm of Reaction in *The Ambassadors*' that Max Patrick
over in the Seventeenth Century loudly proclaimed utterly brilliant—
gay old coot that he was—allowing that had the like of it been written
for his Milton course he'd have had it published in the *PMLA*.

"*Alors*, there was Madam Professor suddenly inquiring of my
pale reflection in the glass, *What more than vain appearance does the
wisest of us know?* It so happened I'd put the book down practically
on the very sentence, so conversation got going. I said that Lamebrain
Stretcher looking up in what Hattie calls *uncontrollable depraved cu-
riosity* at his quarry's windows on the Boulevard Malesherbes was but
a silhouette compared to Swann looking up in desperation at Odette's.
I opined that for long, hard sentences, psychological insight, and the

wild waving of the wings of utterance, Monsieur Marcel Proust pees all over Mister Henry James—who for me is nothing much more than a desperado appealing mainly to adolescents and refugees who have only ever listened at doorways or peeked through keyholes—one, in his own words, *stuck in the box like a schoolboy wishing not to miss a minute of the show.* Unable to go down-and-out with the gorgeous, prematurely gray-streaked Chapstick into the Parisian night. And that's how the expression *nouvelle interpolée* came up, because Hattie did concoct good stories, implemented in some very gay diction. Such as, *On wet nights after wild pleasures, thinking things over, on the return, in lonely four wheelers,* etcetera. . . . And, of course, most poor fools—most poor American fools—do end up exactly like Lamebrain, with his exasperating jelly-mold of a life. Your mother's been fortunate, and so has her faithful, handsome, auburn-haired cavalier—God between us and all harm. . . .

"I asked the professor what it was like for a foreigner to read Hattie's English and try to understand it. 'It isn't at all necessary you should understand it; it will do well enough if you simply remember it—or remember the travail of it.' Well, that made a little sense, especially since she was clever enough to say *travail* in English. It was rather like what could be said of my mission—then all but done; I hadn't really understood it—I'd have had to be far more empathetic to the dying in their throes to do that—but I shall to my own dying day, of course, remember the travail of it. They needn't, really, have returned the diary; I mean, listen to me remembering it now as we speak—or as *I* do. . . .

"I'll tell you what else I remember, though, in relation to the novels of Henry James. I remember sitting up all night in cold baths that summer when I got through them all one a day for the lectures—and sometimes sitting half-submerged on the steps of the shallow end of the Everard cold plunge, just as you recalled it tonight in the show—and I remember life as a consequence taking on a crazy, heightened *aura,* more-or-less comparable to the *Dress Stage* doodlebug blitz days, and the cognac-and-coffee-drenched Liberation of Paris days, during which any minute at all might, too, be your last.

"The professor then insisted that Hattie knew—really *knew*— about women, but Marcel Proust knew only, really, about duchesses— that is to say, about female killers and female climbers. 'Henry James,' she pronounced, 'understood women as *types*—which was all they were, even in his purview, permitted to be.' *Purview*—she used words like *purview* and *strategy* throughout the entire conversation, al- though, thank God, she never descended to the hideousness of *over and against*. 'Exemplary types, cautionary types—types, to be sure, with many *facets*. He says, for example, that Madame de Vionnet, despite her shoulders, could be fifty women.' "

"Shoulders," I remarked. "Garbo."

"Oh, *exactly* what *I* said," Odette replied. "Garbo—fifty women, or forty, anyway, or let's say thirty-eight: one for each year of her life until her retirement after *Two-Faced Woman*. Wasn't she thirty-eight then?"

"I don't know—I never did know things like that."

"No, dear," she said, "you never needed to: still don't. All you need to know is *you're* thirty-eight—or look it. 'Marcel Proust,' the professor continued, 'on the other hand understood them—women— as *personnages:* each terribly singular and none really so wonderfully faceted—except perhaps Odette, the whore, a type that he felt he understood well enough to transport confidently across gender bar- riers.' 'Whore and proleptic duchess,' I replied sharply, whereupon, despite myself, I blushed, adding in a nearly absent murmur, 'Or merely would-be.' She couldn't have known, of course, what Odette meant to me, onomastically, and, anyway, didn't register notice. 'Henry James,' she concluded, 'was Platonic, if you like, and Proust was Aristotelian—also Cartesian. And the great question that divides us all, still, for all, perhaps, it should not do, is: Is the world Platonic or is the world Aristotelian-Cartesian-Freudian? For the world is both— that is to say, the Western world—*l'Occident*—is both. It is Platonic insofar as Atlantis was a real place, did exist, and did sink into the sea, leaving us everlastingly nostalgic, longing for lost ideals and the other half. It is Aristotelian and Cartesian and Freudian insofar as we must decide what to prepare for dinner and go to the market—arrange things, *sur n'importe quel prétexte,* so that the wits keep the cellular machine, the body envelope, intact—and carry on as if we really credited the teleological principle—as if we believed, after all, that all the individual objects and systems we encounter and participate in somehow subordinate their behavior to an overall plan or destiny which each of us calls his life—each one of which even arranges, *enfin,* its own demise.'

" 'Forty years ago,' I replied, 'in Paris, it was existential.' 'Ah,' she said, 'yes. That was when women went out in the evening wearing only black. That is no longer the case. Saint Laurent is completely crazy—it is only because he is always so depressed that he decrees black. Black is finished, forever. Even the Church knows this. One does not even wear black to funerals.' I thought to myself, well, woman, *you* had a hard time—consequence of all those years as the Black Swan, one supposes—giving up black. It wasn't until I read some very smart young fashion writer going at it with a vengeance that I gave in: saying truly *damning* things like *Only lawyers wear black now, and people who know what* leveraged buyout *means—people who liked* Cats *and people who desperately want to know the Kennedys.* Well, *that* did it: your mother has always been able to read the handwriting on the wall—all the way from *Kilroy was here* to Berlin in the eighties."

" '*Alors,*' I said, '*à propos des femmes,* I do like the women in *The Ambassadors* somewhat better than the men.' 'But, of *course* you do! Those men—at one time or another all of them, even the old duck who seems to be a takeoff on Dr. Watson—they all fall back on their cushions.' She did so—across three seats of the empty compartment—'and they exclaim, *ah, ah, ah,* as if they are either about to have asthma attacks or about to sing the music of Dalila.

All the women, on the other hand—even the little Mélisande figurine of the Vionnet daughter, whom old Dr. Watson calls *Miss Jane,* and even the silent Marie in Notre Dame—they all appear to be ready to roll up their sleeves and churn butter. They are all, as Henry James puts it so brilliantly, *never so lovely as when they are prostrate, and always quietest at feeding time. But,'* she went on, 'I know what you are going to say: you are going to tell me that these women are precisely because of these attributes the breeders and sustainers of that hideous class of clotheshorse vampire he— your Henry James—was devoted to: creatures who do nothing their whole lives long but tear off pieces of one another and eat them. *C'est ça!' 'Was* I going to say all that?' I asked.

" *'Weren't* you?' she replied, and I thought, Oh, well, let her talk; she's doing her Henry James–woman performance. And how remarkable that said woman should end up sounding like an abstract of Alexis Colby—who, of course, would never say *his* life, but for whom all systems and objects are nevertheless manifestly subordinate to same. And what has happened to money, and manufacturing in America. And how I wished Diane DeVors could have heard the conversation—and then I thought, who's to say she hasn't. I mean, I believe in Atlantis, for a gay start, and once you start believing. . . .

"Then she said, 'Henry James was for us a *prophet,* you see.' 'A prophet?' In a sudden flash, I saw—myself as the scourge and despoiler of prophets: Anatole France's Thaïs, or Oscar Wilde's Salome—or, more exactly, as Norma Desmond, both as herself, out for the head, heart, and hand of Erich Von Stroheim, and as Salome . . . babbling, *Valentino always said you could only tango on marble floors* and *It's the* pictures *that got small* and *Who is she, Joe, some carhop, some dress extra?* And, looking at my reflection in the late-afternoon glow of the train window, *I'm ready for my closeup, Mr. De Mille!*

" 'Yes, a prophet. For those of us, that is, who could read

him. For you must read him in English; he absolutely does *not* translate. Trying to read Henry James in French is like trying to read Racine in English. He can be read in German, of course—Henry James, not Racine—but that really is a hilarious case, and I don't think the practice will last, although you never know what practice will appeal to the new Berlin cabaret scene. It could be doing little scenes from Henry James novels, all in modern dress. Nevertheless, although he must be read in English, there is a cult of him growing in France that could in the nineties grow to the proportions of the cult forty years ago of Melville or the cult two centuries ago of Benjamin Franklin.'

" 'A prophet of *what?*' I persisted, having become terribly curious. 'Oh, of the American *advance*, of course.' 'The one, you mean, that started in '44 in Normandy.' 'But *exactly.*' I didn't tell her I'd landed there; it seemed too, I don't know, *complicated.* I'd have had to go into *Dress Stage* and, as it were, unpack—and the pointed costume trunk had been heisted. And I'd have to have introduced Odette, who was in a way still having her nap at the Crillon—waiting in Paris for Danny to join her and tell her all about his adventures on the Grand Tour. Also, checking Norma's closeup in the window, I vainly decided the professor would not credit the gentleman sharing the first-class compartment on the *Etoile du Nord* that afternoon with the requisite number of years to have participated in the landing at Omaha Beach, and, God be good to me, I was right. 'But exactly,' she continued. 'And when they arrived—those Americans, your predecessors, your avant-garde—it was for my parents' generation the landing of the *extra-terrestes—les extraterrestes de l'Amérique sidérale—a bien qui pourra.*' "

" 'For which *bien* we may conclude,' I countered, 'they, having never read Henry James, had never been properly prepared.'

" 'Exactly not.' Then, thinking of what she'd said about Hattie in *German*, I suddenly had this camp vision of her scenes being enacted *en travesti* in the new Berlin cabarets. The Germans think Shakespeare is better in German than in English; maybe they'd think Hattie was, too. Wouldn't it be a *scream?* Hattie Jaques catfights in *German.* Not since that summer Thalia Bridgewood tried *Turn of the Screw* at the Mawrdew Czgowchwz Theater on Manitoy and made it *sound* like German. . . .

" 'Do you in France,' I ventured, 'consider Henry James the Shakespeare of the novel?' *'Mais non!'* replied the professor in that wry manner that suggested she was not to be conned into a joke. *'Non—c'est drôle, ça, mais c'est absolument impossible.* Shakespeare knew all *about* men!'

"Once, on the beach, Miss Charity leafed through my copy of, I think it was *Wings of the Dove,* and remarked, 'Well, *dihr,* I dunno if this is for the ages, but it certainly is for the *aged.'*

"Extraterrestrials from stellar America—funny, that was always more or less how I viewed the supremely, achingly sensitive, finely calibrated American of Hattie's wild imagination. As calibrated and jittery as a fifties 3-D movie image you had to put on special glasses to see come at you, and then you got those fierce headaches. I have never known Americans of any class remotely like them anywhere. And I have been served, as you well know, sit-down supper in the upper Park Avenue salons of Midwestern beer and bacon and coffee and dill-pickle heiresses come to restless roost in this our world capital—maddened, alert, paranoid girls who wear good *old* jewelry and sponsor the dressier literati of our time—hello, there—all of whom they fear secretly and desperately long to do nothing so much as mock them, scourge them, and spit upon them—and they none of them, thank *God,* neither the hostesses nor their wily rattlesnake guests, all coiled on good old settees gazing at one another across great empty double-carpeted spaces—rugs on rugs—none of them talk the Mungo wa-wa Hattie's talking puppets talk.

"Of course, what they *do* do is *worry*—both the hostesses and the guests. Was Hattie *Bloom,* the professor, not right *on* the money all those years ago when he proclaimed *The Anxiety of Influence?*

And how universal the application—for me, as an existentialist, the acid test of anything *able to be believed*. *How* these matrons want to be assured that they are real New Yorkers, as good at what they do—from the catering right through the guest list and the *placement* to the floral arrangements—as their great predecessors. And how their guests want to believe that merely by swanning in, they, too, measure up. . . . How they *all* want to know—and they ask me—are the evenings and is the talk up to the standard of the Countess Madge O'Meagher Gautier's Magwyck in the fifties—when, on the evenings when herself wasn't actually slinging the hash out of the sliding door in the kitchen wall, the catering was Vartenessian, the flowers were from Max Schling, and the critters corralled were the stuff of legend. Similarly, in dealing with the hostesses's anxieties about who they are, after all, *au fond*, in spite of their filthy lucre, I tell them that although God knows I am interested in what money can *do*, circumstantially, I am no more interested in hearing about the provenance of it—beer and skittles, beans, coffee, cocoa, or soy—or even in the process of making it—in those things called futures they deal in Chicago, particularly—than I am in hearing people talk about their colons or their bowel movements. I tell them that's why I did not make a hit with Mae West—and leave them to figure out exactly what that means, existentially. I tell them, in relation to what may have been done to the downtrodden of all races, or what dirty tricks may have been played on their begetters' betters to put them where they are just then, that after all, they didn't *personally* empty the gas tanks themselves. I tell them that as I grow older, I greatly prefer upper Park Avenue to, say, Westbeth—they love hearing that. I tell them that in Westbeth you are likely to run into too many of the Discarded Sensations of Yesteryear, and that even though you are likely to sit down to chicken *mole* with some ethnologist who is just back from New Guinea where he has actually sampled human flesh—which actually *happened*, dear, to your mother not long before she went off on her *année de pèlerinage*—social intercourse above Fifty-seventh

Street is, as a rule, vastly more enriching. . . . I tell them lies, the
heiresses, to encourage them—what else can I do?"

"But, you encourage everybody," I reminded her. "Fuck 'em
if they can't take a joke."

"Oh, *dear*—to be quoted back at oneself on the very same
evening. But, yes, it's true—I lie to them, these daughters of American commerce and industry. I tell them the Countess Madge herself used to wonder—worrying—were her multifarious occasions as
good as Mabel Dodge Luhan's had been. Which is a very big
whopper—and I don't mean the hamburger—because the *only* thing
she or anybody else in that crowd ever pondered about Mabel
Dodge Luhan, really, was whether she and Mawrdew Czgowchwz's
mother had really had a torrid affair. That was the talk—Mawrdew
Czgowchwz's mother's lover having been, for a time, Mabel Dodge
Luhan, and her father's having been, for a time, Ludwig Wittgenstein. Situations worthy, dear, of a stronger pen than that wielded
by the author of *The Ambassadors*. Yes, I lead the matrons on—
but I don't lose my *whole mind.* I don't, for example, try to coach
them in Old New York swagger, or teach them to say 'Ca-*nay*-
gie' and '*Mame*-bocker'—they simply wouldn't *get* it.

"Do you know what my absolute favorite moment is in *The
Ambassadors?* It's when Lamebrain, the old poof, pulls out six-
count-'em-*six* adjectives to describe Chapstick *en toilette* in the a.m.
Strong, sleek, gay, easy, fragrant, and fathomless. What more could
mother desire in a man—especially that *fragrant,* which we *howled*
over: it was in those days the euphemism among the *Seventeen* set
for a delicate condition. Talk about singing the *You-don't-know-the-
half-of-it-dearie* blues like it was a French art song! But the professor
was right: Hattie knew *squat* about the species. Poor Hattie, it got
to her, not getting laid. And in the last analysis, I never did give a
flying rat's-ass fuck what became of a single one of those medioc-
rities in *The Ambassadors,* except perhaps for one little minute
under light—when was in, '71?—at Her Majesty's Theatre, when
Danielle Darrieux impersonated Madeleine Vionnet in the musical.

No Merman, Danielle, but for a single bijou minute, under light. . . .

"That said—not out loud, of course, which would have been offensive and nothing to the purpose, but to my reflection in the now nearly opaque window—I looked up and saw the Eiffel Tower, and soon thereafter the five majestic letters emblazoned on the brick wall. Remember the graffito in the tunnel of the Mosholu Parkway overpass—*Benny, I took the train?* Well, I never enter Paris without thinking of it—and of the first naughty expression I ever learned in high school French: *Je vous donne cinq lettres.* M-E-R-D-E. That's actually only four letters, but there you are. P-A-R-I-S is five letters—although I used to put another *A* and another *D* in parentheses in the middle when I wrote letters home in '44. My parents thought I was inserting *anno domini*, for some reason—in the year of the Lord, as if to celebrate the Liberation in a secret religious way. Then my Aunt May would snap back, 'Sure all *that* means—A.D.—is *accordin' t'Danny!*' And she was right, of course, as usual, because what it meant—that A.D.—was that according to me it was a letter from Paradise I was sending them—the real Paradise on this Earth, and not the Loew's on 188th Street and Fordham Road."

"*Hamp*'n Bays!"

As the *Etoile du Nord* pulled into Paris—or *Paradis*, as Odette would have it—the milk train pulled into exotic Hampton Bays, Gateway to the South Fork, and, after the odd few whose destination it was had detrained, off the single-track main line into a siding, there to await the coming across the Shinnecock Canal of the westbound ghost train: leaving us idled, as it were, but a stone's throw from that fabled—and now much-despoiled—Eden of our youthful dreams: The Hamptons. ("The *Hamptons*," Diane De-

Vors used to say, exactly the way Margo Channing says "The *Cub
Room.*" "The *Hamptons.* I see them as a glittering, dissolute family
of down-and-out theater royalty, *dialyzed* by great influxes of Ma-
fioso drug and Garmento fashion and Rock money . . . and, brooding over them all, like the Angel of the Waters brooding over Holly
Woodlawn as the Broken Goddess at the Bethesda Fountain, who
else but the shade of Hope Hampton—looking, exactly as she did
in life, like an embalmed child.")

Odette, meditating on her reflection in the window, was talking
French.

*"Et dès que j'eus reconnu le goût du morceau de madeleine trempée
dans le tilleul que me donnait ma tante. . . ."*
    "Huh?" Her delivery was too much for me. All I could think
of was *la plume de ma tante. . . .*
    "Proust, dear. Proust and his madeleine—and my old Aunt
May dunking her Dugan's doughnuts in her Tetley tea. It's a funny
old world, all right, and that's gospel truth.
    "Anyway," she continued, "lighter by the weight of the stud-
ded trunk—by that responsibility discharged—your mother and
Miss Faith checked back into the Crillon to regroup their forces
for the last leg of the journey: the shank of it the boat-train trip
to London, and the butt of it the flight from there to Knock, in
County Mayo, hard by Ballintubber. You know, dear, Miss Faith
really did make the strongest impression of them all on me—
always, I suppose, excepting DeVors. I can almost see her now
beside me in this clouded train window, as we sat together in
N.Y.U. hospital—when, as she put it, *la bise fut venue.* Looking
out at the city as the lights came on, as the sky darkened and the
rain kept beating on the windowpane.
    "Then, on impulse, to Oscar Wilde's tomb at Père Lachaise—

festooned with graffiti, one of which, I have to tell you, actually made me cry. It was nearly fresh—dated from early summer—and said, in its entirety, *Love is a Miserable Lie—Finian Lynch.* Can you *stand* it?"

"He must have gone to Lincoln Hall—to the Irish equivalent."

"In that moment I didn't think anything written on a wall since *Benny, I Took the Train* had hit me with such force. I mean, to tell *that* to Oscar Wilde! Yes, of course, it defaced a great monument, but I found it—well, dear, as Gauguin said, an ugly thing can often be beautiful; a pretty thing, never. And I reckon Finian Lynch, whatever else he is or isn't, isn't a pretty thing. I wonder what Oscar would say to him. Probably something elevated he'd read somewhere and appropriated as his own—unless in Purgatory he had gotten over that habit. Probably something like Spinoza's great caution: *Whoever loves God truly should not expect to be loved by God in return.* I'd say from what I remember of Catholicism that's where Finian had started going wrong, over in Holy Ireland—just where Oscar had started going wrong before him. Or how that boy went wrong who threw himself in front of. . . . You know, whenever I was in a train that pulled into a siding like this, or slowed to a dead halt and sat—as generally happens in Europe in the middle of the night—I remembered that time not so many years ago when we were together on this very midnight cannonball, and it stopped and stayed the hour because of that boy who'd gone and sat on the tracks waiting for it to come and kill him, which it did. Remember?"

I remembered.

"The flashing red lights. They came and pulled him—what there was of him—out from under us and took it away on a covered stretcher. He thought love was a miserable lie.

"Well, I walked to the Louvre, and there viewed the sunset from inside the Pei pyramid in the courtyard. Who was it said—

was it Victor Hugo?—that the Renaissance may have been a sunset
rather than a sunrise?"

"Southamp'n *College* next!"

I didn't have the slightest idea. The empty westbound having
passed, our train having backed out of the siding, we gathered
speed, approaching the bridge over the Shinnecock Canal. We
crossed it just as Odette was gathering speed (in narration) on the
Hovercraft from Calais to Dover.

"There's an old joke—which, like the monkey-in-the-bar-with-
his-tail-in-the-martini one, is untranslatable. Two Frenchmen on the
Calais-to-Dover Channel crossing seek distraction from heavy
weather in a philosophical *discours*.

> Pierre: *Du sublime au ridicule il n'y a qu'un pas.*
> Jacques: *Oui, le pas de Calais.*

It's good—it says it, or something like it, don't you think?"

I didn't—know it—and I didn't get it, so therefore had no opinion
on its efficacy in saying whatever the *it* was Odette had in mind.
(But, then, I never have been sure what the *it* in *get it* or *doesn't
get it* is. I always think of Dorothy Parker, who when asked if, in
her opinion, Miss X had *It* replied, *"It? Hell, she has those!"*)
However, I include it in this rondelet because it happened—and
happened to be significant to Odette, who, as we were in life
crossing the Shinnecock Canal on the night of August 11, 1991,
seemed to be again in her mind crossing the English Channel—
which opened up a whole line of questioning concerning the Life

of the Mind, as opposed to (or even, in the very words Odette was
so grateful to the French professor for not using, as *over and
against*. . . . O'Maurigan says that if I'm going to be a writer I
should get used to the fact that my characters are nearly always
going to know more than I do. "Is that *your* secret?" I asked. "As
Morgana Neri once declared," he replied, *"A woman is as sick as
her secrets."*) I've learned one thing, anyway, about being a writer:
never take, and never give, a straight answer. The people don't
want one; the people want the crooked alibi. They do.

"The London stay was ideal and idyllic both—the reality of today's
England hardly impinged upon your mother's progress from hotel
to studio to theater to restaurant and around again. 'I'm very glad
to be here,' I said, truthfully, when interviewed. 'In fact, I'm very
glad to be anywhere.' Then I decreed, when provoked by one of
those little—you know—that names don't drop names, I talk about
my friends. 'You're known as *nice*,' another teased. 'Well, I don't
really know how *that* reputation came about, because I've always
thought of myself as Jack Carson—Wally—in *Mildred Pierce*. Talking about competition, remember? *You know me, Mildred, I see an
opportunity and right away I start getting ready to cut myself a piece
of throat*. But an old and dear friend—whose ashes I have just come
from dumping in a Norwegian fjord—once said these very wise
words to me: *That's all right, dear, you go right along creating the
impression you're demure. So long as we who love you know what a
bitch you are when cornered*. And a very dear one, happily alive,
kicking, and writing the most brilliant theater criticism in New
York, remarked, *You have the patience of Job, Odette—and the temperament of Medea*.' And so forth. . . .

"Next morning, out to the Beeb studios in White City, for
the chat show with Barbara Windsor. I felt exactly like Joan Fontaine in *Letter from an Unknown Woman*—when she and Louis

Jourdan enter the coach in the Prater and the pictures of other countries flash before them out the window, just the way Potemkin villages did when Catherine of Russia traveled, and false fronts did for that old cow Victoria on her Dublin state visit. And as resolutely as I'd fought, time and again, the impulse to throw up recklessly enhanced flashbacks to a fabulous past as a bulwark against the difficult present, I'd not always succeeded—sometimes no more than poor Vana, laughing all night at dimly remembered and embellished whorish gaieties, only to collapse in one's arms over having bought in Padua—and worn to the Lido—that terrible beach costume. It was a struggle—to be there then, in 1990 London, and *not* back in *Dress Stage,* bound for Boeuf sur le Toit, and for the basement flat in Bentinck Street. Or *not* be Stolichnaya twenty years later, giving as good as one got in the angled-chin department to the likes of the Brothers Kray. But to dare to be—excuse me— *me,* twenty years later *again*—again the Unknown Woman, so far as the public was concerned, but for myself emphatically *not.* No dead child—inner or otherwise; no cholera ward, or any other ward, symbolic or otherwise, please God, until the time remaining is—

"Whereas in Ireland, from arrival on, it was all terribly real; one did not attempt to mitigate the sorrow—for there I was, having accomplished my mission at last, standing out on the wide and cloud-swept plain of County Mayo, at the holy well in Ballintubber, thinking, although I have never been here before, yet somehow I *have.* I felt just like you going back to the Mais Oui— which, of course, I go back to, too—but here I was going back to May-*o*—perhaps in the name of, or in the stead of, my people— forebears—and realizing that in the entire universe of beautiful sorrows, both general and particular, there is none more beautiful than memorial Ireland.

"And thinking more about the way stories grow, and concluding that they grow exactly like potatoes in Mayo. You take one old story—with, as it were, eyes in it—and you put it in the ground. In a year—in a season—you've got a tuberous network of—and remember, I'd by then put Miss Faith into the well, which I suppose is analogy enough to planting a potato. She always had a kind of potato face, didn't she?

"Another way of putting it, I thought in the same moment, was analogous to the jigsaw puzzle, but in reverse. You start with the found kernel of the story—center it, with all its jagged edges hanging out—and then it's up to you to craft each piece around that jagged center, until. . . . For example, take these two jagged edges. In the lounge bar of the pub that Miss Faith Healy's cousins own, across the way from Ballintubber Abbey, called, naturally, the Abbeyview, sitting next to the cash register is a pink plastic alarm clock. And in the men's toilet—the gents', as they call it in Ireland—positioned right over the sink is a two-paneled mirror that lets you see *perfectly* what you'd see if you stood at one end of the urinal trough and looked toward the other. No pink plastic triangles in the trough, but nevertheless. . . . Thereafter, every piece of the story would have to fit around—or be cut to fit around—these centerpieces. You could first join the clock on the bar with the missing pink triangles—with Vienna—or you could make the mirrors remind you of a pissoir in Paris and work backward from Oscar Wilde's tomb and Finian Lynch, who found love a—

"*You're* the one," Odette suddenly declared, "to make sense of it. You're the only one I ever came across who could assemble the jigsaw puzzle of *Lavender Mist*. And, of course, *Lavender Mist* could be the title for the story of our lives. Could've been once, anyway. . . ."

"*South*-hamp'n College—*South*-hamp'n next!"

"And, of course, it might be something far more simple than potatoes or jigsaw puzzles—something as simple as Jackson Pollock's stone-dowsing abilities and your connecting them to—how was that you put it—relating to them thereafter. . . . Anyway, talking of digging things up—and becoming proprietary of them, and lusting after the adventure itself of it all—I'd called myself Brigid O'Shaughnessy that once on the train, and now I was feeling as caught as she was, finally—feeling as though I had done something and that I was in some dark sense going to have to *go over for it.* Although actually—to dilute the seriousness a little—I was feeling more like Bridget O'Flynn than Brigid O'Shaughnessy. Remember her?"

I remembered Bridget O'Flynn. She was the heroine of a song, a relic of sometime in the early part of the century, when the Irish were getting, metaphorically, out of the jails and into something like the middle class. Sometimes in the old days—the days of the Eleven against Heaven—at parties, Odette and Miss Faith and I would get shanty-Irish drunk and sing it.

> *Bridget O'Flynn, where've ye been?*
> *This is a fine time fer you t'come in.*
> *Y've been t'see the big Parade?*
> *The big parade me eye*
> *Sure it never did take the big parade*
> *So long in passin' by. . . .*
> *Bridget O'Flynn, I know where y've been*
> *Both yer story and yer shoes is pretty thin.*
> *Sure I know y've been t'th'dancin' hall*
> *Sure there's nobody there worthwhile a-tall*
> *'Tis where I met yer father, Bridget daaarlin'!*

"You did?" I asked. It seemed to me that, if anything, she'd been to the Big Parade—been and back.

"I did. I felt something very like Miss Faith herself being debriefed by old May Healy posing as the true mother, sitting there in Thalia Bridgewood's Sutton Place kitchen late after midnight. Being advised to send the whole thing up and dispel the fear and disgust she, Miss Faith, felt after the clap incident. Mock taken to task, if you like, for pretending to be Cinderella in another life, chasing the likes of her father at the ball—and all the rest of the hatred-and-reconciliation melodrama of an abused Irish Catholic faggot only son with the same name. . . . And all this inwrought and cross-hatched after the son's very cinders had been dumped by me—a fairy, God knows, in no uncertain terms, but something of a bust, after all, as a godmother. Dumped under a slanting sky into the well across the way. Yes, I felt as though a sort of particular judgment were taking place in that lounge bar—that if I looked more closely at the pink plastic clock I'd see no hands on it: understand that *I* was in the eternity's anteroom there in Ballintubber. . . .

"Whereupon to Finian Lynch, who most certainly came from somewhere in Mayo, I wanted to say, 'No, Finian, Love is not just a miserable lie, although prevarication, if you know anything, does come into it. No, it's not a lie just because you feel cheated. Love is not much to do, after all, with how you feel—with whether Eddie Mars lets you win on the red and then gets his goon to hold you up in the parking lot. It's none of that—prearranged or no. All that is sentimental—or, as the girl said in her cups, *Thass sediment.* It's still less to do with what you have to *say* about what you feel, either in or out of your transports—which can be gay— but is like the flower growing out of the girl's ass in *The Garden of Earthly Delights* in the Prado in Madrid—where I didn't go this trip, but it's a detail I've never forgotten. Or like the worm in the apple in Caravaggio's still life at the Pinacoteca Brera in Milan.

The flower growing out of the girl's ass is fascinating, but you'd hesitate to pick it and put it into a vase. . . . No, Finian, love is what you *do*—and what you don't—what you put up with, and why. *That's all love is.* Now go with God.' "

"It'd do poor Finian a lot more good," I offered, "to hear your absolution coming from the other side of the grill rather than the penance of Father Drumgool."

"Well, as to that, I have a new faith in the resilience of the Irish young—epitomized for me in the story of Attracta and Fidelma coming out of the Passionist mission sermon. I heard once, dear, on one of those anthropological head shows, that among the Dayak of Borneo the translation of *to live* is equivalent to *not yet*. Remember the punch line of the story? In a way, dear, Attracta and Fidelma are like Beckett's wayfarers waiting for Godot. Get me?"

All right, if love's not what you feel but what you do, and if I love Odette (I do), then in spite of the fact that I feel not good about once again footnoting the text—and I'm even putting that badly, lazily, perhaps in an attempt to convey a sense of the lateness of the hour (that was) and the fatigue that had me in its grip—I'll tell the Attracta and Fidelma joke.

Fidelma and Attracta—they'd be a redhead and a dark brunette—come out of the church in Ballyblarney or Ballyblahblah or Ballybunghole or wherever, having sat through a young Passionist missionary priest's hour-long sermon on virginity. Being two healthy young women of the Irish country Western world—cognizant, for example, of the ways of men and animals—they light up two cigarettes and wait to see which one of them will initiate comment. It's Fidelma. "Tell me, Attracta, are *you* a virgin?" Attracta, exhaling two thin streams of nostril smoke and looking very self-possessed indeed, replies, *"Not yet."*

"Or could it be," Odette continued to wonder, unfazed by the lateness of the hour—but then, I told myself, firstly, she's in jet-lag overdrive, and tomorrow will undoubtedly sleep the sleep of Dolores Del Rio, and secondly, she hasn't done two shows today. "Could it be merely that the Irish, like the characters in Dostoevsky, and like drag queens, have an inveterate longing for voluptuous suffering? For living in the time remaining in anguish imploring ceaselessly *stay thou art fair*, all the while knowing as the animals do not that to live is only and entirely and incessantly and forever to wish both to die and not to die."

"Whatever."

"Exactly."

"*South*-hamp'n!"

"Of course," she continued—footnoting away, "that's Goethe, not Dostoevsky."

"What?"

"Stay thou art fair."

"Oh." To me, at that hour, it sounded like something nice the handsome man from the East Side who picked me up off the Mais Oui floor might have said to me at breakfast—or something that Phil did say to me that fateful night on the loading platform on Washington Street—and, as such (particularly the latter), I could not then and there declare an invitation to an anguished life. Maybe I was, I thought then and there—maybe I will always be—what O'Maurigan said in the publicity: that good-hearted gold digger who made good—or whatever, I could hardly remember, and the time remaining for me to so much as stay awake on my feet that night was, I felt, pouring through the hourglass faster and faster, the way the sand does when time's nearly up. I seemed to recall I'd promised Odette a cup of cocoa in the kitchen before bed; just then I didn't know if I could make it—either the cocoa, that is, or the way home itself at the wheel of the car from Bridgehampton station to the house in Sagaponack.

Meanwhile, undeterred, she rattled on—I decided, in the manner of a comrade on the beach at Normandy, keeping another awake to stay alive in the coming battle dawn.

"Our lives, darling, are probability distributions for like measurements as functions of space time—or, as Hildegarde Dorsay once put it, 'There is *moab* to God's will than deaths and disappointments.' She was trying in those days to come to terms with Destiny, and had drifted into the metaphysics of science and from there into Shiva's foxtrot and the silky embrace of those Oriental habits of mind which, as I said earlier, never did ravish her. Never did get very far beyond that, except, I suppose, you could say that in the light of what befell her—and the others—in terms of the cloud of unknowing, she went—they all did—all the way.

"Yes," she said then, like the soldierly comrade reading my mind, "it is the lateness of the hour, and my mind *is* spinning—becoming very dynamic random-access memorial D-RAM. I seem to hear in the night outside this whistling train the voices of the Misses Faith, Hope, and Charity harmonizing as they used to and singing in tandem 'Why Did I Choose You?' 'Absentminded Me,' and 'Right as the Rain.' And as Miss Claire Trevor as Velma declares in *Murder My Sweet:* Remembering does something to my stomach. I'm looking forward now to that nice cup of cocoa; there's nothing like hot chocolate, is there, to slake sorrow?"

"*Bridge*-hamp'n next!"

"A voluptuous sorrow that seems to come up out of nowhere—
unless, like in the Parzival story, it comes from the song of the
birds. Do you know the passage? He hears the birdsong and it
pierces his bosom, and he runs weeping to his mother, the queen.
'Who has hurt you?' she demands to know. 'You were only out
in the meadow.' The narrator says, *He could tell her nothing, as is
still the way with children.* He must have had Irish children in
particular in mind.

"I was, anyway, sitting there in the Abbeyview looking out
the window at the sun, so very brilliant after the rain—*with the
sun splitting the rocks*—thinking, no wonder life is like it is here
and not one bit like life in contemporary Britain, where it's all
enacted in imitation of the suet-pudding melodramas of E. M.
Forster and the malt-vinegar moralities of Evelyn Waugh; it's *life
in the raw* here—yet as-yet unwilling to go out into the weather's
clemency and proceed to Crossmolina and Poulaphouca, where
I'd been promised—and would find—rainbow's end. And thinking what a laugh Miss Faith would've had over the presumably
unconscious *placement* of the mirrors in the can. And then thinking, *ghosts appear in mirrors:* wouldn't she have a good time over
here—and *maybe she will*, that is to say, may be about to. . . .
When something else, almost a complete contradiction, a switch-
back in the train of thought, hit me with compelling force. I
realized that I'd always known about her that of all of them she
was, down under, the very most serious. The penchant for Racine and Colette were symptomatic of that, as was, of course,
her incessant replaying of the spring 1956 Metropolitan Opera
broadcast tape of *Pelléas et Mélisande* with Mawrdew Czgowchwz
as Mélisande. Yes, very definitely, underneath all the caw-caw,
she was, as Maeterlinck wrote and Debussy immortalized: *Un
petit être, si tranquille, si timide et si silencieux*—or, to paraphrase
it for our time, place, and climate, what was in the girl was

indeed too soft, too unknown for direct dialing. And speaking of Maeterlinck, let's remember *the* great truth he left us. He declared, *There are no dead.* He was absolutely right; there are no dead; we simply go through life imagining the unlikely, and occupy the time remaining in re-editing, categorizing, and canonizing the attributes and performances of the seemingly disappeared."

"By then the sun was slanting in the windows, and Shea the driver, very good about not overdoing it at the bar, but seeing no reason to stay otherwise, indicated it was time to make for Lough Conn and Poulaphouca while the day was still in it.

"Which would've been that day called itself had your mother not, as we were coming around the green in Castlebar, decided on a sudden impulse—because daylight seems to go on forever in the high Irish summer and undoubtedly because the dump of Miss Faith was so fresh still in my mind—to go and face old May Healy then and there in the county home on the pretext of asking her what *did* she want done anyway with her goddam stock certificates and bonds. I can't say I *wanted* to take the left fork at the end of the green. I *wanted* to do what the witches do at the end of a segment of the Great Work: return all bodies in balance, earth myself, dismantle the temple, and forget it. I felt I'd accomplished my segment. In Classical mythology, you know, shades are unable to cross the river Styx to the Elysian Fields until their bodies have been burned or their deaths avenged. I felt both had been accomplished. I felt like George Brent as Dr. Steele in *Dark Victory*, who if you remember was counseled by the dying Judith Traherne to say each time he made an advance against the thing that would by then have killed her, '*That's* for Judith; that's for my *wife!*' In its way, actually, it was my version of your girl's throwing the drink in the cop's face at the Stonewall: *'That's for Judy!'* Except that the cops were the death squad or the God squad—whatever. Each and every one of the girls had, I felt, crossed the Styx—call it the Liffey, the Seine, the Danube, the Rhine. All rivers are the one river."

"She remembered me perfectly, made no allusion to the falling out, and nodded conspiratorially when I told the full story of switching the ashes, of the funeral at Bagel Nosh and the business of half of Billy in the Liffey and the other half in the holy well, as if that's exactly what she'd have done. Then I asked her about the stocks and bonds. 'I don't give a *shite* what y' do with 'em, so long as the priests don't get their hands on 'em. But tell me, anyway, did Billy have the priest's sendoff on him?' I said he did. 'Well, good for him. I can't decide will I or not,' she said, looking long out the Georgian windows at the shadows stretching on the great green lawn, and creating that suspense which she undoubtedly was wont to create on many a rainy afternoon there, regaling all comers with tales of her years in New York—doing for Thalia Bridgewood and being made party to all the stories of Sutton Place and Willows and the New York Rialto when it was the *Rialto*. 'I suppose I will, so, as it's free, gratis, and fer nuthin', and seein' as I've got nothin' in the world to give him except me sins. In case by then I'm so gaga, y'see, as to make 'em think I'd fall for the tricks that's pulled all the time at that place in New York. Y' *know* the one I mean.' I did."

(So did I, because we used to call it the Mary Magdalene Whorish Home, but I didn't know what—)

———

"I knew the one. I asked her what she meant exactly, and she proceeded to *glare* at me with the one-eye-screwed-up like she used to do to Bridgewood, whenever she'd had enough of Madame's shenanigans, as if to say, *Are ye stupid?* Then delivered herself of her homily in the Mayo voice of her early years—the one that used to erupt sometimes in New York from under the Thelma-Ritter-as-Birdie-Coonan accent she'd adopted in Show Business. 'Ye know as well as *I* do, Danny O'Doyle, what's it these ones do, the slopers. Gettin' the *oulwens* that's gone soft in the head t' make over their wills t'em, an' with the proceeds pocketed so they goin' and gettin' themselves great *cairs* to drive. Like this buckalero was over last month—what's this his name is I won't tell ye, but here's yer hint: his cousin used to be teachin' yer woman at the dime store—the one that had a week t'spare—the groundwork and the walkin'-around work, and tellin' her to take it from there. There was himself, pelting in all directions in his sparklin' new Mer-*cedes*-Benz—not even a black one, but *silver!*' I thought to myself, that's the mournful mothafuckin' truth of the world, all right, and wouldn't my mother have been scandalized. Likely not.

" 'Billy always said you taught him about life,' I said. 'As to that,' she replied, 'sure I didn't have much to teach him. We were alike all right. He didn't give a shite what people said about him, and no more do I. I used to say the only thing I never want to hear anybody say about *me* is *and may she rest in peace,* and so far I haven't.' 'Well,' I said, 'there's only one of you alike left now.' 'Y'know,' she said, 'I always thought *you* were a bit like us, too. Anyway, there's Captain Billywinks gone fer his tea, with a good head start on us both.' "

"*Bridge*-hamp'n!"

"Holy great *heaven,* we're here!" Odette exclaimed. "God between us and all harm, so—as they say in County Mayo—until the return journey, and Himself protect everyone's rearing."

"Blackout, end of story."

"Your mother's stories don't end, dear, they just stop. And nice people don't get on or off trains in blackouts any more—the war's long over."

THE EPILOGUE

As we were walking from the platform to the parking lot, we passed by, of all the significant things in the world, a 1950 Oldsmobile convertible, restored, with a bumper sticker on the back fender: 40 ISN'T OLD—WHEN YOU'RE A TREE. What could it mean? (I knew what it *meant;* it wasn't on the face of it deep or inaccessible—neither was "Benny, I Took the Train"—but what was it telling *me,* just then, if anything?) I wondered who'd left the open convertible there at that hour. Somebody in a blackout getting on the westbound—the one that had passed us at Hampton Bays? Then I thought, Jackson wasn't much over forty when he—and then I heard, *like an old dead tree lying in the brush.* So, I was supposed to make something out of it? Apparently. According to O'Maurigan in all this (you're reading), I am not only not dead, not even sleeping, definitely *not* not there—see above—but rather—do not miss this—the Central Intelligence. (That's what he said, Bub.) The Central Intelligence, transformed into the leading actor, registering and evaluating everything that happens, including what happens to and in myself. How could this be true (I asked myself, seriously)? I didn't make Odette up: she's no fiction. Or, without her words on tape, *is* she, unless . . . what? I get her up with me onstage on Second Avenue? People would be there all night—the way they always are up at Symphony Space on the Upper West Side. (Remember them? Pretending to be poor no more. O'Maurigan goes up there every June 16 to read from *Ulysses.*)

First question (mine): Which is the return journey? The journey to New York, or to Bridgehampton (in my case)? The journey to Europe, or the journey home (in Odette's)? There's no correct answer, is there.

I thought, what, then, about the riderless chariot (the Oldsmobile), and came up in a flash with the following scenario. What if, back in 1956, those extraterrestrials had caught Jackson Pollock as he planed through the air into the woods in Springs? (They were all over the place at the time; there were multiple testimonies in the East Hampton *Star*—and let's not forget *Invaders from Mars, Man from Planet X, The Day the Earth Stood Still*, and, Odette's favorite, *This Island Earth.*) Caught him like a long line drive at the last instant and substituted in the brush a *simulacrum* of his dead body—performing a version of what Jeff Bridges did in *Starman* (through some kind of *ion flow* transformation. I remembered Odette saying something about ion flow. . .). Anyway, something like how Saint Thomas Aquinas explained the Virgin Birth: that Christ passed through the Virgin's hymen like light through the window. Obviously the origin of the practice of stained-glass representation—and it just then suddenly occurred to me that *that's* the kind of Christ picture to make next—*not* just a religious picture, not some sentimental drivel like *Last Temptation*, but how the spacemen filtered the Redeemer into existence. *That'd* bring out the Bayside psychotics to demonstrate in their droves—maybe start another new religion. The world needs a new religion—to replace the Storefront Church of God in the Plate-Glass Window with the Starman who passed like light. . . .

But about Jackson Pollock—what if he's been up there *all along* on the perihelion of the planet Roz, fucking away, getting fucked, whatever. Like Osiris. Risen from the dead. (Maybe, I thought, the extraterrestrials would put us *all* in a heaven movie. I'd willingly step down and let Jackson play Christ. I could play John the Divine—the writer, remember? The three of us—Jackson, Odette, me—in dialogue in heaven, like Martha Graham's *Seraphic Dialogue* or like the angels in Wim Wenders's *Wings of Desire*. Divine. Or, as Odette's suppliant, the coffee, beer, or pork-rind heiress would declare at the opening—at the Ziegfeld, in 70-mm and Dolby—*celestial!* And, of course, the Celestial City must be New York, right? Right. Much location work at the Bethesda, with the Angel of the Waters standing guard. There we'd be, all of us, walking on the Boat Lake waters, and dancing with Lila Aron's Venetian *gondolieri.*)

About questions with no correct answers. In the spirit of moving right along: exactly what I was doing, trying to keep awake, until, driving down Sagg Main Street I felt that first blast of predawn Atlantic air hit me in the face. When you get off at any station but the end of the line, you always wonder who's still on and how far they're going and what they'll do when they get there; whereas when you get off at the terminus you never wonder where anybody is going, or I don't, anyway. So, who *was* that lone passenger remaining in the car when we got off? For that matter, who left the open 1950 Oldsmobile convertible and took the train to New York? (For another, deeper matter, *who took the train* and left the note for Benny? Remember the fifties? Questions like that seemed deep.) This got me as far as the car.

We drove east along the Montauk highway, with the top down, chasing the train until it outran us, disappearing, and we heard its whistle waking the Just in Wainscott. I took the right onto Sagg Main Street, and that blast of Atlantic salt air swept up and made me feel, if not absolutely gorgeous, at the very least *very* alive. First light and cockcrow came together, and as we drove toward the beach, Odette noticed in the rear-view mirror that the ridge of the moraine—where the glacier had halted in the Ice Age— was of a shape roughly parallel to the south face of Nephin, the mountain in northwestern Mayo that guards O'Maurigan's ances-tral pile, Poulaphouca. (Nephin, immortalized by Synge in *The Playboy of the Western World,* and over again by The O in his epic

Under Nephin.) I was glad to hear it: it put me in the mood for a cup of cocoa.

As Odette put it, there's no point in sitting down at the kitchen table to a warm drink unless you're going to have your fortune told. Her specialty has always been the tea leaves. Even if you were at the Riker's or up at Hector's or the Burger Ranch, and got your tea in a bag on the side of the cup of hot water— even if you were staying home and had ordered in Chinese and they'd sent a tea bag in the fortune cookie packet, Odette, after you'd dunk it and drunk it nearly to the bottom, would rip the bag open and swirl the pulp around and around, while mumbling something sonorous under her breath, and then have a go. Failing the presence of tea in any form, she'd improvise. That early morning last August, over cocoa in Sagaponack, she did so with the tarot pack she'd carried about for years, unwrapped from a Charvet silk scarf and laid out on the kitchen table in—what else—the Celtic spread.

I won't go into the details—except to say that the *I* card, the Significator, was the Page of Cups and his cover the King—but the gist of the message was in the card at the top of the cross, the fifth card, specifying *This crowns him* (me: and I could only hope hard *not* with thorns). It represents in Celtic-cross tarot an influence that *may* come into being. I drew the Page of Pentacles reversed: indicating dissipation, luxury, and prodigality, and presaging unfavorable news—*or*, since the subject seeker is in this our life a proclaimed invert (just so you know), the card may be righted, to read respect for learning, new opinions, and ideas. (I figured from the run of the show, right?) The card on the right in the cross, the sixth, *This is before him,* was the Major Arcana Card Eleven, styled variously Justice and Astraea, and read *The elimination of useless, outworn forms of education.* Was this perhaps my future—a final farewell in life (and dream life) to those Mott Street black-bonnet Sisters of Charity, to Saint Augustine, and to those priests at Lin-

coln Hall? Or, for that matter, to those priests at the Mais Oui
and the Cherry Lane and the Everard, and to Trenchy at the Modern? (This was beginning to sound to me like Judy Holliday belting
out "to the Bonjour Tristesse Brassiere Company" at the end of
Bells Are Ringing.) Me, freed and serene, in repose (on the promontory of the Ramble? On the stone jetty at Wainscott? Atop the
Judy float? Hardly, I thought, on the stage—unless I decided, with
my long Irish face, to go in for Beckett opuses that put you in urns
or in sand up to your neck. But could that be called serenity?
Repose? Must ask O'Maurigan—he knew Beckett well). The seventh card, the Four of Wands, representing my negative feelings,
read: *A meeting with one the subject has compromised.* I thought to
myself, somebody will come backstage: the man from the East
Side who never went to the West Side, and who maybe never got
over me? The eighth card, second from the bottom to the right of
the cross, read: *Haven of refuge*, but what the subject wants—the
ninth card, third up in the row—read *Treachery, duplicity, separation, emigration.* Was I (am I) looking for trouble? Looking to be
haunted by the dead for (a) living? The decisive tenth card was the
second of the Major Arcana, the High Priestess, again reversed.
My fate seems to be accepting surface knowledge, sensual enjoy-
ment, conceit. Odette thought again H.P. was reversed for the
same reason the Page of Pentacles was but that if righted, she would
signify an unrevealed future, silence, mystery, and duality. Hidden
influence at work. However, if we were to right the two reversed
cards to try to ameliorate the reading on the principle that faggots
are fundamentally the same as other folk (*bab!*), then wouldn't we
have to invert all the upright ones? (We'd always been told we
couldn't have it both ways—which we'd always defied, saying
we had the pictures to prove you could—meaning, essentially, *we
have fucked men.*)

Odette decided that I was looking to be haunted—that, like
her, I had a case of survivor guilt. "But fundamentally, darling, in

the end it all comes down, doesn't it, to 'if only we knew; if only we knew. . . .' *If only we knew what's to know.*"

"In this our life."

"In this our life." *In this our life* was a phrase Odette and I often repeated in conversation. Years ago I used it randomly, and she asked if I knew it was from a very famous Victorian sonnet sequence called *Modern Love.*

> *Ah, what a dusty answer gets the soul*
> *When hot for certainties in this our life.*

Odette said the couplet had been big with the Cambridge fairies— the spies themselves and their gofers—in London during the war. The author of the sequence, George Meredith, had in his youth posed for a famous painting, *The Death of Chatterton*, which hangs in London's Tate Gallery. (Also a Cambridge icon, it is a favorite Lavender Traveler p.c. still. Remember my telling you Odette had sent it to us?) Chatterton was this failed poet until he faked a poem "rediscovered" as an earlier (it turned out mythical) bard's master-piece. He committed suicide in a London garret—hence the paint-ing. James Schuyler, in his poem "Voyage autour de mes cartes postales," referred to it in the lines

> *The poor dead boy*
> *had his hair in the henna lately*
> *great rings and strings of it*
> *on the thin little pillow propped on a fat bolster.*

It turned out that had reminded Odette of me as a platinum blond, at the time of Judy's death, when "everybody had been so afraid for you," and she'd sent it with a funny message—one, remember, I didn't recall. (This is turning into its own little *nouvelle interpolée*.) I said no, I recognized *In This Our Life* as the title of a Bette Davis picture—not one of her best—in which she'd played a character called Stanley, who, hotter first for her sister's fiancé (the sister, played by Olivia de Havilland, was called Roy) and then for her old uncle's money (the uncle was played by Charles Coburn) than for anything you could call certainty—she had seemed to shelve that question: having become perhaps a despairing existentialist earlier than Odette became a hopeful one—ended her woes by driving off a cliff and getting herself a face full of windshield before her dusty final answer. "Oh, that awful Huston picture!" Odette shot back. "The only reason anybody ever looks at it is it's the only known example on the silver screen of a closeup of a platform shoe on a gas pedal. People now freeze-frame the moment on their VCRs to speculate whether it's actually Davis's foot or did Huston call in an extra? *That's* decadence!"

"Somebody," I suggested, "ought to write a sonnet sequence called *Postmodern Love.*"

"Sonnet sequences are no longer written—they are no longer possible."

"A sonnet *cluster*, then?"

"Perhaps a sonnet *scattering.*"

"But are *sonnets* any longer possible?"

"Not only possible, dear, they're postmodern—like the key of C."

Odette was thinking, I knew, of O'Maurigan's *Magnetic Resonance Imaging Suite.*

"And you," I said, "ought to write philosophy."

"The philosophy of the twentieth century has been written, darling. What your mother ought to do is *read* it, seriously."

"But you have—you were an existentialist."

"May I tell you a disruptive truth? That wasn't exactly philosophy."

"So what was it?"

"It was a—*couture* for the serious-minded."

"You certainly were that—serious-minded."

"We all were—all of a mind to get profoundly serious . . . one of those days. With ourselves—with others. Oh *God!* Remember *that? With yourself, or with others, son?*"

I remembered. "You got pretty serious."

"Let's say I got pretty busy mopping up—an activity one's apt to view as a prelude to seriousness."

"So, what's to know?" I asked. (I was *coming down*—or unraveling.) "Do you think philosophy's what's to know?"

"I think—I suppose—that if I ever got *really* serious—let's say, if I ever really do so, before the allotted biblical span is up and I start bargaining hard for more—more of the same, anything: another Old Fashioned, another bowel movement, another opening of another show, anything but the grave just yet—I'll go back to philosophy, printed, published philosophy; hard, exasperating philosophy. And if I do that, there is only one possible philosopher. Everybody one knows talks about him—on the gossip level, because he was Mawrdew Czgowchwz's father's lover, and this one's this and that one's that—but the plain fact is that he was the greatest philosophical mind of the twentieth century, slow curtain, the end. But he is a *hard* case! O'Maurigan said to me when he was home at Poulaphouca in June, 'Wittgenstein is the fulfillment of Schopenhauer in our time, just as Berg was the fulfillment of Beethoven.' 'Of *Beethoven?*' 'Of Beethoven. Lulu the character is the Leonore, and *Lulu* the work is the *Fidelio* of our time.' And to think, I said to myself, that the whole while I was in Vienna I went neither to Beethoven's house nor to the bushes in the Prater. . . . I wish I *could* learn to understand and to talk about Wittgenstein; he would be so much classier as a subject than Johnny Donovan. Although what I think from what I *have* read of him is that Wittgenstein could have made Johnny Donovan feel *ashamed,* as Socrates supposedly did Alcibiades. Is that too crazy a thought, I wonder. Anyway, he did a lot of his best work in Ireland—some

in the west, and some in Dublin itself. Imagine! Perhaps I'll retire
to Ireland, finish reading *Finnegans Wake* once through, finally,
and start reading late Wittgenstein. The nice thing about a G.I.
pension is you can go anywhere—and pin the little bit of fruit salad
they gave you just for being a good sport on whatever frock you
throw on. . . . What am I saying, anyway—I'll never leave New
York. I shall live there forever, in the same apartment, cultivating
my solitude, and, as Miss Dorsay put it, waxing my nostalgia, and
when they interview *me*, I shall say—when I'm finished talking
about the things I've seen, the troubles and the triumphs—I shall
say what Miss Davis said about her place on North Havenhurst:
*This is one of the old ones—they haven't torn it down yet. Of course,
they haven't torn* me *down yet, either!*

"And if I did write anything, I'd write one of those books—
you know, about how whatever it is that's the matter with you is
ninety-nine percent mental. I actually thought one up in Ireland.
It would be a record of every autoimmune disease and psychoso-
matic nerve and muscle ailment, plus arthritis, rheumatism, what
was once called lumbago, whatever it's called that gives the Inner
Child the croup—the whole shitload. I don't know how to phrase
the matter exactly, but that would be no matter in the New Age.
It's the agent and the publicist that matter—properly represented
and hawked, your mother could become the Mary Baker Eddy,
the Louise Scoville Hicks, the Gaylord Hauser, and the Guru Mei
of the Western world by the year 2000. All that's really needed is
a title—preferably an indicting one—and I've got mine: *Snap Out
of It!* Meanwhile, I've been thinking—just now while talking—of
how relentlessly I do employ the phrase *your mother*. It's peculiar,
dear, because no matter how you look at it, the mother role has
been an ungratifying one, all the way from Saint Monica—as you
point out in the show—to Frau Schopenhauer and beyond. You
know that story? She taunted him once, 'Arthur, your tragedy is
that you'll never be known except as the son of an important

novelist.' To which the great philosopher replied, categorically, 'Mother, you are never going to be so much as *mentioned* except as a footnote in my biography.' Now, consider the upshot. I mean, zip—were you reading Schopenhauer last night, or were you— zip—reading Schopenhauer's mother?''

I was moved, and I thought, wise woman, the only crazy thought you're having is the thought of asking *me* if the thought you're having is crazy. In the meantime, wordlessly, Odette had gone upstairs to the bathroom before turning in, and I sat in silence looking down at my fortune in the tarot spread, and thinking about the Bible I'd never read.

The Bible. Extraterrestrials. There are many who believe, or say they believe, that the Bible's Old Testament was not written by Hebrew priests, or by Professor Bloom's court lady, but was dictated to Sinai Desert nomads by what you might term a *sidérale* crowd calling themselves *elohim* and commanded by the archon Metatron, who simultaneously introduced psychedelic mushrooms to earth. (The same gang, or their cousins, supposedly dictated *Gilgamesh* to one or more scribes in Mesopotamia, *The Mahabharata* to others along the Ganges, and others still the *Nibelungensaga* to secretaries along the Rhine. I particularly like that last image: Lorelei and Rhine Maidens as secretaries. Reminds me of Marlene, or of the girl in the Berlin bunker who, hearing of the Führer's cyanide suicide, exclaimed, ''Thank *God*, now we can *smoke* again!'' and lit up a Lucky Strike.)

In the New Testament, the first three gospels are called synoptic, whereas John's isn't; it's a kind of homely ecstatic's Greek ode. Odette had said she was telling the synoptic version. I started wishing I could take dictation in my sleep or in a trance out on the jetty come Sunday—dictation from heaven or Atlantis or wherever and tell a John-like version, or—can we talk loud?—let's say commensurate with John's reputation, anyway—and including the Apocalypse. But not only am I (in spite of that Bethesda scenario) no John, I have no boyfriend Christ, either, whose breast to lean on, whose mother to console. And as I've said, Phil (more, as I've indicated, the rugged Saint Peter type) has done me fine. And respecting his wishes, I shall not expect his resurrection. There are no resurrected gods or men—there's only Jackson Pollock and the *kouros*. The whole idea of the Resurrection—all the way back to Osiris, Tammuz, Adonis, etcetera—was probably a priests' scheme: to keep their stories not only interesting but never-ending, so they'd hold on to their public. (And maybe they *were* giving the people what they'll always want; maybe their audiences—and religious audiences evermore—clamor for their gods and saints and their own reflections as if they're saying just what I said about my audiences: "What good *are* they to me dead, I'd like to know?" I mean are *you*, who are reading *this* instead of *either* Schopenhauer *or* Schopenhauer's mother, alive or dead?) Imagine believing in eternal life. (I used to say imagine *wanting*—but I finally had to give in and say, "All *right*, I *do!*") O'Maurigan says, "Eternal life is a gorgeous idea, it's only *us* there must be a stop put to." Fine, but then what am I saying when I say the Eleven against Heaven are in heaven? Am I writing fiction for the comfort of the disoriented idle?

I scooped the cards up, put them back in their box, and climbed the stairs myself (each tread a little out of the true, sloping sideways, left, southwest, and back, as it were, toward just yesterday), just in time to bid the Broadway-baby goodnight in bright early-morning daylight.

She was coming from the bathroom and going toward the guest room across the creaky hall floorboards. "Sleep tight," I said, adding, "and don't thank me for giving you a chance to talk. Thank you, for being wise and kind, and for letting me see how you are."

"Oh, dear," she whispered, leaning against the doorjamb of the guest room as the bright yellow sun poured in through the white-curtained windows, *"Marie Theres', wie gut Sie ist. Die alte Marschallin."* Then, wistfully, "Opera is such a scream, dear. The old Marschallin is all of thirty-five, and your mother—let's face it, passport control did—is getting on for twice that. Excuse me, but I've been looking in the bathroom mirror. Remember sufficient reflection? Well, it can be overdone. As can soliloquy—even if, as Professor Bloom so brilliantly remarked, it is the signal mark of both Shakespeare's characters and of Vashti's—that is to say, dear, of the author of *The Book of J*, that they change their ways and moderate their means only after listening to themselves talk. As the girl insisted, *How can I know what I think until I see what I say?* Nevertheless, even if it is true that if one did not exist, Shakespeare, or somebody who holds with him, would have to have invented one, still it is perhaps not the best idea in the world to search out one's mirrored greatness at such an hour, in such true-life light reflected off white walls; one finds instead that secondhand book of dog-eared pages, one's old fat face. However, the pain of regret is, I suppose, far worse than that of remorse—for though you may be sorry for what you have done, you can never get back what you have missed. One is somewhat consoled by Flaubert. *Le soir de la vie apporte avec lui sa lampe.* But don't go lifting the lamp up to the mirror. I've done it four times in the last twenty-four hours. In the can on the plane on the way over, backstage in your dressing-room mirror—I couldn't resist—in the train window, and again just now. I looked hard into those mirrors and I realized—I realize—*Ich weiss gar nichts—gar nichts.* And draw the drape on that sunshine, while you're at it. Photosynthesis is for hardy plants; mother requires more likely the ministrations of the filtered lens. I know no more, but you're a dote to think so—and although I am not good, I may be good tomorrow, for as Oscar pointed out, dear, anybody can be good in the country."

I went into the bathroom. I had a look at myself in the

mirror. I looked like I'd been up two nights—at the prom and at the Ulanova *Giselle*—or three, adding the night of Judy's wake at Campbell's plus the Stonewall and the Everard. Except older—no Golden Boy, just another Danny Boy—yes, Odette and I share the same first name. Certainly no "Donal Og"—Young Daniel—the ballad of whose untimely death O'Maurigan is fond of reciting. Not young—but not dead. Daniel, of whom a man in a room had once advised me, when I expressed a certain nostalgia for Kelly's and the Everard and the Cherry Lane and the Mais Oui, "So far as I ever heard, when Daniel got out of the lion's den, he didn't go back for his hat."

Then, in bed, with Sylvester walking up and down on the counterpane, trying to resettle himself (and with Phil in his sleep mask snoring beside me somewhere, likely with orange trees in bloom. Phil seems immune to complication, awake or asleep), it didn't appear I was going to get lucky, but that was, as it turned out, no sodomite's hellrack, either. I lay listening to the thudding of the surf just down the road and over the dunes, thinking that like de Kooning admitted about his wife's pre-Columbian art, I often don't know what Odette's wisdom is, any more than I know really what her experience was—either in the war or in Europe consigning the girls to the waters. But what I understand is that it all was—is, like her, like the waves that constitute, that compose, the thudding surf—authentic. Then I realized the story was winding down in the mind of the Central Intelligence, with no time for any more sufficient reflection—*with yourself or with others, my son?*—and the details all out of focus and confused. I seemed to have Vana Sprezza and Mercedes del Talgo-Benz screaming at one another about glass slippers, or maybe it was ground glass in evening slippers. I thought I saw the ACT/OUT kids sitting at Diane DeVors's feet, much like the children at the feet of Christ in some oleograph on the wall somewhere at Lincoln Hall. And what was she singing—"Hello, Young Lovers" or "Getting to Know You" or "Whistle a Happy Tune"—but if any of those, why did I think the words I could make out were those of a risqué Frances Faye song or of the fabulously filthy pirated tapes of Mildred Bailey's legendary late-night recording-studio rendition of "Salty Dog"? Then everything stacking up in what O'Maurigan calls the interlude of chordal ideation in the hypnogogic state immediately prior to dial tone. . . .

I could hear the sound of the waves; they carried on, breaking against the wall of my mind.

The Skylark wrote,

> *"Look," the ocean said (it was tumbled, like our sheets),*
> *"look*
>
> *in my eyes"*

The sheets weren't tumbled—I hadn't gotten lucky; they were smooth, like the Venice lagoon on a lazy afternoon.

The stacked chords hummed. I saw myself disembark from a gondola and guessed I was to go yet again under the Scandia duck down by way of Venice to the Land of Nod. I'd descend with Miss Mooney and Odette at Piazza San Marco under the lion on his pedestal, then hurry along to the Fenice, where I'm going on with the Vienna Choir Boys, singing "America, I Love You" in an AIDS benefit. It would be the Christmas season—there would be yuletide festoons everywhere and *pannetone* in the shop windows. As I dashed off, Miss Mooney would call after me, "Break a leg!" Odette would call louder, *"Merde!"*

I'd enter the stage door of the Teatro alla Fenice. Vana Sprezza and the stage-door attendant—Phil—would hail me. *"In bocca al lupo!"* I'd answer, *"Crepi."* (The Italian formula salute and response—used as a matter of course in opera houses—the equivalent of "break a leg" in English and *"merde"* in French. It means, literally, in the wolf's mouth. I forget what *"crepi"* means, only

that it's the response—you know, like *"Ad Deum qui laetificat. . . ."*
Skip it.) I'd go out onstage praying, *San'Antonio della barba bianca,
fami trovare ciò che me manca!* (This is what you pray in Italian
show business so you don't forget your lines. I learned it from the
bit players in the movie I was in with Miss Mooney, Princess
Saroya, and Richard Harris. Is Princess Saroya alive?)

The Vienna Choir Boys would be frolicking like the acolytes
in Tosca. Suddenly, Vana Sprezza would sweep in as Floria and
start vamping them, and they'd—Shazaam!—sprout into the rock-
'n'-rollers. Throwing off their surplices and red cassocks, they'd
stand all naked—no loincloths—with arrows stuck here, there, and
everywhere. (I won't elaborate, but as Gennaio likes to point out,
there's generally not a lot of displacement upward in my fantasy
life and dream product.) Joey Veneziani would jump-start the group
with "Walk Like a Man," shutting Vana out as the audience started
cheering and stomping. Vana, furious, would rally in open-chest
overdrive. They'd hit back at her with "Big Girls Don't Cry."
Gone soprano, she'd rip off with a rendition of "Vissi d'arte," and
if the audience started cat-calling *Vecchia! Strega!* she'd round on
them, scaling the prompter's box, screaming *Voi, giudici a Vana?!*

The revested boys and I, anxious not to miss our train—the
Gondoliere—would already have scooted out through the back stage
door into the motor taxi idling right below the Ponte Malavisa
Vechia, headed for the Santa Lucia train station. We'd see there a
single train: not the *Gondoliere*, the Train to Hell—full of single-
door compartments receiving passengers from the platform. I'd
scream, *"No!"* "Get *on* this train, *all of you*," Saint Augustine
would order. "We'll be late for the Diet of Worms!" I would
scream again, "No!" and Joey Veneziani and I, locking arms, would
lead the others, as the train started to move out of the station,
toward the station buffet. As we entered the buffet it would turn
into the refectory at Lincoln Hall. The boys would strip down
again, and in various stages of undress lounge at long tables, singing

The worms crawl in,
The worms crawl out;
In your stomach and out your mouth!

The whistle of the Train to Hell would sound in the night.

Oblivion is not a stop on thought's train: it can't be called out. Or, if it is, and can, it's a terminus you always seem to sleep through— the way I used to sometimes ride back and forth passed out on the F between Delancey Street and 179th in Jamaica. Nor are the Eleven against Heaven gone anywhere like Oblivion. It still gets me how when I think back, I can *think them not yet dead,* and if I write this down—although they are dead, as I've said right at the beginning—that there will be in the telling a point at which *they will not yet have been dead.*

Am I really going to tell more stories—put more of it down? Do I really think that my looking up at the windows of the Everard after the fire can compete with the old queen in *The Ambassadors* looking up at—or, even (worse?), with Swann looking up at Odette's? Apparently.
  Give the people what they want: the alibi.
  Tick-tock; this-that.
  Not atomic fission, but the labyrinthine circuitry of the human mind.
  The stories, dear, and the stories within the—

I say my story isn't about to end. What do I know—right?—it could at any minute. In fact, for years that's all it looked like, that's all I expected. I used to dream of hurtling off precipices.

And, in fact, one Saturday night, having been to the movies in East Hampton, at the old post office on Newtown Lane, unable to scare up a cab afterwards to drive me to the Millstone, and having closed Wolfie's tavern across from the train station, I staggered on blind drunken impulse onto the westbound (the train that passes the eastbound usually at Hampton Bays, as it had that very night) and headed for New York. For what? To go to the Little Church Around the Corner? To revisit old St. Patrick's on Mott Street? A wisecracking onlooker leaving Wolfie's who saw me lurching across the street (and who might have, I remember thinking later, in charity cajoled me into his car and dropped me, if not at our driveway, at least in Doug's vegetable patch on the highway to sleep it off) remarked, "It looked like an outtake from *Beyond East Hampton.*" Anyway, on the ride I became convinced—if that's the word—as the train barreled into the tunnel toward Penn Station that it was going to crash into the wall (an accident of that nature having just occurred in London, at Victoria or Waterloo station), and accordingly went demented. I can still see my face in the dark train window, waiting to die. When it didn't—crash—I was so freaked I staggered out into the morning . . . and now my mind wavers still: was it that morning or was it another that I found myself standing in front of the still-burning Everard and imagining flaming bodies leaping out the windows? Anyway, I was lying there telling Gennaio all this, and he said to me, "You weren't frightened enough." *"What?"* "You weren't— you had a strong mental reservation, and were having a very good time." *"What?!"* "What is there about Penn Station that is unlike other terminuses—unlike Grand Central, unlike Victoria, unlike Waterloo?" I thought only a minute, and it hit me, as he knew it would. Penn Station has no wall! The train would have simply sailed past the platform, out into the yard, all the way over to Jersey (and, if you go on with it, all the way down the coast at least as far as Palm Beach. Imagine passing out in East

Hampton and waking up in Palm Beach. Of course, one's heard . . .). And that's why I suppose I feel my story won't end crashed into a wall. Is that an Allegory?

In the old days we used to say, *I can't kill myself, I have tickets.* I said, *I can't die in my sleep—I have a performance to give.* . . .

A NOTE ON THE TYPE

This book was set in a digitized version of Janson. The hot-metal version of Janson was a recutting made direct from type cast from matrices long thought to have been made by the Dutchman Anton Janson, who was a practicing type founder in Leipzig during the years 1668–1687. However, it has been conclusively demonstrated that these types are actually the work of Nicholas Kis (1650–1702), a Hungarian, who most probably learned his trade from the master Dutch type founder Dirk Voskens. The type is an excellent example of the influential and sturdy Dutch types that prevailed in England up to the time William Caslon (1692–1766) developed his own incomparable designs from them.

Composed by Creative Graphics,
Allentown, Pennsylvania

Printed and bound by The Haddon Craftsmen,
Scranton, Pennsylvania

Designed by Cassandra J. Pappas